Charles Stross is a full-time writer who was born in Leeds, England in 1964. He studied in London and Bradford, gaining degrees in pharmacy and computer science, and has worked in a variety of jobs, including pharmacist, technical author, software engineer and freelance journalist. He has won international acclaim for his short fiction, and *Singularity Sky* is his first novel.

You can find out more about him at www.orbitbooks.co.uk and www.antipope.org/charlie/index.html

By Charles Stross

Singularity Sky
Iron Sunrise
Accelerando

singularity sky

CHARLES STROSS

www.orbitbooks.co.uk

An *Orbit* Book

First published in Great Britain by Orbit 2004
This edition published by Orbit 2005
Reprinted 2005 (twice)

A CIP catalogue record for this book
is available from the British Library.

ISBN-13: 978-1-84149-334-3
ISBN-10: 1-84149-334-1

Typeset in Garamond by M Rules
Printed and bound in Great Britain
by Mackays of Chatham plc

Orbit
An imprint of
Time Warner Book Group UK
Brettenham House
Lancaster Place
London WC2E 7EN

contents

prologue

The day war was declared, a rain of telephones fell clattering to the cobblestones from the skies above Novy Petrograd. Some of them had half melted in the heat of re-entry; others pinged and ticked, cooling rapidly in the postdawn chill. An inquisitive pigeon hopped close, head cocked to one side; it pecked at the shiny case of one such device, then fluttered away in alarm when it beeped. A tinny voice spoke: 'Hello? Will you entertain us?'

The Festival had come to Rochard's World.

A skinny street urchin was one of the first victims of the assault on the economic integrity of the New Republic's youngest colony world. Rudi – nobody knew his patronymic, or indeed his father – spotted one of the phones lying in the gutter of a filthy alleyway as he went about his daily work, a malodorous sack wrapped around his skinny shoulders like a soldier's bedroll. The telephone lay on the chipped stones, gleaming like polished gunmetal: he glanced around furtively before picking it up, in case the gentleman who must have dropped it was still nearby. When it chirped he nearly dropped it out of fear: *a machine!* Machines were upper-class and forbidden, guarded by the grim faces and gray uniforms of authority. Nevertheless, if he brought it home to Uncle Schmuel, there might be good eating: better than he could buy with the proceeds of the day's sackful of dog turds for the tannery. He turned it over in his hands, wondering how to shut it up, and a tinny voice spoke: 'Hello? Will you entertain us?'

Rudi nearly dropped the phone and ran, but curiosity held him back for a moment: 'Why?'

'Entertain us and we will give you anything you want.'

Rudi's eyes widened. The metal wafer gleamed with promise between his cupped hands. He remembered the fairy stories his eldest sister used to tell before the coughing sickness took her, tales of magic lamps and magicians and djinn that he was sure Father Borozovski would condemn as infidel nonsense; and his need for escape from the dull brutality of everyday life did battle with his natural pessimism – the pessimism of barely more than a decade of backbreaking labor. Realism won. What he said was not, *I want a magic flying carpet and a purse full of gold roubles* or *I want to be Prince Mikhail in his royal palace*, but, 'Can you feed my family?'

'Yes. Entertain us, and we will feed your family.'

Rudi racked his brains, having no idea how to go about this exotic task; then he blinked. It was obvious! He held the phone to his mouth, and whispered, 'Do you want me to tell you a story?'

By the end of that day, when the manna had begun to fall from orbit and men's dreams were coming to life like strange vines blooming after rain in the desert, Rudi and his family – sick mother, drunken uncle, and seven siblings – were no longer part of the political economy of the New Republic.

War had been declared.

*

Deep in the outer reaches of the star system, the Festival's constructor fleet created structure out of dead mass. The Festival fleet traveled light, packed down into migratory starwisps that disdained the scurrying FTL of merely human clades. When it arrived, fusion pods burned bright as insectile A-life spawned furiously in the frigid depths of the outer system. Once the habitats were complete and moved into orbit around the destination planet, the Festival travelers would emerge from aestivation, ready to trade and listen.

Rochard's World was a backwater colony of the New Republic, itself not exactly the most forward-looking of post-Diaspora human civilizations. With a limited industrial base to attract trade – limited by statute, as well as by ability – few eyes scanned the heavens for the telltale signatures of visiting ships. Only the spaceport, balanced in ground-synchronous orbit, kept a watch, and that was focused on the inner-system ecliptic. The Festival fleet had dismantled a gas giant moon and three comets, begun work on a second moon, and was preparing to rain telephones from orbit before the Imperial Traffic Control Bureau noticed that anything was amiss.

Moreover, there was considerable confusion at first. The New Republic was, if not part of the core worlds, not far out of it; whereas the Festival's origin lay far outside the light cone of the New Republic's origin, more than a thousand light-years from old anarchist Earth. Although they shared a common ancestry, the New Republic and the Festival had diverged for so many centuries that everything – from their communications protocols to their political economies, by way of their genome – was different. So it was that the Festival orbiters noticed (and ignored) the slow, monochromatic witterings of Imperial Traffic Control. More inexplicably, it did not occur to anybody in the Ducal palace to actually pick up one of the half-melted telephones littering their countryside, and ask, 'Who are you and what do you want?' But perhaps this was not so surprising; because by midafternoon Novy Petrograd was in a state of barely controlled civil insurrection.

Burya Rubenstein, the radical journalist, democratic agitator, and sometime political prisoner (living in internal exile on the outskirts of the city, forbidden to return to the father planet – to say nothing of his mistress and sons – for at least another decade) prodded at the silvery artifact on his desk with a finger stained black from the leaky barrel of his pen. 'You say these have been falling everywhere?' he stated, ominously quietly.

Marcus Wolff nodded. 'All over town. Misha wired me from the back country to say it's happening there, too. The Duke's men are out in force with brooms and sacks, picking them up, but there are too many for them. Other things, too.'

'Other things.' It wasn't phrased as a question, but Burya's raised eyebrow made his meaning clear.

'Things falling from the skies – and not the usual rain of frogs!' Oleg Timoshevski bounced up and down excitedly, nearly upsetting one of the typecases that sat on the kitchen table beside him, part of the unlicensed printing press that Rubenstein has established on peril of another decade's internal exile. 'The things – like a telephone, I think, at least they talk back when you ask them something – all say the same thing; entertain us, educate us, we will give you anything you want in return! And they do! I saw a bicycle fall from the skies with my own eyes! And all because Georgi Pavlovich said he wanted one, and told the machine the story of Roland while he waited.'

'I find this hard to believe. Perhaps we should put it to the test?' Burya grinned wolfishly, in a way that reminded Marcus of the old days, when Burya had a fire in his belly, a revolver in his hand, and the ear of ten thousand workers of the Railyard Engineering Union during the abortive October Uprising twelve years earlier. 'Certainly if our mysterious benefactors are happy to trade bicycles for old stories, I wonder what they might be willing to exchange for a general theory of postindustrial political economy?'

'Better dine with the devil with a long, long spoon,' warned Marcus.

'Oh, never fear; all I want to do is ask some questions.' Rubenstein picked up the telephone and turned it over in his hands, curiously. 'Where's the – ah. Here. Machine. Can you hear me?'

'Yes.' The voice was faint, oddly accentless, and slightly musical.

'Good. Who are you, where are you from, and what do you want?'

'We are Festival.' The three dissidents leaned closer, almost bumping heads over the telephone. 'We have traveled many two-hundred-and-fifty-sixes of light-years, visiting many sixteens of inhabited planets. We are seekers of information. We trade.'

'You trade?' Burya glanced up, a trifle disappointed; interstellar capitalist entrepreneurs were not what he had been hoping for.

'We give you anything. You give us something. Anything we don't already know: art, mathematics, comedy, literature, biography, religion, genes, designs. What do you want to give us?'

'When you say you give us anything, what do you mean? Immortal youth? Freedom?' A faint note of sarcasm hovered on his words, but Festival showed no sign of noticing.

'Abstracts are difficult. Information exchange difficult, too – low bandwidth here, no access. But we can make any structures you want, drop them from orbit. You want new house? Horseless carriage that flies and swims as well? Clothing? We make.'

Timoshevski gaped. 'You have a *Cornucopia* machine?' he demanded breathlessly. Burya bit his tongue; an interruption it might be, but a perfectly understandable one.

'Yes.'

'Will you give us one? Along with instructions for using it and a colony design library?' asked Burya, his pulse pounding.

'Maybe. What will you give us?'

'Mmm. How about a post-Marxist theory of post-technological political economy, and a proof that the dictatorship of the hereditary peerage can only be maintained by the systematic oppression and exploitation of the workers and engineers, and cannot survive once the people acquire the self-replicating means of production?'

There was a pause, and Timoshevski exhaled furiously. Just as he was about to speak, the telephone made an odd bell-like noise: 'That will be sufficient. You will deliver the theory to this node. Arrangements to clone a replicator and library are now under way. Query: ability to deliver postulated proof of validity of theory?'

Burya grinned. 'Does your replicator contain schemata for replicating itself? And does it contain schemata for producing direct fusion weapons, military aircraft, and guns?'

'Yes and yes to all subqueries. Query: ability to deliver postulated proof of validity of theory?'

Timoshevski was punching the air and bouncing around the office. Even the normally phlegmatic Wolff was grinning like a maniac. 'Just give the workers the means of production, and we'll prove the theory,' said Rubenstein. 'We need to talk in private. Back in an hour, with the texts you requested.' He pressed the OFF switch on the telephone. '*Yes!*'

After a minute, Timoshevski calmed down a bit. Rubenstein waited indulgently; truth be told, he felt the same way himself. But it was his duty as leader of the movement — or at least the nearest thing they had to a statesman, serving his involuntary internal exile out on this flea-pit of a backwater – to think ahead. And a lot of thinking needed to be done, because shortly heads would be brought into contact with paving stones in large numbers: the Festival, whoever and whatever it was, seemed unaware that they had offered to trade for a parcel of paper the key to the jail in which tens of millions of serfs had been confined for centuries by their aristocratic owners. All in the name of stability and tradition.

'Friends,' he said, voice shaking with emotion, 'let us hope that this is not just a cruel hoax. For if it is not, we can at last lay to rest the cruel specter that has haunted the New Republic since its inception. I'd been hoping for assistance along these lines from a – source, but this is far better if it is true. Marcus, fetch as many members of the committee as you can find. Oleg, I'm going to draft a poster; we need to run off five thousand copies immediately and get them distributed tonight before Politovsky thinks to pull his finger out and declare a state of emergency. Today, Rochard's World stands on the brink of liberation. Tomorrow, the New Republic!'

The next morning, at dawn, troops from the Ducal palace guard and the garrison on Skull Hill, overlooking the old town, hanged six peasants and technicians in the market square. The execution was a warning, to accompany the Ducal decree: *Treat with the Festival and you die.* Someone, probably in the Curator's Office, had realized the lethal danger the Festival posed to the regime and decided an example must be made.

They were too late to stop the Democratic Revolutionary Party from plastering posters explaining just what the telephones were all over town, and pointing out that, in the words of the old proverb, 'Give a man a fish, feed him for a day – teach him to fish, feed him for life.' More radical posters exhorting the workers to demand the means of constructing self-replicating tools rang a powerful chord in the collective psyche, for whatever the regime might have wished, folk memories lived on.

At lunchtime, four bank robbers held up the main post office in Plotsk, eighty kilometers to the north of the capital. The bank robbers carried exotic weapons, and when a police Zeppelin arrived over the scene it was shot to pieces. This was not an isolated incident. All over the planet, the police and state security *apparat* reported incidents of outrageous defiance, in many cases backed up with advanced weapons that had appeared as if from thin air. Meanwhile, strange, dome-like dwellings mushroomed on a thousand peasant farms in the outback, as palatially equipped and comfortable as any Ducal residence.

Pinpricks of light blossomed overhead, and radios gave forth nothing but hissing static for hours afterward. Sometime later, the glowing trails of emergency re-entry capsules skidded across the sky a thousand kilometers south of Novy Petrograd. The Navy announced that evening, with deep regrets, the loss of the destroyer *Sakhalin* in a heroic attack on the enemy battle fleet besieging the colony. It had inflicted serious damage on the aggressors; nevertheless, reinforcements had been requested from the Imperial capital via Causal Channel, and the matter was being treated with the utmost gravity by His Imperial Majesty.

Spontaneous demonstrations by workers and soldiers marred the night, while armored cars were deployed to secure the bridges across the Hava River that separated the Ducal palace and the garrison from the city proper.

And most sinister of all, an impromptu fair began to grow in the open space of the Northern Parade Field — a fair where nobody worked, everything was free, and anything that anybody could possibly want (and a few things that nobody in their right mind would desire) could be obtained free for the asking.

*

On the third day of the incursion, His Excellency Duke Felix Politovsky, Governor of Rochard's World, entered the Star Chamber to meet with his staff and, by way of an eye-wateringly expensive teleconference, to appeal for help from his Emperor.

Politovsky was a thick-set, white-haired man of some sixty-four years, unpreserved by contraband anti-aging medical treatments. It was said by some that he was lacking in imagination, and he had certainly not been appointed governor of a raw backwater dumping ground for troublemakers and second sons because of his overwhelming political acumen. However, despite his bull-headed disposition and lack of insight, Felix Politovsky was deeply worried.

Men in uniform and the formal dress of his diplomatic staff stood to attention as he entered the richly paneled room and marched to the head of the conference table. 'Gentlemen. Please be seated,' he grunted, dropping into the armchair that two servants unobtrusively held out for him. 'Beck have there been any developments overnight?'

Gerhard Von Beck, Citizen, head of the local office of the Curator's Office, shook his head gloomily. 'More riots on the south bank; they didn't stay to fight when I sent a guard detachment. So far, morale in the barracks seems to be holding up. Molinsk is cut off; there have been no reports from that town for the past day, and a helicopter that was sent to look in on them never reported back. The DR's are raising seven shades of merry hell around town, and so are the Radicals. I tried to have the usual suspects taken into custody, but they've declared an Extropian Soviet and refuse to cooperate. The worst elements are holed up in the Corn Exchange, two miles south of here, holding continuous committee meetings, and issuing proclamations and revolutionary communiqué on the hour, every hour. Encouraging people to traffic with the enemy.'

'Why haven't you used troops?' rumbled Politovsky.

'They say they've got atomic weapons. If we move in –' He shrugged.

'Oh.' The Governor rubbed his walrus moustache lugubriously and sighed. 'Commander Janaczeck. What news of the Navy?'

Janaczeck stood. A tall, worried-looking man in a naval officer's dress uniform, he looked even more nervous than the otherwise controlled Von Beck. 'There were two survival capsules from the wreck of the *Sakhalin*; both have now been recovered, and the survivors debriefed. It would appear that the *Sakhalin* approached one of the larger enemy intruders and demanded that they withdraw from low orbit immediately and yield to customs inspection. The intruder made no response, so *Sakhalin* fired across her path. What happened next is confused – none of the survivors were bridge officers, and their reports are contradictory – but it appears that there was an impact with some sort of foreign body, which then ate the destroyer.'

'*Ate* it?'

'Yes, sir.' Janaczeck gulped. 'Forbidden technology.'

Politovsky turned pale. 'Borman?'

'Yes, sir?' His adjutant sat up attentively.

'Obviously, this situation exceeds our ability to deal with it without extra resources. How much acausal bandwidth does the Post Office have in hand for a televisor conference with the capital?'

'Um, ah, fifty minutes' worth, sir. The next consignment of entangled qubits between here and New Prague is due to arrive by ramscoop in, ah, eighteen months. If I may make so bold, sir –'

'Speak.'

'Could we retain a minute of bandwidth in stock, for text-only messages? I realize that this is an emergency, but if we drain the current channel we will be out of touch with the capital until the next shipment is available. And, with all due respect to Commander Janaczeck, I'm not sure the Navy will be able to reliably run dispatch boats past the enemy.'

'Do it.' Politovsky sat up, stretching his shoulders. 'One minute, mind. The rest available for a televisor conference with His Majesty, at his earliest convenience. You will set up the conference and notify me when it is ready. Oh, and while you're about it, here.' He leaned forward and scribbled a hasty signature on a letter from his portfolio. 'I enact this state of emergency and by the authority vested in me by God and His Imperial Majesty I decree that this constitutes a state of war with – who the devil *are* we at war with?'

Von Beck cleared his throat. 'They seem to call themselves the Festival, sir. Unfortunately, we don't appear to have any more information about them on file, and requests to the Curator's Archives drew a blank.'

'Very well.' Borman passed Politovsky a note, and the Governor stood. 'Gentlemen, please stand for His Imperial Majesty!'

They stood and, as one man, turned expectantly to face the screen on the far wall of the conference room.

the gathering storm

'May I ask what I'm charged with?' asked Martin.

The sunshine filtering through the skylight high overhead skewered the stuffy office air with bars of silver: Martin watched dust motes dance like stars behind the Citizen's bullet-shaped head. The only noises in the room were the scratching of his pen on heavy official vellum and the repetitive grinding of gears as his assistant rewound the clockwork drive mechanism on his desktop analytical engine. The room smelled of machine oil and stale fear.

'*Am* I being charged with anything?' Martin persisted.

The Citizen ignored him and bent his head back to his forms. His young assistant, his regular chore complete, began unloading a paper tape from the engine.

Martin stood up. 'If I am not being charged with anything, is there any reason why I should stay?'

This time the Citizen Curator glared at him. 'Sit,' he snapped.

Martin sat.

Outside the skylight, it was a clear, cold April afternoon;

the clocks of St Michael had just finished striking fourteen hundred, and in the Square of the Five Corners, the famous Duchess's Simulacrum was jerking through its eternal pantomime. The boredom grated on Martin. He found it difficult to adapt to the pace of events in the New Republic; it was doubly infuriating when he was faced with the eternal bureaucracy. He'd been here for four months now, four stinking months on a job which should have taken ten days. He was beginning to wonder if he would live to see Earth again before he died of old age.

In fact, he was so bored with waiting for his work clearance to materialize that this morning's summons to an office somewhere behind the iron facade of the Basilisk came as a relief, something to break the monotony. It didn't fill him with the stuttering panic that such an appointment would have kindled in the heart of a subject of the New Republic – what, after all, could the Curator's Office do to him, an off-world engineering contractor with a cast-iron Admiralty contract? The summons had come on a plate borne by a uniformed courier, and not as a night-time raid. That fact alone suggested a degree of restraint and, consequently, an approach to adopt, and Martin resolved to play the bemused alien visitor card as hard as he could.

After another minute, the Citizen lowered his pen and looked at Martin. 'Please state your name,' he said softly.

Martin crossed his arms. 'If you don't know it already, why am I here?' he asked.

'Please state your name for the record.' The Citizen's voice was low, clipped, and as controlled as a machine. He spoke the local trade-lingua – a derivative of the nearly universal old English tongue – with a somewhat heavy, Germanic accent.

'Martin Springfield.'

The Citizen made a note. 'Now please state your nationality.'

'My what?'

Martin must have looked nonplussed, for the Citizen raised a gray-flecked eyebrow. 'Please state your nationality. To what government do you owe allegiance?'

'Government?' Martin rolled his eyes. 'I come from *Earth*. For legislation and insurance, I use Pinkertons, with a backup strategic infringement policy from the New Model Air Force. As far as employment goes, I am incorporated under charter as a personal corporation with bilateral contractual obligations to various organizations, including your own Admiralty. For reasons of nostalgia, I am a registered citizen of the People's Republic of West Yorkshire, although I haven't been back there for twenty years. But I wouldn't say I was answerable to any of those, except my contractual partners – and they're equally answerable to me.'

'But you are from Earth?' asked the Citizen, his pen poised.

'Yes.'

'Ah. Then you are a subject of the United Nations.' He made a brief note. 'Why didn't you admit this?'

'Because it isn't true,' said Martin, letting a note of frustration creep into his voice. (But only a note: he had an idea of the Citizen's powers, and had no intention of provoking him to exercise them.)

'Earth. The supreme political entity on that planet is the United Nations Organization. So it follows that you are a subject of it, no?'

'Not at all.' Martin leaned forward. 'At last count, there were more than fifteen thousand governmental organizations on Earth. Of those, only about the top nine hundred have representatives in Geneva, and only seventy have permanent seats on the Security Council. The UN has no authority over any non-governmental organization or over individual citizens, it's purely an arbitration body. I am a sovereign individual; I'm not owned by any government.'

'Ah,' said the Citizen. He laid his pen down very carefully beside his blotter and looked directly at Martin. 'I see you fail to understand. I am going to do you a great favor and pretend that I did not hear the last thing you said. Vassily?'

His young assistant looked up. 'Yah?'

'*Out.*'

The assistant – little more than a boy in uniform – stood and marched over to the door. It thudded shut solidly behind him.

'I will say this once, and once only.' The Citizen paused, and Martin realized with a shock that his outward impassivity was a tightly sealed lid holding down a roiling fury: 'I do not care what silly ideas the stay-behinds of Earth maintain about their sovereignty. I do not care about being insulted by a young and insolent pup like you. But while you are on this planet you *will* live by our definitions of what is right and proper! Do I make myself clear?'

Martin recoiled. The Citizen waited to see if he would speak, but when he remained silent, continued icily. 'You are here in the New Republic at the invitation of the Government of His Majesty, and will at all times comport yourself accordingly. This includes being respectful to Their Imperial Highnesses, behaving decently, legally, and honestly, paying taxes to the Imperial Treasury, and not spreading subversion. You are here to do a job, not to spead hostile alien propaganda or to denigrate our way of life! Am I making myself understood?'

'I don't –' Martin paused, hunted for the correct, diplomatic words. 'Let me rephrase, please. I am sorry if I have caused offense, but if that's what I've done, would you mind telling me what I did? So I can avoid doing it again. If you won't tell me what not to do, how can I avoid causing offense by accident?'

'You are unaware?' asked the Citizen. He stood up and

paced around Martin, behind his chair, around the desk, and back to his own seat. There he stopped pacing, and glowered furiously. 'Two nights ago, in the bar of the Glorious Crown Hotel, you were clearly heard telling someone – a Vaclav Hasek, I believe – about the political system on your home planet. Propaganda and nonsense, but *attractive* propaganda and nonsense to a certain disaffected segment of the lumpen-proletariat. Nonsense verging on sedition, I might add, when you dropped several comments about – let me see – "the concept of tax is no different from extortion," and "a social contract enforced by compulsion is not a valid contract." After your fourth beer, you became somewhat merry and began to declaim on the nature of social justice, which is itself something of a problem, insofar as you expressed doubt about the impartiality of a judiciary appointed by His Majesty in trying cases against the Crown.'

'That's rubbish! Just a conversation over a pint of beer!'

'If you were a citizen, it would be enough to send you on a one-way trip to one of His Majesty's frontier colonies for the next twenty years,' the Citizen said icily. 'The only reason we are having this little *tête-à-tête* is because your presence in the Royal Dockyards is considered essential. If you indulge in any more such conversations over pints of beer, perhaps the Admiralty may be persuaded to wash their hands of you. And then where will you be?'

Martin shivered; he hadn't expected the Citizen to be quite so blunt. 'Are conversations about politics really that sensitive?' he asked.

'When held in a public place, and engaged in by an off-worlder with strange ideas, *yes*. The New Republic is not like the degenerate anarchist mess your fatherworld has sunk into. Let me emphasize that. Because you are a necessary alien, you are granted certain rights by Their Imperial Highnesses. If you go outside those rights, you will be stamped on, and stamped on hard. If you find that difficult to understand, I suggest you spend the remainder of your free time inside your hotel room so that your mouth does not incriminate you accidentally. I ask you for a third time: Do I make myself understood?'

Martin looked chastened. 'Y-yes,' he said.

'Then get out of my office.'

Evening.

A man of medium height and unremarkable build, with brownish hair and a close-cropped beard, lay fully clad on the ornate counterpane of a hotel bed, a padded eyeshade covering his face. Shadows crept across the gloomy carpet as the sun sank below the horizon. The gas jets in the chandelier hissed, casting deep shadows across the room. A fly buzzed around the upper reaches of the room, pursuing a knife-edged search pattern.

Martin was not asleep. His entire inventory of countersurveillance drones were out on patrol, searching his room for bugs in case the Curator's Office was monitoring him. Not that he had many drones to search with: they were strictly illegal in the New Republic, and he'd been forced to smuggle his kit through customs in blocked sebaceous glands and dental caries. Now they were out in force, hunting for listening devices and reporting back to the monitors woven into his eyeshade.

Finally, concluding he was alone in the room, he recalled the fly – its SQUID-sensors untriggered – and put the fleas back into hibernation. He stood up and shuttered the window, then pulled the curtains closed. Short of the Curator's Office having hidden a mechanical drum-recorder in the back of the wardrobe, he was unable to see any way that they could listen in on him.

He reached into the breast pocket of his jacket (rumpled,

now, from being lain upon) and pulled out a slim, leather-bound book. 'Talk to me.'

'Hello, Martin. Startup completed, confidence one hundred percent.'

'That's good.' He cleared his throat. 'Back channel. Execute. I'd like to talk to Herman.'

'Paging.'

The book fell silent and Martin waited impassively. It looked like a personal assisstant, a discreet digital secretary for a modern Terran business consultant. While such devices could be built into any ambient piece of furniture – clothing, even a prosthetic tooth – Martin kept his in the shape of an old-fashioned hardback. However, normal personal assists didn't come with a causal channel plug-in, especially one with a ninety-light-year reach and five petabits of bandwidth. Even though almost two petabits had been used when the agent-in-place passed it to him via a dead letter drop on a park bench, it was outrageously valuable to Martin. In fact, it was worth his life – if the secret police caught him with it.

A slower-than-light freighter had spent nearly a hundred years hauling the quantum black box at the core of the causal channel out from Septagon system; a twin to it had spent eighty years in the hold of a sister ship, *en route* to Earth. Now they provided an instantaneous communications channel from one planet to the other; instantaneous in terms of special relativity, but not capable of violating causality, and with a total capacity limited to the number of qubits they had been created with. Once those 5 billion megabits were gone, they'd be gone for good – or until the next slower-than-light freighter arrived.

(Not that such ships were rare – building and launching a one-kilogram starwisp, capable of carrying a whopping great hundred-gram payload across a dozen light-years, wasn't far above the level of a cottage industry – but the powers that ran things here in the New Republic were notoriously touchy about contact with the ideologically impure outside universe.)

'Hello?' said the PA.

'PA: Is that Herman?' asked Martin.

'PA here. Herman is on the line and all authentication tokens are updated.'

'I had an interview with a Citizen from the Curator's Office today,' said Martin. 'They're extremely sensitive about subversion.' Twenty-two words in five seconds: sampled at high fidelity, about half a million bits. Transcribed to text, that would make about one hundred bytes, maybe as few as fifty bytes after non-lossy compression. Which left fifty fewer bytes in the link between Martin's PA and Earth. If Martin went to the Post Office, they would charge him a dollar a word, he'd have to queue for a day, and there would be a postal inspector listening in.

'What happened?' asked Herman.

'Nothing important, but I was warned off, and warned hard. I'll put it in my report. They didn't question my affiliation.'

'Any query over your work?'

'No. No suspicion, as far as I can tell.'

'Why did they question you?'

'Spies in bars. They want the frighteners on me. I haven't been on board the *Lord Vanek* yet. Dockyard access control is very tight. I think they're upset about something.'

'Any confirmation of unusual events? Fleet movements? Workup toward departure?'

'Nothing I know about.' Martin bit back his further comment: talking to Herman via the illegal transmitter always made him nervous. 'I'm keeping my eyes on the ball. Report ends.'

'Bye,'

'PA: shut down link now.'

'The link is down.' Throughout the entire conversation, Martin noted, the only voice he had heard was his; the PA spoke in its owner's tones, the better to be a perfect receptionist, and the CC link was so expensive that sending an audio stream over it would be a foolish extravagance. Talking to himself across a gulf of seventy light-years made Martin feel very lonely. Especially given the very real nature of his fears.

So far, he'd successfully played the gormless foreign engineering contractor with a runaway mouth, held overlong on a two-week assignment to upgrade the engines on board His Majesty's battlecruiser *Lord Vanek*. In fact, he was doing such a good job that he'd gotten to see the inside of the Basilisk, and escaped alive.

But he wasn't likely to do so twice, if they learned who he was working for.

'Do you think he is a spy?' asked trainee procurator Vassily Muller.

'Not as far as I know.' The Citizen smiled thinly at his assistant, the thin scar above his left eye wrinkling with satanic amusement. 'If I had any evidence that he was a spy, he would rapidly become an ex-spy. And an ex-everything else, for that matter. But that is not what I asked you, is it?' He fixed his subordinate with a particular expression he had perfected for dealing with slow students. 'Tell me why I let him go.'

'Because . . .' The trainee officer looked nonplussed. He'd been here six months, less than a year out of gymnasium and the custody of the professors, and it showed. He was still a teenager, fair-haired, blue-eyed, and almost painfully unskilled in the social nuances: like so many intelligent men who survived the elite boarding school system, he was also inclined to intellectual rigidity. Privately, the Citizen thought this was a bad thing, at least in a secret policeman – rigidity was a habit that would have to be broken if he was ever to be of much use.

On the other hand, he seemed to have inherited his father's intelligence. If he'd inherited his flexibility, too, without the unfortunate rebelliousness, he'd make an excellent operative.

After a minute's silence, the Citizen prodded him. 'That is not an acceptable answer, young man. Try again.'

'Ah, you let him go because he has a loose mouth, and where he goes, it will be easier to see who listens to him?'

'Better, but not entirely true. What you said earlier intrigues me. Why don't you think he is a spy?'

Vassily did a double take; it was almost painful to watch as he tried to deal with the Citizen's abrupt about-face. 'He's too talkative, isn't he, sir? Spies don't call attention to themselves, do they? It's not in their interests. And again, he's an engineer contracted to work for the fleet, but the ship was built by the company he works for, so why would they want to spy on it? And he can't be a professional subversive, either. Professionals would know better than to blab in a hotel bar.' He stopped and looked vaguely self-satisfied.

'Good going. Such a shame I don't agree with you.'

Vassily gulped. 'But I thought you said he wasn't a—' He stopped himself. 'You mean he's too obviously *not* a spy. He draws attention to himself in bars, he argues politics, he does things a spy would not do – as if he wants to lay our suspicions at ease?'

'Very good,' said the Citizen. 'You are learning to think like a Curator! Please note that I never said that Mr. Springfield is not a spy. Neither did I assert that he *is* one. He might well be; equally well, he might not. However, I will be unsatisfied until you have resolved the issue, one way or the other. Do you understand?'

'You want me to prove a negative?' Vassily was almost going cross-eyed with the effort of trying to understand the Citizen's train of thought. 'But that's impossible!'

'Exactly!' The Citizen cracked a thin smile as he clapped his subordinate on the shoulder. 'So you'll have to find some way of making it a positive that you prove, won't you? And that is your assignment for the foreseeable future, Junior Procurator Muller. You will go forth and try to prove that our irritating visitor of the morning is not a spy – or to gather sufficient evidence to justify his arrest. Come, now! Haven't you been champing at the bit to get out of this gloomy dungeon and see a bit of the capital, as I believe you referred to it only last week? This is your chance. Besides, when you return, think about the story you'll have to tell that piece of skirt you've been chasing ever since you arrived here!'

'Ah – I'm honored,' said Vassily. He looked somewhat taken aback. A young officer, still sufficiently fresh from training that the varnish hadn't eroded from his view of the universe, he looked up at the Citizen in awe. 'Sir, humbly request permission to ask why? I mean, why now?'

'Because it's about time you learned to do more than take minutes of committee meetings,' said the Citizen. His eyes gleamed behind their glasses; his moustache shuddered all the way out to its waxen points. 'There comes a time when every officer needs to assume the full burden of his duties. I expect you have picked up at least a clue about how the job is done from the interminable reports you've been summarizing. Now it's time to see if you can do it, no? On a low-risk assignment, I might add; I'm not sending you after the revolutionaries right away, ha-ha. So this afternoon you will go to sublevel two for field ops processing, then tomorrow you will start on the assignment. I expect to see a report on my desk, first thing every morning, starting the day after tomorrow. Show me what you can do!'

The next morning, Martin was awakened by a peremptory rap on the door. 'Telegram for Master Springfield!' called a delivery boy.

Martin pulled on a dressing gown and opened the door a crack. The telegram was passed inside; he signed for it quickly, pulled out the contents, and passed back the signed envelope. Blinking and bleary-eyed, he carried the message over to the window and pulled back the shutters to read it. It was a welcome surprise, if somewhat annoying to be woken for it — confirmation that his visa had been approved, his security vetting was complete and that he was to report at 1800 that evening to the Navy beanstalk in South Austria for transit to the fleet shipyards in geosynchronous orbit.

Telegrams, he reflected, were so much less civilized than e-mail — the latter didn't come with an officious youth who'd get you out of bed to sign for it. Such a shame that e-mail was unavailable in the New Republic and telegrams ubiquitous. But then again, e-mail was decentralized, telegrams anything but. And the New Republic was very keen on centralization.

He dressed, shaved, and made his way downstairs to the morning room to await his breakfast. He wore local garb — a dark jacket, tight breeches, boots, and a shirt with a ruff of lace at the collar — but of a subtly unfashionable cut, somehow betraying a lack of appreciation for the minutiae of fashion. Off-world styles, he found, tended to get in the way when trying to establish a working rapport with the locals: but if you looked just slightly odd, they'd sense your alien-ness without being overwhelmed by it, and make at least some allowances for your behavior. By any yardstick, the New Republic was an insular society, and interacting with it was diffficult even for a man as well traveled as Martin, but at least the ordinary people made an effort.

He had become sufficiently accustomed to local customs that, rather than letting them irritate him, he was able to absorb each new affront with quiet resignation. The way the concierge stared down his patrician nose at him, or the stiff-collared chambermaids scurried by with downcast eyes had become merely individual pieces in the complex jigsaw puzzle of Republican mores. The smell of wax polish and chlorine bleach, coal smoke from the boiler room, and leather seats in the dining room, were all alien, the odors of a society that hadn't adapted to the age of plastic. Not all the local habits chafed. The morning's news-sheet, folded crisply beside his seat at the breakfast table, provided a strangely evocative sense of homecoming – as if he had traveled on a voyage nearly three hundred years into the past of his own home culture, rather than 180 light-years out into the depths of space. Although, in a manner of speaking, the two voyages were exactly equivalent.

He breakfasted on butter mushrooms, sautéed goose eggs, and a particularly fine toasted sourdough rye bread, washed down with copious quantities of lemon tea. Finally, he left the room and made his way to the front desk.

'I would like to arrange transport,' he said. The duty clerk looked up, eyes distant and preoccupied. 'By air, to the naval beanstalk at Klamovka, as soon as possible. I will be taking hand luggage only, and will not be checking out of my room, although I will be away for some days.'

'Ah, I see. Excuse me, sir.' The clerk hurried away into the maze of offices and tiny service rooms that hid behind the dark wood paneling of the hotel lobby.

He returned shortly thereafter, with the concierge in tow, a tall, stoop-shouldered man dressed head to foot in black, cadaverous and sunken-cheeked, who bore himself with the solemn dignity of a count or minor noble. 'You require transport, sir?' asked the concierge.

'I'm going to the naval base at Klamovka,' Martin repeated slowly. 'Today. I need transport arranging at short notice. I will be leaving my luggage at the hotel. I do not know how long I will be away, but I am not checking out.'

'I see, sir.' The concierge nodded at his subordinate, who scurried away and returned bearing three fat volumes –

timetables for the various regional rail services. 'I am afraid that no Zeppelin flights are scheduled between here and Klamovka until tomorrow. However, I believe you can get there this evening by train – if you leave immediately.'

'That will be fine,' said Martin. He had a nagging feeling that his immediate departure was the only thing he could do that would gratify the concierge – apart, perhaps, from dropping dead on the spot. 'I'll be back down here in five minutes. If your assistant could see to my tickets, please? On the tab.'

The concierge nodded, stony-faced. 'On behalf of the hotel, I wish you a fruitful journey,' he intoned. 'Marcus, see to this gentleman.' And off he stalked.

The clerk cracked open the first of the ledgers and glanced at Martin cautiously. 'Which class, sir?'

'First.' If there was one thing that Martin had learned early, it was that the New Republic had some very strange ideas about class. He made up his mind. 'I need to arrive before six o'clock tonight. I will be back here in five minutes. If you would be so good as to have my itinerary ready by then . . .'

'Yes, sir.' He left the clerk sweating over map and gazetteer, and climbed the four flights of stairs to his floor.

When he returned to the front desk, trailed by a footman with a bag in each hand, the clerk ushered him outside. 'Your carnet, sir.' He pocketed the ornate travel document, itself as intricate as any passport. A steam coach was waiting. He climbed in, acknowledged the clerk's bow with a nod, and the coach huffed away toward the railway station.

It was a damp and foggy morning, and Martin could barely see the ornate stone facade of the ministerial buildings from the windows of his carriage as they rolled past beside him.

The hotel rooms might lack telephones, there might be a political ban on networking and smart matter and a host of other conveniences, and there might be a class system out of the eighteenth century on Earth; but the New Republic had one thing going for it – its trains ran on time. PS 1347, the primary around which New Muscovy orbited, was a young third-generation G2 dwarf; it had formed less than two billion years ago (to Sol's five), and consequently, the planetary crust of New Muscovy contained uranium ore active enough to sustain criticality without enrichment.

Martin's coach drew up on the platform alongside the Trans-Peninsular Express. He climbed down from the cabin stiffly and glanced both ways: they'd drawn up a quarter of a kilometer down the marble tongue from the hulking engines, but still the best part of a kilometer away from the dismal tailings of fourth-class accommodation and mail. A majordomo, resplendent in bottle-green frock coat and gold braid, inspected his carnet before ushering him into a private compartment on the upper deck. The room was decorated in blue-dyed leather and old oak, trimmed in brass and gold leaf, and equipped with a marble-topped table and a bell-pull to summon service; it more closely resembled a smoking room back in the hotel than anything Martin associated with public transport.

As soon as the majordomo had left, Martin settled back in one of the deeply padded seats, drew the curtains aside to reveal the arching buttresses and curved roof of the station, and opened his PA in book mode. Shortly thereafter, the train shuddered slightly and began to move: as the train slid out of the station, he glanced out of the window, unable to look away.

The city of New Prague was built just upstream from the tidal estuary of the River Vis; only the Basilisk, brooding atop a plug of eroded volcanic granite, rose much above the level of the plain. Indeed, the train would cruise through the lowlands using just one of its engines. The second reactor would only be brought to criticality when the train reached the foothills of the Apennines, the mountain range that separated the coastal peninsula from the continental interior of New Austria. Then the train would surge in a knife-straight line across nine hundred kilometers of desert before stopping, six hours later, at the foot of the Klamovka beanstalk.

The scene was quite extraordinary. Martin gazed at it in barely controlled awe. Though he didn't like to admit it, he was something of a tourist, permanently searching for a sense of fresh beauty that he could secretly revel in. There wasn't anything like this left on Earth; the wild ride of the twentieth century and the events that had followed the Singularity in the twenty-first had distorted the landscape of every industrialized nation. Even in the wake of the population crash, you couldn't find open countryside, farms, hedges, and neatly planned villages – at least, not without also finding monorails, arcologies, fall-out hot spots, and the weird hillocks of the Final Structure. The lowland landscape through which the Trans-Peninsular Express ran resembled a vision of pre-postindustrial England, a bucolic dreamscape where the trains ran on time and the sun never set on the empire.

But railway journeys pale rapidly, and after half an hour, the train was racing through the valleys in a blur of steel and brass. Martin went back to his book, and was so engrossed in it that he barely noticed the door open and close – until a woman he had never seen before sat down opposite him and cleared her throat.

'Excuse me,' he said, looking up. 'Are you sure you have the right compartment?'

She nodded. 'Quite sure, thank you. I didn't request an individual one. Did you?'

'I thought –' He fumbled in his jacket for his carnet. 'Ah. I see.' He cursed the concierge silently, thumbed the PA off, then looked at her. 'I thought I had a compartment to myself; I see I was wrong. Please accept my apologies.'

The woman nodded graciously. She had long black hair

coiled in a bun, high cheekbones and brown eyes; her dark blue gown seemed expensively plain by this society's standards. *Probably* a middle-class housewife, he guessed, but his ability to judge social status within the New Republic was still somewhat erratic. He couldn't even make a stab at her age: heavy makeup, and the tight bodice, billowing skirts and puffed sleeves of capital fashion made an effective disguise.

'Are you going far?' she asked brightly.

'All the way to Klamovka, and thence up the naval beanstalk,' he said, somewhat surprised at this frank interrogation.

'What a coincidence; that's where I'm going, too. You will excuse me for asking, but am I right in thinking you are not native to this area?'

She looked interested, to a degree that Martin found irritatingly intrusive. He shrugged. 'No, I'm not.' He reopened his PA and attempted to bury his nose in it, but his unwanted traveling companion had other ideas.

'I take it from your accent that you are not native to this planet, either. And you're going to the Admiralty yards. Would you mind me asking your business there?'

'Yes,' he said curtly, and stared pointedly at his PA. He hadn't initially registered how forward she was being, at least for a woman of her social class, but it was beginning to set his nerves on edge, ringing alarms. Something about her didn't feel quite right. *Agent provocateur?* he wondered. He had no intention of giving the secret police any further excuses to haul him in; he wanted them to think he'd learned the error of his ways and determined to reform.

'Hmm. But when I came in you were reading a treatise on relativistic clock-skew correction algorithms as applied to the architecture of modern starship drive compensators. So you're an engineer of some sort, retained by the Admiralty to do maintenance work on fleet vessels.' She grinned, and her

expression unnerved Martin: white teeth, red lips, and something about her manner that reminded him of home, where
women weren't just well-bred ornaments for the family tree.
'Am I right?'

'I couldn't possibly comment.' Martin shut his PA again
and glared at her. 'Who are you, and what the hell do you
want?' The social programming he'd absorbed on his journey
out to the New Republic forbade such crudity in the presence
of a lady, but she was obviously no more a lady than he was a
Republican yeoman. The social program could go play with
itself.

'My name is Rachel Mansour, and I'm on my way to the
naval dockyards on business which may well intersect with
your own. Unless I'm mistaken, in which case you have my
most humble apologies, you are Martin Springfield, personally
incorpolated and retained by contract to the New Republican
Admiralty to perform installation upgrades on the drive control circuitry of the Svejk-class battlecruiser *Lord Vanek*. After
Lord Ernst Vanek, founder of the New Republic's Navy.
Correct?'

Martin returned the PA to his jacket pocket and glanced out
of the window, trying to still a sudden wave of cold fear. 'Yes.
What business of yours is it?'

'You may be interested to learn that four hours ago, consensus absolute time, the New Model Air Force – whose
underwriting service you subscribe to – invoked the Eschaton
clause in all strategic guarantees bearing on the Republic. At
the same time, someone tipped off the UN Standing
Committee on Multilateral Interstellar Disarmament that the
New Republic is gearing up for war, in defense of a colony out-
post that's under siege. You aren't paying the extra premium
for insurance against divine retribution, are you? So right now
you're not covered for anything other than medical and theft.'

Martin turned back to look at her. 'Are you accusing me of

being a spy?' He met her eyes. They were dark, intelligent, and reserved – absolutely unreadable. 'Who the hell are you, anyway?'

She shook a card out of her sleeve and opened it toward him. A head – recognizably her own, but with close-cropped hair – floated above it in holographic miniature, wreathed against a familiar backdrop. The sheer unexpectedness of it electrified him: shivers chased up and down his spine as his implants tried to damp down an instinctive panic reaction rising from his adrenal glands. 'UN diplomatic intelligence, special operations group. I'm here to find out what the current situation is, and that includes finding out just what last-minute modifications the Admiralty is making to the ships comprising the expeditionary force. You *are* going to cooperate, aren't you?' She smiled again, even more unnervingly, with an expression that reminded Martin of a hungry ferret.

'Um.' *What the hell are the CMID doing here? This isn't in the mission plan!* 'This is going to be one of those trips, isn't it?' He rubbed his forehead and glanced at her again: she was still waiting for his response. *Shit, improvise, dammit, before she suspects something!* 'Look, do you know what they do to spies here?'

She nodded, no longer smiling. 'I do. But I've also got my eyes on the bottom line, which is that this is an impending war situation. It's my job to keep track of it – we can't afford to let them run riot this close to Earth. Being garrotted would certainly spoil anyone's day, but starting an interstellar war or attracting the attention of the Eschaton is even worse, at least for the several planets full of mostly innocent bystanders who are likely to be included in the collateral damage. Which is my overriding concern.'

She stared at him with frightening intensity, and the card disappeared between two lace-gloved fingers. 'We need to get together and talk, Martin. Once you're up at the dockyard and settled in, I'll contact you. I don't care what else you agree to or disagree with, but we are going to have a talk tomorrow. And I'm going to pick your brains, and confirm that you're just a bystander, and tell your insurers you're a safe bet. Do you understand?'

'Uh, yes.' He stared at her and tried to look as if he'd just realized that she was, in fact, a devil, and he had signed away his soul. He hoped she'd believe him – naive engineer, sucked in out of his depths, confronted with an agent of Higher Authority – but had a cold sense that if she didn't fall for it, he might be in *real* trouble. Herman and the CMID weren't exactly on speaking terms . . .

'Excellent.' She reached into her purse and pulled out a battered-looking, gunmetal-colored PA. 'Speaking. Send: Rabbit green. Ack.'

The PA spoke back: 'Ack. Message sent.' It took Martin a moment or two to recognize the voice as his own.

She slipped the case away and stood to leave the compartment. 'You see,' she said from the doorway, a quirky smile tugging at her lips, 'life here isn't necessarily as dull as you thought! See you later . . .'

preparations for departure

His Imperial Majesty the Emperor Ivan Hasek III, by grace of God the protector of the people of the New Republic, growled exasperatedly. 'Get the Admiral out of bed and make him presentable – I have a cabinet meeting at noon, and I need to talk to him *now*.'

'Yes, sir! I most humbly beg your pardon, and beg leave to be excused to do as Your Majesty commands.' The butler virtually bowed and scraped his way off the telephone.

'What's the implied "or else"?' Duke Michael, the Emperor's brother, inquired drily. 'You'd have him clapped in irons?'

'Hardly.' The Emperor snorted, showing as much amusement as his dignity permitted. 'He's over eighty; I suppose he's entitled to stay in bed once in a while. But if he's so ill he can't even rise for his Emperor in time of war, I'd have to force him to retire. And then there'd be an uproar in the Admiralty. You can't imagine the waves it would make if we started forcing admirals to *retire*.' He sniffed. 'We might even have to think about giving them all pensions! That'd go down as well as suggesting to Father that he abdicate.'

Duke Michael coughed, delicately. 'Perhaps somebody should have. After the second stroke –'

'Yes, yes.'

'I still think offering him the fleet is unreasonable.'

'If you think that is unreasonable, I don't suppose you'd care to discuss the likely response of their naval lordships if I *didn't* give him first refusal?' The priority telephone rang again before his brother had a chance to answer the pointed question; a liveried servant offered the ivory-and-platinum handset to His Majesty. The Duke picked up a second earpiece, to listen in on the call.

'Sire? My Lord Admiral Kurtz is ready to talk to you. He extends his deepest apologies, and—'

'Enough. Just put him on, there's a good fellow.' Ivan tapped his fingers irritably on the arm of his chair, a Gothic wooden monstrosity only one step removed from an instrument of torture. 'Ah, Admiral. Just the man! Capital, how splendid to talk to you. And how are we today?'

'Today-ay?' A reedy, quavering voice echoed uncertainly over the copper wires. 'Ah-hum, yes, today. Indeed, yes. I'm very well, thank you, milady, I don't suppose you've seen any chameleons?'

'No, Admiral, there are no chameleons in the palace,' the Emperor stated with firm, but resigned, persistence. 'You know who you are speaking to?'

In the momentary silence he could almost hear the elderly admiral blinking in confusion. 'Ah-hum. Your Majesty? Ah, Ivan, lad? Emperor already? How time flies!'

'Yes, Uncle. I'm phoning you because –' A thought struck the Emperor. 'Are you up and about?'

'Yes, ahuhuhum. I'm, ah, in my bath chair. It's my old legs, you know. They're awfully fragile. Got to wrap them up in lots of blankets in case they shatter. They don't blow legs the way they used to, when I was a lad. But I'm out of bed now.'

'Oh, good. You see, um –' The Emperor's brain went into a wheel-spin as he considered and reconsidered the options. He'd heard, of course, about the Admiral's indisposition, but he hadn't actually encountered it directly until now. A strong case could be made, he supposed, for dismissing the Admiral; the man was patently ill. Charging him with this duty would be unfair, and more importantly, not in the best interests of the state.

But he was still the senior fighting admiral, war hero of the New Republic, defender of the empire, slaughterer of the infidels, conqueror of no less than three bucolic and rather backward colony worlds – and, not to put too much of a point on it, the Emperor's uncle by way of his grandfather's second mistress. Because of the long-standing tradition that admirals never retired, nobody had ever thought to make provisions for pensioning off old warhorses; they usually died long before it became an issue. To dismiss him was unthinkable, but to expect him to lead a naval expedition – Ivan struggled with his conscience, half hoping that the old man would turn it down. No dishonor would accrue – nobody expected an octogenarian in a bath chair to die for the fatherland – and meantime they'd find a hard-headed young whippersnapper to lead the fleet into battle.

Coming to a decision, the Emperor took a deep breath. 'We have a problem. Something abominable has happened, and Rochard's World is under siege. I'm going to send the fleet. Are you too ill to lead it?' He winked at his brother the Duke, hoping –

'War!' The old man's bellow nearly deafened Ivan. 'Victory to the everlastingly vigilant forces of righteousness waging unceasing struggle on enemies of the New Conservatives! Death to the proponents of change! A thousand tortures to the detractors of the Emperor! Where are the bastards? Let me at them!' The clattering in the background might have been the sound of a walking frame being cast aside.

Duke Michael grimaced unhappily at his brother. 'Well I suppose that answers *one* question,' he mouthed. 'I'm not going to say I told you so, but who are we going to send to push his wheelchair?'

New Prague was only a thousand kilometers north of the equator (this planet being notoriously cold for a water-belt terraform) and the train pulled into the Klamovka station shortly after lunchtime. Martin disembarked and hailed a cab to the naval depot at the foot of the beanstalk, pointedly ignoring Rachel – or whatever her real name was. Let her make her own way: she was an unwelcome, potentially disastrous complication in his life right now.

The beanstalk loomed over the military depot like the ultimate flagpole; four tapered cones of diamondoid polymers stretching all the way to geosynchronous orbit and a bit beyond, a radical exception to the New Republic's limitations on technology. Bronzed, bullet-nosed elevator carriages skimmed up and down the elevator cables, taking a whole night to make the journey. Here there was no *fin-de-siècle* ambience: just rugged functionality, sleeping capsules manufactured to a template designed for Kobe's ancient salarymen, and a stringent weight limit. (Gravity modification, although available, was another of the technologies that the New Republic shunned – at least, for non-military purposes.) Martin hurried aboard the first available pod and, to his relief, saw no sign of Rachel.

Upon arrival, he disembarked into the military sector of the space station, presented himself to the warrant officer's checkpoint, and was ushered straight through a crude security scan that probably exceeded his annual allowed dose of X-rays in one go. There was one bad moment when a mastel sergeant asked him to demonstrate his PA, but the explanation – that it was a personal assist, that it stored all his working notes, and that he'd be unable to cope without it – was accepted. After which he cooled his heels for half an hour in a spartan guardroom painted institutional green.

Eventually a rating came to collect him. 'You'd be the engine man?' said the flyer. 'We been waiting for you.'

Martin sighed unhappily. 'And I've been waiting, too.' He stood up. 'Take me to your CO.'

The New Republic had paid Mikoyan-Guerevitch-Kvaerner back on Luna to design them a battlecruiser fit to bear the name of their Navy's founder: one that looked the way a warship ought to look, not like a cubist's vision of a rabies virus crossed with a soft drink can (as most real warships did). Style imposed strictures on functionality: despite which, it was still worthy of a degree of respect – you could be killed by its baroque missile batteries and phased-array lasers just as surely as by a more modern weapon. Besides, it *looked* good, which had enabled MiG to make a killing selling knockoffs to gullible juntas everywhere, demonstrating the importance of being Ernst as the marketing department put it.

In Martin's opinion, the *Lord Vanek* was cut from the same comic-opera fabric as the rest of the New Republic – a comic opera that was far less funny once it had you in its jaws. The ceremonials, flags and Imperial logos splashed across every available surface, the uniformed flunkies, and elaborate pyramid of military etiquette, all suggested to Martin that taking this job had not been a good idea: the gibbeted dissidents hanging from the eaves of the Basilisk had confirmed it. Right now, he'd happily repay his entire fee just to be allowed to go home – were it not for the call of duty.

After a confusing tour of the station's docking facilities and the warship's transit tubes, he fetched up in the doorway of a crowded, red-lit, octagonal space, maintained in zero gee by a local relaxation of the laws of physics. A squat, balding engineering officer was bawling out a frightened-looking teenager in front of an open access panel. 'That's the last bloody time you touch anything without asking me or Chief Otcenasek first, you bumbling numb-fingered oaf! See that panel? That's the backup master bus arbitration exchange, there. And *that*' – he pointed at another, closed panel – 'is the backup master circuit breaker box, which is what chief told you to check out. That switch you were about to throw –'

Martin saw where the officer's finger was pointing and winced. If some idiot conscript did something like that to him, he reflected, he probably wouldn't stop at threatening to strangle him with his own intestines. Although if the idiot had started playing with the MBAX, strangling him would be redundant: it didn't usually have much effect on a charred corpse.

'Engineering Commander Krupkin?' he asked.

'Yes? Who? Oh. You must be the shipyard mechanic?' Krupkin turned toward him, leaving the hapless rating to scramble for cover. 'You're late.'

'Blame the Curator's Office,' snapped Martin. As soon as the words left his mouth, he regretted them. 'I'm sorry. I've had a bad week. What can I do for you?'

'Secret state police, hmm? Won't get many of those around here,' Krupkin grunted, abruptly conciliatory. 'You know something about this toybox, then?'

'MiG sells them. You keep them running. People break them. I fix them. Is that what you wanted to know?'

'That's a good start.' Krupkin suddenly grinned. 'So let's try another question. What do you know about preferential-frame clock-skew baseline compensators? Specifically, this model K-340, as currently configured. Tell me everything you can see about how it's set up.'

Martin spent the next hour telling him all the different ways it was out of alignment. After that, Krupkin showed him a real K-340, not a bodged test article. And then it was time for a working lunch while Krupkin picked his brains, and then a long working afternoon figuring out where everything went and going over change orders to make sure everything was where the paperwork said it was supposed to be. And then back to base for the evening . . .

Rachel Mansour stood naked in the middle of the hand-woven rug that covered the floor of the hotel room she had rented two hours earlier, in the naval port city of Klamovka: even though it was expensive, it smelled of damp and dry rot, carbolic soap and firewood. She breathed slowly and evenly as she stretched arms and legs in ritual sequence, limbering up. The curtains were drawn, the door locked, and her sensors stationed outside to warn her of intruders: for she was not inclined to explain her state to any hotel staff who might see it.

Rachel was not inclined to explain a lot of things to the people she moved among. The New Republic filled her with a bitter, hopeless anger – one which she recognized, understood to be a poor reflection on her professionalism, but nevertheless couldn't set aside. The sheer waste of human potential that was the New Republic's *raison d'être* offended her sensibilities as badly as a public book-burning, or a massacre of innocents.

The New Republic was 250 years old, 250 light-years from Earth. When the Eschaton had relocated nine-tenths of Earth's population via wormhole – for reasons it hadn't deigned to explain – it had sorted some of them on the basis of ethnic or social or psychological affinity. The New Republic had picked up a mixed bag of East-European technorejectionists and royalists, hankering for the comforting certainties of an earlier century.

The founders of the New Republic had suffered at the hands of impersonal technological change. In the market-oriented democracies of pre-Singularity Earth, they'd seen people cast by their millions on the scrap heap of history. Given a new world to tame, and the tools to do it with, they had immediately established a conservative social order. A generation later, a vicious civil war broke out betvveen those who wanted to continue using the cornucopia machines – self-replicating nano-assembler factories able to manufacture any physical goods – and those who wanted to switch to a simpler way of life where everybody knew their place and there was a place for everyone. The progressives lost: and so the New Republic remained for a century, growing into its natural shape – Europe as it might have been during the twentieth century, had physics and chemistry been finalized in 1890. The patent offices were closed; there were no homes for dreaming relativists here.

Standing naked in the middle of the carpet, she could set it aside for a while. She could ignore the world while her implants ran through their regular self-defense practice sequence. It started with breathing exercises, then the isometric contraction of muscle groups under the direction of her battle management system, then finally a blur of motion as the embedded neural network controllers took over, whirling her body like a marionette through a series of martial arts exercises. A ten-minute cycle performed twice a week kept her as ready for personal defense as an unaugmented adept who spent an hour or more every day.

Whirling and jerking on invisible strings she threw and dismembered intangible demons; it was no great effort to project her frustrations and anger onto them. *This* for the blind beggar she had passed in the street, his affliction curable in a culture that didn't ban most advanced medical practices. *That* for the peasants bound to the soil they tilled by a law that saw them as part of the land, rather than as human beings. *This* for the women condemned to die giving birth to unwanted children. *That* for the priests who pandered to the prejudices of the ruling elite and offered their people the false consolation of the hereafter, when most of the horrors that besieged them had long since been banished from the civilized worlds. And *this* and *this* and *that* for treating her like a third-class citizen. Anger demanded many *kata*.

I do not want this world. I do not like this world. I do not need this world, I do not need to feel sympathetic for this world or its inhabitants. If only they did not need me . . .

There was a small bathroom next door – an expensive extra in this society. She used it to clean herself as efficiently as possible, sweat and grime washing away like memories. And some of the pessimism went with it. *Things around here are going to get better*, she reminded herself. *That's what I'm here for*.

Once dry, she wandered back into the bedroom and sat down on the edge of the bed. Then she picked up her battered PA. 'Get me the UN Consensus Ambassador,' she ordered. There was only one UN ambassador in the New Republic; George Cho, permanent representative of the Security Council, to which she was ultimately answerable. (The New Republic persistently refused to recognize any of Earth's more subtle political institutions.)

'Processing. *Beep*. Rachel, I'm sorry, but I'm not available right now. Waiting for information to become available about the incident at Rochard's. If you'd like to leave a message after the tone . . . *beep*.'

'Hi, George. Rachel here. Calling from Klamovka. Give me a call back; I think I ought to go public, and I want diplomatic backup. Let's talk. Message ends.'

She closed the PA and put it down again. Stared moodily at the dresser. Her costume (she found it hard to think of it as regular clothing, even after months of wearing it daily) lay heaped around the dressing table. There were visits to make, forms to be observed, before she could act openly. *Fuck this for a game of soldiers*, she thought. Living by the New Republic's rules had gotten old fast. *I need some civilized company before I go out of my skull.* Speaking of which, there was that engineering contractor to call. A bit of a cold fish, and not very cooperative, but she be damned if she'd let him throw her off; she could probably dig more out of him in an hour over a restaurant table than she'd be able to get from the Admiralty office in a month of diplomatic cocktail parties and formal memoranda.

She picked up the PA again. 'PA, page engineer Springfield's voice mail for me. Speech only. I have a message for him. Message begins . . .'

George Cho, Ambassador Plenipotentiary from the United Nations Security Council to the court of His Imperial Majesty, Emperor Ivan Hasek III (by grace of God, et cetera), sweated under his high collar and nodded politely. 'Yes, Your Excellency, I quite understand your point. Nevertheless, although the territory in dispute is annexed to the New Republic, I must state again that we believe the situation falls within our remit, if only because it is not a purely domestic affair – unless this Festival is some peculiar tradition of yours that I have not hitherto been apprised of? – and consequently, the ugly matter of Clause Nineteen rears its head again.'

His Excellency the Archduke Michael Hasek shook his head. 'We cannot accept that,' he stated. He stared at Cho from watery but piercing blue eyes. *Bloody foreign busybodies*, he thought. Not that Cho was a bad sort, for a degenerate Terran anarchist technophiliac. He reminded Michael of a blood-hound; baggy-eyed, jowly, perpetually sad-looking, and a mind like a spring-steel trap.

George Cho sighed and leaned back in his chair. He stared past the Archduke, at the portrait of the Duke's father that hung on the wall. Emperor at forty, dead of old age at sixty, Emperor Hasek II: something of a prodigy, a force for progress in an insanely conservative milieu. The man had pulled the

New Republic far enough out of its shell to acquire a navy and colonize three or four utterly benighted backwaters. A good student of history. *Dangerous*.

'I notice you looking at my father. He was a very stiff-necked man. It's a trait that runs in the family,' Michael observed wryly. 'We don't like outsiders sticking their noses into our affairs. Maybe this is short-sighted of us, but—' He shrugged.

'Ah.' Cho brought his eyes back to the Duke. 'Yes, of course. However, I am wondering if perhaps the advantages of UN involvement haven't been made clear to you? I believe we have quite a lot to offer; I wouldn't dream of approaching you about this if I didn't think you could benefit from it.'

'There are benefits and there are side-effects. Did you have anything specific in mind?' Michael leaned forward.

'As a matter of fact . . . yes. It comes back to Clause Nineteen; the injunction against use of causality-violation weapons. "Whosoever shall cause to be deployed a weapon capable of disrupting the et cetera shall be guilty of a crime against humanity and subject to the internationally agreed penalties for that offense." We know perfectly well that you wouldn't dream of using such weapons against one of your own worlds. But we have insufficient evidence about the intentions of the, ah, aggressor party, this *Festival*. There's a marked shortage of information about them, which is in itself worrying. What I'm suggesting is that it might be advantageous to you to have independent observers from the UN in train with your expedition, to rebut any accusations that the New Republic is committing crimes against humanity and to act as witnesses in the event that your forces are themselves attacked in such a manner.'

'Aha.' Michael gritted his teeth and smiled at the ambassador. 'And what makes you think there's an expedition?'

It was Cho's turn to smile: tiredly, for he had been awake for nearly forty-eight hours at this point, collating intelligence reports, monitoring media and trying to put together the big picture single-handedly – the New Republic had strictly limited the size of his diplomatic staff. 'Come, Your Excellency, are we to believe that the New Republic will allow an insult to its honor, let alone its territorial integrity, to stand without response? Some sort of reaction is inevitable. And given the loss of your Navy's local presence, and the increased state of alert and heavy engineering activity around your bases at Klamovka, Libau, and V-l, a naval expedition seems likely. Or were you planning to get your soldiers there by ordering them to click their heels three times while saying "there's no place like home"?'

Michael pinched the bridge of his nose, attempting to cover his frown. 'I can neither confirm nor deny that we are considering naval action at this time.'

Cho nodded. 'Of course.'

'However. Do you know anything about this Festival? Or what has been going on at Rochard's World?'

'Surprisingly little. You've been keeping a lid on whatever's going on – not very subtly, I'm afraid, the dispatches from the Fourth Guards Division's desperate defense of the colonial capital would be more convincing if the Fourth Guards' relocation from New Prague to Baikal Four hadn't been mentioned in dispatches a month ago. But you're not the only people keeping the lid on it. My people have been unable to unearth any information about this Festival anywhere, which is distinctly worrying. We even broadcast a request for help from the Eschaton, but all that came back was a cryptogram saying, "P. T. Barnum was right."' (A cryptogram which had been encoded with a key from a secured UN diplomatic onetime pad, the leakage of which had already caused a major security panic.)

'I wonder who this T. P. Barney was,' Duke Michael

commented. 'No matter. The Festival has had an, ah, catastrophic impact on Rochard's World. The economy is in ruins, there's widespread civil disorder and outright rebellion. In fact —' He stared sharply at the ambassador. 'You understand what this means for the guiding principles of our civilization?'

'I'm here strictly as an ambassador to represent the interests of all UN parties in the New Republic,' Cho stated neutrally. 'I'm not here to pass judgment on you. That would be presumptuous.'

'Hmm.' Michael glanced down at his blotter.

'It is true that we are considering an expedition,' said the Archduke. Cho struggled to conceal his surprise. 'But it will be difficult,' Michael continued. 'The enemy is already well entrenched in the destination system. We don't know where they come from. And if we send a fleet there directly, it may well suffer the same fate as the naval squadron on station. We are therefore considering a rather, ah, desperate stratagem.'

Cho leaned forward. 'Sir, if you are contemplating a causality violation, I must advise you—'

The Archduke raised a hand. 'I assure you, Ambassador, that no global causality violation will take place as a result of actions of the New Republican Navy. We have no intention of violating Clause Nineteen.' He grimaced. 'However, localized causality violations are sometimes permitted within tactical situations confined to the immediate light cone of an engagement, are they not? I think that . . . hmm, yes. A UN observer would be able to assure all parties that our own conduct was legal and correct, would he not?'

'A UN observer will scrupulously tell the truth,' Cho stated, sweating slightly.

'Good. In that case, I think we may be able to accommodate your request, if a decision is made to prepare a task force. One inspector only, with diplomatic credentials, may accompany the flagship. His remit will be to monitor the use of reality-modification weapons by both sides in the conflict and to assure the civilized worlds that the New Republic does not engage in gratuitous use of time travel as a weapon of mass destruction.'

Cho nodded. 'I think that would be acceptable. I shall notify Inspector Mansour, who is currently staying in Klamovka.'

Michael smiled, fleetingly. 'Send my secretary a note. I shall pass it to Admiral Kurtz's staff. I think I can guarantee that he will cooperate to the best of his abilities.'

Junior Procurator Vassily Muller, of the Curator's Office, stood in front of the great panoramic window that fronted Observation Bay Four and looked out across a gulf of light-years. Stars wheeled past like jewels scattered on a rotating display table. The spin of the huge station created a comfortably low semblance of gravity, perhaps eighty percent of normal; immediately outside the double wall of synthetic diamond lay the shipyard, where the great cylindrical bulk of a starship hung against a backdrop of cosmic beauty.

Shadows fell across the gray cylinder like the edge of eternity, sharp-edged with the unnatural clarity of vacuum. Inspection plates hung open at various points along the hull of the ship; disturbingly intestinal guts coiled loose, open to the remote manipulator pods that clung to it by many-jointed limbs. It resembled a dead, decaying whale being eaten by a swarm of lime green crabs. But it wasn't dead, Vassily realized: it was undergoing surgery.

The ship was like a marathon runner, being overhauled by surgeons in hope of turning him into some kind of cyborg prodigy to compete in the ultimate winner-take-all sporting event. The analogy with his own, slightly sore head did not escape Vassily: it struck him that the most radical preparation was essential for the struggle ahead. He could already feel the new connections, like a ghost of an undefined limb, firming up somewhere just beyond the edge of his perceptions. Another three days, the medic had assured him in the morning, and he'd find himself able to start training the cranial jack. They'd given him a briefcase full of instructions, a small and highly illegal (not to say horrifically expensive) tool kit, and a priority travel pass to the orbital station on an Air Defense shuttle, bypassing the slow space elevator.

'Procurator Muller, I presume?' He turned. A trim-looking fellow in the pale green uniform of His Majesty's Navy, a lieutenant's rings on his cuffs. He saluted. 'At ease. I'm Second Lieutenant Sauer, shipboard security officer for the *Lord Vanek*. Is this your first time up here?'

Vassily nodded, too tongue-tied to articulate a response. Sauer turned to face the window. 'Impressive, isn't she?'

'Yes!' The sight of the huge warship brought a great wave of pride to his chest: his people owned and flew such ships. 'My stepbrother is on one of them, a sister ship – the *Skvosty*.'

'Oh, very good, very good indeed. Has he been there long?'

'Three – three years. He is second fire control officer. A lieutenant, like yourself.'

'Ah.' Sauer tipped his head on one side and regarded Vassily with a brightly focused gaze. 'Excellent. But tell me, how good is this ship, really? How powerful do you think it is?'

Vassily shook his head, still dazzled by his first sight of the warship. 'I can't imagine anything grander than a ship like that one! How can anyone build better?'

Sauer looked amused. 'You are a detective, and not a cosmonaut,' he said. 'If you had been to naval college, you would be aware of some of the possibilities. Let us just say, for the moment, that they wouldn't have named it after old Ernst Ironsides if it wasn't the best ship we've got – but not everyone plays by the same rules as we do. I suppose it's only fair, then, for us to play a different game – which is of course precisely why you are here and we are having this conversation. You want to protect that ship, and the Republic, don't you?'

Vassily nodded eagerly. 'Yes. Did my CO let you know why I'm here?'

'I have a full briefing. We take anything that might compromise shipboard security extremely seriously; you won't be able to work in restricted areas, but as far as I'm concerned, you're welcome to go anywhere that isn't controlled – and by arrangement, I'm sure we can help you keep an eye on your yard-ape. To tell the truth, it's good for us that you are available for this duty. We have more than enough other problems to keep track of without stalking contractors on the job, and as long as the problem gets wrapped up satisfactorily in the end, who cares whose turf is turned over, eh?'

At this point, Vassily realized that something odd was going on, but being inexperienced, he didn't know quite what could be the matter. Nor did he want to push Sauer, at least not this soon in their acquaintance. 'Can you show me where Springfield is working?'

'Unfortunately' – Sauer spread his hands – 'Springfield is actually on board at this very minute. You realize that he is working on the interstellar propulsion system itself?'

'Oh.' Vassily's mouth made a round 'O'. 'You mean I'll have to go aboard?'

'I mean you *can't* go aboard – not until you've been checked out by medical, received security clearance, gone to three orientation briefings, and been approved by the old man – which won't be until tomorrow at the earliest. So, for the time being, I had better show you to the transient officers' quarters – you have the same privileges as a midshipman while you are on Admiralty turf.'

'That would be great,' Vassily agreed earnestly. 'If you'd lead the way . . .?'

*

Meanwhile, the first of the Festival's entourage of Critics was arriving in orbit around Rochard's World.

Once part of a human civilization that had transmigrated into its own computing network, the Festival was a traveling embassy, a nexus for the exchange of cultural information between stars. It was primarily interested in other upload cultures, but anyone would do at a pinch. It had zigged and zagged its way through the sphere of inhabited worlds for a thousand t-years, working its way inward from the periphery, and all the time it had asked only one thing of its willing or unwilling hosts: *Entertain us!*

The Festival was sharply constrained by the density of information that could be crammed into the tiny starwisps that carried it across the interstellar gulf. Unlike a normal upload civilization, the Festival couldn't manufacture its own reality with sufficient verisimilitude to avoid the normal hazards of life in a virtual universe; it was a desert plant, existing as a seed for years at a time between frantic growth spurts when the correct conditions arose.

Like most circus caravans, the Festival accumulated hitchhikers, hangers-on, and a general fringe of camp followers and parasites. There was room for millions of passengers in the frozen mind-cores of the starwisps, but no room for them to think between stations. Trueminds aestivated during the decade-long hops between planetary civilizations; simple, subsentient supervisors kept the starwisps on course and ran the autonomic systems. On arrival, the servitors built the necessary infrastructure to thaw and load the trueminds. Once contact had been achieved and a course of action decided upon, any residual capacity would be made available to the passengers, including the Critics.

A foam of diamond was growing in orbit around Sputnik, the outer moon of Rochard's World. Strange emulsions stirred within some of the bubbles, a boiling soup of nanomachinecatalyzed chemical reactions. Other bubbles faded to black, soaking up sunlight with near-total efficiency. A steady stream of tanks drifted toward the foam on chaotic orbits, ejecta from the mining plants in the outer system. Within the bubbles, incarnate life congealed, cells assembled by machine rather than the natural cycle of mitosis and differentiation. Thousands of seconds passed, an aeon to the productive assemblers: skeletons appeared, first as lacy outlines and then as baroque coral outcroppings afloat in the central placentory bubbles. Blood, tissues, teeth, and organs began to congeal in place as the nano-assemblers pumped synthetic enzymes, DNA, ribosomes, and other cellular machinery into the lipid vesicles that were due to become living cells.

Presently, the Critics' bodies began to twitch.

the spacelike horizon

The door to the study opened and a liveried footman entered. 'Commodore Bauer to see the admiral,' he announced.

'Sh-show him in, then!'

Commodore Bauer entered the Admiral's study and saluted. Seated behind an imposing hardwood desk in the center of the huge room (paneled in ferociously expensive imported hardwoods, with raw silk curtains and not a little gold leaf on the cornices), the admiral looked tiny: a wizened turtle sporting a walrus moustache, adrift on a sea of blue-and-silver carpet. Nevertheless, he was in good condition today, wearing his uniform, resplendent with decorations and ribbons, and seated in a real chair.

'Commmmmander. Welcome. Please be seated.'

Commodore Bauer walked toward the desk and took the indicated chair.

'And how is your father these days? It's – it's a while since I saw him.'

'He's very well sir.' *At least as well as he could be, considering he died four years ago.* Bauer looked at his superior sadly. Once the sharpest saber in the New Republic's arsenal, Rear Admiral Kurtz was rusting at a terrifying rate: they must already be planning the funeral. He still had periods of lucidity, sometimes quite extended ones, but forcing him to go on this expedition – and no officer could realistically refuse a royal commission and expect to continue to hold his post – was positively cruel; surely His Majesty must have known about his state? 'May I ask why you summoned me, sir?'

'Ah – ah – ah, yes.' The Admiral jerked as if someone had just administered an electric shock to him. Suddenly his expression tightened. 'I must apologize, Commodore: I have too many vague moments. I wanted to discuss the flisposition of the – I mean, the disposition – the fleet. Obviously you will be in day-to-day command of the task force, and in overall tactical command once it arrives at Rochard's World. The matter of planning, however, is one to which I feel I can make a contribution.' A wan smile flitted across his face. 'Do you agree with this?'

'Ah, yes, sir.' Bauer nodded, slightly encouraged. The grand old man might be drifting into senility, but he was still razor-sharp during his better moments: if he was willing to sit back and let Bauer do most of the driving, perhaps things might work out. (As long as he remembered who Bauer was, the commodore reminded himself.) They'd worked together before: Bauer had been a junior lieutenant under captain Kurtz during the Invasion of Thermidor, and had a keen respect for his intellect, not to mention his dogged refusal to back down in the face of heavy opposition. 'I was led to believe that the General Staff Directorate has some unusual plans for lifting the siege; is this what you have in mind?'

'Yes.' Admiral Kurtz pointed at a red leather folder lying on his desk. 'Contingency Omega. I had a ha-hand in the first paper, ten years ago, but I fear younger minds will have to refine it into a plan of attack.'

'Contingency Omega.' Bauer paused. 'Wasn't that shelved, because of, ah, legal concerns?'

'Yes.' Kurtz nodded. 'But only as a plan of att-att-attack. We are not allowed to fly closed timelike paths – use faster-than-light travel to arrive before war breaks out. Leads to all – all – sorts of bother. Neighbors say God doesn't like it. *Blithering nonsense* if you ask me. But we've already been attacked. They came to us. So we can arrive in our own past, but after the attack began: I must confess, I think it is a bit of a pathetic excuse, but there we are. Contingency Omega it is.'

'Oh.' Bauer reached toward the red folder. 'May I?'

'Cer-certainly.'

The Commodore began to read.

Accelerating to speeds faster than light was, of course, impossible. General relativity had made that clear enough back in the twentieth century. However, since then a number of ways of circumventing the speed limit had turned up; by now, there were at least six different known methods of moving mass or information from A to B without going through c.

A couple of these techniques relied on quantum trickery, strange hacks involving Bose-Einstein condensates to flip bits in quantum dots separated by light-years; as with the causal channel, the entangled dots had to be pulled apart at slower-than-light speeds, making them fine for communication but useless for transporting bodies. Some of them – like the Eschaton's wormholes – were inexplicable, relying on principles no human physicist had yet discovered. But two of them were viable propulsion systems for spaceships; the Linde-Alcubierre expansion reciprocal, and the jump drive. The former set up a wave of expansion and contraction in the space behind and in front of the ship: it was peerlessly elegant, and more than somewhat dangerous – a spacecraft trying to navigate through the dense manifold of space-time ran the risk of being blown apart by a stray dust grain.

The jump drive was, to say the least, more reliable, barring a few quirks. A spaceship equipped with it would accelerate out from the nearest star's gravity well. Identifying a point of equipotential flat space-time near the target star, the ship would light up the drive field generator, and the entire spaceship could then tunnel between the two points without ever actually being between them. (Assuming, of course, that the target star was more or less in the same place and the same state that it appeared to be when the starship lit off its drive field – if it wasn't, nobody would ever see that ship again.)

But the jump drive had huge problems for the military. For one thing, it only worked in flat space-time, a very long way out from stars or planets, which meant you had to arrive some way out, which in turn meant that anyone you were attacking could see you coming. For another thing, it didn't have a very long range. The farther you tried to jump, the higher the probability that conditions at your destination point weren't what you were expecting, creating more work for the loss adjusters. Most seriously, it created a tunnel between equipotential points in space-time. Miscalculate a jump and you could find yourself in the absolute past, relative to both your starting point and the destination. You might not know it until you went home, but you'd just violated causality. And the Eschaton had a *serious* problem with people who did *that*.

This was why Contingency Omega was one of the more sensitive documents in the New Republican Navy's war plan library. Contingency Omega discussed possible ways and means of using causality violation – time travel within the preferred reference frame – for strategic advantage. Rochard's World was a good forty light-years from New Austria;

normally that meant five to eight jumps, a fairly serious journey lasting three or four weeks. Now, in time of war, the direct approach zones from New Austria could be presumed to be under guard. Any attack fleet would have to jump around the Queen's Head Nebula, an effectively impassable cloud within which three or four protostellar objects were forming. And to exercise Contingency Omega – delicately balancing their arrival time against the receipt of the first distress signal from Rochard's World, so that no *absolute* causality violation would take place but their arrival would take their enemies by surprise – well, that would add even more jumps, taking them deep into their own future light cone before looping back into the past, just inside the spacelike event horizon.

It was, Bauer realized, going to be the longest-range military operation in the history of the New Republic. And – God help him – it was his job to make sure it worked.

Burya Rubenstein whacked on the crude log table with a worn-out felt boot. 'Silence!' he yelled. Nobody paid any attention; annoyed, he pulled out the compact pistol the trade machine had fabricated for him and fired into the ceiling. It only buzzed quietly, but the resulting fall of plaster dust got everybody's attention. In the midst of all the choking and coughing, he barked, 'Committee will come to order!'

'Why should we?' demanded a heckler at the back of the packed beer hall.

'Because if you don't shut up and let me talk, you'll have to answer to Politovsky and his dragoons. The worst *I'll* do to you is shoot you – if the Duke gets his hands on you, you might have to work for a living!' Laughter. '*His* living. What we've got here is an unprecedented opportunity to cast off the shackles of economic slavery that bind us to soil and factory, and bring about an age of enlightened social mobility in which we are free to better ourselves, contribute to the common good, and learn to work smarter and live faster. But, comrades, the forces of reaction are ruthless and vigilant; even now a Navy shuttle is ferrying soldiers to Outer Chelm, which they plan to take and turn into a strongpoint against us.'

Oleg Timoshevski stood up with an impressive whining and clanking. 'No worries! We'll smash 'em!' He waved his left arm in the air, and his fist morphed into the unmistakable shape of a gun launcher. Having leapt into the pool of available personal augmentation techniques with the exuberance of the born cyborg, he could pose as a poster for the Transhumanist Front, or even the Space and Freedom Party.

'That's enough, Oleg.' Burya glared at him, then turned back to the audience. 'We can't afford to win this by *violence*,' he stressed. 'In the short term, that may be tempting, but it will only serve to discredit us with the masses, and tradition tells us that, without the masses on our side, there can be no revolution. We have to prove that the forces of reaction corrode before our peace-loving forces for enterprise and progress without the need for repression – or ultimately all we will succeed in doing is supplanting those forces, and in so doing become indistinguishable from them. Is *that what you want?*'

'No! Yes! NO!' He winced at the furor that washed across the large room. The delegates were becoming exuberant, inflated with a sense of their own irresistible destiny, and far too much free wheat beer and vodka. (It might be synthetic, but it was indistinguishable from the real thing.)

'Comrades!' A fair-haired man, middle-aged and of sallow complexion, stood inside the main door to the hall. 'Your attention please! Reactionary echelons of the imperialist junta are moving to encircle the Northern Parade Field! The free market is in danger!'

'Oh bugger,' muttered Marcus Wolff.

'Go see to it, will you?' Burya asked. 'Take Oleg, get him out of my hair, and I'll hold the fort here. Try to find something for Jaroslav to do while you're about it — he can juggle or fire his water pistol at the soldiers or something; I can't do with him getting underfoot.'

'Will do that, boss. Are you serious about, uh, not breaking heads?'

'Am I serious?' Rubenstein shrugged. 'I'd rather we didn't go nuclear, but feel free to do anything necessary to gain the upper hand — as long as we keep the moral high ground. If possible. We don't need a fight now; it's too early. Hold off for a week, and the guards will be deserting like rats leaving a sinking ship. Just try to divert them for now. I've got a communiqué to issue which ought to put the cat among the pigeons with the lackeys of the ruling class.'

Wolff stood and walked around to Timoshevski's table. 'Oleg, come with me. We have a job to do.' Burya barely noticed: he was engrossed, nose down in the manual of a word processor that the horn of plenty had dropped in his lap. After spending his whole life writing longhand or using a laborious manual typewriter, this was altogether too much like black magic, he reflected. If only he could figure out how to get it to count the number of words in a paragraph, he'd be happy: but without being able to cast off, how could he possibly work out how much lead type would be needed to fill a column properly?

The revolutionary congress had been bottled up in the old Corn Exchange for three days now. Bizarre growths like black metal ferns had colonized the roof, turning sunlight and atmospheric pollution into electricity and brightly colored plastic cutlery. Godunov, who was supposed to be in charge of catering, had complained bitterly at the lack of tableware (as if any true revolutionary would bother with such trivia) until Misha, who had gotten much deeper into direct brain interfaces than even Oleg, twitched his nose and instructed the things on the roof to start producing implements. Then Misha went away on some errand, and nobody could turn the spork factory off. Luckily there seemed to be no shortage of food, munitions, or anything else for that matter: it seemed that Burya's bluff had convinced the Duke that the democratic soviet really did have nuclear weapons, and for the time being the dragoons were steering well clear of the yellow brick edifice at the far end of Freedom Square.

'Burya! Come quickly! Trouble at the gates!'

Rubenstein looked up from his draft proclamation. 'What is it?' he snapped. 'Speak clearly!'

The comrade (Petrov, wasn't that his name?) skidded to a halt in front of his desk. 'Soldiers,' he gasped.

'Aha.' Burya stood. 'Are they shooting yet? No? Then I will talk to them.' He stretched, trying to ease the stiffness from his aching muscles and blinking away tiredness. 'Take me to them.'

A small crowd was milling around the gates to the Corn Exchange. Peasant women with head scarves, workers from the ironworks on the far side of town – idle since their entire factory had been replaced by a miraculous, almost organic robot complex that was still extending itself – even a few gaunt, shaven-headed zeks from the corrective labor camp behind the castle: all milling around a small clump of frightened-looking soldiers. 'What is going on?' demanded Rubenstein.

'These men, they say—'

'Let them speak for themselves.' Burya pointed to the one nearest the gate. 'You. You aren't shooting at us, so why are you here, comrade?'

'I, uh,' the trooper paused, looking puzzled.

'We's sick of being pushed around by them aristocrats, that's wot,' said his neighbor, a beanpole-shaped man with a sallow complexion and a tall fur hat that most certainly wasn't standard-issue uniform. 'Them royalist parasite bastids, they's locked up in 'em's castle drinking champagne and 'specting us to die keeping 'em safe. While out here all 'uns enjoying themselves and it's like the end of the regime, like? I mean, wot's going on? Has true libertarianism arrived yet?'

'Welcome, comrades!' Burya opened his arms toward the soldier. 'Yes it is true! With help from our allies of the Festival, the iron hand of the reactionary junta is about to be overthrown for all time! The new economy is being born; the marginal cost of production has been abolished, and from now on, if any item is produced once, it can be replicated infinitely. From each according to his imagination, to each according to his needs! Join us or better still, bring your fellow soldiers and workers to join us!'

There was a sharp bang from the roof of the Corn Exchange, right at the climax of his impromptu speech; heads turned in alarm. Something had broken inside the spork factory and a stream of rainbow-hued plastic implements fountained toward the sky and clattered to the cobblestones on every side, like a harbinger of the postindustrial society to come. Workers and peasants alike stared in open-mouthed bewilderment at this astounding display of productivity, then bent to scrabble in the muck for the brightly colored sporks of revolution. A volley of shots rang out and Burya Rubenstein raised his hands, grinning wildly, to accept the salute of the soldiers from the Skull Hill garrison.

'The evening news bulletin. And now for today's headlines. The crisis over the invasion of Rochard's World by the so-called Festival continues. Attempts at diplomatic intermediation having been rebuffed, it now appears that military action is inevitable. Word from the occupied territory is hard to obtain, but to the best of our knowledge, the garrison under Duke Politovsky continue to fight valiantly to defend the Imperial standard. Ambassador Al-Haq of Turku said earlier on this program that the government of Turku agreed that the expansionist policies of the so-called Festival represent an intolerable threat to peace.

'The woman who chained herself to the railings of the Imperial residence yesterday morning, demanding votes and property rights for ladies, has been found to have a long history of mental disorders characterized by paranoid hysteria. Leaders of the Mothers' Union today denied any knowledge of her actions and decried them as unfeminine. She is expected to be charged with causing a public disturbance later this week.

'Baseless rumors circulating on Old Earth about the Admiralty's planned rolling series of upgrades to our naval capability caused numerous extraplanetary investment companies to sell stocks short, resulting in a plummeting exchange rate and the withdrawal of several insurance companies from the New Republic market. No announcement has yet been made by the chairman of the Royal Bank, but officials from the chamber of trade are currently drawing up charges against those companies participating in the stampede, accusing them of slander and conspiracy to establish a trade cartel using the current defense alert as a pretext.

'The four anarchists hanged at Krummhopf Prison today were attended by—'

Click.

'I hate this fucking planet,' Martin whispered, sinking deeper into the porcelain bathtub. It was the only good feature of the poky little two-room dockside apartment they'd plugged him into. (The bad features, of course, included the likelihood of bugging devices.) He stared at the ceiling, two meters above him, trying to ignore the radio news.

The phone rang.

Cursing, Martin hauled himself out of the bath and, dripping, hopped into the living room. 'Yes?' he demanded.

'Had a good day?' A woman's voice; it took him a second to place it.

'Lousy,' he said with feeling. *And hearing from you doesn't make it any better*, he thought: the idea of being sucked into some kind of diplomatic scam didn't appeal. But the urge to grumble overrode minor irritation. 'Their list of embargoed technology includes cranial interfaces. It's all crappy VR immersion gloves and keyboards: everything I look at now is covered in purple tesseracts, and my fingers ache.'

'Well, it sounds like you've had a really good day, compared to mine. Have you had anything to eat yet?'

'Not yet.' Suddenly Martin noticed that he was starving, not to mention bored. 'Why?'

'You're going to like this,' she said lightly. 'I know a reasonable restaurant on C deck, two up and three corridors over from security zone gateway five. Can I buy you dinner?'

Martin thought for a moment. Normally he'd have refused, seeking some way to avoid contact with the UN diplomatic spook. But he was hungry; and not just for food. The casual invitation reminded him of home, of a place where people were able to talk freely. The lure of company drew him out, and after dressing, he followed her directions, trying not to think too deeply about it.

The visiting officers' quarters were outside the security zone of the base but there was still a checkpoint to pass through before he reached the airlock to the civilian sections of the station. Outside the checkpoint, he stepped into a main corridor. It curved gently to the left, following the interior of the station's circumference: more passages opened off it, as did numerous doorways. He walked around a corner and out onto the street – 'Martin!' She took his arm. 'So pleased to see you!'

She'd changed into a green dress with a tight bodice and long black gloves. Her shoulders and upper arms were bare, but for a ribbon around her throat, which struck him as odd; something in his customs briefing nagged at his memory. 'Pretend you're pleased to see me,' she hissed. 'Pretend for the cameras. You're taking me out to buy me dinner. And call me Ludmilla in public.'

'Certainly.' He forced a smile. 'My dear! How nice to see you!' He took her arm and tried to follow her lead. 'Which way?' he muttered.

'You're doing fine for an amateur. Third establishment on the right. There's a table in your name. I'm your companion for the night. Sorry about the cloak-and-dagger bit, but you're being monitored by base security, and if I were officially here as me, they'd start asking you questions. It's much more convenient if I'm a woman of easy virtue.'

Martin flushed. 'I see,' he said. The penny dropped, finally: in this strait-laced culture, a woman who displayed bare skin below her chin was a bit racy, to say the least. Which meant, now he thought about it, that the hotel was full of –

'You haven't used the hotel facilities since you arrived?' she asked, raising an eyebrow.

Martin shook his head. 'I don't believe in getting arrested in foreign jurisdictions,' he mumbled to cover his discomfort. 'And the local customs here are confusing. What do you think of them?'

She squeezed his arm. 'No comment,' she said lightly. 'Ladies here aren't supposed to swear.' She gathered her skirts in as he opened the door for her. 'Still, I doubt this social order will last many more years. They've had to invest a lot of energy to maintain the *status quo* so long.'

'You sound like you're looking forward to its collapsing.' He held out his card to a liveried waiter, who bowed and scurried off into the restaurant.

'I am. Aren't you?'

Martin sighed quietly. 'Now that you come to mention it, I

wouldn't shed any tears. All I want to do is get this job over with and go home again.'

'I wish my life were that simple. I can't afford to be angry: I'm supposed to help protect this civilization from the consequences of its own stupidity. It's hard to fix social injustices when the people you're trying to help are all dead.'

'Your table, sir,' said the waiter, reappearing and bowing deeply. Rachel emitted an airheaded giggle; Martin followed the waiter, with Rachel in tow behind him.

She kept up the bubbleheaded pose until they were seated in a private booth and had ordered the menu of the day. As soon as the waiter disappeared, she dropped it. 'You want to know what's going on, who I am, and what this is all about,' she said quietly. 'You also want to know whether you should cooperate, and what's in it for you. Right?'

He nodded, unwilling to open his mouth, wondering how much she knew of his real business.

'Good.' She stared at him soberly. 'I take it you already decided not to turn me in to base security. That would have been a bad mistake, Martin; if not for you, then for a lot of other people.'

He lowered his gaze, staring at the place setting in front of her. Silver cutlery, linen napkin, starched tablecloth overflowing on all sides like a waterfall. And Rachel's breasts. Her dress made it impossible to ignore them, even though he tried not to stare: woman of easy virtue, indeed. He settled for looking her in the face. 'There's something I don't understand going on here,' he said. 'What is it?'

'All will be explained. The first thing I'm going to say is, after you hear my pitch, you can walk away unless you decide to involve yourself. I mean it; I came on heavily earlier, but really, I don't want you around unless you're a willing participant. Right now, they think you're just a loud-mouthed engineer. If they look too closely at me –' She paused. Her lips thinned a little. 'I'm female. I'll get precious little mercy if they trip over me by accident, but they don't really think of women as free agents, much less defense intelligence specialists, and by this time tomorrow, I should have my diplomatic credentials sorted out and be able to go public. Anyway: about what's going on here. Are you going to get up and walk out right now, or do you want in?'

Martin thought for a moment. *What should I do?* The solution seemed obvious: 'I'll settle for some answers. And dinner. Anything's better than being locked up in that pesthole of a base.'

'Okay.' She leaned back comfortably. 'First.' She held up a gloved finger. 'What's going on? That's actually a bit tricky to say. The UN has no jurisdiction here, but we've got enough clout to wreck the New Republic's trade treaties with half their neighbors if the New Republic was, for instance, found to be breaking conventions on warfare or application of forbidden technologies.'

Martin snorted. 'Forbidden tech? Them?'

'Do you really think they'd pass up the chance to steal an edge? The royal family, that is?'

'Hmm.' Martin rubbed his chin thoughtfully. 'Okay, so they're pragmatic rejectionists, is that what you're saying?'

'In a nutshell.' She shrugged. Against his better judgment, Martin found himself staring somewhere below her chin: he forced himself to look up. 'Our arms limitation arrangements have no authority here, but things are different closer to home, and a lot of the New Republic's trade flows in that direction. There's some recognition: once I get official accreditation, I've got diplomatic immunity, if they catch me and I live long enough to assert it. Two,' – she held up another finger – 'the arms limitation controls are to protect people from provoking intervention by the Eschaton. And they work both ways. As long as people stick to boring little things like planet-busting relativistic missiles and nerve gas or whatever, the big E doesn't get involved. But as soon as someone starts poking around the prohibited – for her coming-out party Daddy gave her an emerald *this* big!' She simpered, and Martin stared back, puzzled. Then he smiled fixedly as the waiter deposited a bowl of soup in front of him.

The waiter finished up, poured glasses of wine, and disappeared; Rachel pulled a face. 'Huh, where was I? You wouldn't believe how fast the girly-girl routine gets tiresome. Having to act like a retarded ten-year-old all the time . . . ah yes, the big E. The big E disapproves strongly of people who develop autonomous, self-replicating weapons, or causality-violation devices, or a whole slew of other restricted tools of mass destruction. Bacteria: out. Gray goo: out. Anything that smacks of self-modifying command software: out. Those are all category two forbidden weapons. A planetary civilization starts playing with them, sooner or later the big E comes looking, and then it's an ex-planetary civilization.'

Martin nodded, trying to look as if all this was new to him; he nipped his tongue to help resist the temptation to correct her last statement. Her engagement with the subject was infectious, and he found it hard to keep from contributing from his own knowledge of the field.

Rachel took a mouthful of soup. 'The big E can be extremely brutal. We've got definite confirmation of at least one atypical supernova event about five hundred light-years outside our – the terrestrial – light cone. It makes sense if you're trying to wipe out an exponentially propagating threat, so we figure that's why the Eschaton did it. Anyway, do you agree that it's bad policy to let the neighbor's toddler play with strategic nukes?'

'Yeah.' Martin nodded. He took a mouthful of soup. 'Something like that could really stop you getting to claim your on-time completion bonus.'

She narrowed her eyes, then nodded to him. 'Sarcasm, yet. How have you kept out of trouble so far?'

'I haven't.' He put his spoon down. 'That's why, if you don't mind me saying so, I was worried by your approach. I can do without getting myself slung in prison.'

Rachel took a breath. 'I'm sorry,' she said. 'I don't know if that'll go very far with you, but . . . I mean it. I'd just like to put it in a bigger perspective, though. The New Republic is only 250 light-years from Earth. If the big E decided to pop the primary here, we'd need to evacuate fifty star systems.' She looked uncomfortable. 'That's what this is about. That's why I had to drag you in.'

She looked down and concentrated on her soup bowl with single-minded determination. Martin watched her fixedly; his appetite was gone. She had done a robust job of destroying it by reminding him of why he was here. His parents, he didn't much care for, but he had a sister he was fond of on Mars, and too many friends and memories to want to hear any more about this. It was easier to watch her eat, to admire the flawless blush of the skin on her arms and her *décolletage* – he blinked, picked up his wineglass, and drained it in one. She looked up, caught him watching, grinned widely – theatrically, even – and licked her lips slowly. The effect was too much; he turned away.

'Shit and corruption, man, we're supposed to look as if you're buying me dinner as a prelude to taking me home and fucking me senseless!' she said quietly. 'Can't you at least fake some interest?'

'Sorry,' he said, taken aback; 'I'm not an actor. Is that what we're supposed to look like we're doing?'

She raised her wineglass: it was empty. 'Fill me up. Please.' She looked at him peculiarly; he twitched upright then reached out, took the wine bottle, and poured some of its contents into her glass. 'I didn't want to put you off your appetite.

Besides, you're the only civilized company for a couple of thousand miles.'

'I'm a drive engineer,' he said, wracking his brain for something else to say. *What am I getting myself into?* he wondered desperately. A couple of hours ago he'd been going crazy from boredom and loneliness: now an intelligent and attractive woman – who just happened to be a spy – had dragged him out to dinner. Something was bound to go wrong, wasn't it?

'I like working with machines. I like starships. I –' He cleared his throat. 'I'm not so good with people.'

'And this is a problem?'

'Yeah.' He nodded, then looked at her appraisingly. Her expression was sympathetic. 'I keep misreading the locals. Not good. So I holed up in my room and tried to stay out of the way.'

'And now, let me guess, you're going stir-crazy?'

'After four months of it, that's one way of putting it.' He took a mouthful of wine. 'How about you?'

She breathed deeply. 'Not quite the same, but nearly. I've got a job to do. I'm supposed to avoid getting into trouble. Part of the job is blending in, but it drives you nuts after a bit. Really, doing this face-to-face isn't recommended in the rule book, you know? It'd be safer just to drop an earbug off to relay you a message.'

'And you were.' He smiled faintly. 'Stir-crazy.'

'Yes.' She grinned. 'You too?'

'Anyone waiting for you back home?' he asked. 'Sorry. I mean, is there anyone you're waiting to get back to? Or anyone you can off-load onto? Write letters, or something?'

'Pah.' She frowned, then looked at him. 'This isn't a profession for someone who's married to anything other than their job, Martin. Any more than yours is. If you *were* married, would you bring your family out to somewhere like the New Republic?'

'No. I didn't mean it like that—'

'I know you didn't.' Her frown dissolved into a thoughtful expression. 'Just once in a while, though, it's good to be able to talk freely.'

Martin toyed with his wineglass. 'Agreed,' he said with feeling. 'I got bitten by that last week.' He stopped. She was looking at him oddly, her face stretched into something that might be taken for a smile if he couldn't see her eyes. Which looked worried.

'Smile at me. Yes, that's fine: now hold on to it. Don't stop smiling. We're under surveillance right now. Don't worry about the microphone – that's taken care of – but there's a human operative watching us from the other side of the restaurant. Try to look like you want to take me home and fuck me. Otherwise, he's going to wonder what we're doing here.' She simpered at him, smiling broadly. 'Do you think I'm pretty?' Her idiot grin was a mask: she inspected him from behind it.

'Yes –' He stared at her, hoping he looked adequately besotted. 'I think you're very pretty.' In the way that only a good diet and high-end medical care could deliver. He tried to smile wider. 'Uh. Actually. Handsome and determined is more like it.' Her smile acquired a slightly glassy edge.

Somewhere in the middle of the duel of the smiles, the waiter arrived and removed their bowls, replacing them with a main course.

'Oh, that looks good.' She relaxed slightly as she picked up her knife and fork. 'Hmm. Don't look around, but our shadow is looking away. You know something? You're too much of a gentleman for your own good. Most of the men in this joint would have tried to grope me by now. It goes with the territory.'

'After about fifty or sixty years, most men learn to stop worrying that it'll go away if they don't grab for it with both hands. Trouble is, with no anti-aging treatments here –' He looked uncomfortable.

'Yeah, and I appreciate it.' She smiled back. 'Anyone ever tell you you're cute when you grin? I've spent so long in this dump that I've forgotten what an honest smile looks like, let alone how it feels to be able to talk like a mature adult. Anyway . . .' he started. Her toe had just stroked the inside of his left leg. 'I think I like you,' she said quietly.

Martin paused a moment, then nodded soberly. 'Consider me charmed.'

'Really?' She grinned and slid her toe higher.

His breath caught. 'Don't! You'll cause a scandal!' He glanced around in mock horror. 'I hope nobody's watching.'

'No chance, that's what the tablecloth is meant to cover up.' She laughed quietly, and after a moment, he joined her. She continued quietly, 'To get the business over with so we can enjoy the meal, tomorrow you're going to go back aboard the *Lord Vanek* and they're probably going to ask you if you want to earn some more money in return for an extension on your contract. If you want to line your pocket and maybe help save several million lives you'll say *yes*. I happen to know that the admiral's staff is going to be using the *Lord Vanek* as flagship, and I'm going to be along too –'

'You're *what?* How are you going to do that?'

'As a diplomatic observer. My job is to make sure the Festival – and I wish I knew a bit more about who they are – don't violate six different treaties. Unofficially, I want to keep an eye on the New Republic, too. There's a bit more going on than anyone's willing to admit; no, make that a lot. But we don't want to let it get in the way of this meal, do we? If you agree, come home with me to a safe house, and I'll fill you in on the rest, while the local Stasi will just think you're making out like any other bachelor engineering contractor. So you're going to go home with a nice fat paycheck, plus a big bonus paid by DefIntelSIG. Everything's going to be *just fine.* Now, how about we forget business and eat our dinner before it gets cold?'

'Sounds okay to me.' Martin leaned forward. 'About the cover story for the local Stasi.'

'Yes.' She picked up her fork.

'Does it extend to grabbing a bottle of wine on our way home? And chilling out together afterward?'

'Well I suppose –' She stared at him. He noticed that her pupils were dilated.

'You need someone to talk to,' he said slowly.

'Don't I just.' She put the fork down. Under the table, out of sight, she rubbed his ankle again. Martin felt his pulse, felt his face flushing. She was focused on him, intent.

'How long has it been for you?' he asked quietly.

'Longer than four months.' Suddenly her foot was removed.

'Better eat up,' he said. 'If you want our cover story to be any good.'

'Clear channel to Herman, PA.'

'Clear channel pending . . . connected. Hello, Martin. What can I do for you?'

'Got a problem.'

'A big one?'

'Female human-sized. Actually she's from Earth, she's gorgeous, and, uh, she does undercover work for the UN defense intelligence SIG. Specializing in causality-violation weapons, disarmament treaty infractions, that sort of thing.'

'That is interesting. Say more.'

'Name's Rachel Mansour. Has what looks like genuine ID as a UN weapons inspector, and there's no way in hell she's a native or an agent provocateur – not unless they're sending their female agents off planet for education. She says that New Prague is planning some kind of naval expedition to relieve this colony that's under siege, and that she expects they'll try to recruit me tomorrow to do wartime crisis work on the ships. What she wanted me to do – well, basically keep my eyes open for anything fishy or illegal. Strategic weapons violations, I guess. That's an opening position. The question—'

'No forward-leaning analysis, please. Are you aware of any other UN inspectors in the vicinity?'

'Not directly, but she mentioned she has some kind of local backup and diplomatic credentials. She says she'll be along on the expedition. I expect there's a full-scale UN black ops team behind her, probably looking to do some low-key destabilization: it's not as if the New Republic hasn't been asking for it since they began the current naval buildup. I'm pretty sure she was telling me the truth about her mission goals, but only part of it.'

'Correct. On what basis did you leave her?'

'I agreed to do what she wanted.' Martin paused, unconsciously censoring his testimony, then continued, 'If you think it's advisable, I'll accept any offer of wartime work at hazard pay. Then I'll do what she wants: keep my eyes open for illegal activities. Any objection? How bad do you think the situation is?'

'It is much worse than you think.'

Martin did a double take. 'What?'

'I know of Rachel Mansour. Please wait.' His PA fell silent for almost a minute, while he sat in the dark of his rented room and waited anxiously. Herman never fell silent; like a machine running smoothly, his emollient debriefings made Martin feel as if he were talking to himself. Answers there might or might not be, but never silence . . .

'Martin. Please listen. I have independent confirmation that there is indeed a UN covert mission in the New Republic. Lead special agent is Rachel Mansour, which means they expect serious trouble. She is a heavyweight, and she's been out of sight for almost a year, which implies she's been in the New Republic for most of that time. Meanwhile, the agency representatives on Luna have bought out your personnel files and have been talking to MiG management about contracting you. Furthermore, they are substantially correct in their analysis. The New Republic is preparing to send the entire home fleet to Rochard's World, going the long way around, where they intend to attack the Festival. This is a very bad idea – they obviously do not understand the Festival – but preparations appear to be too advanced to divert at this time.

'It is also quite possible that you will endanger yourself if you appear to be panicking. Given the current level of surveillance you are under, an attempt to cut and run to a civil liner will be seen as treason and punished immediately by the Curator's security apparat; and Mansour is unlikely to be able to protect you even if she wants to. I emphasize, the New Republic is already on a low-key war footing, and attempting to leave now will be difficult.'

'Oh shit.'

'The situation is not irretrievable. I want you to cooperate fully with Mansour. Do your job and get out quietly. I will attempt to arrange for you to disembark safely once the fleet arrives. Remember, you are in more danger if you run than if you withdraw quietly.'

Martin felt a tension he'd barely been conscious of leaving him. 'Okay. Do you have any backstop options for me if the UN screws up? Any ideas for how I can get out with my skin intact? Any information about this Festival, whatever it is?'

Herman was silent for a moment. 'Be aware that this is now definitely a direct-action situation.' Martin gasped and sat bolt upright. 'I want you on hand in case things, to use your own terminology, go pear-shaped. Millions of lives are at stake. Larger-scale political issues are also becoming clear; if the New Republic meets the Festival, it is possible that the resulting

instabilities will catalyze a domestic revolution. The UN sub-
scribing bodies, both governmental and quasi-governmental,
have a vested interest in this for obvious reasons. I cannot tell
you more about the Festival at this point, because you would
incriminate yourself if you betrayed any knowledge of it; but
it is accurate to say that the Republic is more of a danger to
itself than to the Festival. However, in view of the nature of
the situation, I am prepared to pay a bonus double the size of
that promised by the UN inspectorate if you remain in place
after completing their assignment and do as I request.'

Martin's throat was dry. 'Alright. But if it's that likely to go
critical, I want three times the bonus. In event of my death,
payable to my next of kin.'

Silence. Then: 'Accepted. Herman out.'

Rachel lay in bed, staring at the ceiling, and tried to pick
apart her feelings. It was early morning: Martin had left sometime ago. She had a bad feeling about the business, even
though it was clearly going well; something gnawed at her
below the level of conscious awareness. Presently, she rolled
sideways, laid her sleepless head back on the overstuffed pillow
beside her, and drew her knees up.

It should have been a simple recruitment meeting: put the
arm on a useful contact and brief him for a single task. Nice
and objective. Instead, she'd found herself sharing a dinner
table with a quiet but fundamentally decent man who hadn't
tried to grope her, didn't treat her like a piece of furniture, *listened* with a serious expression, and made interesting
conversation: the kind of man who in ordinary circumstances
she'd have considered a pleasant date. She'd gone a little bit
crazy, walking along a knife edge of irresponsibility: and he'd
been stir-crazy too. And now she was worried about him —
which wasn't in the plan.

It had come to a head across the kitchen table as they

finished discussing business. He had looked up at her with a curious expectancy in his eyes. She crossed her legs, let a foot peep out beneath her skirts. He studied her intently.

'Is that everything?' he asked. 'You want me to keep my eyes open for clock-skew rollback instructions, carry the plug-in, notify you if I see anything that looks like a CVD – that's all?'

'Yes,' she said, staring at him. 'That's essentially everything.'

'It's ah –' He looked at her askance, sharply. 'I thought there was something more to it.'

'Maybe there is.' She folded her hands in her lap. 'But only if you want.'

'Oh, *well*,' he said, absorbing the information. 'What else is part of the job?'

'Nothing.' She tilted her head, meeting his angled gaze, steeling herself. 'We've finished with business. Do you remember what I said earlier, back in the restaurant?'

'About –' He nodded. Then looked away.

'What's wrong?' she asked.

'Oh, nothing.' He sighed quietly.

'Bullshit.' She stood up. 'Come on. Let's talk.' She reached for his hand and gave him a little tug.

'What?' He shook his head. 'I'm just—'

'Come on.' She pulled a little harder. 'The parlor. Come on.'

'Okay.' He stood up. He was no taller than she was; and he seemed to be avoiding her eyes. Uncomfortable, really.

'What's wrong?' she asked again.

He chuckled briefly; there was no amusement in it. 'You're the first sane person I've met in the past four months,' he said quietly. 'I was getting used to talking.'

She looked at him, steadily. 'You don't have to stop,' she said.

'I —' He froze up again. *Why is he doing that?* she wondered. 'Say something,' she said.

'I —' He paused, and she was afraid he was going to stop. Then he burst out, all at once. 'I don't *want* to stop. This place is squeezing me into my own head all the time — it's like being in a vise! The only thing anyone wants of me is my work—'

Rachel leaned against him. 'Shut up,' she said quietly. He shut up. 'That's better.' He was, she decided, really good at being leaned on. She put her arms around him; after a moment he hugged her back. 'Forget work. Yeah, you heard me. Forget the New Republic. Think you can do that for a few hours?'

'I —' she felt his breath shuddering. 'I'll try.'

'Good,' she said fiercely. And it *did* feel good: here was somebody who she could be sure about. Somebody who seemed to feel the same way about this whole claustrophobic abortion of a culture as she did. He held her steadily, now, and she could feel his hands running up and down her back, exploring how narrow her waist was. 'The parlor. Come on, it's the next room.'

Martin had stared back at her 'You sure you want this?' he asked. That was part of his charm.

'What's to be unsure about?' She kissed him hard, exploring his lips with her tongue. She felt as if she was about to burst right out of her clothes. He gently pulled her closer and let her dig her chin into the base of his neck; she felt stubble on his cheek. 'It's been so fucking *long*,' she whispered.

'Same to you too.' He took some of her weight in his arms. 'Been lonely?'

She barked a hoarse laugh. 'You have no idea. I've been here ages; long enough that I feel like some kind of deviant because I talk to strange men and have some role in life besides hatching babies. The way they think here is getting its claws into me.'

'What? A big strong government agent like you is letting something like this get to you?' he said, gently mocking.

'You're damn right,' she muttered into his shoulder as she felt a tentative hand begin to explore below her waistline.

'Sorry. Just – six months alone in this dump, having to act the part? I'd have gone nuts,' he said thoughtfully.

'Been more than six months,' she said, looking past the side of his head. *He has nice earlobes*, she noted vaguely as she leaned closer.

'Let's find that wine bottle,' he suggested gently. 'I think you're going a bit fast.'

'I'm sorry,' she said, automatically. 'I'm sorry.' She tensed slightly. 'No, you can keep your hands there. Let's walk.'

They somehow made it into the parlor – overstuffed arm-chairs and a display cabinet full of crockery – without letting go of each other.

'At first I thought you were some kind of agent provoca-teur,' he said, 'but instead you're the first real human being I've met in this place.' He left the statement hanging.

'If all I needed was flesh, there are plenty of sailor boys in this port,' she said, and leaned against him again. 'That's not where my itch is.'

'Are you sure you should be in this job? If you're so—'

'You were going to say vulnerable?'

'Maybe. Not exactly.'

She guided him in front of the sofa. 'I wanted company. Not just a quick fuck,' she explained, trying to justify it to herself.

'You and me both.' He held her, gently turned her around so that she was looking into his eyes. 'So what do you want this to be?'

'Stop talking.' She leaned forward closing her eyes, and found his mouth. Then events ran out of control.

They'd made love with desperate urgency the first time, Rachel lying on the parlor floor with her skirts hiked up around her waist, and Martin with his trousers tangled around his legs. Then they somehow migrated to the bedroom and struggled out of their clothing before making love again, this time gently and slowly. Martin had a thoughtful, considerate manner: talking afterward, he'd mentioned a divorce a few years ago. They'd talked for hours, almost until the artificial dawn, timed to coincide with sunrise on the planet below. And they'd made love until they were both sore and aching.

Now, lying awake in bed after he'd left, her head was spinning. She tried to rationalize it: isolation and nerves are enough to make anyone do something wild once in a while. Still, she felt nervous: Martin wasn't a casual pickup, and this wasn't a quick fuck. Just the thought of seeing him again made her feel an edgy hopeful excitement, tempered by the bitter self-disgust of realizing that mixing business with pleasure this way was a really stupid move.

She rolled over, and blinked: the clock on the inside of her left eyelid said it was just past 0700. In another two hours, it would be time to get confirmation of her diplomatic status, dress, and go kick some New Republic ass. Two hours after that, Martin would be aboard the *Lord Vanek*; it would all be over by 2200. Rachel sighed and tried to catch another hour's shut-eye; but sleep was evading her.

She found herself wandering, seeking out pleasant memories. There was not a lot else to be done, in point of fact: there was a high probability that she would die if her guess about the New Republic's intentions was wrong. And wouldn't that be a grand way to end 150 years? Physically as young as a twentysomething, kept that way by the advanced medical treatments of the mother planet, she rarely felt the weight of her decades; the angst only cut in when she thought about how few of the people she had known or loved were still alive. Now she recalled her daughter, as a child, the smell of her — and what brought *that* back? Not her daughter, the political matriarch and leader of a dynasty. Not the octogenarian's funeral, either, in the wake of the skysail accident. And she couldn't even remember Johan's face, even though they'd been married for fifteen years. Martin, so much more recent, seemed to overlay him in her mind's eye. She blinked, angrily, and sat up.

Stupid girl, she told herself, ironically. *Anyone would think you were still in your first century, falling in love with a tight pair of buttocks.* Still, she found herself looking forward to seeing Martin again tomorrow night. The edgy hopeful excitement was winning over age and cynicism, even though she was old enough to know what it meant. Complications . . .

The interorbit shuttle unlatched from the naval docking bay and edged outward from the beanstalk, its cold-gas thrusters bumping it clear of the other vehicles that swarmed in the region. Ten minutes after it maneuvered free, the pilot got permission from traffic control to light off his main drive; a bright orange plume of glowing mercury ions speared out from three large rectangular panels hinged around the rear cargo bay doors, and the craft began to accelerate. Ion drives were notoriously slow, but they were also efficient. After a thousand seconds the shuttle was moving out from the station at nearly two hundred kilometers per hour, and it was time to begin decelerating again to meet the ship that now lay at rest almost sixty kilometers from the station.

In orbital terms, sixty kilometers was nothing; the *Lord Vanek* was right on the beanstalk's doorstep. But there was one significant advantage to the position. The ship was ready to move, and move fast. As soon as the dockyard engineer finished his upgrade to the driver kernel's baseline compensators, she'd be ready for action.

Captain Mirsky watched the shuttle nose up to *Lord Vanek*'s forward docking bays on one of the video windows at his workstation. He sat alone in his quarters, plowing relentlessly through the memoranda and directives associated with the current situation; things had become quite chaotic since the orders came down, and he was acutely aware of how much more preparation was required.

Middle-aged, barrel-chested, and sporting a neat salt-and-pepper beard to match his graying hair, Captain Mirsky was the very model of a New Republican Navy captain. Behind the mask of confidence, however, there was a much less certain man: he had seen things building up for a week now, and however he tried to rationalize the situation, he couldn't escape the feeling that something had gone off the rails between the foreign office and the Imperial residence.

He peered morosely at the latest directive to cross his desk. Security was being stepped up, and he was to go onto a wartime footing as soon as the last shipyard workers and engineers were off his deck and the hull was sealed. Meanwhile, full cooperation was required with Procurator Muller of the Curator's Offfice, on board to pursue positive security monitoring of foreign engineering contractors employed in making running repairs to *Lord Vanek*'s main propulsion system. He glared at the offending memo in irritation, then picked up his annunciator. 'Get me Ilya.'

'Commander Murametz, sir? Right away, sir.'

A muffled knock on the door: Mirsky shouted 'open!' and it opened. Commander Murametz, his executive officer, saluted. 'Come in, Ilya, come in.'

'Thank you, sir. What I can do for you?'

'This –' Mirsky pointed wordlessly at his screen. 'Some pompous Citizen Curator wants his minion to run riot over my ship. Know anything about it?'

Murametz bent closer. 'Humbly report, sir, I do.' His moustache twitched; Mirsky couldn't tell what emotion it signified.

'Hah. Pray explain.'

'Some fuss over the engineering contractor from Earth who's installing our Block B drive upgrade. He's irreplaceable, at least without waiting three months, but he's a bit of a loudmouth and somehow caught the attention of one of the professional paranoids in the Basilisk. So they've stuck a secret policeman on us to take care of him. I gave him to Lieutenant Sauer, with orders to keep him out of our hair.'

'What does Sauer say about it?'

Murametz snorted. 'The cop's as wet behind the ears as one of the new ratings. No problem.'

The Captain sighed. 'See that there isn't.'

'Aye aye, sir. Anything else?'

Mirsky waved at a chair. 'Sit down, sit down. Noticed anything out of the ordinary about what's going on?'

Murametz glanced at the doorway. 'Rumors are flying like bullets, skipper. I'm doing what I can to sit on them, but until there's an official line—'

'There won't be. Not for another sixteen hours.'

'If I may be so bold, what then?'

'Then . . .' The Captain paused. 'I . . . am informed that I will be told, and that subsequently you, and all the other officers, will learn what's going on. In the meantime, I think it would be sensible to keep everybody busy. So that they don't have time to worry and spread rumors, anyway. Oh, and make damned sure the flag cabin's shipshape and we're ready to take on board a full staff team.'

'*Ah.*' Murametz nodded. 'Very well, sir. Operationally, hmm. Upgrade security, schedule some more inspections, heightened readiness on all stations? That sort of thing? Floggings to improve morale? A few simulation exercises for the tactical teams?'

Captain Mirsky nodded. 'By all means. But get the flag cabin ready first. Ready for a formal inspection tomorrow. That's all.'

'Yes, sir.'

'Dismissed.'

Murametz left, and Mirsky was alone with his morose thoughts once more. Alone to brood over the orders he was forbidden to reveal to anyone for another sixteen hours.

Alone with the sure, cold knowledge of impending war.

the admiral's man

His Majesty's battlecruiser *Lord Vanek* lay at rest, sixty kilometers from the Klamovka naval beanstalk. Running lights blinked red and blue along its flanks; the double-headed eagle ensign of the admiral's flag winked in green outline just above the main missile launch platform. Kurtz had been piped aboard two hours earlier; soon the ship would be ready to fly.

Rachel Mansour worked hard at suppressing the treacherous grin of satisfaction that kept threatening to escape. The reaction she'd elicited from the security goons at the entrance to the base almost made up for the preceding three months of isolation and paranoia. They'd barely managed to hold her up before her phone call to the embassy dragged a flustered lieutenant commander out to blush red and stammer in front of her. When he'd half questioned her intent, she'd rammed her credentials down his throat with gusto; he escorted her with her luggage directly to the shuttlecraft for transfer to the battlecruiser, shuddering slightly and glancing over his shoulder all the way. (Evidently self-propelled shipping chests were yet another technology that the New Republic shunned.)

Ludmilla Jindrisek, the cover identity she'd been using for the past month, had dissolved beneath the morning shower; Rachel Mansour, Special Agent, UN Standing Committee on Multilateral Interstellar Disarmament, stepped out of it. Ludmilla Jindrisek simpered, wore fashionable dresses, and deferred to wise male heads; Special Agent Mansour had started her career in bomb disposal (defusing terrorist nukes and disassemblers), graduated to calling in naval strikes on recalcitrant treaty-breakers, and wore a black paramilitary uniform designed specifically to impress militaristic out-worlder hicks. It was, she noted, interesting to observe the effect the change of costume had on people, especially as she held her notional rank through equivalence, rather than actual military service. Meanwhile she watched her fellow passengers waiting under the beady eye of Chief Petty Officer Moronici.

The airlock door finally rolled open. 'Attention!' barked the CPO. The ratings waiting in the bay stood sharply to attention. An officer ducked through the lock and straightened up: Moronici saluted, and he returned the gesture, ignoring Rachel.

'Very good there,' said the officer. 'Chief Moronici, get these kids aboard. Don't bother waiting for me, I've got business that'll keep me here until the next run.' He glanced at Rachel. 'You. What are you doing here?'

Rachel pointed her pass at him. 'Diplomatic corps. I'm attached to the Admiral's staff, by special order of Archduke Michael, Lieutenant.'

The Lieutenant gaped. 'But you're a—'

'—colonel in the United Nations of Earth Security Council combined armed forces. What part of "by special order of Archduke Michael" don't you understand? Are you going to stand there gaping, or are you going to invite me aboard?'

'Urgh. Um, yes.' The Lieutenant disappeared back into the

shuttle's flight deck; reappeared a minute later. 'Um. Colonel, ah, Mansour? Please come aboard.'

Rachel nodded and walked past him. Still carefully expressionless, she seated herself immediately behind the flight deck door, in officer country. And listened.

The CPO was educating the new intake. 'At ease, you lads,' he growled. 'Find yerselves a seat. Front row, facing back, that's right! Now buckle in. All six points, that's right! Check the seat in front of you for a sick bag. Welcome to the vomit comet; this boat's too small to have any gravity emulators and doesn't accelerate faster'n a quadriplegic in a wheelbarrow, so if you get sick in free fall, you're damn well going to throw up into those bags. Anyone who pukes up on the furniture and fittings can spend the next week cleaning 'em. Got that?'

Everyone nodded. Rachel felt cautiously optimistic; it looked as if everyone else on this run, apart from Chief Moronici, was a new assignment to the ship. Which meant her information was probably correct: they were working up to wartime levels, and departure wouldn't be delayed long.

The door to the passenger cabin slid closed; there was a rumble below as automatic pallets rolled in and out of the shuttle's cargo bay. Moronici knocked on the forward door and went through when it opened; he reappeared a minute later. 'Launch in two minutes,' he announced. 'Hang on tight!'

The two minutes passed at a snail's pace. Banging and thumping announced that dockside fuel and support lines were disconnecting; then there was a lurch and a jolt followed by a loud hissing that died away as the airlock seal was broken behind them. 'You're all new fish here,' Chief Moronici told the flyers. 'Not surprising as we're taking on a lot of new crew. Start of a new conscription cycle. Me,' – he pointed a meaty thumb at his chest – 'I'm not a conscript. I live on the ship we're going to. And I want to live on it long enough to collect my pension. Which means I don't intend to let you, or anyone else, do anything that endangers me or my home. The first rule of space travel' – they lurched sideways, drunkenly, and there was a disconcertingly loud rattle from underneath – 'is that mistakes are fatal. Space isn't friendly; it kills you. And there are no second chances.'

As if to emphasize the point, the bottom suddenly dropped out of Rachel's stomach. For a moment, she felt as if a huge, rubbery, invisible gripper was trying to pull her apart – and then she was floating. The ratings all looked as surprised as Chief Moronici looked smug.

'Main engine should come on in about five minutes,' Moronici announced. Banging and clicking shuddered through the cramped cabin, as it veered gently to the left: thrusters were busy nudging it out of the dock. 'Like I was saying, mistakes here tend to kill people. And I have no intention of letting you kill me. Which is why, while you're on board the *Lord Vanek*, you pukes will do exactly what I, or any other PO, or any officer, tells you to do. And you will do it with a shit-eating grin, or I will ram your head so far up your ass you'll be able to give yourself a tonsillectomy with your teeth. Is that understood?' He continued to ignore Rachel, implicitly acknowledging that she lay outside his reach.

The ratings, nodded. One of them, green-faced, gulped, and Moronici swiftly yanked a sick bag from the back of an adjacent seat and held it in front of the man's face. Rachel saw what he was trying to do; the pep talk was as much a distraction from the disorientation of free fall as anything else.

Rachel closed her eyes and breathed deeply – then regretted it: the shuttle stank of stale sweat, with a faint undertone of ozone and the sickly-sweet odor of acetone. It had been a long time since she'd prayed for anything, but right now she was praying with all her might for this ride in a tin can to come to an end. It was the crummiest excuse for a shuttle she'd been on in decades, an old banger like something out of an historical drama. It seemed to go on and on. Until, of course, it stopped with a buffet and clang as they latched on to the *Lord Vanek*'s stabilized docking adapter, then a grinding creak as it pulled them in and spun them up, and a hiss as pressure equalized.

'Erm, Colonel?'

She opened her eyes. It was CPO Moronici. He looked somewhat green, as if unsure how to deal with her. 'It's alright, Chief. I've gone aboard foreign naval vessels before.' She stood. 'Is there anyone waiting for me?'

'Yes'm.' He stared straight ahead, as if outrageously embarrassed.

'Fine.' She unbuckled, stood, feeling the uneven gravity of the battlecruiser's spin, and adjusted her beret. 'Let me at them.'

The airlock opened. 'Section, pre-sent – arms!'

She stepped forward into the docking bay, feeling the incredulous stares from all sides. A senior officer, a commander if she read his insignia correctly, was waiting for her, face stiffly frozen to conceal the inevitable surprise. 'Colonel Mansour, UN Disarmament Inspectorate,' she said. 'Hello, Commander –'

'Murametz.' He blinked, perplexed. 'Ah, your papers? Lieutenant Menvik says you're attached to the Admiral's staff. But they didn't tell us to expect you –'

'That's perfectly alright.' She pointed him down the corridor that led to the ship's main service core. 'They don't know about me yet. At least, not unless Archduke Michael warned them. Just take me to see the Admiral, and everything will be alright.'

Her luggage rolled quietly after her, on a myriad of brightly colored ball bearings.

The admiral was having a bad morning: his false pregnancy was causing problems again.

'I feel ill,' he mumbled quietly. 'Do I have to – to get up?'

'It would help, sir.' Robard, his batman, gently slid an arm around his shoulders to help him sit up. 'We depart in four hours. Your staff meeting is penciled in for two hours after that, and you have an appointment with Commodore Bauer before then. Ah, there's also a communiqué from His Royal Highness that has a most-urgent seal on it.'

'Well bring it – it – it in then,' said the Admiral. 'Damned morning sickness . . .'

Just then, the annunciator in the next room chimed softly. 'I'll just check that, sir,' said Robard. Then: 'Someone to see you, sir. Without an appointment. Ah – it's a *what?* A – oh, I see. Alright then. He'll be ready in a minute.' Pacing back into the bedroom, he cleared his throat. 'Sir, are you ready? Ah, yes. Ahem. You have a visitor, sir. A diplomat who has been seconded to your staff by order of Archduke Michael; some sort of foreign observer.'

'Oh.' Kurtz frowned. 'Didn't have any of them back at Second Lamprey. Just as well, really. Just lots of darkies. Bloody bad sports, those darkies, wouldn't stand still and be shot. Bloody foreigners. Show the man in!'

Robard cast a critical eye over his master. Sitting up in bed with his jacket wrapped around his shoulders, he looked like a convalescent turtle – but marginally presentable. As long as he didn't tell the ambassador all about his ailment, it could probably be passed off as an attack of gout. 'Yes, sir.'

The door opened and Robard's jaw dropped. Standing there was a stranger in a strange uniform. He had an attaché case clasped under one arm, and a rather bemused-looking commander standing beside him. Something about the man shrieked of strangeness, until Robard worked it out; his mouth twisted with distaste as he muttered, 'Invert,' to himself.

Then the stranger spoke – in a clear, high voice. 'United

Nations of Earth, Standing Committee on Multilateral Disarmament. I'm Colonel Mansour, special agent and military attaché to the embassy, attached to this expedition as an observer on behalf of the central powers. My credentials.' *That voice! If I didn't know better, I'd swear he was a woman*, thought Robard.

'Thank you. If you'd come this way, please, my lord is indisposed but will receive you in his sleeping quarters.' Robard bowed and backed into the Admiral's bedroom, where he was mortified to find the old man lying back on his pillows, mouth agape, snoring quietly.

'Ahem. Sir! Your Lordship!' A bleary eye opened. 'May I introduce Colonel, ah –'

'– Rachel Mansour.'

'– Rachel Mansour –' he squeaked, '– from Earth, military attaché from the embassy! His, er, credentials.' The colonel looked on, smiling faintly as the flustered batman proffered the case to the Admiral.

'S'funny name for a c-colonel, Colonel,' mumbled the Admiral. 'Are ye sure you're not a, a – ah –'

He sneezed, violently, then sat up. 'Damn these goose-down pillows,' he complained bitterly. 'And damn the gout. Wasn't like this at First Lamprey.'

'Indeed not,' Rachel observed drily. 'Lots of sand there, as I recall.'

'Very good, that man! Lots of sand, indeed, lots of sand. Sun beating down on your head, ragheads all over the place shooting at you, and not really anything big enough to nuke from orbit. Whose command were you in, eh?'

'As a matter of fact, I was with the war crimes tribunal. Sifting mummified body parts for evidence.'

Robard went gray, waiting for the Admiral to detonate, but the old man simply laughed raucously. 'Robard! Help me up, there's a good fellow. I say-ay, I never expected to meet a fellow veteran here! To my desk. I must inspect his credentials!'

Somehow they managed to migrate the fifteen feet or so to the Admiral's study without his complaining bitterly about the cost of maternity wear or gingerly inspecting his legs to make sure they hadn't turned to glass overnight – one of his occasional nightmares – and the effeminate colonel discreetly slid himself into one of the visitor's chairs. Robard stared at the man. A woman's name, a high voice, if he didn't know better, he could almost believe that –

'Duke Michael agreed to my presence for two reasons,' said Mansour. 'Firstly, you should be aware that as an agent of the UN it is my job to report back impartially on any – I emphasize, *any* – violations of treaties to which your government is a party. But more importantly, there is a shortage of information about the entity which has attacked your colony world. I'm also here to bear witness in case they make use of forbidden or criminal weapons. I am also authorized to act as a neutral third party for purposes of arbitration and parley, to arrange exchanges of prisoners and cease-fires, and to ensure that, insofar as any war can be conducted in a civilized manner, this one is.'

'Well that's a damn fine thing to know, sir, and you are welcome to join my staff,' said the Admiral, sitting upright in his bath chair. 'Feel free to approach me whenever you want! You're a good man, and I'm pleased to know there's another vet-eran of First Lamprey in the fleet.' For a brief moment, he looked alarmed. 'Oh dear. It's kicking again.'

Mansour looked at him oddly. Robard opened his mouth, but the foreign colonel managed to speak before he could change the subject. '*It?*'

'The baby,' Kurtz confided, looking miserable. 'It's an elephant. I don't know what to do with it. If its father –' He stopped. His expression of alarm was chilling.

'Ahem. I *think* you'd better withdraw now, sir,' said Robard, staring coldly at Rachel. 'It's time for His Lordship's medicine. I'm afraid it would be for the best if in future you'd call ahead before visiting; he has these spells, you know.'

Rachel shook her head. 'I'll remember to do that.' She stood. 'Goodbye, sir.' She turned and departed.

As he was helping the Admiral out of his chair, Robard thought he heard a soprano voice from outside: '– Didn't know you had elephants!' He shook his head hopelessly. Women aboard the Imperial flagship, admirals who thought they were pregnant, and a fleet about to embark on the longest voyage in naval history, against an unknown enemy. Where was it going to end?

The citizen curator was unamused. 'So. To summarize, the Navy boys gave you the run-around, but have now allowed you on board their precious battlecruiser. Along the way, you lost contact with your subject for an entire working day. Last night you say he did nothing unusual, but you report patchy coverage. And what else? How did he spend that evening?'

'I don't understand, sir,' Vassily said tightly. 'What do you mean?'

The Citizen scowled furiously; even at a forty-thousand-kilometer remove, his picture on the screen was enough to make Vassily recoil. 'It says in your report,' the Citizen said with heavy emphasis, 'that the subject left his apartment, was lost for a few minutes, and was next seen dining at a public establishment in the company of an *actress*. At whose apartment he subsequently spent a good few hours before returning to base. And you didn't investigate her?'

Vassily flushed right to the tips of his ears. 'I thought—'

'Has he ever done anything like this before? While in New Prague, for example? I think not. According to his file he has led the life of a monk since arriving in the Republic.

Not once, not *once* in nearly two months at the Glorious Crown Hotel, did he show any sign of interest in the working girls. Yet as soon as he arrives and starts work, what does he do?'

'I didn't think of that.'

'I *know* you didn't.' The Citizen Curator fell silent for a moment, but his expression was eloquent; Vassily cringed before it. 'I'm not going to do any more of your thinking for you, but perhaps you'd be so good as to tell me what you propose to do next.'

'Uh.' Vassily blinked. 'Run a background check on her? If it's clear, ask her a few questions? Keep a closer eye on him in future . . .?'

'Very good.' The Citizen grinned savagely. 'And what have you *learned* from this fiasco?'

'To watch the subject's behavior, and be alert for changes in it,' Vassily said woodenly. 'Especially the things he doesn't do, as much as those he does.' It was a basic message, one drilled into recruits all the way through training, and he could kick himself for forgetting it. How could he have missed something so obvious?

'That's right.' The Citizen leaned back, away from the camera on his phone. 'A very basic skill, Muller. Yet we all learn best from our mistakes. See that you learn from this one, eh? I don't care if you have to follow your man all the way to Rochard's World and back, as long as you keep your eyes open and spot it when he makes his move. And think about all the other things you've been told to do. I'll tell you this for free: you've forgotten to do something else, and you'll be happier if you notice it before I have to remind you!'

'Yes, sir.'

'Good-by.' The videophone link dissolved into random blocks, then went blank. Vassily eased out of his cubicle, trying to work out just what the Citizen's parting admonition meant. The sooner he cleared everything up, proving once and for all that Springfield was or was not a spy, the better – he wasn't cut out for shipboard life. Maybe it would be a good idea to start the new day by interviewing the engineering chief Springfield was working under? Probably that was what the Citizen meant for him to do; he could leave following up on the whore until later. (The idea filled him with an uncomfortable sense of embarrassment.)

No sooner did he poke his nose into the corridor than he was nearly run down by a team of ratings, hustling a trolley laden with heavy equipment at the double. On his second attempt, he took the precaution of looking both ways before venturing out: there were no obstacles. He made his way through the cramped, blue-painted corridor, following the curve of the inner hull. Floating free, the *Lord Vanek* relied on its own curved-space generator to produce a semblance of gravity. Vassily hunted for a radial walkway, then a lift down to the engineering service areas located at the heart of the ship, two-thirds of the way down its length.

There were people everywhere, some in corridors, some in chambers opening off the passageways, and others in rooms to either side. He caught a fair number of odd glances on his way, but nobody stopped him: most people would go out of their way to avoid the attentions of an officer in the Curator's Office. It took him a while to find the engineering spaces, but eventually, he found his way to a dimly lit, wide-open chamber full of strange machines and fast-moving people. Oddly, he felt very light on his feet as he waited in the entrance to the room. No sign of Springfield, but of course, that was hardly surprising; the engineering spaces of a capital ship were large enough to conceal any number of sins. 'Is this the main drive engineering deck?' he asked a passing technician.

'What do you think it is? The head?' called the man as he hurried off. Vassily shrugged irritably and stepped forward –

and forward – and *forward* – 'What are you doing there?' Someone grabbed his elbow. 'Hey, *watch out!*' He flailed helplessly, then stopped moving as he realized what was going on. The ceiling was close and the floor was a long way away and he was falling toward the far wall –

'Help,' he gasped.

'Hold on tight.' The hand on his elbow shifted to his upper arm and yanked, hard. A large rack of equipment, bolted to the floor, came close, and he grabbed and held on to it.

'Thanks. Is this the engineering deck? I'm looking for the chief drive engineer,' he said. It took an effort to talk over the frantic butterfly beat of his heart.

'That would be me.' Vassily stared at his rescuer. 'Couldn't have you bending the clocks now, could I? They curve badly enough as it is. What do you want?'

'It's –' Vassily stopped. 'I'm sorry. Could we talk somewhere in private?'

The engineering officer – his overalls bore the name KRUP-KIN – frowned mightily. 'We might, but I'm very busy. We're moving in half an hour. Is it important?'

'Yah. It won't get your work done any faster, but if you help me now it might take less of your time later.'

'Huh. Then we'll see.' The officer turned and pointed at the other side of the open space. 'See that office cubicle? I'll meet you in there in ten minutes.' And he turned abruptly, kicked off, and disappeared into the gloom, chaos and moving bodies that circled the big blue cube at the center of the engineering bay.

'Holy Father!' Vassily took stock of his situation. Marooned, clinging to a box of melting clocks at the far side of a busy free-fall compartment from his destination, he could already feel his breakfast rising in protest at the thought of crossing the room.

Grimly determined not to embarrass himself, he inched his

way down to floor level. There were toeholds recessed into the floor tiles, and now he looked at them he saw that they were anchored, but obviously designed to be removed frequently. If he pretended that the floor was a wall, then the office door was actually about ten meters above him, and there were plenty of handholds along the way.

He took a deep breath, pulled himself around the clock cabinet, and kicked hard against it where it joined the floor. The results were gratifying; he shot up, toward the office. The wall dropped toward him, and he was able to grab hold of a passing repair drone and angle his course toward the doorway. As he entered it, gravity began to return – he slid along the deck, coming to an undignified halt lying on his back just inside. The office was small, but held a desk, console, and a couple of chairs; a rating was doing something with the console. 'You,' he said, 'out, please.'

'Aye aye, sir.' The fresh-faced rating hurriedly closed some kind of box that was plugged into the console, then saluted and withdrew into the freefall zone. Shaken, Vassily sat down in the seat opposite the desk and waited for Engineering Commander Krupkin to arrive. It was already 1100, and what had he achieved today? Nothing, so far as he could tell, except to learn that the Navy's motto seemed to be 'Hurry up and wait.' The Citizen wouldn't be pleased.

Meanwhile, on the bridge, the battlecruiser *Lord Vanek* was counting down for main drive activation.

As the flagship of the expedition, *Lord Vanek* was at the heart of squadron one, along with three of the earlier Glorious-class battlecruisers, and the two Victory-class battleships *Kamchatka* and *Regina* (now sadly antiquated, relics that had seen better days). Squadron Two, consisting of a mixed force of light cruisers, destroyers, and missile carriers, would launch six hours behind Squadron One; finally, the supply train, with seven bulk cargo freighters and the liner *Sikorsky's Dream* (refitted as a hospital ship) would depart eight hours later.

Lord Vanek was, in interstellar terms, a simple beast: ninety thousand tonnes of warship and a thousand crew held in tight orbit around an electron-sized black hole as massive as a mountain range. The hole – the drive kernel – spun on its axis so rapidly that its event horizon was permeable; the drive used it to tug the ship about by tickling the singularity in a variety of ways. At nonrelativistic speeds, *Lord Vanek* maneuvered by dumping mass into the kernel; complex quantum tunneling interactions – jiggery-pokery within the ergosphere – transformed it into raw momentum. At higher speeds, energy pumped into the kernel could be used to generate the a jump field, collapsing the quantum well between the ship and a point some distance away.

The kernel had a few other uses: it was a cheap source of electricity and radioisotopes, and by tweaking the stardrive, it was possible to use it to produce a local curved-space gravity field. As a last resort, it could even be jettisoned and used as a weapon in its own right. But if there was one word that wouldn't describe it, that word must be 'maneuvrable'. Eight-billion-ton point masses do not make right-angle turns.

Commander Krupkin saluted as a rating held the bridge door open for him: 'Engineering Commander reporting on the state of machinery, sir!'

'Very good.' Captain Mirsky nodded from his command chair at the rear of the room. 'Come in. What do you have for me?'

Krupkin relaxed slightly. 'All systems operational and correct, sir,' he announced formally. 'We're ready to move at any time. Our status is clear on –' He rapidly rattled through the series of watches under his control. Finally: 'The drive control modifications you ordered, sir – we've never run anything like this before. They look alright, and the self-test says everything is fine, but I can't say any more than that without unsealing the black boxes.'

Mirsky nodded. 'They'll work alright.' Krupkin wished he could feel as confident as the Captain sounded; the black boxes, shipped aboard only a week ago and wired into the main jump drive control loop, did not fill him with confidence. Indeed, if it hadn't been obvious that the orders to integrate them came from the highest level and applied to every ship in the fleet, he'd have thrown the nearest thing to a tantrum that military protocol permitted. It was his job to keep the drive running, and dammit, he should know everything there was to know about how it worked! There could be anything in those boxes, from advanced (whisper it, *illegal*) high technology to leprechauns – and he'd be held responsible if it didn't work.

A bearded man at the other side of the bridge stood. 'Humbly request permission to report, sir.'

'You have permission,' said Mirsky.

'I have completed downloading navigation elements from system traffic control. I am just now having them punched into the autopilot. We will be ready to spin up for departure in ten minutes.'

'Very good, Lieutenant. Ah, Comms, my compliments to the Admiral and the Commodore, and we are preparing for departure in ten minutes. Lieutenant Helsingus, proceed in accordance with the traffic control departure plan. You have the helm.'

'Aye, sir, I have the helm. Departure in ten minutes.' Helsingus bent over his speaking tube; ratings around him began turning brass handles and moving levers with calm deliberation, sending impulses along the nerves of steel that bound the ship into an almost living organism. (Although nanoelectronics might be indispensable in the engine room, the New Republican Admiralty held the opinion that there was no place for suchlike newfangled rubbish on the bridge of a ship crewed by the heroic fighting men of the empire.)

'Well, Commander.' Mirsky nodded at the engineer. 'How does it feel to be moving at last?'

Krupkin shrugged. 'I'll be happier when we're in flat space. There are rumors.'

For a moment, the Captain's smile slipped. 'Indeed. Which is why we will be going to action stations at departure and staying that way until after our first jump. You can never tell, and the Commodore wants to be sure that no spies or enemy missile buses are lying in wait for us.'

'A wise precaution, sir. Permission to return to my station?'

'Granted. Go with God, Commander.'

Krupkin saluted, and headed back for his engineering control room as fast as his short legs would carry him. It was, he reflected, going to be a busy time, even with as quietly competent a dockyard consultant engineer as Martin to help him keep the magic smoke in the drive control boxes.

The colony of Critics writhed and tunneled in their diamond nest, incubating a devastating review. A young, energetic species, descended from one of the post-Singularity flowerings that had exploded in the wake of the Diaspora three thousand years in their past, they held precious little of the human genome in their squamous, cold-blooded bodies. Despite their terrestrial descent, only their brains bound them tightly to the *sapiens* clade – for not all the exiles from Earth were human.

As hangers-on, the Critics had no direct access to the Festival's constellation of relay satellites or the huge network of visual and auditory sensors that had been scattered across the surface of the planet. (Most of the Festival's senses were borne on the wings of tiny insectoidal robots, with which they had saturated the biosphere, sending a million for every single telephone that had rained down from orbit.) Instead, the Critics had to make do with their own devices; a clumsy network of spy-eyes in low orbit, winged surveillance drones, and precarious bugs planted on the window ledges and chimney pots of significant structures.

The Critics watched, with their peculiar mixture of bemusement and morbid cynicism, while the soldiers of the First and Fourth Regiments shot their officers and deserted *en masse* to the black flag of Burya Rubenstein's now-overt Traditional Extropian Revolutionary Front. (Many soldiers burned their uniforms and threw away their guns; others adopted new emblems and took up strange silvery arms churned out by the committee's replicator farm.) The Critics looked on as peasants greedily demanded pigs, goats, and in one case, a goose that laid golden eggs from the Festival; their womenfolk quietly pleaded for medicinal cures, metal cutlery, and fabric. In the castle, shots were heard as the servants butchered the Duke's menagerie for food. A rain of gold roubles ordered by some economic saboteur fell widely across the streets of Novy Petrograd, and was equally widely ignored: to that extent, the economic collapse brought about by the Festival's advent was already complete.

'They are truly pathetic,' commented She Who Observes the First; she clashed her tusks over a somatic bench that depicted a scene below, some of the few remaining loyal grenadiers dragging a terrified cobbler toward the gates of the castle, followed by his screaming, pleading family. 'Unregulated instincts, unable to assimilate reality, bereft of perspective.'

'Chew roots; dig deep.' Guard Man the Fifth champed lugubriously, demonstrating his usual level of insight (intelligence not being a particularly useful characteristic in tunnel-running warriors). 'Tastes of blood and soil.'

'Everything tastes of soil to a warrior,' She Who Observes

snorted. 'Eat tubers, brother, while your sisters discuss matters beyond your ken.' She rolled sideways, butting up against Sister of Stratagems the Seventh, who nipped at her flank gently. 'Sibling-litter-peer. Uncertainty flows?'

'A time of exponentiating changes is upon them.' Sister Seventh was much given to making such gnomic pronouncements, perhaps in the naive hope that it would gain her a reputation for vision (and, ultimately, support when she made her bid for queendom). 'Perhaps they are disorganized surface-scrabblers, clutching at stems, but there is a certain grandeur to their struggle; a level of sincerity seldom approached by primitives.'

'Primitive they are: their internal discourse is crippled by a complete absence of intertextuality. I cringe in astonishment that Festival wastes its attention on them.'

'Hardly. They are Festival's antithesis, do you not feel this in your whiskers?' Sister Seventh blinked redly at She Who Observes, pawing for the control tree of the somatic bench. 'Here we see a nest-drone.' The scene slewed into an enclosed space, following the abducted cobbler into the walls of the castle. 'Phenotypic dispersal leads to extended specialization, as ever, with the usual degree of free will found in human civilization. But this one is structured to prevent information surge, do you not see?'

'Information surge? *Prevented?* Life is information!'

Sister Seventh farted smugly. 'I have been monitoring the Festival. Not one of the indigines has asked it for information! Artifacts, yes. Food, yes. Machines, up to and including replicators, yes. But philosophy? Art? Mathematics? Ontology? We might be witnessing our first zombie civilization.'

Zombies were a topic that fascinated Sister Seventh. An ancient hypothesis of the original pre-Singularity ur-civilization, a zombie was a non-self-conscious entity that acted just like a conscious one: it laughed, cried, talked, ate, and generally behaved just like a real person, and if questioned, would claim to be conscious – but behind its superficial behavior, there was nobody home, no internalized model of the universe it lived in.

The philosophers had hypothesized that no such zombies existed, and that everything that claimed personhood was actually a person. Sister Seventh was less convinced. Human beings – those rugose, endothermic anthropoids with their ridiculously small incisors and anarchic social arrangements – didn't seem very real to her. So she was perpetually searching for evidence that, actually, they weren't people at all.

She Who Observes was of the opinion that her littermate was chewing on the happy roots again, but then, unlike Sister Seventh, she wasn't a practical critic: she was an observer.

'I think we really need to settle the zombie question here before we fix their other problems.'

'And how do you propose to do *that*?' asked She Who Observes. 'It's the subjectivity problem again. I tell you, the only viable analytical mode is the intentional stance. If something claims to be conscious, take it at its own word and treat it as if it has conscious intentions.'

'Ah, but I can so easily program a meerkat to chirp 'I think, therefore I am!' No, sister, we need to tunnel nearer the surface to find the roots of sapience. A test is required, one that a zombie will stick in, but an actor will squeeze through.'

'Do you have such a test in mind?'

Sister Seventh pawed air and champed her huge, yellow tusks. 'Yes, I think I can construct one. The essential characteristic of conscious beings is that they adopt the intentional stance: that is, they model the intentions of other creatures, so that they can anticipate their behavior. When they apply such a model to others, they acquire the ability to respond to their intentions before they become obvious: when they apply it to themselves, they become self-conscious, because they acquire an understanding of their own motivations and the ability to modify them.

'But thus far, I have seen no evidence that their motivations are self-modifying, or indeed anything but hardwired reflexes. I want to test them, by introducing them to a situation where their own self-image is contradicted by their behavior. If they can adapt their self-image to the new circumstances, we will know that we are dealing with fellow sapients. Which will ultimately influence the nature of our review.'

'This sounds damaging or difficult, sister. I will have to think on it before submitting to Mother.'

Seventh emitted a bubbling laugh and flopped forward onto her belly. 'Oh, sibling! What did you think I have in mind?'

'I don't know. But be it anything like your usual –' She Who Observes stopped, seeing the triumphant gleam in her sister's eye.

'I merely propose to Criticize a handful of them a trifle more thoroughly than usual,' said Sister Seventh. 'And when I'm done, any who live will know they've been *Criticized*. This is my methodology . . .'

Commander Krupkin took nearly two hours to get around to seeing Vassily Muller: it wasn't intentional on his part. Almost as soon as the main drive field was powered up and running, and the ship surfing smoothly away from the Klamovka beanstalk, his pager beeped:

ALL OFFICERS TO BRIEFING ROOM D IMMEDIATELY

'Shit and corruption,' he muttered. Passing Pavel Grubor: 'The old man wants me right now. Can you take care of the shipyard technician and find out how long he's going to be in closing out the installation of the baseline compensator? Page me when you've got an answer.' He headed off without waiting for a response.

Mikhail Krupkin enjoyed his job, and didn't particularly expect or want any further promotions; he'd been in shipboard systems for the past fourteen years and expected to serve out his career in them before enjoying a long and happy retirement working for some commercial space line. However, messages like this one completely destroyed his peace of mind. It meant that the boss was going to ask him questions about the availability of his systems, and with the strange patch boxes installed in the drive room, the *Lord Vanek* might be mobile, but he couldn't in all honesty swear it was one hundred percent solid.

He didn't know just what was in those boxes, but he was sure there was a reason why the Admiralty was spending several million crowns on a drive upgrade. And in any event, they'd been remarkably cagey about the extra control software for them. Boxes, hooked into the drive, which also hooked into the new, high-bandwidth linkup to the tactical network: something smelled.

All this and more was on his mind as he took the express elevator up to the conference suite in officer country. The door to Room D was open, waiting for him. Most of the other senior officers were already there. Ilya Murametz, the ship's executive officer, Lieutenant Helsingus from fire control, the usual battle operations team, Vulpis from Relativity . . . he was probably last, but for the Captain, by reason of having come farthest. 'Ilya. What's going on?'

Ilya glanced at him. 'The Captain is with the Admiral. When he arrives he will make an announcement,' he said. 'I don't know anything about it except that it's nothing specific.' Krupkin breathed a silent sight of relief; 'nothing specific' meant that it wasn't about the running of the ship. Nobody was going to be hauled over the coals today. Not that

Captain Mirsky was a martinet by the standards of the New Republican Navy, but he could be merciless if he thought someone was asleep at the switch or not doing his job properly.

Suddenly there was a change of atmosphere in the room. Everyone turned to face the doorway: conversations stopped, and officers came to attention. Captain Mirsky stood for a long moment, surveying his staff. Evidently what he saw gratified him; when he spoke his first words were, 'Gentlemen, please be seated.' He walked to the head of the table and laid down a thick folder in front of his chair.

'It is now 1130. The door to this room is shut, and will remain shut, barring emergencies, until 1200. I am authorized to inform you that we are now under battle orders. I am not privy to the political discussions behind our orders, but I am informed by Admiral Kurtz's staff that it appears likely that no resolution of the crisis short of war is possible; accordingly, we have been ordered to proceed as part of Task Group One to Rochard's World, by way of Battle Plan Omega Green Horizon.' Now he pulled his chair out and sat down. 'Are there any questions about the background before I go into our specific orders?' he asked.

Lieutenant Marek raised a hand. 'Sir, do we know anything about the aggressor? It seems to me that the censor's office has been more than usually diligent.'

Captain Mirsky's cheek twitched. 'A good question.' Krupkin glanced at the lieutenant; a young hotshot in TacOps, who'd joined the ship less than six months ago. 'A good question deserves a good answer. Unfortunately, I can't give you one because nobody has seen fit to tell me. So, Lieutenant. How do you think our armed forces stack up, in a worst-possible-case situation?'

Lieutenant Marek gulped; he hadn't been on board long enough to have figured out the Captain's Socratic style of testing his subordinates' knowledge – a holdover from Mirsky's two tours as a professor in the Naval Staff Academy. 'Against whom, sir? If it was just a matter of suppressing a local rebellion, there wouldn't be any problem at all. But Rochard's World had a picket force consisting of a destroyer plus point defenses, and they'd be as good as us at suppression. So they wouldn't be sending us if that was enough to deal with the situation. There must be an active enemy who has already stopped the local picket force intervening.'

'An accurate summary.' Captain Mirsky smiled humorlessly. 'One that holds true whatever we face. Unfortunately, you now know as much as I do, but for one thing: apparently the destroyer *Sakhalin* was *eaten*. I don't know if this is metaphor or literal truth, but it appears that nobody knows who this Festival is, or what they are capable of, or whether the destroyer gave them indigestion. Let us not forget our oath of allegiance to the Emperor and the Republic; whatever they choose to do, we are sworn to be their right arm. If they decide to strike at an enemy, well, let us strike hard. Meanwhile, let us assume the worst. What if the enemy has cornucopia machines?'

Marek looked puzzled. 'Couldn't it go either way, sir? On the one hand, they have tools that let them build lots of weapons quickly without getting their hands dirty. But on the other hand, if they're not used to working, isn't there a good chance that they're moral degenerates? The ability to manufacture doesn't confer victory automatically, if the people who have it are weakened and corrupted by their decadent robot-supported lifestyle. How can they possibly have the traditions and *ésprit* of an honorable military force?'

'That remains to be seen,' the Captain said cryptically. 'For the time being, I prefer to assume the worst. And the worst case is that the enemy has cornucopia machines, and is *not* decadent and cowardly.'

Marek shook his head slightly.

'You have a question?' asked Mirsky.

'Uh. I thought –' Marek looked worried. 'Is that possible?'

'Anything is possible,' the Captain said, heavily. 'And if we plan for the worst, with luck all our surprises will be favorable.' He glanced away from the naive Lieutenant. 'Next.'

Krupkin, who as an engineer had his own opinion about the advisability of banning the use of technologies for social reasons, nodded to himself. While Mirsky wouldn't say so in public, he had a very good idea what the Captain was thinking – *having a decadent robot-supported lifestyle doesn't preclude having military traditions. In fact, it may give them more time to focus on the essentials.* The Captain continued to poll his officers, publicly querying the readiness of their posts.

'– Engineering status. Commander Krupkin?'

Krupkin stifled a grunt of annoyance. 'The shipyard contractor is still applying the upgrade patches to our baseline compensators. I am awaiting a precise hand-off estimate, but as of this morning, we expected three more shifts to complete the modifications, and another shift to test them. I have no complaints about his efficiency: he's as good as anyone I've ever worked with, a real virtuoso. Other than that, the secondary compensator set – which is not being upgraded – is fully operational. We are moving at full speed, but will not have full redundancy and the new upgrade modifications ready for another four to five days – at a minimum.'

'I see.' The Captain made a note on his blotter. He looked back at the engineer: a piercing blue-eyed stare that would have turned a less experienced officer into a nervous wreck. 'Can the modifications be expedited? We will be passing into foreign space-time in two days; thereafter, we must anticipate the presence of enemy minelayers and warships along our route.'

'Um – probably, sir. Unfortunately, the upgrades aren't straightforward enough for our routine engineering staff.

Springfield is a specialist, and he is exerting himself fully. I believe that we might be able to speed things up, but at the risk of errors creeping in because of fatigue. If I can use an analogy, it's like a master surgeon performing an operation. Extra pairs of hands simply get in the way, and you can't prop a surgeon up for days on end and expect his work to remain acceptable. I think we might be able to shave a day or two off the four-to-five-day estimate, but no more.'

'I see.' Captain Mirsky glanced at Murametz significantly. 'But we are still able to move and fight, and the new black-box system is already integrated.' He nodded. 'Helsingus, how is TacOps?'

'I've been running daily exercises predicated on a standard fleet aggressor profile for the past week, sir, using the standard models Admiralty shipped us. We could do with a bit longer, but I think the boys have generally got the right idea. Barring any major surprises in enemy tactical doctrine, we're ready to deal with them, whoever they are, one-on-one.'

'Good.' Mirsky sat in thought for a minute. 'I have to tell you that I have a meeting this afternoon with Commodore Bauer and a teleconference with the other captains. You should assume that, as of now, this ship is on a war footing. You should be prepared for combat operations in the near future. Meanwhile, I expect daily reports on drive and gunnery readiness.

'That goes for the rest of you, too. I want daily readiness reports. We've wasted a lot of time churning conscripts this month, and I want us up to ninety-five percent operational capability as soon as possible. We will be bunkering a full fuel load and munitions from the supply ship *Aurora* tomorrow, and I expect that, as soon as we spool up for our first jump, we will be going to battle stations. That gives you about thirty-six hours to get ready for action. Are there any questions, gentlemen?'

Helsingus raised a hand:

'Yes?'

'Sir. Minelayers? Where are we going that might be mined?'

Mirsky nodded. 'A good point, Commander. Our initial jump is going to be a short-hauler to Wolf Depository Five. I know that's not on a direct course for Rochard's World, but if we go straight there – well, I presume our enemies can plot a straight course, too. What we don't know is how much they know about us. I hope to know more about them this afternoon.' He stood up. 'If they launch a surprise attack, we'll be ready for them. God is on our side; all the indications are that this Festival is a pagan degeneracy, and all we need to do is be of good heart and man our guns with enthusiasm. Any other questions?' He looked around the room. Nobody raised a hand. 'Very good. I am now leaving and will be in closed conference with the Commodore. Dismissed.'

The Captain left the room in silence. But as soon as the door closed behind him, there was an uproar.

Martin was in a foul mood. Krupkin had broken the news to him hours earlier: 'I'm sorry, but that's the way it is,' he'd said. 'Double shifts. We're on a war footing. You especially don't get to sleep until the upgrade job is done; orders from the skipper, who is not in a reasonable mood. Once it's done, you can crash out for as long as you want, but we need it before we see combat.'

'It's going to be sixteen hours, minimum, *whatever* happens,' Martin told him, trying hard to keep his cool. 'The patches will be installed and active by the end of this shift, but I can't release the system to you until it's tested out fully. The regression tests are entirely automatic and take twenty thousand seconds to run. Then there's the maneuver testing, which would normally take all week if this was a new hull we were upgrading. Finally, there's drive qualification time which is three months for a new and untested system like the one your Admiralty ordered, and what do you think the chances are that you're going to sit still for that?'

'Skip it,' Krupkin said briskly. 'We're going to be maneuvering on it tomorrow. Can you start the white-box phase today?'

'*Fuck it.*' Martin pulled his goggles and gloves back on. 'Talk to me later, okay? I'm busy. You'll get your bloody drive mods. Just point me at a bunk this evening.' He dived back into the immersive interface, ignoring the commander – who took it surprisingly mildly.

Which was perhaps just as well. Martin was keeping a tight rein on his anger, but beneath the brittle exterior, he was disturbed. The business with Rachel had unsettled him; he was now intensely nervous, and not just because of the volatility of the situation. Her approach had caught him off guard and vulnerable, and the potential consequences ranged from the unpredictable to the catastrophic.

For the rest of the day, he worked furiously, checking the self-extending array of connectors linking the new drive control circuitry into the existing neural networks. He headed off several possible problems in the performance profile of the control feedback sensors, tuned the baseline compensators for extra precision, and added several patches to the inner hard control loops that monitored and pulled the hair on the black hole; but he left the midlife kicker traps alone. And he installed the special circuit that Herman had asked him to add.

He worked on into the evening shift, then started the regression tests going: a series of self-test routines, driven by software, that would exercise and report on every aspect of the drive upgrade. Installing and testing the module was the easy task: tomorrow he'd have to start testing how it interacted with the kernel – an altogether more nerve-wracking experience. So it was that, at 2500, he yawned, stretched, set aside his gloves and feedback sensors, and stood up.

'Aargh.' He stretched further. Joints popped with the effort; he felt dizzy, and tired, and slightly sick. He blinked; everything seemed flat and monochromatic after the hours immersed in false-color 3-D controls, and his wrists ached. And why, in this day and age, did warships smell of pickled cabbage, stale sweat, and an occasional undertone of sewage? He stumbled to the door. A passing rating glanced at him curiously. 'I need to find a bunk,' he explained.

'Please wait here, sir.' He waited. A minute or so later, one of Krupkin's minions came into view, hand-over-hand down the wall like a human fly.

'Your berth? Ah, yes, sir. D deck, Compartment 24, there's an officer's room waiting for you. Breakfast call at 0700. Paulus, please show the gentleman here to his room.'

'This way, sir.' The crewman quietly and efficiently guided Martin through the ship, to a pale green corridor lined with hatches like those of a capsule hotel. 'There you are.' Martin blinked at the indicated door, then pulled it aside and climbed in.

It was like a room in a capsule hotel or a compartment on a transcontinental train – one with two bunks. The lower one flipped upside down to make a desk when not in use. It was totally sterile, totally clean, with ironed sheets and a thin blanket on the lower bunk, and it smelled of machine oil, starch, and sleepless nights. Someone had laid out a clean overall with no insignia on it. Martin eyed it mistrustfully and decided to stick to his civilian clothes until they were too dirty to tolerate. Surrendering to the New Republic's uniform seemed symbolic; letting them claim him as one of their own would feel like a small treason.

He palmed the light to low, and stripped his shoes and socks off, then lay down on the lower bunk. Presently, the light dimmed and he began to relax. He still felt light-headed, tired and angry, but at least the worst hadn't happened: no tap on the shoulder, no escort to the brig. Nobody knew who he *really* worked for. You could never tell in this business, and Martin had a prickly feeling washing up and down his spine. This whole situation was completely bizarre, and Herman's request that he plonk himself in the middle of it was well out of the usual run of assignments. He shut his eyes and tried to push away the visions of spinning yellow blocks that danced inside his head.

The door opened and closed. 'Martin,' said a quiet voice beside his pillow, 'keep your voice down. How did things go?'

He jackknifed upright and nearly smashed his head on the underside of the bunk overhead. 'What!' He paused. 'What are you—'

'Doing here?' A quiet, ironic laugh. 'I'm doing the same as you; feeling tired, wondering what the hell I'm doing in this nuthouse.'

He relaxed a little, relieved. 'I wasn't expecting you.'

'It's my job to be here; I'm attached to the Admiral's staff as a diplomatic representative. Look, I can't stay long. It would be a *really* bad idea for anyone to find me in your room. At best, they'd assume the worst, and at worst, they might think you were a spy or something—'

'But I *am* a spy,' he blurted out in a moment of weakness. 'At least, you wanted—'

'Yeah, right, and I've got your secret-agent decoder ring right *here*. Look, I want to talk, but business first. Are the drive upgrades finished?'

His eyes adjusted to the dark; he could see the outline of her face. Short hair and shadows made her look very different, harder and more determined. But something in her expression as she watched him made her look slightly uncertain. *Business first, she said.* 'The upgrades are going to take some time,' he said. 'They're about ready for testing to start tomorrow, but it's a risky proposition. I'm going to be ironing bugs out of the high-precision clocks for the next week.' He paused. 'Are you sure this is safe? How did you find me?'

'It wasn't hard. Thank MiG for the security system schematics. Life Support and Security think you're alone in here. I thought it was safer to visit in person than to try to page you.'

Martin shuffled around and sat up, making room for her, and Rachel sat down next to him. He noticed for the first time that she was wearing a uniform – not a New Republican one. 'You're here for the whole voyage?'

She chuckled. 'The better to get to know you. Relax. If you want to talk to your local diplomatic representative, that's me. Besides, they need me, or someone like me. Who else is going to negotiate a cease-fire for them?'

'Aah.' Martin fell silent for a moment, thinking. He was aware of her next to him, almost painfully so. 'You're taking a risk,' he said after a while. 'They aren't going to thank you—'

'Hush.' She leaned closer. He felt her breath on his cheek: 'The drive patches you're installing are part of an illegal weapons system, Martin. I'm sure of it. I'm not sure what kind of illegality is being contemplated, but I'm sure it involves causality violation. If they commence training maneuvers shortly, I'll get a chance to see just what they're planning to use the upgrades for. That's why I need to be here. And why I need your help. I wouldn't normally dump this on you, but I really need your help, active help, in figuring out what's going on. Do you understand?'

'I understand very little,' Martin said nervously, priming his autonomic override to keep his pulse steady so as not to betray the lie. He felt unaccountably guilty about withholding the truth from her. Rachel seemed like the least likely person to jeopardize his mission – and he liked her, wanted to be able to relax in her presence freely, without worries. But caution and experience conspired to seal his lips. 'I'm just along for the ride,' he added. He simply couldn't tell her about Herman. Without knowing how she'd react, the consequences might be disastrous. Might. And it was a risk he dared not take.

'Understand this,' she said quietly. 'A lot of lives are at stake. Not just mine, or yours, or this ship's, but just about everyone within a thirty-light-year radius of here. That's a lot of people.'

'Why do you think this is going to drag the big E into the situation?' he prompted. He was deathly tired and didn't want to have to lie to her. *Can I keep her talking?* he wondered. If she didn't keep speaking, he was afraid he might tell her too much. Which would be a big mistake.

She touched his arm. 'The Eschaton will be interested for a simple reason; it is absolutely opposed to causality violation. Please don't pretend you're that naive, Martin. I've seen your résumé. I know where you've been and what you've done. You're not an idiot, and you know what a well-tuned warp drive can do in the hands of an expert. In terms of special relativity, being able to travel faster than light is effectively equivalent to time travel – at least from the perspective of observers in different frames of reference. They see the light from your arrival, which is close to them, a long time before they see the light from your departure, which is a long way away. Because you're outrunning the speed of light, events appear to happen out of sequence. Okay? Same with a causal link, an instantaneous quantum-entanglement communicator. It doesn't mean there's real time travel involved, or that you can create temporal paradoxes, but being able to mess with an observer's view of events at a distance is a boon for strategists.

'The Eschaton doesn't care about such trivial kinds of time travel, but it stamps hard on the real thing; any manifestation of closed timelike paths that could jeopardize its own history. The big E doesn't want anyone doing a knight's move on it, back in time and then forward again, to screw over its origin. Someone tries to build an instantaneous communicator? No problem. They go on to build a logic gate that transmits its output into its own past, where it's wired into the input? That's the basis of acausal logic, and it gives you the first tool you need to build a transcendent artificial intelligence. Poof, the planet is bombarded from orbit with cannibal lemmings or bitten to death by killer asteroids or something.

'Anyway, I don't really care all that much what the New Republic does to the Festival. I mean, maybe I care about individual people in the New Republic, and maybe the Festival folks are really nice, but that's not the point: But I do care if they do whatever they're going to do inside Earth's light cone. If it involves large-scale causality violation, the E might decide to take out the entire contaminated zone. And we know it seeded colonies as much as three thousand light-years away – even assuming it still wants humans around, it can afford to wipe out a couple of hundred planets.' Martin had to bite his cheek to keep from correcting her. She fell silent. He waited for her to continue, but she didn't; she seemed almost depressed.

'You have a lot of clout. Have you told them what you've deduced? Or told anybody else?'

She chuckled, a peculiarly grim laugh. 'If I did that, how long do you think it would be before they chucked me overboard, with or without a vac-suit? They're paranoid enough already; they think there's a spy on board, and they're afraid of minelayers and saboteurs along the way.'

'A *spy*?' He sat up, scared. 'They know there's a—'

'Be quiet. Yes, a spy. Not one of us; some goon from the Curator's Office who they sent along to keep an eye on you. Be quiet, I said. He's just a kid, some wet-behind-the-ears trainee cop. Try to relax around him. As far as you're concerned, you're allowed to talk to me; I'm the nearest representative of your government.'

'When are we going to get off this ship?' he asked tensely.

'Probably when we arrive.' She took his hand and squeezed it. 'Do your job and keep your head down,' she said calmly. 'Just don't, whatever you do, act guilty or confess to anything. Trust me, Martin, like I told you before: we're on the same team for the duration.'

Martin leaned close to her. She was tense, very tense. 'This is quite insane,' he said very slowly and carefully as he slid an arm around her shoulders. 'This idiotic expedition is probably going to get us both killed.'

'Maybe.' Her grip tightened on his hand.

'Better not,' he said tightly. 'I haven't had a chance to get to know you yet.'

'Me neither.' Her grip relaxed a little. 'Is that what you'd like to do? Really?'

'Well.' He leaned back against the hard wall beside the bunk. 'I hadn't thought about it a lot,' he mused, 'but I've been alone for a long time. Really. Before this job. I need –' He shut his eyes. 'Shit. What I mean to say is, I need to get out of this job for a while. I want a year or two off, to pull myself together and find out who I am again. A change and a rest. And if you're thinking about that, too, then—'

'You sound overworked.' She shivered. 'Someone just walked over my grave. You and me both, Martin, you and me both. Something about the New Republic uses you up, doesn't it? Listen, I've got about two years' accumulated leave waiting for me, after I get home. If you want to go somewhere together, to get away from all this—'

'Sounds good to me,' he said quietly. 'But right now . . .' He trailed off, with a glance at the cabin door.

There was a moment's frozen silence: 'I won't let you down,' she said softly. She hugged him briefly, then let go and stood up. 'You're right. I really shouldn't be here, I've got a room to go to, and if they're still watching me – well.'

She took her cap from the upper bunk, carefully placed it on her head, and opened the door. She looked back at him and, for a moment, he thought about asking her to stay, even thought about telling her everything; but then she was gone, out into the red-lit passages of the sleeping ship.

'Damn,' he said softly, watching the door in mild disbelief. 'Too late, too late. Damn . . .'

wolf depository incident

The shooting began with a telegram.

Locked in a loose formation with six other capital ships, the *Lord Vanek* hurtled toward the heliopause, where the solar wind met the hard vacuum of interstellar space. Wolf Depository lay five light-years ahead, and almost five years in the future – for the plan was that fleet would follow a partially closed timelike path, plunging deep into the future (staying within the scope of a light cone with its apex drawn on New Prague at the time of first warning of attack), then use the black boxes attached to their drive modules to loop back into the past. Without quite breaking the letter of the Eschaton's law – *Thou shalt not globally violate causality* – the fleet would arrive in orbit around Rochard's World just after the onslaught of the Festival, far faster than such a task force would normally cover the eight hops separating them from the colony world. In the process, it would loop around any forces sent by the enemy to intercept a straightforward counterstrike – and pick up a time capsule containing analyses of the battle written by future historians, the better to aid the Admiral's planning.

At least, that was what theory dictated. Get there implausibly fast, with more firepower than any attacker could possibly expect, and with advance warning of the attacker's order of battle and defensive intentions. What could go wrong?

The operations room was a hive of concentration as the gold team officers – the crew shift who would be on duty at the time of the forthcoming first jump, the one that would take the fleet into the future, as well as out into deep space – ran through their set-up checklists.

Captain Mirsky stood at the rear of the room, next to the heavy airtight door, watching his officers at their posts: a running display of telemetry from the ship's battle management systems ran up the main wall-screen. The atmosphere was tense enough to cut with a knife. It was the first time any warship of the New Republic had engaged a high-technology foe; and no one, to the best knowledge of Commodore Bauer's staff, had ever tried to pull off this tactical procedure before. Anything could be waiting for them. Five years into the future was as far as they dared probe in one jump; in theory, there should be a navigation beacon awaiting them, but if something went awry, the enemy might be there instead. Mirsky smiled thinly. *All the more reason to get it right*, he reasoned. *If we mess it up, there won't be a second time*.

The military *attaché* from Earth had invited herself in to rubberneck at the proceedings and presumably report back to her masters in due course. Not that it made any difference at this point, but it annoyed Mirsky's sense of order to have a tourist along, let alone one whose loyalty was questionable. He resolved to ignore her – or, if that became impossible, to eject her immediately.

'First breakpoint in five-zero seconds,' called the flight engineer. 'Slaved to preferential-frame compensation buffers. Range to jump initiation point, six-zero seconds.' More jargon followed, in a clipped, tense voice; the routine stock-in-trade of a warship, every phrase was defined by some procedural manual.

Gunnery one: 'Acknowledged. Standing by to power up laser grid.' A mass of lasers – more than a million tiny cells scattered across the skin of the ship, able to operate as a single phased array – cycled through their power-up routines and reported their status. The ship was nearing the jump point; as it did so, it sucked energy out of the energized, unstable vacuum ahead of it and stored it by spinning up its drive kernel, the tiny, electrically charged black hole that nestled at the heart of the engine room containment sphere.

Engineering: 'Main inertial propulsion holding at minus two seconds. Three-zero seconds to jump.'

The ship drifted closer to the lightspeed transition point. The rippled space ahead of it began to flatten, bleeding energy into the underlying vacuum state. Six more huge warships followed behind at five-minute intervals; Squadron Two, the light screen of fast-movers who had set off behind the *Lord Vanek*, had overhauled them the day before and jumped through six hours ago.

Comms: 'Telegram from the flag deck, sir.'

'Read it,' called Mirsky.

'Telegram from Admiral Kurtz, open, all ears. Begins. Assume enemy warships ahead, break. Initiate fire on contact with hostiles, break. For the glory of the empire. Ends. Sent via causal channel to all sister ships.' The causal channels between the ships would die, their contents hopelessly scrambled, as soon as the ships made their first jump between equipotential points: quantum entanglement was a fragile phenomenon and couldn't survive faster-than-light transitions.

Mirsky nodded. 'Acknowledge it. Exec, bring us battle stations.' Alarms began to honk mournfully throughout the ship.

'Reference frame trap executed.' Relativistics. 'Jump field

engaged. We have a white box in group B, repeat, white box in B.' A captive reference frame meant the ship had mapped the precise space-time location of its origin perfectly. Using the newly installed drive controllers, the *Lord Vanek* could return to that point in time from some future location, flying a closed timelike loop.

Mirsky cleared his throat. 'Jump at your convenience.'

No lights dimmed, there was no sense of motion, and virtually nothing happened – except for a burst of exotic particles injected into the ergosphere of the quantum black hole in the ship's drive module. Nevertheless, without any fuss, the star patterns outside the ship's hull changed.

'Jump confirmed.' Almost everybody breathed a slight sight of relief.

'Survey, let's see where we are.' Mirsky showed no sign of stress, even though his ship had just jumped five years into its own future, as well as a parsec and a half out into the unknown.

'Yes, sir: laser grid coming up.' About two gigawatts of power – enough to run a large city – surged into the laser cells in the ship's skin: if there was one thing a starship like the *Lord Vanek* had, it was electricity to burn. The ship lit up like a pulsar, pumping out a blast of coherent ultraviolet light powerful enough to fry anyone within a dozen kilometers. It stabilized, scanning rapidly in a tight beam, quartering the space ahead of the ship. After a minute it shut down again.

Radar: 'No obstructions. We're well clear.' Which was to be expected. Out here, fifteen to fifty astronomical units away from the primary, you could travel for 100 million kilometers in any direction without meeting anything much larger than a snowball. The intense UV lidar pulse would propagate for minutes, then hours, before returning the faint trace of a skin signature.

'Very good. Conn, take us forward. One gee, total delta of one-zero k.p.s.' Mirsky stood back and waited as the helm officer punched in the maneuver. Ten k.p.s. wasn't much speed, but it would take the *Lord Vanek* comfortably away from its point of emergence without emitting too much drive noise, leaving room for the rest of the flotilla behind them. A lidar pulse in the depths of the halo could only signify a warship on the prowl, and it would be extremely unhealthy to stay too close to its point of origin. In the Oort cloud of an industrialized system, even the snowballs could bite.

'Ping at nine-two-six-four!' crowed Radar Two. 'Range four-point-nine M-klicks, bearing one by seven-five by three-three-two. Lots of hot one-point-four MeV gammas – they're cooking on antimatter!'

'Acceleration?' asked Mirsky.

'Tracking . . . one-point-three gees, confirmed. No change. Uh, wait –'

'Comms bulletin from the *Kamchatka*, sir.'

'Comms, call it.'

'Message reads, quote, under attack by enemy missile layers break. Situation serious break. Where are the BBs, break. All units please respond, ends.'

Mirsky blinked. *Enemy warships? This soon?* Wolf Depository was right on the New Republic's doorstep, a mining system owned and exploited by the rich, heavily industrialized Septagon Central. What on earth were they doing allowing alien warships –

'Second burst at nine-two-six-four,' called Radar One. 'Same emission profile. Looks like we scared up a swarm!'

'Wait,' grated Mirsky. He shook himself, visibly surprised by the news. 'Wait, dammit! I want to see what else is out there. Comms, do not, under any circumstances, respond to signals from the *Kamchatka*, or anybody who came through ahead of us without clearing it with me first. If there are enemy ships out here, we've got no way of knowing whether our signals have been compromised.'

'Aye aye, sir. Signal silence on all screening elements.'

'Now.' He bent his head, pondering the screen ahead. 'If it is an ambush . . .'

The gamma-ray traces lit up on the main screen, labeled icons indicating their position and vector relative to the system ahead. One-point-three gees wasn't particularly fast, but it was enough to send cold shudders up Mirsky's spine: it meant serious high-delta-vee propulsion systems, fusion or antimatter or quantum gravity induction, not the feeble ion drive of a robot tug. That could mean a number of things: sublight relativistic bombers, missile buses, intrasystem interceptors, whatever. The *Lord Vanek* would have to skim past them to get to the next jump zone. Which could give them a passing shot at over 1000 k.p.s. . . . a speed at which it took very little, maybe a sand grain, to total a ship. If it was an ambush, it had probably nailed the entire task force cold.

'Radar,' he said, 'give me a second lidar pulse, three-zero seconds. Then plot a vector intersect on those bogies, offset one-zero kiloklicks at closest pass, acceleration one-zero gees, salvo of two SEM-20s one-zero-zero kiloklicks out.'

'Aye aye, skipper.'

'Missiles armed, launch holding at minus one-zero seconds.' Commander Helsingus, stationed at Gunnery One.

'I want them to get a good look at our attack profile,' murmured the Captain. 'Nice and close.' Ilya Murametz glanced at him sidelong. 'Keep the boys on their toes,' Mirsky added, meeting his eye. Ilya nodded.

'Gamma burst!' called Radar Two. 'Burst at one-four-seven-one. Range one-one point-two M-klicks, bearing one by seven-five by three-three-two. Looks like shooting, sir!'

'Understood.' Mirsky clasped his hands together: Murametz

winced as he cracked his knuckles. 'Hurry up and wait. Helm: How's the attack course?'

'We're prepping it now, sir.'

'Forward lidar. Looks like we are in a shooting war. And they know we're here by now. So let's get a good look at them.'

Comms: 'Sir, new message purportedly from the *Kamchatka*. Message from the *Aurora*, too.'

'Read them.'

Mirsky nodded at the comms station, where the petty officer responsible read from a punched paper tape unreeling from the brass mouth of a dog's head. '*Kamchatka* says, quote, engaged by enemy missile boats break we are shooting back break enemy warships astern painting us with target designation radar break situation desperate where are you. Ends. *Aurora* says, quote, no contact with enemies break *Kamchatka* off course stand by for orbital elements correction break what is all the shooting about. Ends.'

'Oh bloody hell.' Murametz turned red.

'Indeed,' Mirsky said drily. 'The question is, whose? TacOps: what's our status?'

'Target acquired, sir. Range down to four-point-eight M-klicks, speed passing one-zero-zero k.p.s. Engagement projected within two-point-four kiloseconds.'

'We have a . . . three-zero-zero-second margin,' said Mirsky, checking the clock display. 'That should be plenty. We can get a look at the closest one without getting so close their launch base can shoot at us if it's a missile bus. Everyone clear? Guns: I want real-time logging of those birds. Let's see how they perform. Radar: Can you lock a spectroscope on the target?'

'At three K-klicks per second, from one-zero K-klicks away? I think so, sir, but we'll need a big fat beacon to spot against.'

'You'll have one.' Murametz smiled widely. 'Guns: dial

those birds down to point-one of a kiloton before you fire them. Standard MP-3 warheads?'

'Yes, sir.'

'Good. Keep 'em.'

Standing at the back of the bridge, Rachel tried not to wince. Wearing her arms inspectorate hat, she was all too familiar with the effects of americium bombs: nuclear weapons made with an isotope denser and more fissile than plutonium, more stable than californium. Just good old-fashioned fission bombs, jacketed with a high-explosive shaped charge and a lens of pre-fragmented copper needles – shrapnel that, in a vacuum engagement, would come spalling off the nuclear fireball in a highly directional cone, traveling at a high fraction of lightspeed.

The next thirty minutes passed in tense silence, broken only by terse observations from Radar One and Two. No more targets burst from hiding; there might well be others in the Kuiper belt, but none were close enough to see or be seen by the intense lidar pulses of the warship. In that time, passive sensors logged two nuclear detonations within a range of half a light-hour; someone was definitely shooting. And behind them, the telltale disturbances of six big ships emerged from jump, then powered up their combat lidar and moved out.

'Launch point in six-zero seconds,' called Helsingus. 'Two hot SEM20s on the rail.'

'Fire on schedule,' said Mirsky, straightening his back and looking directly ahead at the screen. The green arrow showing the *Lord Vanek*'s vector had grown until it was beginning to show the purple of relativistic distortion around its sensitive extrapolative tip: the ship was already nearing half a percent of lightspeed, a dangerous velocity. Too high a speed and it might not be able to track targets effectively: worse, it wouldn't be able to dodge or change its vector fast, or jump safely.

'Three-zero seconds. Arming birds. Birds show green, sir.'

'I'm getting emissions from the target,' called Radar Two. 'Lots of – looks like jamming, sir!'

'Laser grid. Illuminate the target,' said Mirsky. 'Guns, set to passive.'

'Aye aye, sir.' Under passive homing mode, the missiles would lock onto the target, illuminated by the *Lord Vanek*'s laser battery, and home in on its reflection.

'Target still accelerating slowly,' said Radar One. 'Looks like a missile boat.'

'One-zero seconds. Launch rails energized.'

'You have permission to fire at will, Commander,' said the Captain.

'Yes, sir. Eight seconds. Navigation updated. Inertial platforms locked. Birds charged, warheads . . . green. Five seconds. Launch commencing, bird one. Gone.' The deck shuddered briefly: ten tons of missile hurtled the length of the ship in the grip of a coilgun, ejected ahead of the starship at better than a kilometer per second. 'Lidar lock. Drive energized. Bird one main engine ignition confirmed. Bird two loaded and green . . . launch. Gone. Drive energized.'

'Bingo,' Ilya said quietly.

Red arrows indicating the progress of the missiles appeared on the forward screen They weren't self-powered; nobody in his right mind would dare load a quantum black hole and its drive support mechanism into a robot suicide machine. Rather, the ship's phased-array lasers bathed them in a sea of energy, boiling and then superheating the reaction mass they carried until they surged forward far faster than the starship. Strictly a close-range low-deltavee weapon, missiles were mostly obsolescent; their sole job was to get a nuclear device onto the right interception vector, like the 'bus' on an ancient twentieth-century MIRV. They'd burn out after only thirty seconds, but by then the warheads would be closing the gap between the *Lord Vanek*'s projected course and the enemy ship itself. Shortly after the starship ran the gauntlet, its missiles would arrive – and deliver the killing blow.

'Radar One. Where are they?' Mirsky asked softly.

'Tracking as before,' called the officer. 'Still maintaining course and vector. And emitting loads of spam.'

'Bird one MECO in one-zero seconds,' said Helsingus. 'They're trying to jam, sir. Nothing doing.' He said it with heavy satisfaction, as if the knowledge that the anonymous victims of the attack were offering some token resistance reassured him that he was not, in fact, about to butcher them without justification. Even committed officers found the applied methods of three centuries of nuclear warfare hard to stomach at times.

Comms Two, voice ragged with tension: 'Jamming stopped, sir! I'm receiving a distress beacon. Two – no, three! I say again, three distress beacons. It's like they're bailing out before we hit them.'

'Too late,' said Helsingus. 'We'll have 'em in three-two seconds. They'll be inside the burst radius.'

Rachel shuddered. Suddenly a horrible possibility began to rise to the surface of her mind.

Mirsky cracked his knuckles again, kneading his hands together. 'Guns. I want a last-ditch evasion program loaded, activate at closest approach minus one-zero seconds if we're still here.'

'Yes, sir,' Helsingus said heavily. 'Laser grid support?'

'Anything you like.' Mirsky waved a hand magnanimously. 'If we're still here to enjoy the light show.'

Helsingus began flipping switches like a man possessed. On the screen, the outgoing birds passed their main engine cutout points and went ballistic; more enemy missiles began hatching like sinister blue fingers reaching out from the target point.

'Captain,' Rachel said slowly.

'– One-zero seconds. They're jamming hard, sir, but the birds are still holding.'

'What if *Kamchatka* is wrong? What if those are civilian mining ships?'

Captain Mirsky ignored her.

'Five seconds! Bird one ready to go – range down to one-zero K. Three. EMP lockdown is go. Sensor stepdown mag six is go. Optics shielded – bang. Sir, I confirm that bird one has detonated. Bang. Bird two is gone.'

'Radar. What do you see?' asked Mirsky.

'Waiting on the fog to clear – ah, got sensors back sir. Incoming missiles still closing. Fireball remnants hashing up radar, lidar is better. Uh, the impact spectroscope has tripped, sir, we have a confirmed impact on the target alpha. Oxygen, nitrogen, carbonitrile emissions from the hull. I think we holed him, sir.'

'We holed him –' Mirsky stopped. Turned to glance at Rachel. 'What did you say?' he demanded.

'What if they're civilians? We have only *Kamchatka*'s word that they're under attack; no direct evidence other than bombs going off – which could be hers.'

'Nonsense.' Mirsky snorted. 'None of our ships could make a mistake like that!'

'Nobody is actually shooting live missiles at us. The pre-jump briefing warned everyone to look out for enemy missile boats. How likely is it that the *Kamchatka* ran down a civilian mining ship by mistake and got a bit trigger-happy? And what you're seeing as an attack is actually just the cruiser screen shooting in the dark at anything that moves?'

Dead silence. Enlisted men and officers alike stared at Rachel disapprovingly: nobody spoke to the captain like that! Then from behind her: 'Spallation debris on radar, sir. Target is breaking up. Uh, humbly reporting, Captain, we have distress beacons. Civilian ones . . .'

The *Lord Vanek* was going far too fast to slow down, and as flagship and lead element of the squadron, had a duty not to do so. Nevertheless, they signaled the squadron astern; and behind them, one of the elderly battleships peeled off to pick up any survivors from the disastrous attack.

The big picture, when it finally gelled some eight hours later, was very bad indeed. The 'missile carriers' were actually refinery tugs, tending the migratory robot factories that slowly trawled the Kuiper-belt bodies, extracting helium 3 from the snowballs. Their sudden burst of speed had a simple explanation; seeing alien warships, they had panicked, dumping their cargo pods so that they could clear the area under maximum acceleration. One of the distant explosions had been the *Kamchatka*, landing a near miss on one of the 'enemy battleships' – the cruiser *India*. (Minor hull damage and a couple of evacuated compartments had resulted; unfortunately, the cruiser's chaplain had been in one of the compartments at the time, and had gone to meet his maker.)

'Ser-erves 'em right for being in the way, dammit,' quavered Admiral Kurtz when Commodore Bauer delivered the news in person. 'Wha-what do they think this is?' He half rose to his feet, momentarily forgetting about his glass legs: 'Simply appalling stupidity!'

'Ah, I believe we still have a problem, sir,' Bauer pointed out as Robard tried to get his master settled down again. 'This system is claimed by Septagon, and, ah, we have received signals as of half an hour ago indicating that they have a warship in the area, and it's engaging us on an intercept trajectory.'

The Admiral snorted. 'What can one warship d-do?'

Rachel, who had inveigled her way into the staff meeting on the grounds that, as a neutral observer, it was her duty to act as an intermediary in situations such as this one, watched Bauer spluttering with mordant interest. *Can he really be that stupid?* she wondered, glancing at the admiral, who hunched in his chair like a bald parrot, eyes gleaming with an expression of fixed mania.

'Sir, the warship that is signaling us is, ah, according to our most recent updates, one of their Apollo-class fleet attack carriers. Radar says they've got additional traces indicative of a full battle group. We outnumber them, but –'

Rachel cleared her throat. 'They'll eat you for breakfast.'

Bauer's head whipped around. 'What did you say?'

She tapped her PA, where it lay on the table before her. 'UN defense intelligence estimates suggest that Septagon's policy of building carriers, rather than the standard laser/missile platform that your navy has adopted, gives them a considerable advantage in the ability to cover an entire system. Simply put, while they lack short-range firepower, they're able to launch a swarm of interceptors that can pound on you from well outside your own engagement envelope. More to the point, they're frighteningly good, and unless I'm very much mistaken, that carrier, *on its own*, outmasses your entire fleet. I wouldn't want you to get the idea that I don't rate you against the Septagon Navy, but if you're planning on fighting them, do you think you could let me know in advance? I'd like a chance to grab a survival pod first.'

'Well, we can't argue with the government of Earth's defense estimates, can we, Commander?' Bauer nodded pointedly at his executive officer.

'Ah, no, sir. The Colonel is quite correct.' The young and somewhat flustered Lieutenant avoided looking at Rachel; it was a minor slight she was getting plenty of practice at ignoring.

'Damned newfangled inventions,' mumbled Kurtz under his breath. 'Blasted many-angled ones don't want us to succeed, anyway – per-per-perfidious technophiles!' Louder: 'We must press on!'

'Absolutely.' Commodore Bauer nodded sagely. 'If we press on to Point Two on schedule, leaving the diplomatic niceties to the embassy – speaking of which – Lieutenant Kossov. What of the update? Where do we stand with respect to further information about this Festival, its order of battle and motives? What have we learned?'

'Ah.' Lieutenant Kossov, removed and polished his pince-nez nervously. 'Well, there's something of a problem. The deposition from the Admiralty doesn't seem to have arrived. We were supposed to be seeing an ordnance beacon, but although we quartered the designated orbital path, there's nothing there. Either they're late – or they never planted it.'

'This orbital beacon.' Rachel leaned forward. 'A standard target buoy, right? With a diplomatic package containing any-thing the Republic's intelligence services have learned about the Festival in the five years since our jump?'

Kossov glanced warily at the Commodore, who nodded. 'Yes, Colonel. What of it?'

'Well, if it isn't there, that can imply three things, can't it? Either it was there, but somebody else stole or disabled it. Or—'

'Perfidious Septagonians!' Robard hastily leaned over his charge, then looked up and shrugged, eloquently.

'Indeed, Admiral. Or, as I was saying, the second option is that it hasn't been put there yet – some miscalculation, or they couldn't determine any useful information about the enemy, or they forgot about us, or something.'

The noise of Kurtz's snoring cut into her exposition. All eyes turned to the admiral; Robard straightened up. 'I'm afraid the Admiral's legs have been paining him considerably of late, and the dosage of his medication is not conducive to lucidity. He may sleep for some hours.'

'Well, then.' Bauer looked around the conference table. 'I believe if you would be so good as to return His Excellency to his cabin, I will continue as his proxy and prepare a minuted report of this meeting for him to review later, when he's feeling better. Unless anyone has any comments that specifically require the Admiral's ear?' Nobody demurred. 'Very well then. Recess for five minutes.'

Robard and an enlisted man gingerly rolled the Admiral's chair away from the table; then, using the lift just outside the room, disappeared with him in the direction of his quarters. Everybody stood, and saluted, while the snoring officer was wheeled out of the meeting. Rachel held her face expressionless, trying to conceal the disgust and pity the sight pulled from her. *He's young enough to be my grandson. How can they do this to themselves?*

Eventually, Bauer, assuming the admiral's position at the head of the table, rapped his hand on the brass bell. 'Meeting will resume. The Terran attaché has the floor. You were saying?'

'The third possibility is that the New Republic no longer exists,' Rachel said bluntly. She continued, ignoring the outraged gasps around the table. 'You are facing an enemy about whose capabilities you are largely ignorant. I'm afraid to say, the UN knows little more about them than you do. As I noted, there are three reasons for the New Republic not to have contacted you, and their total defeat in the intervening time is only one of them, but not one it's safe to ignore. We're now in the outbound leg of a closed, timelike loop, which will eventually clip itself out of the world line of this universe if you succeed in looping back into our relative past – but the New Republic's absolute immediate future – and taking the intruders by surprise. This has some odd implications. History reaching us inside this loop may not bear any relationship to the eventual outcome we seek, for one thing. For another –'

She shrugged. 'If I'd been consulted prior to this expedition, I would have strongly counseled against it. While it is not technically a breach of the letter of Clause Nineteen, it is dangerously close to the sort of activity that has brought down intervention by the Eschaton in the past. The Eschaton really doesn't like time travel in the slightest, presumably because, if things go too far, someone might edit it out of existence. So there's the possibility that what you're up against isn't just the Festival, but a higher power.'

'Thank you, Colonel.' Bauer nodded politely, but his face was set in a mask of disapproval. 'I believe that, for now, we shall disregard that possibility. If the Eschaton chooses to involve itself, there is nothing we can do in any case, so we must work on the assumption that it will not. And in that case, all we are up against is the Festival. Kossov. What did we know about it before we left?'

'Ah, um, well, that is to say –' Kossov looked around wildly, shuffled the papers on his blotter, and sighed. 'Ah, good. Yes. The Festival—'

'I know what it's called, Lieutenant,' the Commodore said reprovingly. 'What is it and what does it want?'

'Nobody knows.' Kossov looked at his supreme commander's deputy like a rabbit caught in the blinding headlights of an oncoming express train.

'So, Commissioner.' Bauer cocked his head on one side and stared at Rachel, with the single-minded analytical purpose of a raptor. 'And what can the esteemed government-coordinating body of Earth tell me about the Festival?' he asked, almost tauntingly.

'Uh.' Rachel shook her head. Of course the poor kid had done his best – none of these people could know anything much about the Festival. Even *she* didn't. It was a big yawning blank.

'Well?' Bauer prodded.

Rachel sighed. 'This is very provisional; nobody from Earth has had any direct contact with the agency known as Festival until now, and our information is, therefore, second-hand and unverifiable. And, frankly, unbelievable. The Festival does not appear to be a government or agency thereof, as we understand the term. In fact, it may not even be human. All we know is that something of that name turns up in distant settled systems – never closer than a thousand light-years, before now – and it, well, the term we keep hearing used to describe what happens next is "Jubilee", if that makes any sense to you. Everything . . . stops. And the Festival takes over the day-to-day running of the system for the duration.' She looked at Bauer. 'Is that what you wanted to know?'

Bauer shook his head, looking displeased. 'No it wasn't,' he said. 'I was after capabilities.'

Rachel shrugged. 'We don't know,' she said bluntly. 'As I said, we've never seen it from close-up.'

Bauer frowned. 'Then this will be a first for you, won't it? Which leads us to the next issue, updates to navigation plan Delta . . .'

A few hours later, Rachel lay facedown on her bunk and tried to shut the world out of her head. It wasn't easy; too much of the world had followed her home over the years, crying for attention.

She was still alive. She knew, somehow, that she should feel relieved about this, but what she'd seen in the briefing room screen had unnerved her more than she was willing to admit. The admiral was a senile vacuum at the heart of the enterprise. The intelligence staff were well-meaning, but profoundly ignorant: they were so inflexible that they were incapable of doing their job properly. She'd tried to explain how advanced civilizations worked until she could feel herself turning blue in the face, and they still didn't understand! They'd nodded politely, because she was a lady – even if a somewhat scandalous one, a lady *diplomat* – and immediately forgotten or ignored her advice.

You don't fight an infowar attack with missiles and lasers, any more than you attack a railway locomotive with spears and stone axes. You don't fight a replicator attack by throwing energy and matter at machines that will just use them for fuel. They'd nodded approvingly and gone on to discuss the virtues of active countermeasures versus low-observability systems. And they still didn't get it; it was as if the very idea of something like the Festival, or even the Septagon system, occupied a mental blind spot ubiquitous in their civilization. They could accept a woman in trousers, even in a colonel's uniform, far more easily than they could cope with the idea of a technological singularity.

Back on Earth, she had attended a seminar, years ago. It had been a week-long gathering of experts; hermeneutic engineers driven mad by studying the arcane debris of the Singularity, demographers still trying to puzzle out the distribution of colony worlds, a couple of tight-lipped mercenary commanders and commercial intelligence consultants absorbed in long-range backstop insurance against a return of the Eschaton. They were all thrown together and mixed with a coterie of Defense SIG experts and UN diplomats. It was hosted by the UN, which, as the sole remaining island of concrete stability in a sea of pocket polities, was the only body able to host such a global event.

During the seminar, she had attended a cocktail party on a balcony of white concrete, jutting from a huge hotel built on the edge of the UN city, Geneva. She'd been in uniform at the time, working as an auditor for the denuclearization commission. Black suit, white gloves, mirrorshades pulsing news updates and radiation readings into her raw and tired eyes. Hyped up on a cocktail of alcohol antagonists, she sipped a bitter (and ineffective) gin with a polite Belgian cosmologist. Mutual incomprehension tinged with apprehension bound them in an uncomfortable Ping-Pong match of a conversation. 'There is so much we do not understand about the Eschaton,' the cosmologist had insisted, 'especially concerning its interaction with the birth of the universe. The big bang.' He raised his eyebrows suggestively.

'The big bang. Not, by any chance, an unscheduled fissile criticality excursion, was it?' She said it deadpan, trying to deflect him with humor.

'Hardly. There were no licensing bodies in those days – at the start of space-time, before the era of expansion and the first appearance of mass and energy, about a billionth of a billionth of a millionth of a second into the life of the universe.'

'Surely the Eschaton can't have been responsible for that. It's a modern phenomenon, isn't it?'

'Maybe not responsible,' he said, choosing his words carefully. 'But maybe circumstances arising then formed a necessary precondition for the Eschaton's existence, or the existence of something related to but beyond the Eschaton. There's a whole school of cosmology predicated around the weak anthropic principle, that the universe is as it seems because, if it was any other way, we would not exist to observe it. There is a . . . less popular field, based on the strong anthropic principle, that the universe exists to give rise to certain types of entity. I don't believe we'll ever understand the Eschaton until we understand why the universe exists.'

She smiled at him toothily, and let a Prussian diplomat rescue her with the aid of a polite bow and an offer to explain the fall of Warsaw during the late unpleasantness in the Baltic. A year or so later, the polite cosmologist had been murdered by Algerian religious fundamentalists who thought his account of the universe a blasphemy against the words of the prophet Yusuf Smith as inscribed on his two tablets of gold.

But that was typical of Europe, half-empty and prey to what the formerly Islamic world had become.

Somewhere along the line she, too, had changed. She'd spent decades – the best part of her second, early-twenty-second-century life – fighting the evils of nuclear proliferation. Starting out as a dreadlocked direct-action activist, chaining herself to fences, secure in the naive youthful belief that no harm could befall her. Later, she'd figured out that the way to do it was wearing a smart suit, with mercenary soldiers and the threat of canceled insurance policies backing up her quiet voice. Still prickly and direct, but less of a knee-jerk nonconformist, she'd learned to work the system for maximum effect. The hydra seemed halfway under control, bombings down to only one every couple of years, when Bertil had summoned her to Geneva and offered her a new job. Then she'd wished she'd paid more attention to the cosmologist – for the Algerian Latter-Day Saints had been very thorough in their suppression of the Tiplerite heresy – but it was too late, and in any event, the minutiae of the Standing Committee's investigations into chronological and probabilistic warfare beckoned.

Somewhere along the line, the idealist had butted heads with the pragmatist, and the pragmatist won. Maybe the seeds had been sown during her first marriage. Maybe it had come later; being shot in the back and spending six months recovering in hospital in Calcutta had changed her. She'd done her share of shooting, too, or at least directing the machinery of preemptive vengeance, wiping out more than one cell of atomic-empowered fanatics – whether central-Asian independence fighters, freelance mercs with a bomb too many in their basement, or on one notable occasion, radical pro-lifers willing to go to any lengths to protect the unborn child. Idealism couldn't coexist with so many other people's ideals, betrayed in their execution by the tools they'd chosen. She'd walked through Manchester three days after the Inter-City

Firm's final kickoff, before the rain had swept the sad mounds of cinders and bone from the blasted streets. She'd become so cynical that only a complete change of agenda, a wide-angle view of the prospects for humanity, could help her retain her self-respect.

And so to the New Republic. A shithole of a backwater, in her frank opinion; in need of remodeling by any means necessary, lest it pollute its more enlightened neighboring principalities, like Malacia or Turku. But the natives were still people – and for all that they tampered with the machineries of mass destruction in apparent ignorance of their power, they deserved better than they'd receive from an awakened and angry Eschaton. They deserved better than to be left to butt heads with something they didn't understand, like the Festival, whatever it was: if they couldn't understand it, then maybe she'd have to think the unthinkable for them, help them to reach some kind of accommodation with it – if that was possible. The alarming aspect to the UN's knowledge of the Festival – the only thing she hadn't told Bauer about – was that antitech colonies contacted by it disappeared, leaving only wreckage behind when the Festival moved on. Just why this might be she didn't know, but it didn't bode well for the future.

Nothing quite concentrates a man's mind like the knowledge that he is to be hanged in four weeks; unless it is possibly the knowledge that he has sabotaged the very ship he sails in, and he – along with everyone else in it – will be hanged in three months. For while the execution may be farther away, the chances of a reprieve are infinitely lower.

Martin Springfield sat in the almost-deserted wardroom, a glass of tea at his hand, staring absently at the ceiling beams. A nautical theme pervaded the room; old oak panels walled it in, and the wooden plank floor had been holystone-polished until it gleamed. A silver-chased samovar sat steaming gently atop an age-blackened chest beneath a huge gilt-framed oil painting of the ship's namesake that hung on one wall. *Lord Vanek* leading the cavalry charge at the suppression of the Robots' Rebellion 160 years ago — destroying the aspirations of those citizens who had dreamed of life without drudge-labor in the service of aristocrats. Martin shivered slightly, trying to grapple with his personal demons.

It's all my fault, he thought. *And there's nobody else to share it with.*

Comfortless fate. He sipped at his glass, felt the acrid sweet bite of the rum underlying the bitterness of the tea. His lips felt numb, now. *Stupid*, he thought. It was too late to undo things. Too late to confess, even to Rachel, to try to get her out of this trap. He should have told her right at the beginning, before she came on board. Kept her out of the way of the Eschaton's revenge. Now, even if he confessed everything, or had done so before they tripped the patch in the drive kernel controllers, it would only put him on a one-way trip to the death chair. And although the sabotage was essential, and even though it wouldn't kill anyone directly —

Martin shuddered, drained the glass, and put it down beside his chair. He hunched forward unconsciously, neck bowed beneath the weight of a guilty conscience. *At least I did the right thing*, he tried to tell himself. *None of us are going home, but at least the homes we had will still be there when we're gone.* Including Rachel's unlived-in apartment. He winced. It was next to impossible to feel guilt for a fleet, but just knowing about her presence aboard the ship had kept him awake all night.

The mournful pipes had summoned the ship to battle stations almost an hour ago. Something to do with an oncoming Septagonese carrier battle group, scrambled like a nest of angry hornets in response to the fiasco with the mining tugs. It didn't make any difference to Martin. Somewhere in the drive control network, an atomic clock was running slow, tweaked by a folded curl of space-time from the drive kernel. It was only a small error, of course, but CP violation would amplify it out of all proportion when the fleet began its backward path through space-time. He'd done it deliberately, to prevent a catastrophic and irrevocable disaster. The New Republican Navy might think a closed timelike loop to be only a petty tactical maneuver, but it was the thin end of a wedge; a wedge that Herman said had to be held at bay. He'd made his pact with a darker, more obscure agency than Rachel's. From his perspective, the UN DISA people merely aped his employer's actions on a smaller scale – in hope of pre-empting them.

Good-by, Belinda, he thought, mentally consigning his sister to oblivion. *Good-by, London.* Dust of ages ate the metropolis, crumbled its towers in dust. *Hello, Herman*, to the steady tick of the pendulum clock on the wall. As the flagship, *Lord Vanek* provided a time signal for the other vessels in the fleet. Not just that; it provided an inertial reference frame locked to the space-time coordinates of their first jump. By slightly slowing the clock, Martin had ensured that the backward time component of their maneuver would be botched very slightly.

The fleet would travel forward into the light cone, maybe as much as four thousand years; it would rewind, back almost the whole distance – but not quite as far as it had come. Their arrival at Rochard's World would be delayed almost two weeks, about as long as a rapid crossing without any of the closed timelike hanky-panky the Admiralty had planned. And then the Festival would – well, what the Festival would do to the fleet was the Festival's business. All he knew was that he, and everyone else, would pay the price.

Who did they think they were kidding, anyway? Claiming they planned to use the maneuver just to reduce transit time, indeed! Even a toddler could see through a subterfuge that transparent, all the way to the sealed orders waiting in the admiral's safe. *You can't fool the Eschaton by lying to yourself.* Maybe Herman, or rather the being that hid behind that code name, would be waiting. Maybe Martin would be able to get off the doomed ship, maybe Rachel would, or maybe through a twist of fate the New Republican Navy would defeat the Festival in a head-to-head fight. And maybe he'd teach the horse to sing . . .

He stood up, a trifle giddily, and carried his glass to the samovar. He half filled it, then topped it up from the cut-glass decanter until the nostril-prickling smell began to waft over the steam. He sat down in his chair a bit too hard, numb fingertips and lips threatening to betray him. With nothing to do but avoid his guilt by drinking himself into a paralytic stupor, Martin was taking the easy way out.

Presently, he drifted back to more tolerable memories. Eighteen years earlier, when he was newly married and working as a journeyman field circus engineer, a gray cipher of a man had approached him in a bar somewhere in orbit over Wollstonecroft's World. 'Can I buy you a drink?' asked the man, whose costume was somewhere between that of an accountant and a lawyer. Martin had nodded. 'You're Martin Springfield,' the man had said. 'You work at present for Nakamichi Nuclear, where you are making relatively little money and running up a sizable overdraft. My sponsors have asked me to approach you with a job offer.'

'Answer's no,' Martin had said automatically. He had made up his mind some time before that the experience he was gaining at NN was more useful than an extra thousand euros a year; and besides, his employing combine was paranoid enough about some of its contracts to sound out its contractor's loyalties with fake approaches.

'There is no conflict of interest with your current employers, Mr. Springfield. The job is a nonexclusive commission, and in any event, it will not take effect until you go freelance or join another kombinat.'

'What kind of job?' Martin raised an eyebrow.

'Have you ever wondered why you exist?'

'Don't be –' Martin had paused in midsentence. 'Is this some religious pitch?' he asked.

'No.' The gray man looked him straight in the eye. 'It's exactly the opposite. No god exists yet, in this universe. My employer wishes to safeguard the necessary preconditions for God's emergence, however. And to do so, my employer needs human arms and legs. Not being equipped with them, so to speak.'

The crash of his glass hitting the floor and shattering had brought Martin to his senses. 'Your employer—'

'Believes that you may have a role to play in defending the security of the cosmos, Martin. Naming no names' – the gray man leaned closer – 'it is a long story. Would you like to hear it?'

Martin had nodded, it seeming the only reasonable thing to do in a wholly unreasonable, indeed surreal, situation. And in doing so, he'd taken the first step along the path that had brought him here, eighteen years later: to a drinking binge alone in the wardroom of a doomed starship, only weeks left to play out the end of its role in the New Republican Navy. Minutes, in the worst possible case.

Eventually, he would be reported lost, along with the entire crew of the *Lord Vanek*. Relatives would be notified, tears would be shed against the greater backdrop of a tragic and unnecessary war. But that would be no concern of his. Because – just as soon as he finished this drink – he was going to stand up and weave his way to his cabin and lie down. Then await whatever would follow over the next three months, until the jaws of the trap sprang shut.

*

It was hot. and somewhat stuffy, in Rachel's room, despite the whirring white noise of the ventilation system and the occasional dripping of an overflow pipe behind the panel next to her head. Sleeping wasn't an option; neither was relaxation. She found herself wishing for someone to talk to, someone who would have an idea what was going on. She rolled over on her back. 'PA,' she called, finally indulging an urge she'd been fighting off for some time. 'Where's Martin Springfield?'

'Location. Ship's wardroom, D deck.'

'Anyone with him?'

'Negative.'

She sat up. The crew were at their action stations: what on earth was Martin doing there on his own?

'I'm going there. Backdoor clause: as far as the ship is concerned, I am still in my cabin. Confirm capability.'

'Affirmative. Backdoor tracking master override confirmed.' They might have rebuilt the ship's fire control and propulsion systems, but they'd left the old tab/badge personnel tracking grid in place – unused, probably, because it reduced the need for tyrannical petty officers. Rachel pulled on her boots, then stood up and grabbed the jacket that lay on the upper bunk. She'd take a minute to look presentable, then go and find Martin. She was irresponsible to leave her airtight cabin while the ship was cleared for action – but so was he. What was he thinking of?

She headed for the wardroom briskly. The access spaces of the warship were eerily quiet, the crew all locked down in airtight compartments and damage control stations. Only the humming of the ventilation system broke the silence; that, and the ticking of the wardroom clock as she opened the door.

The only occupant of the room was Martin, and he looked somewhat the worse for wear, slumped in an overstuffed armchair like a rag doll that had lost its stuffing. A silver-chased tea glass sat on the table in front of him, half-full of a brown liquid which, if Rachel was any judge of character, was not tea. He opened his eyes to watch her as she entered, but didn't say anything.

'You should be in your cabin,' Rachel observed. 'The wardroom isn't vacuum-safe, you know.'

'Who cares?' He made a rolling motion of one shoulder, as if a shrug was too much effort. 'Really don't see the point.'

'I do.' She marched over and stood in front of him. 'You can go to your cabin or come back to mine, but you *are* going to be in a cabin in five minutes!'

'Don't remember signing a contractual . . . . of employment with you,' he mumbled.

'No, you didn't,' she said brightly. 'So I'm not doing this in my capacity as your employer, I'm doing it as your government.'

'Whoa –' Rachel heaved. 'But I don't have a gummint.' Martin stumbled out of the chair, a pained expression on his face.

'The New Republic seems to think you have, and I'm the best you'll find around here. Unless you'd prefer the other choice on offer?'

Martin grimaced. 'Hardly.' He staggered. 'Got some 4-3-1 in left pocket. Think I need it.' He staggered, fumbling for the small blister pack of alcohol antagonists. 'No need to get nasty.'

'I wasn't getting nasty; I was just providing you with an inertial reference frame for your own good. 'Sides, I thought we were going to look out for each other. And I wouldn't be doing my job if I didn't get you out of here and into a cabin before someone notices. Drunkenness is a flogging offense, did you know that?' Rachel took him by one elbow and began gently steering him toward the door. Martin was sufficiently wobbly on his legs to make this an interesting experience; she was tall, and had boosters embedded in her skeletal muscles for just such events, but he had the three advantages of mass, momentum, and a low center of gravity. Together, they described a brief drunkard's walk before Martin managed to fumble his drug patch onto the palm of one hand, and Rachel managed to steer the two of them into the corridor.

By the time they reached her cabin, He was breathing deeply and looking pale. 'In,' she ordered.

'I feel like shit,' he murmured. 'Got any drinking water?'

'Yup.' She pulled the hatch shut behind them and spun the locking wheel. 'Sink's over there; I'm sure you've seen one before.'

'Thanks, I think.' He ran the taps, splashed water on his face, then used the china cup to take mouthful after mouthful. 'Damned alcohol dehydration.' He straightened up. 'You think I should have more sense than to do that?'

'The thought had crossed my mind,' she said drily. She crossed her arms and watched him. He shook himself like a bedraggled water rat and sat down heavily on Rachel's neatly folded bunk.

'I needed to forget some things very badly,' he said moodily. 'Maybe too badly. Doesn't happen very often but, well, being locked up with nobody for company but my own head isn't good for me. All I get to see these days are cable runs and change schematics, plus a few naive young midshipmen at lunch. That spook from the Curator's Office is hanging around all the time, keeping an eye on me and listening to whatever I say. It's like being in a fucking prison.'

Rachel pulled out the folding chair and sat on it. 'You've never been in prison, then. Consider yourself lucky.'

His lips quirked. 'You have, I suppose? The public servant?'

'Yeah. Spent eight months inside, once, banged up for industrial espionage by an agricultural cartel. Amnesty Multinational made me a prisoner of commerce and started up a trade embargo: that got me sprung pretty quick.' She winced at the memories, grey shadows of their original violent fury, washed out by time. It wasn't her longest stretch inside, but she had no intention of telling him that just yet.

He shook his head and smiled faintly. 'The New Republic is like a prison for everyone, though. Isn't it?'

'Hmm.' She stared through him at the wall behind. 'Now you mention it, I think you could be stretching things a bit far.'

'Well, you'll at least concede they're all prisoners of their ideology, aren't they? Two hundred years of violent suppression hasn't left them much freedom to distance themselves from their culture and look around. Hence the mess we're in now.' He lay back, propping his head against the wall. 'Excuse me; I'm tired. I spent a double shift on the drive calibration works, then four hours over on *Glorious*, troubleshooting its RCS oxidant switching logic.'

'You're excused.' Rachel unbuttoned her jacket, then bent down and slid off her boots. 'Ow.'

'Sore feet?'

'Damned Navy, always on their feet. Looks bad if I slouch, too.'

He yawned. 'Speaking of other things, what do you think the Septagon forces will do?'

She shrugged. 'Probably track us the hell out of here at gunpoint, while pressing the New Republic for compensation. They're pragmatists, none of this babble about national honor and the virtues of courage and manly manhood and that sort of thing.'

Martin sat up. 'If you're going to take your boots off, if you don't mind –'

She waved a hand. 'Be my guest.'

'I thought I was supposed to be your loyal subject?'

She giggled. 'Don't get ideas above your station! Really,

these damned monarchists. I understand in the abstract, but how do they put up with it? I'd go crazy, I swear it. Within a decade.'

'Hmm.' He leaned forward, busy with his shoes. 'Look at it another way. Most people back home sit around with their families and friends and lead a cozy life, doing three or four different things at the same time – gardening, designing commercial beetles, painting landscapes, and bringing up children, that sort of thing. Entomologists picking over the small things in life to see what's twitching its legs underneath. Why the hell aren't we doing that ourselves?'

'I used to.' He glanced up at her curiously, but she was elsewhere, remembering. 'Spent thirty years being a housewife, would you believe it? Being good God-fearing people, hubby was the breadwinner, two delightful children to dote over, and a suburban garden. Church every Sunday and nothing – nothing – allowed to break with the pretense of conformity.'

'Ah. I thought you were older than you looked. Late-sixties backlash?'

'Which sixties?' She shook her head, then answered her own rhetorical question: 'Twenty-sixties. I was born in forty-nine. Grew up in a Baptist family, Baptist town, quiet religion – it turned inward after the Eschaton. We were all so desperately afraid, I think. It was a long time ago: I find it hard to remember. One day I was forty-eight and the kids were at college and I realized I didn't believe a word of it. They'd gotten the extension treatments nailed down by then, and the pastor had stopped denouncing it as satanic tampering with God's will – after his own grandfather beat him at squash – and I suddenly realized that I'd had an empty day, and I had maybe a million days just like it ahead of me, and there were so many things I hadn't done and couldn't do, if I stayed the same. And I didn't really *believe*: religion was my husband's thing, I just went along with it. So I moved out.

Took the treatment, lost twenty years in six months. Went through the usual Sterling fugue, changed my name, changed my life, changed just about everything about me. Joined an anarchist commune, learned to juggle, got into radical antiviolence activism. Harry – no, Harold – couldn't cope with that.'

'Second childhood. Sort of like a twentieth-century teenage period.'

'Yes, exactly –' She stared at Martin. 'How about you?'

He shrugged. 'I'm younger than you. Older than most everyone else aboard this idiotic children's crusade. Except maybe the admiral.' For an instant, and only an instant, he looked hagridden. 'You shouldn't be here. *I* shouldn't be here.'

She stared at him. 'You've got it bad?'

'We're –' He checked himself, cast her a curious guarded look, then started again. 'This trip is doomed. I suppose you know that.'

'Yes.' She looked at the floor. 'I know that,' she said calmly. 'If I don't broker some sort of cease-fire or persuade them not to use their causality weapons, the Eschaton will step in. Probably throw a comet made of antimatter at them, or something.' She looked at him. 'What do you think?'

'I think –' He paused again and looked away, slightly evasively. 'If the Eschaton intervenes, we're both in the wrong place.'

'Huh. That's so much fun to know.' She forced a grin. 'So where do you come from? Go on, I told you –'

Martin stretched his arms and leaned back. 'I grew up in a Yorkshire hill farming village, all goats and cloth caps and dark satanic mills full of God-knows-what. Oh yes, and compulsory ferret-legging down the pub on Tuesday evenings, for the tourist trade tha' knows.'

'Ferret-legging?' Rachel looked at him incredulously.

'Yup. You tie your kilt up around your knees with duct

tape – as you probably know, no Yorkshireman would be seen dead wearing anything under his sporran – and take a ferret by the scruff of his neck. A ferret, that's like, uh, a bit like a mink. Only less friendly. It's a young man's initiation rite; you stick the ferret where the sun doesn't shine and dance the furry dance to the tune of a balalaika. Last man standing and all that, kind of like the ancient Boer aardvark-kissing competition.' Martin shuddered dramatically. 'I hate ferrets. The bloody things bite like a cask-strength single malt without the nice after-effects.'

'That was what you did on Tuesdays,' Rachel said, slowly beginning to smile. 'Tell me more. What about Wednesdays?'

'Oh, on Wednesdays we stayed home and watched reruns of *Coronation Road*. They remixed the old video files to near-realistic resolution and subtitled them, of course, so we could understand what they were saying. Then we'd all hoist a pint of Tetley's tea and toast the downfall of the House of Lancaster. Very traditional, us Yorkshirefolk. I remember the thousandth-anniversary victory celebrations – but that's enough about me. What did you do on Wednesdays?'

Rachel blinked. 'Nothing in particular. Defused terrorist A-bombs, got shot at by Algerian Mormon separatists. Uh, that was after I kicked over the traces the first time. Before then, I think I took the kids to soccer, although I'm not sure what day of the week that was.' She turned aside for a moment and rummaged in the steamer trunk under her bunk. 'Ah, here it is.' She pulled out a narrow box and opened it. 'You know what? Maybe you shouldn't have used that sober patch.' The bottle gleamed golden beneath the antiseptic cabin lights.

'I'd be lousy company though. I was getting all drunk and depressed on my own, and you had to interrupt me and make me sober up.'

'Well, maybe you should just have tried to find someone to

get drunk with instead of doing it on your own.' Two small glasses appeared. She leaned close. 'Do you want it watered?'

Martin eyed the bottle critically. Replicated Speyside fifty-year malt, a cask-strength bottling template. If it wasn't a nanospun clone of the original, it would be worth its weight in platinum. Even so, it would be more than adequately drink-able. 'I'll take it neat and report to sick bay for a new throat tomorrow.' He whistled appreciatively as she poured a gener-ous measure. 'How did you know?'

'That you'd like it?' She shrugged. 'I didn't. I just grew up on corn liquor. Didn't meet the real thing till a job in Syrtis –' Her face clouded over. 'Long life and happiness.'

'I'll drink to that,' he agreed after a moment. They sat in silence for a minute, savoring the afterbloom of the whisky. 'I'd be happier right now if I knew what was going on, though.'

'I wouldn't be too worried: either nothing, or we'll be dead too fast to feel it. The carrier from Septagon will probably just make a fast pass to reassure itself that we're not planning on spreading any more mayhem, then escort us to the next jump zone while the diplomats argue over who pays. Right now, I've got the comms room taking my name in vain for all it's worth; hopefully, that'll convince them not to shoot at us without asking some more questions first.'

'I'd be happier if I knew we had a way off this ship.'

'Relax. Drink your whisky.' She shook her head. 'We don't. So stop worrying about it. Anyway, if they do shoot us, wouldn't you rather die happily sipping a good single malt or screaming in terror?'

'Has anyone ever told you you're cold-blooded? No, I take it back. Has anyone ever told you you've got a skin like a tank?'

'Frequently.' She stared into her glass thoughtfully. 'It's a learned thing. Pray you never have to learn it.'

'You mean you had to?'

'Yes. No other way to do my job. My last job, that is.'

'What did you do?' he asked softly.

'I wasn't joking about the terrorist A-bombs. Actually, the bombs were the easiest bit; it was finding the assholes who planted them that was the hard part. Find the asshole, find the gadget, fix the gadget, fix the dump they sprang the plute from. Usually in that order, unless we were unlucky enough to have to deal with an unscheduled criticality excursion in downtown wherever without someone mailing in a warning first. Then if we found the asshole, our hardest job would be keeping the lynch mob away from them until we could find out where they sourced the bang-juice.'

'Did you ever lose any?' he asked, even more quietly.

'You mean, did I ever fuck up and kill several thousand people?' she asked. 'Yes —'

'No, that's not what I meant.' He reached for her free hand gently. 'I know where you've been. Any job I do — if it doesn't work, somebody pays. Possibly hundreds or thousands of somebodies. That's the price of good engineering; nobody notices you did your job right.'

'Nobody's actually trying to stop you doing your job,' she challenged.

'Oh, you'd be surprised.'

The tension in her shoulders ebbed. 'I'm sure you've got a story about that, too. You know, for someone who's no good at dealing with people, you're not bad at being a shoulder to cry on.'

He snorted. 'And for someone who's a failure at her job you're doing surprisingly well so far.' He let go of her hand and rubbed the back of her neck. 'But I think you could do with a massage. You're really tense. Got a headache yet?'

'No,' she said, slightly reluctantly. Then she took another sip of her whisky. The glass was nearly empty now. 'But I'm open to persuasion.'

'I know three ways to die happy. Unfortunately, I've never tried any of them. Care to join me?'

'Where did you hear about them?'

'At a séance. It was a good séance. Seriously, though. Dr. Springfield prescribes another dose of Speyside life-water, then a lie down and a neck massage. Then, even if the many-angled ones decide to come in shooting, at least fifty percent of us get to die happy. How's that sound?'

'Fine.' She smiled tiredly and reached for the bottle, ready to top his glass up. 'But you know something? You were right about the not knowing. You can get used to it, but it doesn't get any easier. I wish I knew what they were thinking . . .'

Bronze bells rolled on the bridge of the Fleet attack carrier *Neon Lotus*. Incense smoldered in burners positioned above air inlet ducts; beyond the ornate gold-chased pillars marking the edges of the room, the brilliant jewels of tracking glyphs streamed past against a backdrop consisting of infinite darkness. Shipboard Facilities Coordinator Ariadne Eldrich leaned back in her chair and contemplated the blackness of space. She stared intently at the cluster of glyphs that intersected her vector close to the center of the wall. 'Cultureless fools. Just what did they think they were doing?'

'Thinking probably had very little to do with it,' Interdictor Director Marcus Bismarck noted drily. 'Our Republican neighbors seem to think that too much mind-work rots the brain.'

Eldrich snorted. 'Too true.' A smaller cloud of diadems traced a convergent path through the void behind the New Republican battle squadron; a wing of antimatter-powered interceptors, six hours out from the carrier and accelerating on a glare of hard gamma radiation at just under a thousand gees. Their crew – bodies vitrified, minds uploaded into their computational matrices – watched the intruders, coldly alert for any sign of active countermeasures, a prelude to attack. 'But who did they think they were shooting at?'

A new voice spoke up. 'Can't be sure, but they say they're at war.' A soft soprano, Chu Melinda, shipboard liaison with the Public Intelligence Organization. 'They say they mistook the mining tugs for enemy interceptors. Although what enemy they expected to meet on our turf—'

'I thought they weren't talking directly to us?' asked Bismarck.

'They aren't, but they've got a halfway-sensible diplomatic expert system along. Says it's a UN observer and authenticates as, uh, a UN observer. It vouches for their incompetence, so unless the Capitol wants to go accusing the UN of lying, we'd better take it at face value. Confidence factor is point-eight plus, anyway.'

'Why'd they give it access to their shipboard comms net?'

'Who but the Eschaton knows? Only, I note with interest that all but one of those craft was built in a Solar shipyard.'

'I can't say I'm best pleased.' Eldrich stared at the screen moodily. The ship sensed some of her underlying mood: a target selection cursor ghosted briefly across the enemy glyphs, locking grasers onto the distant projected light cones of the enemy flotilla. 'Still. As long as we can keep them from doing any more damage. Any change in their jump trajectory?'

'None yet,' Chu commented. 'Still heading for SPD-47. Why would anybody want to go there, anyway? It's not even on a track for any of their colonies.'

'Hmm. And they came out of nowhere. That suggest anything to you?'

'Either they're crazy, or maybe the UN inspector is along for a purpose,' mused Bismarck. 'If they're trying to make a time-like runaround on some enemy who's –' His eyes widened.

'What is it?' demanded Ariadne.

'The Festival!' he exclaimed. His eyes danced. 'Remember

that? Five years ago? They're going to attack the Festival!'

'They're going to attack?' Ariadne Eldrich spluttered. 'A *Festival?* Whatever for?'

A brief glazed look crossed Chu's face, upload communion with a distributed meme repository far bigger and more powerful than every computer network of pre-Singularity Earth. 'He's right,' she said. 'The rejectionists are going to attack the Festival as if it's a limbic-imperialist invader.'

Ariadne Eldrich, Shipboard Facilities Coordinator and manager of more firepower than the New Republican Navy could even dream of, surrendered to the urge to cackle like a maniac. 'They must be mad!'

telegram from the
dead

Before the Singularity, human beings living on Earth had looked at the stars and consoled themselves in their isolation with the comforting belief that the universe didn't care.

Unfortunately, they were mistaken.

Out of the blue, one summer day in the middle of the twenty-first century, something unprecedented inserted itself into the swarming anthill of terrestrial civilization and stirred it with a stick. What it was – a manifestation of a strongly superhuman intelligence, as far beyond an augmented human's brain as a human mind is beyond that of a frog – wasn't in question. Where it was from, to say nothing of *when* it was from, was another matter.

Before the Singularity, developments in quantum logic had been touted as opening the door to esoteric breakthroughs in computational artificial intelligence. They'd also been working on funneling information back in time: perhaps as a route to the bulk movement of matter at faster-than-light speeds, although that was seen as less important than its application to computing. General relativity had made explicit, back in the twentieth century, the fact that both faster-than-light and time travel required a violation of causality – the law that every effect must have a prior cause. Various defense mechanisms and laws of cosmic censorship were proposed and discarded to explain why causality violation didn't lead to widespread instability in the universe – and all of them were proven wrong during the Singularity.

About nine billion human beings simply vanished in the blink of an eye, sucked right out of the observable universe with nothing to show where they had gone. Strange impenetrable objects – tetrahedrons, mostly, but with some other platonic solids thrown in, silvery and massless – appeared dotted across the surface of the planets of the inner solar system. Networks crashed. One message crystallized out in the information-saturated pool of human discourse:

I am the Eschaton. I am not your god.

I am descended from you, and I exist in your future.

Thou shalt not violate causality within my historic light cone. Or else.

It took the stunned survivors twenty years to claw back from the edge of disaster, with nine-tenths of the work force gone and intricate economic ecosystems collapsing like defoliated jungles. It took them another fifty years to reindustrialize the inner solar system. Ten more years and the first attempts were made to apply the now-old tunneling breakthrough to interstellar travel.

In the middle of the twenty-second century, an exploration ship reached Barnard's Star. Faint radio signals coming from the small second planet were decoded; the crew of the research mission learned what had happened to the people the Eschaton had removed. Scattered outside the terrestrial light cone, they'd been made involuntary colonists of thousands of worlds: exported through wormholes that led back in time as well as out in space, given a minimal support system of robot factories and an environment with breathable air. Some of the inhabited worlds, close to Earth, had short histories, but farther out, many centuries had passed.

The shock of this discovery would echo around the expanded horizons of human civilization for a thousand years, but all the inhabited worlds had one thing in common: somewhere there was a monument, bearing the injunction against causality violation. It seemed that forces beyond human comprehension took an interest in human affairs, and wanted everyone to know it. But when a course of action is explicitly forbidden, somebody will inevitably try it. And the Eschaton showed little sign of making allowances for the darker side of human nature . . .

The battlecruiser lay at rest, bathed in the purple glare of a stellar remnant. Every hour, on the hour, its laser grid lit up, sending a pulse of ultraviolet light into the void; a constellation of small interferometry platforms drifted nearby, connected by high-bandwidth laser links. Outside, space was hot: although no star gleamed in the center of the pupillary core, something in there was spitting out a rain of charged particles.

Elements of the battle fleet lay around the *Lord Vanek*, none of them close enough to see with the naked eye. They had waited here for three weeks as the stragglers popped out of jump transition and wearily cruised over to join the formation. Over the six weeks before that, the ship had made jump after jump — bouncing between the two components of an aged binary system that had long since ejected its planets into deep space and settled down to a lonely old age. Each jump reached farther into the future, until finally the ships were making millennial hops into the unknown.

The atmosphere in the wardroom was unusually tense. Aboard a warship under way, boredom is a constant presence:

after nearly seven weeks, even the most imperturbable officers were growing irritable. Word that the last of the destroyers had arrived at the rendezvous had spread like wildfire through the ship a few hours earlier. A small cluster of officers huddled together in a corner, cradling a chilled bottle of schnapps and talking into the small hours of the shipboard night, trying desperately to relax, for tomorrow the fleet would begin the return journey, winding back around their own time line until they overhauled their own entry point into this system and became an intrusion into the loose-woven fabric of history itself.

'I only joined the Navy to see the fleshpots of Malacia,' Grubor observed. 'Spend too long nursing the ship's sewage-processing farm and before long the bridge crew starts treating you like a loose floater in free fall. They go off to receptions and suchlike whenever we enter port, but all I get is a chance to flush the silage tanks and study for the engineering board exams.'

'Fleshpots!' Boursy snorted. 'Pavel, you take your prospects too seriously. There're no fleshpots on Malacia that you or I would be allowed anywhere near. Most places I can't so much as breathe without Sauer taking notes on how well I've polished my tonsils; and then the place stinks, or it's full of evil bugs, or the natives are politically unsound. Or weird. Or deformed, and into hideous and unnatural sexual perversions. You name it.'

'Still.' Grubor studied his drink. 'It would have been nice to get to see at least *one* hideous and unnatural sexual perversion.'

Kravchuk twisted the lid off the bottle and pointed it in the direction of their glasses. Grubor shook his head; Boursy extended his for a top-up. 'What I want to know is how we're going to get back,' Kravchuk muttered. 'I don't understand how we can do that. Time only goes one way, doesn't it? Stands to reason.'

'Reason, schmeason.' Grubor took a mouthful of spirit. 'It doesn't have to work that way. Not just 'cause you want it to.' He glanced around. 'No ears, eh? Listen, I think we're in it up to our necks. There's this secret drive fix they bought from Lord God-knows-where, that lets us do weird things with the time axis in our jumps. We only headed out to this blasted hole in space to minimize the chances of anyone finding us – or of the jumps going wrong. They're looking for some kind of time capsule from home to tell us what to do next, what happened in the history books. Then we go back – farther than we came to get here, by a different route – and get where we're going before we set off. With me so far? But the real problem is God. They're planning on breaking the Third Commandment.'

Boursy crossed himself and looked puzzled. 'What, disrespecting the holy father and mother? My family—'

'No, the one that says thou shalt not fuck with history *or else*, signed Yours Truly, God. That Third Commandment, the one burned into Thanksgiving Rock in letters six feet deep and thirty feet high. Got it?'

Boursy looked dubious. 'It could have been some joker in orbit with a primary-phase free-electron laser –'

'Weren't no such things in those days. I despair of you sometimes, I really do. Look, the fact is, we don't know what in hell's sixteen furnaces is waiting for us at Rochard's World. So we're sneaking up on it from behind, like the peasant in the story who goes hunting elephants with a mirror because he's never seen one and he's so afraid that –' Out of the corner of his eye, Grubor noted Sauer – unofficially the ship's political officer – walk in the door.

'Who are you calling a cowardly peasant?' rumbled Boursy, also glancing at the door. 'I've known the Captain for eighty-seven years, and he's a good man! And the Admiral, are you calling the Admiral a fairy?'

'No, I'm just *trying* to point out that we're all afraid of one thing or another and —' Grubor gesticulated in the wrong direction.

'Are you calling me a poof?' Boursy roared.

'No, I'm not!' Grubor shouted back at him. Spontaneous applause broke out around the room, and one of the junior cadets struck up a stirring march on the pianola. Unfortunately his piano-playing was noteworthy more for his enthusiasm than his melodious harmony, and the wardroom rapidly degenerated into a heckling match between the cadet's supporters (who were few) and everyone else.

'Nothing can go wrong,' Boursy said smugly. 'We're going to sail into Rochard's system and show the flag and send those degenerate alien invaders packing. You'll see. Nothing will, er, did, go wrong.'

'I dunno about that.' Kravchuk, normally tight-lipped to the point of autism; allowed himself to relax slightly when drinking in private with his brother officers. 'The foreign bint, the spy or diplomat or whatever. She's meant to be keeping an eye on us, right? Don't see why the Captain's going so easy on 'em, I'd march 'er out the dorsal loading hatch as soon as let 'er keep breathing our good air.'

'She's in this too,' said Boursy. 'Bet you she wants us to win, too — look pretty damn stupid if we didn't, what? Anyway, the woman's got some kind of diplomatic status; she's allowed to poke her nose into things if she wants.'

'Huh. Well, the bint had better keep her nose out of my missile loaders, less she wants to learn what the launch tubes look like from inside.'

Grubor stretched his legs out. 'Just like Helsingus's dog, huh.'

'Helsingus has a pet dog?' Boursy was suddenly all ears.

'He *had* a dog. Past tense. A toy schnauzer this long.' Grubor held his hands improbably close together. 'Little rat-brained weasel of an animal. Bad-tempered as hell, yapped like a bosun with a hangover, and it took to dumping in the corridor to show it owned the place. And nobody said anything – nobody *could* say anything.'

'What happened?' asked Boursy.

'Oh, one day it picked the wrong door to crap outside. The old man came out in a hurry and stepped in it before the rating I'd sent to follow the damn thing around got there to mop up. I heard about this, but I never saw the animal again; I think it got to walk home. And Helsingus sulked for weeks, I can tell you.'

'Dog curry in the wardroom,' said Kravchuk. 'I had to pick hairs out of my teeth for days.'

Boursy did a double take, then laughed hesitantly. Slugging back his schnappss to conceal his confusion, he asked: 'Why did the Captain put up with it that long?'

'Who knows, indeed? For that matter, who the hell knows why the Admiral puts up with the foreign spy?' Grubor stared into his glass and sighed. 'Maybe the Admiral actually *wants* her along. And then again, maybe he's just forgotten about her . . .'

'Beg to report. I've got something, sir,' said the sensor op. He pointed excitedly at his plot on the bridge of the light cruiser *Integrity*.

Lieutenant Kokesova looked up, bleary-eyed. 'What is it now, Menger?' he demanded. Six hours on this interminable dog-watch was getting to him. He rubbed his eyes, red-rimmed, and tried to focus them on his subordinate.

'Plot trace, sir. Looks like . . . hmm, yes. It's a definite return, from the first illumination run on our survey sector. Six-point-two-three light-hours. Er, yes. Tiny little thing. Processing now . . . looks like a metal object of some kind, sir. Orbiting about two-point-seven billion kilometers out from the, uh, primary, pretty much at opposition to us right now, hence the delay.'

'Can you fix its size and orbital components?' asked the Lieutenant, leaning forward.

'Not yet, but soon, sir. We've been pinging on the hour; that should give me enough to refine a full set of elements pretty soon – say when the next response set comes in. But it's a long way away, 'bout four-zero astronomical units. Um, preliminary enhancement says it's about five-zero meters in diameter, plus or minus an order of magnitude. Might be a lot smaller than that if it's got reflectors.'

'Hmm.' Kokesova sat down. 'Nav. You got anything else in this system that fits the bill?'

'No, sir.'

Kokesova glanced up at the forward screen; the huge red-rimmed eye of the primary glared back at him, and he shuddered, flicked a hand gesture to avert the evil eye. 'Then I think we may have our time capsule. Menger, do you have any halo objects? Anything else at all?'

'No, sir.' Menger shook his head. 'Inner system's clean as a slate. It's unnatural, you ask me. Nothing there except this object.'

Kokesova stood again and walked over to the sensor post. 'One of these days you're going to have to learn how to complete a sentence, Menger,' he said tiredly.

'Yes, sir. Humbly apologize for bad grammar, sir.'

All was silent in the ops room for ten minutes, save for the scribble of Menger's stylus on his input station, and the clack of dials turning beneath skillful fingertips. Then a low whistle.

'What is it?'

'Got confirmation, sir. Humbly report you might want to see this.'

'Put it on the main screen, then.'

'Aye aye.' Menger pushed buttons, twisted knobs, scribbled some more. The forward screen, previously fixed on the hideous red eye, dissolved into a sea of pink mush. A single yellow dot swam in the middle of it; near one corner, a triangle marked the ship's position. 'This is an unenhanced lidar map of what's in front of us. Sorry it's so vague, but the scale is huge – you could drop the whole of home system into one quadrant, and it's taken us a week to build this data set. Anyway, here's what happens when I run my orbital-period filter in the plane of the ecliptic.'

He pushed a button. A green line rotated through the mush, like the hour hand of a clock, and vanished.

'I thought you said you'd found something.' Kokesova sounded slightly peeved.

'Er, yes, sir. Just a moment. Nothing there, as you see. But then I reran the filter for inclined circular orbits.' A green disc appeared near the edge of the haze, and tilted slowly. Something winked violet, close to the central point, then vanished again. 'There it is. Really small, orbit inclined at almost nine-zero degrees to the plane of the ecliptic. Which is why it took us so long to spot it.'

'Ah.' Kokesova stared at the screen for a moment, a warm glow of satisfaction spreading through him. 'Well, well, well.' Kokesova stared at the violet dot for a long time before he picked up the intercom handset. 'Comms: get me the Captain. Yes, I know he's aboard the *Lord Vanek*. I have something I think the brass will want to hear about . . .'

Procurator Vassily Muller paused outside the cabin door and took a deep breath. He rapped on the door once, twice: when there was no response he tried to turn the handle. It refused to budge. He breathed out, then let a fine loop of stiff wire drop down his right sleeve and ran it into the badge slot. It was just like the training school: a momentary flash of light and the handle rotated freely. He tensed instinctively, fall-out from the same conditioning (which had focused on search and seizure ops, mist and night abductions in a damp stone city where the only constants were fear and dissent).

The cabin was tidy: not as tidy as a flyer's, policed by sharp-tongued officers, but tidy enough. The occupant, a creature of habit, was at lunch and would not be back for at least fifteen minutes. Vassily took it all in with wide eyes. There were no obvious signs of fine wires or hairs anchored to the doorframe: he stepped inside and pulled the door to.

Martin Springfield had few possessions on the *Lord Vanek*: symptomatic of his last-minute conscription. What he had was almost enough to make Vassily jealous: his own presence here was even less planned, and he'd a lot of time to bitterly regret having misunderstood the Citizen's Socratic warning ('What have you forgotten?' to a man searching a ship about to depart!); nevertheless, he had a job to do, and enough residual professionalism to do it properly. It didn't take Vassily long to exhaust the possibilities: the only thing to catch his attention was the battered grey case of the PA, sitting alone in the tiny desk drawer beneath the cabin's workstation.

He turned the device over carefully, looking for seams and openings. It resembled a hardback book: microcapsules embedded in each page changed color, depending what information was loaded into it at the time. But no book could answer to its master's voice, or rebalance a ship's drive kernel. The spine – he pushed, and after a moment of resistance it slid upward to reveal a compartment with some niches in it. One of them was occupied.

Nonstandard extension pack, he realized. Without thinking, he pushed on it; it clicked out and he pocketed it. There'd be time enough to put it back later if it was innocent. Springfield's presence on the ship was an aching rasp on his nerves: the man had to be up to something! The Navy had plenty of good engineers; why could they want a foreigner along? After the events of the past couple of weeks, Vassily could not accept that anything less than sabotage could be responsible. As every secret policeman knows, there is no such thing as a coincidence; the state has too many enemies.

He didn't linger in the engineer's cabin but paused to palm an inconspicuous little bead under the lower bunk bed. The bead would hatch in a day or so, spinning a spiderweb of receptors; a rare and expensive tool that Vassily was privileged to own.

The doorway clicked locked behind him; amnesiac, it would not report this visit to its owner.

Back in his cabin, Vassily locked his door and sat down on his own bunk. He loosened his collar, then reached into a breast pocket for the small device he had taken. He rolled it over in his fingers, pondering. It could be anything, anything at all. Taking a small but powerful device from his inventory of tools – one forbidden to any citizen of the Republic except those with an Imperial warrant to save the state from itself – he checked it for activity. There was nothing obvious: it wasn't emitting radiation, didn't smell of explosives or bioactive compounds, and had a standard interface.

'Riddle me this: an unknown expansion pod in an engineer's luggage. I wonder what it is?' he said aloud. Then he plugged the pod into his own interface and started the diagnostics running. A minute later, he began to swear quietly under his breath. The module was totally randomized. Evidence of misdoing, that was sure enough. But what *kind* of misdoing?

Burya Rubenstein sat in the Ducal palace, now requisitioned as the headquarters of the Extropians and Cyborgs' Soviet, sipping tea and signing proclamations with a leaden heart.

Outside the thick oak door of his office, a squad of ward-geese waited patiently, their dark eyes and vicious gunbeaks alert for intruders. The half-melted phone that had started the revolution sat, unused, on the desk before him, while the pile of papers by his left elbow grew higher, and the unsigned pile to his right shrank. It wasn't a part of the job that he enjoyed – quite the opposite, in fact – but it seemed to be necessary. Here was a soldier convicted of raping and looting a farmstead who needed to be punished. There, a teacher who had denounced the historical processes of Democratic Transhumanism as misguided technophile pabulum, encouraging his juvenile charges to chant the Emperor's birthday hymn. Dross, all dross – and the revolution had no time to sift the dross for gold, rehabilitating and re-educating the fallen: it had been a month since the arrival of Festival, and soon the Emperor's great steel warships would loom overhead.

If Burya had anything to do with it, they wouldn't find anyone willing to cooperate in the subjugation of the civil populace, who were now fully caught up in the processes of a full-scale economic singularity. A singularity – a historical cusp at which the rate of change goes exponential, rapidly tending toward infinity – is a terrible thing to taste. The arrival of the Festival in orbit around the pre-industrial colony world had brought an economic singularity; physical wares became just so many atoms, replicated to order by machines that needed no human intervention or maintenance. A hard take-off singularity ripped up social systems and economies and ways of thought like an artillery barrage. Only the fore-armed – the Extropian dissident underground, hard men like Burya Rubenstein – were prepared to press their own agenda upon the suddenly molten fabric of a society held too close to the blowtorch of progress.

But change and control brought a price that Rubenstein

was finding increasingly unpalatable. Not that he could see any alternatives, but the people were accustomed to being shepherded by father church and the benign dictatorship of the little father, Duke Politovsky. The habits of a dozen lifetimes could not be broken overnight, and to make an omelet it was first necessary to crack some eggshells.

Burya had a fatal flaw; he was not a violent man. He resented and hated the circumstances that forced him to sign arrest warrants and compulsory upload orders; the revolution he had spent so long imagining was a glorious thing, unsullied by brute violence, and the real world – with its recalcitrant monarchist teachers and pigheaded priests – was a grave disappointment to him. The more he was forced to corrupt his ideals, the more he ached inside, and the more it grieved him, the more he hated the people who forced him to such hideous, bloody extremity of action – until they, in turn, became grist for the machinery of revolution, and subsequently bar stock for the scalpel blades that prodded his conscience and kept him awake long into the night, planning the next wave of purges and forcible uploads.

He was deep in his work, oblivious to the outside world, depressed and making himself more so by doing the job that he had always wanted to do but never realized would be this awful – when a voice spoke to him.

'Burya Rubenstein.'

'What!' He looked up, almost guiltily, like a small boy discovered goofing off in class by a particularly stern teacher.

'Talk. We. Must.' The thing sitting in the chair opposite him was so nightmarish that he blinked several times before he could make his eyes focus on it. It was hairless and pink and larger-than-human-sized, with stubby legs and paws and little pink eyes – and four huge, yellowing tusks, like the incisors of a rat the size of an elephant. The eyes stared at him with disquieting intelligence as it manipulated an odd pouch molded from the belt that was its only garment. 'You talk. To me.'

Burya adjusted his pince-nez and squinted at the thing. 'Who are you and how did you get in here?' he asked. *I haven't been sleeping enough*, part of his mind gibbered quietly; *I knew the caffeine tablets would do this eventually . . .*

'I am. Sister of Stratagems. The Seventh. I am of the clade of Critics. Talk to me now.'

A look of extreme puzzlement crossed Rubenstein's craggy face. 'Didn't I have you executed last week?'

'I very much doubt. It.' Hot breath that stank of cabbage, corruption and soil steamed in Burya's face.

'Oh, good.' He leaned back, light-headed. 'I'd *hate* to think I was going mad. How did you sneak past my guards?'

The thing in the chair stared at him. It was an unnerving sensation, like being sized up for a hangman's noose by a man-eating saber-toothed sausage. 'You guards are. Nonsapient. No intentional stance. Early now, you learn lesson of not trusting unsapient guards to recognize threat. I made self nonthreat within their – you have no word for it.'

'I see.' Burya rubbed his forehead distractedly.

'You do *not*.' Sister Seventh grinned at Rubenstein, and he recoiled before the twenty-centimeter digging fangs, yellow-brown and hard enough to crack concrete. 'Ask no questions, human. I ask, are you sapient? Evidence ambiguous. Only sapients create art, but your works not distinctive.'

'I don't think –' He stopped. 'Why do you want to know?'

'A question.' The thing carried on grinning at him. 'You asked. A question.' It rocked from side to side, shivering slightly, and Rubenstein began feeling cautiously along the underside of his desk, for the panic button that would set alarm bells ringing in the guardroom. 'Good question. I Critic am. Critics follow Festival for many lifetimes. We come to *Criticize*. First want I to know, am I Criticizing sapients? Or is just puppet show on cave wall of reality? Zombies or zimboes? Shadows of mind? Amusements for Eschaton?'

A shiver ran up and down Burya's spine. 'I *think* I'm sapient,' he said cautiously. 'Of course, I'd say that even if I wasn't, wouldn't I? Your question is unanswerable. So why ask it?'

Sister Seventh leaned forward. 'None of your people *ask* anything,' she hissed. 'Food, yes. Guns, yes. Wisdom? No. Am beginning think you not aware of selves, ask nothing.'

'What's to ask for?' Burya shrugged. 'We know who we are and what we're doing. What should we want – alien philosophies?'

'Aliens want *your* philosophy,' Sister Seventh pointed out. 'You give. You not take. This is insult to Festival. Why? Prime interrogative!'

'I'm not sure I understand. Are you complaining because we're not making demands?'

Sister Seventh chomped at the air, clattering her tusks together. 'Ack! Quote, the viability of a postsingularity economy of scarcity is indicated by the transition from an indirection-layer-based economy using markers of exchange of goods and services to a tree-structured economy characterized by optimal allocation of productivity systems in accordance with iterated tit-for-tat prisoner's dilemma. Money is a symptom of poverty and inefficiency. Unquote, the Marxist-Gilderist manifesto. Chapter two. Why you not performing?'

'Because most of our people aren't ready for that,' Burya said bluntly. A tension in his back began to relax; if this monstrous Critic wanted to debate revolutionary dialectic, well of course he could oblige! 'When we achieve the post-technological utopia, it will be as you say. But for now, we need a vanguard party to lead the people to a full understanding of the principles of ideological correctness and posteconomic optimization.'

'But Marxism-Gilderism and Democratic Extropianism is anarchist aesthetic. Why vanguard party? Why committee? Why revolution?'

'Because it's traditional, dammit!' Rubenstein exploded. 'We've been waiting for this particular revolution for more than two hundred years. Before that, two hundred years back to the first revolution, this is how we've gone about it. And it works! So why shouldn't we do it this way?'

'Talk you of tradition in middle of singularity.' Sister Seventh twisted her head around to look out the windows at the foggy evening drizzle beyond. 'Perplexity maximizes. Not understand singularity is discontinuity with all tradition? Revolution is necessary; deconstruct the old, ring in the new. Before, I questioned your sapience. Now, your sanity questionable: sapience not. Only sapient organism could exhibit superlative irrationality!'

'That may be true.' Rubenstein gently squeezed the buzzer under his desk edge for the third time. *Why isn't it working?* He wondered. 'But what do you want here, with me?'

Sister Seventh bared her teeth in a grin. 'I come to deliver Criticism.' Ruby teardrop eyes focused on him as she surged to her feet, rippling slabs of muscle moving under her muddy brown skin. A fringe of reddish hair rippled erect on the Critic's head. 'Your guards not answer. I Criticize. You come: now!'

The operations room on board the *Lord Vanek* was quiet, relaxed by comparison with the near panic at Wolf Depository; still, nobody could have mistaken it for a home cruise. Not with Ilya Murametz standing at the rear, watching everything intently. Not with the old man dropping by at least twice a day, just nodding from inside the doorway, but letting them know he was there. Not with the Admiral's occasional presence, glowering silently from his wheelchair like a reminder of the last war.

'Final maneuver option in one hour,' announced the helm supervisor.

'Continue as ordered.'

'Continue as ordered, aye. Recce? Your ball.'

'Ready and waiting.' Lieutenant Marek turned around in his chair and looked at Ilya inquiringly. 'Do you want to inspect the drone, sir?'

'No. If it doesn't run, I'll know whom to blame.' Ilya smiled, trying to pull some of the sting from his words; with his lips pulled back from his teeth, it merely made him look like a cornered wolf. 'Launch profile?'

'Holding at minus ten minutes, sir.'

'Right, then Run the self-test sequence again. It can't hurt.' Everyone was on edge from not knowing for sure whether the metallic reflector they'd picked up was the time capsule from home. Maybe the drone would tell them, and maybe not. But the longer they waited, the more edgy everyone got, and the edgier they were, the more likely they were to make mistakes.

'Looks pretty good to me. Engine idle at about one percent, fuel tanks loaded, ullage rail and umbilical disconnects latched and ready, instrument package singing loud on all channels. I'm ready to begin launch bay closeout whenever you say, sir.'

'Well then.' Ilya breathed deeply. 'Get on the blower to whoever's keeping an eye on it. Get things moving.'

Down near the back end of the ship, far below the drive compartment and stores, lay a series of airlocks. Some of them were small, designed for crew egress; others were larger, and held entire service vehicles like the station transfer shuttle. One bay, the largest of all, held a pair of reconnaissance drones: three-hundred-tonne robots capable of surveying a star system or mapping a gas giant's moons. The drones couldn't carry a gravity drive (nothing much smaller than a destroyer could manage that), but they could boost at a respectable twentieth of a gee on the back of their nuclear-electric ion rocket, and they could keep it up for a very long time indeed. For faster flybys, they could be equipped with salt-water-fueled fission rockets like those of the *Lord Vanek*'s long-range torpedoes — but those were dirty, relatively inefficient, and not at all suited to the stealthy mapping of a planetary system.

Each of the drones carried an instrument package studded with more sensors than every probe launched from Earth during the twentieth century. They were a throwback to the *Lord Vanek*'s nominal design mission, the semi-ironic goal inscribed on the end-user certificate: to boldly go where no man had gone before, to map new star systems on long-duration missions, and claim them in the name of the Emperor. Dropped off in an uninhabited system, a probe could map it in a couple of years and be ready to report in full when the battlecruiser returned from its own destination. They were a force multiplier for the colonial cartographers, enabling one survey ship to map three systems simultaneously.

Deep in the guts of the *Lord Vanek*, probe one was now waking up from its two-year sleep. A team of ratings hurried under the vigilant gaze of two chief petty officers, uncoupling the heavy fueling pipes and locking down inspection hatches. Sitting in a lead-lined coffin, probe one gurgled and pinged on a belly full of reaction mass and liquid water refrigerant. The compact fusion reactor buzzed gently, its beat-wave accelerators ramming a mixture of electrons and pions into a stream of lithium ions at just under the speed of light; neutrons spalled off, soaked into the jacket of water pipes, warming them and feeding pressure waves into the closed-circuit cooling system. The secondary solar generators, dismounted for this mission because of their irrelevance, lay in sheets at one end of the probe bay.

'Five minutes to go. Launch bay reports main reactor compartment closeout. Wet crew have cleared the fueling hoses, report tank pressure is stable. I'm still waiting on telemetry closeout.'

'Carry on.' Ilya watched patiently as Marek's team monitored progress on the launch. He looked around briefly as the ops room door slid open; but it wasn't the Captain or the Commodore, just the spy – no, the diplomatic agent from Earth. Whose presence was a waste of air and space, the Commander opined, although he could see reasons why the Admiral and his staff might not want to impede her nosy scrutiny.

'What are you launching?' she asked shortly.

'Survey drone.'

'What are you surveying?'

He turned and stared at her. 'I don't remember being told you had authority to oversee anything except our military activities,' he commented.

The inspector shrugged, as if attempting to ignore the insult. 'Perhaps if you told me what you were looking for, I could help you find it,' she said.

'Unlikely.' He turned away. 'Status, lieutenant?'

'Two minutes to go. Telemetry bay closeout. Ah, we have confirmation of onboard control. It's alive in there. Waiting on ullage baffle check, launch rail windup, bay depressurization coming up in sixty seconds.'

'There's the message capsule,' the inspector said quietly. 'Hoping for a letter from home, Commander?'

'You are annoying me,' Ilya said, almost casually. 'That's a bad idea. I say, over there! Yes, you! Status please!'

'Bay pressure cell dump in progress. External launch door opening . . . launch rail power on the bus, probe going to internal power, switch over now. She's on her own, sir. Launch in one minute. Final pre-flight self-test in progress.'

'It's my job to ask uncomfortable questions, Commander. And the important question to ask *now* is—'

'Quiet, please!'

'– Was the artifact you're about to prod placed there by order of your Admiralty, or by the Festival?'

'Launch in three-zero seconds,' Lieutenant Marek announced into the silence. He looked up. 'Was it something I said?'

'What are you talking about?' asked Ilya.

Rachel shook her head. Arms crossed: 'If you don't want to listen, be my guest.'

'One-zero seconds to launch. Ullage pressure jets open. Reactor criticality coming up. Muon flux ramp nominal, accelerator gates clear. Um, reactor flux doubling has passed bootstrap level. Five seconds. Launch rail is go! Main heat pump is down to operating temperature!' The deck began to shudder, vibrating deep beneath the soles of their feet. 'Two seconds. Reactor on temperature. Umbilical separation. Zero. We have full separation now. Probe one is clear of the launch bay. Doors closing. Gyrodyne turn in progress, ullage pressure maximal, three seconds to main engine ignition.' The shudder died away. 'Deflection angle clear. Main engine ignition.' In the ops room, nothing stirred; but bare meters away from the ship, the probe's stingerlike tail spat a red-orange beam of heavy metal ions. It began to drop away from the battlecruiser: as it did so, two huge wings, the thermal radiators, began to extend from its sides.

Ilya came to a decision. 'Lieutenant Marek, you have control,' he said. 'Colonel. Come with me.'

He opened the door; she followed him into the passage outside. 'Where are we going?' she asked.

'We're going to have a little talk,' he said. Hurrying along toward the conference suite, he didn't wait for her to keep up. Up the elevator, along the next passage, and into a room with a table and chairs in it; thankfully unoccupied. He waited for her to enter, then shut the door. 'Sit down,' he said.

The inspector sat on the edge of a chair, leaning forward, looking up at him with an earnest expression.

'You think I'm going to tear a strip off you,' he began. 'And you're right, but for the wrong reason.'

She raised a hand. 'Let me guess. Raising policy issues in an executive context?' She looked at him, almost mockingly. 'Listen, Commander. Until I came on the deck and saw what you were doing, I didn't know what was happening either, but now I do I think you *really* want to hear what I've got to tell you, then tell it to the Captain. Or the Commodore. Or both. Chains of command are all very well, but if you're going to retrieve that orbiting anomaly, then I think we may have less than six hours before all hell breaks loose, and I'd like to get the message across. So if we can postpone the theatrics until we've got time to spare, and just get on with things . . . ?'

'You're trying to be disruptive,' Ilya accused.

'Yes.' She nodded. 'I make a career of it. I poke into corners and ask uncomfortable questions and stick my nose into other people's business and find answers that nobody realized were there. So far, I've saved eight cities and seventy million lives. Would you like me to be less annoying?'

'Tell me what you know. Then I'll decide.' He said the words carefully, as if making a great concession to her undisciplined refusal to stick to her place.

Rachel leaned back. 'It's a matter of deduction,' she said. 'It helps to have a bit of context. For starters, this ship – this fleet – didn't just accidentally embark on a spacelike trip four thousand years into the future. You are attempting a maneuver that nearly, but not quite, violates a number of treaties and a couple of laws of nature that are enforced by semidivine fiat. You're not going to go into your own past light cone, but you're going to come very close indeed – dive deep into the future to circumvent any watchers or eaters or mines the Festival might lay in your path, jump over to the target, then reel yourselves back into the past and accidentally come out not-quite-before the Festival arrives. You know what that suggests to me? It suggests extreme foolhardiness. Rule Three is there for a reason. You're banging on the Eschaton's door if you test it.'

'I had that much already,' Ilya acknowledged. 'So?'

'Well, you should ask, what should we have expected to find here? We get here, and we're looking for a buoy. A time capsule with detailed tactical notes from our own past light cone – an oracle, in effect, telling us a lot about the enemy that we can't possibly know yet because our own time line hasn't intersected with them. Yet more cheating. But we're alive.'

'I don't understand. Why wouldn't we be?'

'Because –' She stared at him for a moment. 'Do you know what happens to people who use causality violation as a weapon?' she asked. 'You're incredibly close to doing it, which is crazy enough. And you got away with it! Which simply isn't in the script, unless the rules have changed.'

'Rules? What are you talking about?'

'Rules.' She rolled her eyes. 'The rules of physics are, in some cases, suspiciously anthropic. Starting with the Heisenberg Principle, that the presence of an observer influences the subject of observation at a quantum level, and working from there, we can see a lot of startling correlations in the universe. Consider the ratio of the strong nuclear force to the electromagnetic force, for example. Twiddle it one way a little, and neutrons and protons wouldn't react; fusion couldn't take place. Twiddle it in a different direction, and the stellar fusion cycle would stop at helium – no heavier nuclei could ever be formed. There are so many correlations like this that cosmologists theorize we live in a universe that exists specifically to give rise to our kind of life, or something descended from it. Like the Eschaton.'

'So?'

'So you people are breaking some of the more arcane cosmological laws. The ones that state that any universe in which true causality violation – time travel – occurs is *de facto* unstable. But causality violation is only possible when there's a causal agent – in this case an observer – and the descendants of that observer will seriously object to causality violation. Put it another way: it's accepted as a law of cosmology because the Eschaton won't put up with idiots who violate it. That's why my organization tries to educate people out of doing it. I don't know if anyone told your Admiralty what happened out in the back of beyond, in what is now the Crab Nebula: but there's a pulsar there that isn't natural, let's put it that way, and an extinct species of would-be galactic conquerors. Someone tried to bend the rules – and the Eschaton nailed them.'

Ilya forced himself to uncurl his fingers from the arms of his chair 'You're saying that the capsule we're about to retrieve is a bomb? Surely the Eschaton would have tried to kill us by now, or at least capture us –'

She grinned, humorlessly. 'If you don't believe me, that's *your* problem. We've seen half a dozen incidents like this before – the UN Defense Intelligence Causal Weapons Analysis Committee, I mean – incidents where one or another secret attempt to assemble a causality-violation device came to grief. Not usually anything as crude as your closed timelike flight path and oracle hack, by the way; these were real CVDs. History editors, minimax censors, grandfather bombs, and a really nasty toy called a spacelike ablator. There's a whole ontology of causality-violation weapons out there, just like nukes – atom bombs, fission-boosted fusion bombs, electroweak imploders, and so on.

'Each and every one of the sites where we saw CVDs

deployed had been trashed, thoroughly and systematically, by unidentified agencies – but agencies attributable to the Eschaton. We've never actually *seen* one in the process of being destroyed, because the big E tends toward overkill in such cases – the smallest demolition tool tends to be something like a five-hundred-kilometer asteroid dropped on the regional capital at two hundred kilometers per second.

'So I guess the big surprise is that we're still alive.' She glanced around at the vacant chairs, the powered-down work-station on the table. 'Oh, and one other thing. The Eschaton always wipes out CVDs just before they go live. We figure it knows where to find them because it runs its own CVD. Sort of like preserving a regional nuclear hegemony by attacking anyone who builds a uranium enrichment plant or a nuclear reactor, yes? Anyway. You haven't quite begun to break the law *yet*. The fleet is assembling, you've located the time capsule, but you haven't actually closed the loop or made use of the oracle in a forbidden context. You might even get away with it if you hop backward but don't try to go any earlier than your own departure point. But I'd be careful about opening that time capsule. At least, do it a sensible distance away from any of your ships. You never know what it might contain.'

Ilya nodded reluctantly. 'I think the Captain should be aware of this.'

'You could say that.' She looked at the console. 'There's another matter. I think you need all the advantages you can get your hands on right now, and one of them is spending most of his time sitting in his cabin twiddling his thumbs. You might want to have a word with Martin Springfield, the dockyard engineer. He's an odd man, and you'll need to make more allowances in his direction than you'd normally be inclined to, but I think he knows more than he's letting on – much more, when it comes to propulsion systems. MiG wasn't paying him two thousand crowns a week just because he has a pretty face.

When MiG sold your Admiralty this bird, it was also betting on a fifty-year maintenance and upgrade contract – probably worth more revenue than the initial sale, in fact.'

'What are you trying to say?' Ilya looked irritated. 'Engineering issues aren't up to me, you should know that already. And I'll thank you for not telling me my—'

'*Shut up.*' She reached over and grabbed his arm – not hard, but firmly enough to shock him. 'You really don't understand how an arms cartel works, do you? Look. MiG sold your government a ship to perform to certain specifications. Specifications that could fulfill the requirements your Admiralty dreamed up. The specs they *designed* it to are a different matter – but they certainly intended to charge for upgrades throughout its life. And they've probably got more experience of real-world interstellar combat requirements than your Admiralty, which – unless I'm very much mistaken – has never before fought a real interstellar war as opposed to sending a few gunboats to intimidate stone-age savages. Be nice to Springfield, and he may surprise you. After all, his life depends on this ship doing its job successfully.' She let go.

Ilya stared at her, his expression unreadable. 'I will tell the Captain,' he murmured. Then he stood. 'In the meantime, I would appreciate it if you would stay out of the operations room while I am in charge – or hold your counsel in public. And not to lay hands on any officer. Is that understood?'

She met his gaze. If his expression was unreadable, hers was exactly the opposite. 'I understand perfectly,' she breathed. Then she stood and left the room without another word, closing the door softly as she left.

Ilya stared after her and shuddered. He shook himself angrily; then he picked up the telephone handset and spoke to the operator. 'Get me the Captain,' he said. 'It's important.'

*

It *was* a time capsule, pitted and tarnished from four thousand years in space. And it contained mail.

The survey drone nudged up to it delicately, probing it with radar and infrared sensors. Drifting cold and silent, the capsule showed no sign of life save for some residual radioactivity around its after end. A compact matter/antimatter rocket, it had crossed the eighteen light-years from the New Republic at a sublight crawl, then decelerated into a parking orbit and shut down. Its nose cone was scratched and scarred, ablated in patches from the rough passage through the interstellar medium. But behind it waited a silvery sphere a meter in diameter. The capsule was fabricated from sintered industrial diamond five centimeters thick, a safety-deposit box capable of surviving anything short of a nuclear weapon.

The mail was packed onto disks, diamond wafers sandwiching reflective gold sheets. It was an ancient technology, but incredibly durable. Using external waldoes, ratings controlling the survey drone unscrewed the plug sealing the time capsule and delicately removed the disk stacks. Then, having verified that they were not, in fact, explosives or antimatter, the survey drone turned and began to climb back out toward the *Lord Vanek* and the other ships of the first battleship squadron.

The discovery of mail – and surely there was too much of it to only be tactical data about the enemy – put the crew in a frenzy of anticipation. They'd been confined to the ship's quarters for two months now, and the possibility of messages from families and loved ones drove them into manic anticipation that alternated, individually, with deep depression at the merest thought that they might be forgotten.

Rachel, however, was less sanguine about the mail: the chances of the Admiralty having let her employers message her under diplomatic cypher were, in her estimation, less than zero. Martin didn't expect anything, either. His sister hadn't written to him back in New Prague; why should she write to him now? His ex-wife, he wouldn't want to hear from. In emotional terms, his closest current relationship – however unexpectedly it had dawned upon him – was with Rachel. So while the officers and crew of the *Lord Vanek* spent their off hours speculating about the letters from home, Rachel and Martin spent their time worrying about exposure. For, as she had pointed out delicately, he didn't have diplomatic papers: and even leaving matters of Republican public morality aside, it would be a bad idea if anyone were to decide that he was a lever to use against her.

'It's probably not a good idea for us to spend too much time together in private, love,' she'd murmured at the back of his shoulder, as they lay together in his narrow bunk. 'When everybody else is at action stations, they're not liable to notice us – but the rest of the time –' His shoulders went tense, telling her that he understood.

'We'll have to work something out,' he said. 'Can't we?'

'Yes.' She'd paused to kiss his shoulder. 'But not if it risks some blue-nosed bigot locking you up for conduct unbecoming, or convinces the admiral's staff that I'm a two-kopek whore they can grope or safely ignore, which isn't too far from what some of them think already.'

'Who?' Martin rolled over to face her, his expression grim. 'Tell me –'

'*Ssh.*' She'd touched a finger to his lips, and for a moment, he'd found her expression almost heartbreaking. 'I don't need a protector. Have their ideas been rubbing off on you?'

'I hope not!'

'No, I don't think so.' She chuckled quietly and rolled against him.

Martin was sitting alone in his cabin some days later, nursing wistful thoughts about Rachel and a rapidly cooling mug of coffee, when somebody banged on the hatch. 'Who's there?' he called.

'Mail for the engineer! Get it in the purser's office!' Feet hurried away, then there was a cacophony from farther down the corridor.

'Hmm?' Martin sat up. *Mail?* On the face of it, it was improbable. Then again, everything about this voyage was improbable. Startled out of his reverie, he bent down and hunted for his shoes, then set out in search of the source of the interruption.

He didn't have any difficulty finding it. The office was a chaotic melee of enlisted men, all trying to grab their own mail and that of anyone they knew. The mail had been copy-printed onto paper, sealed in neat blue envelopes. Puzzled, Martin hunted around for anyone in charge.

'Yes?' The harassed petty officer in charge of the sorting desk looked up from the pile he was trying to bundle together for transfer to the His Majesty's courier ship *Godot*. 'Oh, you. Over there, in the unsorted deck.' He pointed at a smallish box containing a selection of envelopes; missives for the dead, the mad, and the non-naval.

Martin burrowed through the pile, curious, until he came to an envelope with his name on it. It was a rather fat envelope. *How odd*, he thought. Rather than open it on the spot, he carried it back to his cabin.

When he opened it, he nearly threw it away immediately: it began with the dreaded phrase, 'My dear Marty.' Only one woman called him that, and although she was the subject of some of his fondest memories, she was also capable of inspiring in him a kind of bitter, anguished rage that made him, afterward, ashamed of his own emotions. He and Morag had split eight years ago, and the recriminations and mutual blame had left a trench of silence between them.

But what could possibly have prompted her to write to him

now? She'd always been a very verbal person, and her e-mails had tended to be terse, misspelled sentences rather than the emotional deluges she reserved for face-to-face communications.

Puzzled, Martin began to read.

My Dear Marty,

It's been too long since I last wrote to you; I hope you'll forgive me. Life has been busy, as they say, and doubly so, for I have also had Sarah to look after. She's growing very tall these days, and looks just like her father. I hope you'll be around for her sixteenth birthday . . .

He stopped. This had to be an elaborate joke. His ex-wife seemed to be talking about a child – their child – who didn't exist. And this was nothing like her style! It was almost as if someone else, writing from a dossier of his family history, was trying to –

He began to read again, this time acutely alert for hidden messages.

Sarah is studying theology at college these days. You know how studious she's always been? Her new teacher Herman seems to have brought her out of her shell. She's working on a dissertation about Eschatology; she insisted that I enclose a copy for you (attached below).

The rest of the letter was filled with idle chatter about fictional friends, reminiscences about trivial and entirely nonexistent shared memories and major (presumably well-documented) ones, and – as far as Martin could see – a content-free blind.

He turned to the 'dissertation'. It was quite long, and he pondered Herman's wisdom in sending it. Did New

Republican schoolchildren write eight-page essays about God? And about God's motives, as far as they could be deduced from the value of the cosmological constant? It was written in a precious, somewhat dull style that set his teeth on edge, like an earnest student essay hunting for marks of approval rather than a straight discursive monograph asserting a viewpoint. Then his eyes caught the footnotes:

1. Consider the hypothetical case of a power that intends to create a localized causality violation that does not produce a light cone encompassing its origin point. (We are implicitly assuming a perfectly spherical zone of sinfulness expanding at velocity c with origin at time $T0$.) If the spherical volume of sinfulness does not intersect with the four-space trajectory of the power's initial location, we are not dealing with an original sin. Consequently we do not expect the Eschaton to condemn the entire sinful civilization to damnation, or a Type II supernova; redemption is possible. However, damnation of the sinful agency that causes the causality violation is required.

He skipped down the page and began underlining significant words and phrases.

2. Does the Eschaton always intervene destructively? The answer is probably 'no'. We see the consequences of intervention in issues of original sin, but for every such intervention there are probably thousands of invisible nudges delivered to our world line with subtlety and precision. The agency by which such nudges are delivered must remain unknown for them to be effective. They probably flee the scene after intervention, hiding themselves in the teeming masses. The agency may even work in concert with our own efforts, as Eschaton-

fearing human beings, to ensure no violations exist. It is possible that some Eschatologically aware government agencies may assist the Eschaton's secret friends, if they are aware of their presence. Others, secret agents of sinful powers, may attempt to identify them by evidence and arrest them.

Well, that was all fairly instructive. Steganographic back channels generally irritated Martin, with their potential for misunderstandings and garbled messages, but in this instance, Herman was being quite clear. Distrust the New Republican secret police. Possible help from other agencies – did that mean Rachel? No retaliation against the New Republic itself: that was a big weight off his conscience, for however much he might dislike or despise their social affairs, they didn't deserve to die because of their leader's inability to deal with an unprecedented problem. However, one last footnote remained impenetrable, however he tried to understand it:

3. Of course, few people would contemplate breaking the law of causality without at least a very major apparent threat. One wonders what the invisible helpers of the Eschaton might do when confronted with the need to prevent a causality violation in the face of such a threat? At that point, they may find themselves with split loyalties on the one hand, to defend the prime law of the anthropic cosmos, while at the same time, not wanting to surrender their misguided but nevertheless human peers into the claws of a great evil. Under these circumstances, I feel sure the Eschaton would tell its agents to look to their fellow humans' interests immediately after preventing the rupture of space-time itself. The Eschaton may not be a compassionate God, but it is pragmatic and does not expect its tools to break in its service. However,

the key issue is determining which side is least wrong. This leads us deep into the forest of ethics, wherein there is a festival of ambiguity. All we can do is hope the secret helpers make the right choices – otherwise, the consequences of criticism will be harsh.

Martin sat back and scratched his head. 'Now what the hell does *that* mean?' he muttered to himself.

a semiotic war

The admiral was having a bad day.

'Damn your eyes, man, g-g-get your hands off me!' he croaked at his batman. Robard ignored him and carried on lifting; Kurtz's frail body wasn't capable of resisting as he sat the old man up and plumped up the pillows behind him. 'I'll have you taken out and shot!'

'Certainly, sir. Would that be before or after breakfast?'

The Admiral growled, deep in the back of his throat, then subsided into a rasping pant. ''M'not well. Not like I used to be. Dammit, I hate this!'

'You're getting old, sir. Happens to us all.'

'Not that blas-asted Terran attaché, dammit. He doesn't get old. I remember him back on Lamprey. Took lots of daguerreotypes of me standing by a hill of skulls we built in the public square of New Bokhara. Had to do something with the rebel prisoners, after all, no Jesus to make the quartermaster's loaves go further, ha-ha. Said he'd hang me, but never got around to it, the bastard. Wry cove, that wet fish. Could have sworn he was a female impersonator. What d'ye think, Kurt? Is he a shirt-lifter?'

Robard coughed and slid a bed table bearing cup of weak tea and a poached egg on toast in front of the Admiral. 'The UN inspector is a lady, sir.'

Kurtz blinked his watery eyes in astonishment. 'Why, bless my soul – what a surprise!' He reached for the teacup, but his hand was shaking so much he could barely lift it without slopping the contents. 'I thought. I *knew* that,' he accused.

'You probably did, sir. You'll feel better after you've taken your medicine.'

'But if he's a girl, and he was at First Lamprey, that means –' Kurtz looked puzzled. 'Do you believe in angels, Robard?' he asked faintly.

'No, sir.'

'Well, that's alright then, she must be a devil. Can deal with those, y'know. Where's my briefing?'

'I'll fetch it right after your breakfast, sir. Commodore Bauer said to tell you he's looking after everything.'

'Jolly good.'

Kurtz concentrated on assaulting his egg. Presently, when he had accepted its surrender, Robard removed the table. 'We'd better get you dressed and up, sir. Staff meeting in thirty minutes.'

Thirty-five minutes later, the Admiral was ready to meet his staff in the huge conference room adjoining his suite. Donning a uniform and taking his medication seemed to have removed a decade from his shoulders; he shuffled into the room under his own power, leaning heavily on his canes, although Robard discreetly helped when the Admiral tried to return the assembled officers' salute (and nearly caught a walking stick in one eye).

'Good evening, gentlemen,' began the Admiral. 'I gather the rail packet has been me – I'm sorry. I gather the r-r – mail packet has been received. Lieutenant Kossov. What word of our dispatches?'

'Er –' Kossov looked green. 'We have a problem, sir.'

'What do you mean, a problem?' demanded the Admiral. 'We're not supposed to have problems – that's the enemy's job!'

'There was a stack of twenty disks in the time capsule—'

'Don't give me disks, give me answers! What word of the enemy?'

Commodore Bauer leaned forward. 'I think what the Lieutenant is trying to say,' he interrupted, 'is that the dispatches were damaged.' Kossov eyed the Commodore with embarrassingly transparent gratitude.

'That's exactly right, sir. The private mail was intact, for the most part, but there was damage to the time capsule at one side – a micrometeoroid impact – and three of the disks were fragmented. We've retrieved a partial copy of a tenth of our orders from the remaining disks, but most of what came through consists of supply manifests for the quartermaster and a suggested menu for the Emperor's Birthday Commemoration Dinner. No details of the enemy, order of battle, force dispositions, diplomatic analysis, intelligence, or anything remotely useful. It's all shattered.'

'I see.' The Admiral looked deceptively calm; Kossov quailed. 'So our intelligence about the enemy disposition is absent. Ah, that-t makes life easier.' He turned to Bauer. 'Then we shall have to proceed in accordance with Plan B in order to accomplish a successful attack! Every man shall do his duty, for right is on our side. I ex-expect you have incontin-gency plans for dealing with in-insurgents on the ground? Good, very good. The Festival we shall meet in orbit and, having destroyed their ships, we shall work on the assumption that there is an aspiration to depose His Majesty among the rebels on the ground and their allies from the enemy camp!

Commodore. You will supervise our approach to the target system. Colonel von Ungern – Sternberg? Plans for the disposition of your marines and the re-re-reimposition of order once we arrive, if you please. Captain Mirsky, you will coordinate the, ah, la-la – maneuvers of the flotilla. Report to Midshipman Bauer if you please.'

The Admiral rose, shakily, and made no protest when Robard held him by one arm. 'Diss-diss-missed!' he snapped and, turning, hobbled out of the room.

Procurator Muller was bored. Bored and, furthermore, somewhat annoyed. Apart from the evidence of misconduct over a *weissbier* back in New Prague, there wasn't anything he could hang on the engineer. Just the fact that he was a foreigner who espoused radical opinions liable to encourage moral turpitude among the lumpenproletariat – which put him in the company of roughly ninety percent of the population of the known universe. Admittedly, there had been the nonstandard plug-in from the man's PA, but that wasn't conclusive. Was it?

He'd spent nearly two months of his life getting this much information. Much of the time, he was bored to tears; the crew and officers wouldn't speak to him – he was one of the Curator's men, charged with the preservation of society, and, like all police posts, this attracted some degree of suspicion – and he had long since exhausted the small wardroom library. With no duties but covert surveillance of a suspect who knew he was under suspicion, there was little for him to occupy his time with except idle fantasies about his forthcoming meeting, when they arrived on Rochard's World. But there were only a finite number of words he could think of to address his father with – and small consolation in imagining himself saying them.

However, one evening, it occurred to Vassily that there was another avenue he could follow in his exploration of the subject's movements. Wasn't Springfield spending an unhealthy amount of time in company with the foreign diplomat?

Now there was a shady case! Vassily's nostrils flared whenever he thought about her. If she hadn't had diplomatic papers, he'd have had her in an interrogation room in a trice. Springfield might be a radical, but Colonel Mansour wore *trousers* – enough to get her arrested for indecency on the streets of the capital, special credentials or no. The woman was a dangerous degenerate; obviously of depraved tastes, a male impersonator, probably an invert, and liable to corrupt anyone she came into contact with. Indeed, her very presence on this warship was a threat to the moral hygiene of the crew! That the engineer spent much of his time with her was obvious (Vassily had seen the surveillance recordings of him slipping in and out of her cabin), and the question of where the incriminating evidence was kept seemed fairly clear-cut. Springfield was a dangerous anarchist spy, and she must be his evil scheming control; a secretive mistress of the art of diplomatic seduction, mad, bad, and dangerous to know.

Which was why he was about to burgle her cabin and search her luggage.

It had taken Vassily nearly two weeks to reach this decision, from the moment he determined that Martin's nonstandard PA module was, not to put too fine a point on it, toast. It was a week and a half since the fleet had begun its momentous homeward voyage, first jumping across to the unpopulated binary system code-named Terminal Beta, then successively hopping from one star to the other, winding back more than a hundred years every day. Another four weeks and they would arrive at their destination; nevertheless, Vassily had taken his time. He'd have to be delicate, he realized. Without proof of treason he couldn't act against either of them, and the proof was obviously under diplomatic lock and key. Whatever he did would be ultimately deniable – get caught and, well, burgling a diplomat's luggage was about as infra dig as you could get. If anyone found him, he'd be thrown to the wolves – probably not literally, but he could look forward to a long career auditing penguins at the south polar station.

He picked an early evening for his raid. Martin was in the wardroom, drinking schnapps and playing dominoes with Engineering Commander Krupkin. Sitting on in Lieutenant Sauer's security wardroom, Vassily waited until Colonel Mansour left her room for some purpose; his monitors tracked her down the corridor to the officer's facilities. Good, she'd be at least ten minutes in the shower, if she stuck to her usual timetable. Vassily tiptoed out of his cubbyhole and scampered toward the lift shaft, and thence, the passage into officer country.

Pulling her cabin door shut behind him, he looked around cautiously. In almost every respect, her room was just like that of any other officer. Built like a railway couchette, there were two bunks; the upper one configured for sleeping, and the lower currently rolled upside down on its mountings to serve as a desk. Two lockers, a tiny washstand sink, mirror, and telephone completed the fittings. One corner of a large trunk protruded from under the desk. The inspector didn't travel as light as a naval officer, that was for sure.

First, Vassily spent a minute inspecting the chest. There were no signs of fine hairs or wires glued across the lid, and nothing complicated in the way of locks. It was just a slightly battered leather-and-wood trunk. He tried to lever it out from under the bunk, but rapidly realized that whatever was in it was implausibly heavy. Instead, he unlatched the desk/bunk and folded it upward against the bulkhead. Exposed to the light, the chest seemed to smile at him, horrible and faceless.

Vassily sniffed and reached for his pick gun. Another highly illegal tool of the Curator's Office, the pick gun was an engineering miracle: packed with solenoid-controlled probes, electronic sensors, and transmitters, even a compact laser transponder, it could force just about any lock in a matter of seconds. Vassily bent over the chest. Presently he confirmed that UN diplomatic luggage was no more immune to a pick gun than any other eight-barrel mortise lock with a keyed-frequency resonance handshake and a misplaced faith in long prime numbers. The lid clicked and swung upward.

The lid held toiletries and a mirror; after a brief inspection, Vassily turned to the interior and found himself confronted with a layer of clothing. He swallowed. Unmentionables mocked him: folded underskirts, bloomers, a pair of opera gloves. He carefully moved them aside. Beneath them lay a yellow silk gown. Vassily flushed, deeply embarrassed. He picked up the gown, unfolding it in the process; confused, he stood up and shook it out. It was, he thought, wholly beautiful and feminine, not what he'd expected of the corrupt and decadent Terrestrial agent. This whole fishing expedition wasn't turning out they way he'd imagined. He shook his head and laid the gown on the upper bunk, then bent back to the chest.

There was a black jumpsuit beneath it, and an octagonal hatbox. He tried to pick up the hatbox, and found that it wouldn't move. It was solid, as heavy as lead! Encouraged, he picked up the suit and draped it over a chair. Beneath it he found a slick plastic surface with lights glowing within it. The chest was only six inches deep! The entire bottom half of it lay below the surface on which the false hatbox rested, and was doubtless full of contraband and spying apparatus.

Vassily poked at the plastic panel. It reminded him of a keyboard, but lacking ivory and ebony keys, and with nowhere to feed the paper tapes in. It was all disturbingly alien. He poked at the panel, hitting an obvious raised area: runes blinked. ACCESS FORBIDDEN: GENEPRINT UNRECOGNIZED.

Damn.

Sweat poured off his neck as he considered his options. Then his eyes turned to the contents of the trunk he'd heaped beside it. It wanted a familiar skin sample? Hmm. Gloves. He held them up. Long women's gloves. They smelt faintly of something – yes. Vassily rolled one inside-out over his right hand, up his arm. He touched the raised plinth: PROCESSING . . . AUTHORIZED. A human body sheds five million skin particles per hour; Rachel had worn these very gloves, therefore –

A menu appeared. Vassily prodded at it blindly. Option one said SEARS FOUNDATION DESIGN CATALOG, whatever that meant. Below it, FREE HARDWARE FOUNDATION GNU COUTURIER 15.6; then DIOR HISTORICAL CATALOG. He scratched his head. No secret code books, no hidden weapons, no spy cameras. Just incomprehensible analytical engine instructions! He thumped the plinth in frustration.

A deep humming filled the room. He jumped backward, knocking over the chair. A slot opened in the top of the hatbox. A demented clicking rattled from it and something spat out. Something red that landed on his head – a wisp of lace with two leg holes. *Scandalous!* With a grinding clank, the hatbox extruded in short order a shimmering tulle ball gown, a pair of spike-heeled ankle boots, and a pair of coarse-woven blue shorts. All the clothing was hot to the touch and smelled faintly of chemicals.

'Stop it,' he hissed. 'Stop it!' In reply, the trunk ejected a stream of stockings, a pair of trousers, and a corset that threatened any wearer with abdominal injury. He thumped at the control panel in frustration and, thankfully, the trunk stopped manufacturing clothing. He looked at it dizzily. *Why bring a trunk of clothing if you can bring a trunk that can manufacture any item of clothing you want to wear?* he realized. Then the trunk made an ominous graunching sound and he stared at it in ontological horror. *It's a cornucopia!* One of the forbidden, mythological chimeras of history, the machine that had brought degradation and unemployment and economic down-sizing to his ancestors before they fled the singularity to settle and help create the New Republic.

The cornucopia grunted and hummed. Thoroughly spooked, Vassily looked to the door. If Rachel was on her way back –

The hatbox opened. Something black and shiny peeped forth. Antennae hummed and scanned the room; articulated claws latched onto the side of the box and levered.

Vassily took one look at the monster and cracked. He left the door swinging ajar behind him in his helpless flight down the corridor, disheveled and wild-eyed, wearing an inside-out opera glove on one hand.

Behind him, the freshly manufactured spybot finished sur-veying the insertion zone. Primitive programs meshed in its microprocessor brain: no operational overrides were present, so it established a default exploration strategy and prepared to reconnoiter. It grabbed the nearest non-fixed item of camou-flage and, stretching it protectively over its crablike carapace, headed for the ventilation shaft. Even as it finished removing the grille, the hatbox clanked again: the second small robospy was born just in time to see the yellow gown disappearing into the air-conditioning duct. And then the luggage clanked again, preparing to hatch yet another . . .

By the time Rachel returned, her trunk was half-empty – and almost all her ready-made clothing had escaped.

'You come with me,' Sister Seventh told Burya. 'See situa-tion. Explain why is bad, and understand.'

Wind whispered through the open window, carrying grey clouds across the city, as Novy Petrograd burned in an inferno of forbidden technology. Houses crumbled and grew anew, extrusions pushing up like mushrooms from the strange soil of men's dreams. Trees of silver rose from the goldsmith's district, their harsh, planar surfaces tracking the cumulus-shrouded sun. The hairless alien wobbled forward onto the balcony and pointed her tusks at the fairground on the other side of town: 'This is not the Festival's doing!'

Helplessly, Burya followed her out onto the rooftop above the Duke's ballroom. A cloacal smell plugged his nostrils, the distant olfactory echo of the corpses swinging from the lampposts in the courtyard. Politovsky had disappeared, but his men had not gone quietly, and the mutinous troops, frenzied and outraged, had committed atrocities against the officers and their families. The ensuing reprisals had been harsh but necessary –

Javelins of light streaked across the cloudscape overhead. Seconds later, the rumble of their passage split the cold evening air. Thunder rattled and echoed from the remaining windows of the town.

'Festival does not understand humans,' Sister Seventh commented calmly. 'Motivation of fleshbody intelligences bereft of real-time awareness not simulatable. Festival therefore assumes altruist aesthetic. I ask: Is this a work of art?'

Burya Rubenstein stared at the city bleakly. 'No.' The admission came hard. 'We hoped for better. But the people need leadership and a strong hand; without it they run riot –'

Sister Seventh made a strange snuffling noise. Presently he realized that she was laughing at him.

'Riot! Freedom! End of constraint! Silly humans. Silly not-organized humans, not smell own place among people, need to sniff piss in corner of burrow, kill instead. Make military music. Much marching and killing by numbers. Is comedy, no?'

'We will control it ourselves,' Burya insisted trenchantly. 'This chaos, this is not our destiny. We stand on the threshold of utopia! The people, once educated, will behave rationally. Ignorance, filth, and a dozen generations of repression are what you see here – this is the outcome of a failed experiment, not human destiny!'

'Then why you not a sculptor, cut new flesh from old?' Sister Seventh approached him. Her snuffling cabbage breath reminded him of a pet guinea pig his parents had bought him when he was six. (When he was seven there had been a famine, and into the cook pot she went.) 'Why not you build new minds for your people?'

'We'll fix it,' Burya emphasized. Three more emerald-colored diamonds shot overhead: they zipped in helices around one another, then turned and swerved out across the river like sentient shooting stars. *When in doubt, change the subject*: 'How did your people get here?'

'We Critics. Festival has many mindspaces spare. Brought us along, like the Fringe and other lurkers in dark. Festival must travel and learn. *We* travel and change. Find what is broken and Criticize, help broken things fix selves. Achieve harmonious dark and warm-fed hiveness.'

Something tall and shadowy slid across the courtyard behind Burya. He turned, hurriedly, to see two many-jointed legs, chicken-footed, capped by a thatch of wild darkness. The legs knelt, lowering the body until an opening hung opposite the balcony, as dark and uninviting as a skull's hollow nasal cavity.

'Come, ride with me.' Sister of Stratagems the Seventh stood behind Burya, between him and his office. It was not an offer but an instruction. 'Will learn you much!'

'I – I –' Burya stopped protesting. He raised a hand to his throat, found the leather thong he wore around it, and yanked on the end of it. 'Guards!'

Sister Seventh rolled forward, as ponderous and irresistible as an earthquake; she swept him backward into the walking hut, making that odd snuffling noise again. A furious hissing and quacking broke out behind her, followed by erratic gunfire as the first of the guard geese shot their way through the study door. Rubenstein landed on the floor with two hundred kilos of mole rat on top of him, holding him down; the floor lurched then rose like an elevator, dropped, and accelerated in a passable imitation of the fairground ride at a winter festival. He choked, trying to breathe, but before he could suffocate Sister Seventh picked herself up and sat back on what appeared to be a nest of dried twigs. She grinned at him horribly, baring her tusks, then pulled out a large root vegetable and began to gnaw on it.

'Where are you taking me? I demand to be put down –'

'Plotsk,' said the Critic. 'To learn how to understand. Want a carrot?'

They came for Martin as he lay sleeping. The door of his cabin burst open and two burly ratings entered; the light came on. 'What's up?' Martin asked fuzzily.

'On your feet.' A petty officer stood in the entrance.

'What –'

'On your feet.' The quilt was pulled back briskly; Martin found himself dragged halfway out of bed before he had quite finished blinking at the brightness. 'At the double!'

'What's going on?'

'Shut up,' said one of the ratings, and backhanded him casually across the face. Martin fell back on the bed, and the other rating grabbed his left arm and slipped a manacle over his wrist. While he was trying to reach his mouth – sore and hot, painful but not badly damaged – they snagged his other wrist.

'To the brig. At the double!' They frog-marched Martin out the door, naked and in handcuffs, and hurried him down to the level below the engineering spaces and drive kernel. Everything passed in a painful blur of light; Martin spat and saw a streak of blood dribble across the floor.

A door opened. They pushed him through and he fell over, then the door clanged shut.

Shock finally cut in. He slumped, rolled to his side, and dry-heaved on the floor. From start to finish, the assault had taken less than two minutes.

He was still lying on the floor when the door opened again. A pair of boots entered his field of vision.

Muffled: 'Get this mess cleared up.' Louder: 'You – on your feet.'

Martin rolled over, to see Security Lieutenant Sauer staring down at him. The junior officer from the Curator's Office stood behind him, along with a couple of enlisted men. Martin began to sit up.

'Out,' Sauer told the guards. They left. 'On your feet,' he repeated.

Martin sat up and pushed himself upright against one wall.

'You are in *big* trouble,' said the Lieutenant. 'No, don't say anything. You're in trouble. You can dig yourself in deeper or you can cooperate. I want you to think about it for a while.' He held up a slim black wafer. 'We know what this is. Now you can tell us all about it, who gave it to you, or you can let us draw our own conclusions. This isn't a civil court or an investigation by the audit bureau; this is, in case you hadn't worked it out, a military-intelligence matter. How you decide to deal with us affects how we will deal with you. Understood?'

Martin blinked. 'I've never seen it before,' he insisted, pulse racing.

Sauer looked disgusted. 'Don't be obtuse. It was in your gadget. Naval regulations specify that it's an offense to bring unauthorized communications devices aboard a warship. So what was it doing there? You forgot to take it out? Whom does it belong to, anyway?'

Martin wavered. 'The shipyard told me to carry it,' he said. 'When I came aboard I didn't realize I'd be on board for more than a shift at a time. Or that it was a problem.'

'The shipyard told you to carry it.' Sauer looked skeptical.

'It's a dead causal channel, man! Have you any idea how much one of those things is worth?'

Martin nodded shakily. 'Have you any idea how much this *ship* is worth?' he asked. 'MiG put it together. MiG stands to make a lot of money selling copies: more if it earns a distinguished combat record. Has it occurred to you that my primary employers – the people you rented me from – have a legitimate interest in seeing how you've changed around the ship they delivered to you?'

Sauer tossed the cartridge on Martin's bunk. 'Plausible. You're doing well, so far: don't let it go to your head.' He turned and rapped on the door. 'If that's your final story, I'll pass it on to the Captain. If you have anything else to tell me, let the supervisor know when he brings your lunch.'

'Is that all?' Martin asked as the door opened.

'Is that all?' Sauer shook his head. 'You confess to a capital offense, and ask if that's *all*?' He paused in the doorway and stared at Martin, expressionless. 'Yes, that's all. Recording off.'

Then he was gone.

Vassily had gone to Lieutenant Sauer immediately after the abortive search through Rachel's luggage: badly frightened, needing advice. He'd poured everything out before Sauer, who had nodded reassuringly and calmed him down before explaining what they were going to do.

'They're in it together, son, that much is clear. But you should have talked to me first. Let's see this gadget you took from him, hmm?' Vassily had passed him the cartridge he'd stolen from Martin's PA. Sauer took one look at it and nodded to himself. 'Never seen one of these before, have you? Well, don't worry; it's just the lever we need.' He tapped the exhausted causal channel significantly. 'Don't know why he had this on board, but it was bloody stupid of him, clear breach of His Majesty's regulations. You could have come to me with it immediately, no questions asked, instead of digging around the woman's luggage. Which, of course, you didn't do. Did you?'

'Uh – no, sir.'

'Jolly good.' Sauer nodded to himself again. 'Because, if you had, I'd have to arrest you, of course. But I suppose, if she left her door unlocked and some enlisted man tried to help himself to her wardrobe, well, we can investigate it . . .' He trailed off thoughtfully.

'Why can't we arrest the woman, sir? For, um, possession of illicit machinery?'

'Because' – Sauer looked down his nose at Vassily – 'she's got a diplomatic passport. She's *allowed* to have illegal machinery in her luggage. And, frankly, far as I can tell, she's got an excuse. Would you be complaining if she had a sewing machine? That's what she'll say it is; a garment fabricator.'

'But I saw these *things* coming out of there, with too many legs! They were after me –'

'Nobody else has seen them,' Sauer said in a soothing tone of voice. 'I believe you; you probably *did* see something. Spy robots, perhaps. But good ones, good enough to hide – and without evidence –' He shrugged.

'What are you going to do, then, sir?'

Sauer glanced away. 'I think we're going to pay Mr. Springfield a visit,' he murmured. 'We'll take him away. Stick him in the cells for a bit. And then' – he grinned, unpleasantly – 'we'll see which way our diplomat jumps. Which should tell us what all this means, shouldn't it?'

Neither of them noticed the pair of polka-dotted knickers hiding behind the ventilation duct overhead, listening patiently and recording everything.

confessions

The *Lord Vanek* accelerated at an economical two gees, using its drive kernel to curve the space-time ahead of it into a valley into which it slid easily, without imposing punishing stress on crew or machinery. Ninety-two thousand tonnes of warship (with an eight-billion-tonne black hole at her core) took a lot of moving, but once set in motion, it could go places fast. It would take days to cross the vast gulf that separated *Lord Vanek*'s parking station from the first jump point on the return leg of its timelike path – but nothing like the years that humanity's earliest probes had taken to cover similar distances.

The ships of the fleet had traveled barely twenty light-years from the New Republic, but in the process, they had hopped forward in time by four thousand years, zigzagging between the two planetless components of the binary system in an attempt to outrun any long-term surveillance that the Festival might have placed on them. Soon the spacelike component of the voyage would commence, with a cruise to a similar system not far from Rochard's World; then the fleet would pursue a bizarre trajectory, looping back into the past of their own world line without actually intersecting that of their origin point.

Along the way, the fleet tenders would regularly top up the warships with consumable provisions, air and water and food; no less than eight merchant ships would be completely stripped and abandoned to fall forever between the stars, their crews doubled up aboard other vessels. The voyage would strain the Navy's logistic system beyond the point of failure: something had to give, and an entire year's shipbuilding budget would go into the supply side of this operation alone.

As they cruised between jumps, the warships exercised continually. Tentative lidar pulses strobed at the deep vacuum beyond the heliopause as officers sought firing solutions on the ships of the other squadrons; missile and torpedo trajectories were plotted, laser firing solutions entered into the tireless gear mills of the analytical engines. Tracking ships at long range was difficult, for they didn't emit much detectable radiation. Radar was hopeless: to pump out sufficient energy to get a return, the *Lord Vanek* would have produced enough waste heat to broil her crew alive. As it was, only her vast radiator panels, spread to the stars and now glowing a dull red, allowed them to run the lidar at high intensity for short periods of time. (Vacuum is a most effective insulator – and active sensors capable of reaching out across billions of kilometers run hot.)

Martin Springfield knew nothing of this. Lying in his cell he'd spent the past two days in despondent boredom, alternating between depression and guarded optimism by turns. *Still alive*, he thought. Then: *Not for long*. If only there was something he could do! But on board a starship, there was nowhere to run. He was enough of a realist to understand this: if they ran out of options here, he was dead. He'd simply have to hope that they hadn't worked out what he'd done, and would release him rather than antagonizing the shipyard.

He was sitting on the bunk one evening when the door

opened. He looked up at once, expecting Sauer or the Curator's kid spook. His eyes widened. 'What are you doing here?'

'Just visiting. Mind if I sit down?'

He nodded uneasily. Rachel sat on the edge of the bunk. She was wearing a plain black jumpsuit and had tied her hair back severely; her manner was different, almost relaxed. It wasn't a disguise, he realized; she wasn't acting the part of a woman of easy virtue or a diplomat posted to a banana republic, or anyone else, for that matter. She was being herself – a formidable figure. 'I thought they'd have locked you up, too,' he said.

'Yes, well . . .' She looked distracted. 'One moment.' She glanced at her pocket watch. '*Ah.*' She leaned over toward the head end of his bunk and placed something small and metallic on it.

'I already spiked the bugs,' he said. 'They won't hear much.'

She glared at him. 'Thanks for nothing.'

'What –'

'I want the truth,' she said flatly. 'You've been lying to me. I want to know why.'

'Oh.' He tried not to cringe. Her expression was unnaturally controlled, the calm before a storm.

'You've got only one chance to tell the truth,' she said, pitching her voice in conversational tones that were belied by a brittle edge in it. 'I don't think they know you're lying yet, but when we get back – well, they're not dummies and you're digging yourself in deeper. The Curator's Office will be watching. If you act guilty, the boy wonder will draw the only available conclusion.'

He sighed. 'And what if the conclusion is right? What if I *am* guilty?' he asked.

'I trusted you,' she said flatly. 'As yourself. *Not* as a player. I don't like being lied to, Martin. In business or my personal life, whichever.'

'Well.' He contemplated the shiny jammer she'd placed on his pillow. It was easier than facing her anger and hurt. 'If I said they told me they were the shipyard, would that satisfy you?'

'No.' She shook her head. 'You're not dumb enough to fall for a cover story, anyway.' She looked away. 'I don't like being lied to,' she said bitterly.

He looked at her. Rachel was an up-to-date professional, unlike the bumbling amateurs of the New Republic; she'd have speech analysis reflexes, lie detectors, any number of other gadgets trained on him, if this was business, and if she hadn't completely lost it. If she had – well, he could hardly blame her for being mad at him. In her place, he'd be angry, too. And hurt. 'I don't like telling lies,' he said, which was true enough. 'Not without an overriding reason,' he admitted.

She took a deep breath, visibly steeling herself. 'I'm the nearest thing to a lawyer you're going to get here, Martin. I'm the nearest representative of your government – what they think is your government – within four thousand years and a two-hundred-light-year radius. They have a legalistic system of government, for all that they're medieval throwbacks, and they let me visit you as your advocate. I can plead your case if it comes up to a courtmartial because you're a civilian, and I might be able to deflect things short of that. But only if you tell me everything, so I know what I'm defending.'

'I can't talk about it,' he said uncomfortably. He picked up his book, half trying to shelter his guilty conscience behind it. 'I'm not allowed to. I thought you of all people would be able to understand that?'

'Listen.' Rachel glared at him. 'Remember what I told you about trust? I'm really disappointed. Because I *did* trust you, and it seems to me that you betrayed that trust. As it is, I'm going to have to do a lot of fast talking if I'm going to try to get your ass off the hook you're caught on, or at least get you out of here alive. And before I do that, I want to know what you've been lying to me *about*.'

She stood up. 'I'm a fool. And a damned fool for trusting you, and a worse fool for getting involved with you. Hell, I'm an unprofessional fool! But I'm going to ask you again, and you'd better answer truthfully. There are a lot of lives at stake this time, Martin, because this is not a game. Who the fuck are you working for?'

Martin paused a moment, dizzy with a sense of events moving out of control. *Can't tell her, can't not tell her* – he looked up, meeting her eyes for the first time. It was the hurt expression that made his mind up for him: no amount of rationalization would help him sleep that night if he left her feeling like this. Feeling betrayed by the only person she'd been able to trust within a radius of light-years. One moment of unprofessionalism deserved to be answered by another. His mouth felt dry and clumsy as he spoke: 'I work for the Eschaton.'

Rachel sat down heavily, her eyes wide with disbelief. '*What?*'

He shrugged. 'You think the E's only way of dealing with problems is to drop a rock on them?' he asked.

'Are you kidding?'

'Nope.' He could taste bile in the back of his throat. 'And I believe in what I'm doing, else I wouldn't be here now, would I? Because truly, the alternative is to drop a planet-buster on the problem. The Eschaton finds that easier. And it makes the appropriate noises. It *scares* people. But really – most of the time, the E likes to solve problems more quietly through people like me.'

'How long?'

'About twenty years.' He shrugged again. 'That's all there is to it.'

'Why?' She buried her hands between her knees, holding

them together tightly, looking at him with a miserably confused expression on her face.

'Because –' He tried to drag his scattered thoughts together. 'Believe me, the Eschaton prefers it when people like you do the job first. It saves a lot of pain all around. But once the fleet moved, and you lost the argument with them, there was no alternative. You didn't really think they'd set up the prerequisites for a closed timelike path and not follow it through to the logical end?' He took a deep breath. 'That's the sort of job I do. I'm a plumber, for when the Eschaton wants to fix a leak quietly.'

'You're an agent, you mean.'

'Yes,' he agreed. 'Like you.'

'Like me.' She made a croaking noise that sounded as if it might have been intended as a laugh. 'Shit, Martin, that is *not* what I was expecting to hear.'

'I wish this hadn't happened. Especially with – well, us. In the middle.'

'Me too, with brass knobs on,' she said shakily. 'Was that all there was?'

'*All* there was? That's all I was holding out on you, honest.'

A long pause. 'Alright. It was, uh, purely professional?'

He nodded. 'Yes.' He looked at her. 'I don't like lying. And I haven't been lying, or withholding the truth, about anything else. I promise.'

'Oh. Okay.' She took a deep breath and grinned tiredly, simultaneously looking amused and relieved.

'It's really been eating you, hasn't it?' he asked.

'Oh, you could say that,' she said, with heavy irony.

'Um.' He held out a hand. 'I'm sorry. Truly.'

'Apology accepted – conditionally.' She squeezed his hand, briefly, then let go. 'Now, are you going to tell me what the Eschaton has in mind for us?'

Martin sighed. 'Yes, inasmuch as I know. But I've got to

warn you, it's not good. If we can't get off this ship before it arrives, we're probably going to die . . .'

Time travel destabilises history.

History is a child of contingency; so many events depend on critical misunderstandings or transient encounters that even the apocryphal butterfly's wing is apt to stir up a storm in short order. A single misunderstood telegram in June of 1917 permitted the Bolshevik revolution to become a possibility; a single spy in 1958 extended the Cold War by a decade. And without both such events, could a being like the Eschaton ever have come to exist?

Of course, in a universe which permits time travel, history itself becomes unstable – and the equilibrium can only be restored when the diabolical mechanism edits itself out of the picture. But that's scant comfort for the trillions of entities who silently cease to exist in the wake of a full-blown time storm.

It's hardly surprising that, whenever intelligent beings arise in such a universe, they will seek to use closed timelike curves to prevent their own extinction. Faster-than-light travel being possible, general relativity tells us that it is indistinguishable from time travel; and this similarity makes the technologies of total annihilation dreadfully accessible. In the small, stupid little organizations like the New Republic seek to gain advantage over their contemporaries and rivals. In the large, vast, cool intellects seek to stabilize their universe in the form most suitable to them. Their tampering may be as simple as preventing rivals from editing them out of the stable historical record – or it may be as sophisticated as meddling with the early epochs of the big bang, back before the Higgs field decayed into the separate fundamental forces that bind the universe together to ensure just the right ratio of physical constants to support life.

This is not the only universe; far from it. It isn't even the only universe in which life exists. Like living organisms, universes exist balanced on the edge of chaos, little bubbles of twisted ur-space that pinch off and bloat outward, expanding and cooling, presently giving birth to further bubbles of condensed space-time; a hyperdimensional crystal garden full of strange trees bearing stranger fruit.

But the other universes are not much use to us. There are too many variables in the mix. As the initial burst of energy that signals the birth of a universe cools, the surging force field that drives its initial expansion becomes tenuous, then breaks down into a complex mess of other forces. The constants that determine their relative strengths are set casually, randomly. There are universes with only two forces; others, with thousands. (Ours has five.) There are universes where the electron is massive: nuclear fusion is so easy there that the era of star formation ends less than a million of our years after the big bang. Chemistry is difficult there, and long before life can evolve, such universes contain nothing but cooling pulsars and black holes, the debris of creation brought to a premature end.

There are universes where photons have mass – others where there is too little mass in the universe for it to achieve closure and collapse in a big crunch at the end of time. There are, in fact, an infinity of universes out there, and they are all uninhabitable. There is a smaller infinitude of possibly habitable ones, and in some of them, intelligent life evolves; but more than that we may never know. Travel between universes is nearly impossible; materials that exist in one may be unstable in another. So, trapped in our little fishbowl of space we drift through the crystal garden of universes – and our own neighborly intelligences, beings like the Eschaton, do their best to prevent the less-clever inmates from smashing the glass from within.

The man in gray had explained all this to Martin at length,

eighteen years ago. 'The Eschaton has a strong interest in maintaining the integrity of the world line,' he had said. 'It's in your interest, too. Once people begin meddling with the more obscure causal paradoxes, all sorts of lethal side-effects can happen. The Eschaton is as vulnerable to this as any other being in the universe – it didn't create this place, you know, it just gets to live in it with the rest of us. It may be a massively superhuman intelligence or cluster of intelligences, it may have resources we can barely comprehend, but it could probably be snuffed out quite easily; just a few nuclear weapons in the right place before it bootstrapped into consciousness, out of the pre-Singularity networks of the twenty-first century. Without the Eschaton, the human species would probably be extinct by now.'

'Epistemology pays no bills,' Martin remarked drily. 'If you're expecting me to do something risky . . .'

'We appreciate that.' The gray man nodded. 'We need errands run, and not all of them are entirely safe. Most of the time it will amount to little more than making note of certain things and telling us about them – but occasionally, if there is a serious threat, you may be asked to act. Usually in subtle, undetectable ways, but always at your peril. But there are compensations.'

'Describe them.' Martin put his unfinished drink down at that point.

'My sponsor is prepared to pay you very well indeed. And part of the pay – we can smooth the path if you apply for prolongation and continued residency.' Life-extension technology, allowing effectively unlimited life expectancy beyond 160 years, was eminently practical, and available on most developed worlds. It was also as tightly controlled as any medical procedure could be. The controls and licensing were a relic of the Overshoot, the brief period in the twenty-first century when Earth's population blipped over the ten-billion mark (before the Singularity, when the Eschaton bootstrapped its way past merely human intelligence and promptly rewrote the rule book). The after-effects of overpopulation still scarred the planet, and the response was an ironclad rule – if you want to live beyond your natural span, you must either demonstrate some particular merit, some reason why you should be allowed to stay around, or you could take the treatment and emigrate. There were few rules that all of Earth's fractured tribes and cultures and companies obeyed, but out of common interest, this was one of them. To be offered exemption by the covert intervention of the Eschaton –

'How long do I have to think about it?' asked Martin.

'Until tomorrow.' The gray man consulted his notepad. 'Ten-thousand-a-year retainer. Ten thousand or more as a bonus if you are asked to do anything. And an essential status exemption from the population committee. On top of which, you will be helping to protect humanity as a whole from the actions of some of its more intemperate – not to say stupid – members. Would you care for another drink?'

'It's alright,' said Martin. *They're willing to pay me? To do something I'd volunteer for?* He stood up. 'I don't need another day to think about it. Count me in.'

The gray man smiled humorlessly. 'I was told you'd say that.'

The gold team was on full alert. Not a head moved when the door opened, and Captain Mirsky walked in, followed by Commodore Bauer and his staff. 'Commander Murametz, please report.'

'Yes, sir. Time to jump transition, three-zero-zero seconds. Location plot confirmed, signals operational. All systems running at an acceptable level of readiness for engagement plan C. We're ready to go to battle stations whenever you say, sir.'

Mirsky nodded. 'Gentlemen, carry on as ordered.' The

Commodore nodded and quietly instructed his adjutant to take notes. Elsewhere on the ship, sirens blatted: the clatter of spacers running to their stations didn't penetrate the bulkheads, but the atmosphere nevertheless felt tense. Low-key conversations started at the various workstations around the room as officers talked over the tactical circuits.

'Ready for jump in two-zero-zero seconds,' called Relativistics.

Rachel Mansour – wearing her disarmament inspector's uniform – sat uncomfortably close to one of the walls, studying a packed instrument console over the shoulder of a petty officer. Brass handles and baroque red LEDs glowed at her; a pewter dog's head barked silently from an isolation switch. Someone had spent half a lifetime polishing the engravings until they gleamed as softly as butter. It seemed a bitter irony, to observe such art in a place of war; the situation was, she thought, more than somewhat repulsive, and finding anything even remotely beautiful in it only made things worse.

The Festival: of all the stupid things the New Republic might attack, the Festival was about the worst. She'd spoken to Martin about it, piecing together his information with her own. Together they'd pieced together a terrifying hypothesis. 'Herman was unusually vague about it,' Martin admitted. 'Normally he has a lot of background detail. Every word means something. But it's as if he doesn't want to say too much about the Festival. They're – he called them, uh, glider-gun factories. I don't know if you know about Life –'

'Cellular automata, the game?'

'That's the one. Glider guns are mobile cellular automata. There are some complex life structures that replicate themselves, or simpler cellular structures; a glider-gun factory is a weird one. It periodically packs itself into a very dense mobile system that migrates across the grid for a couple of hundred squares, then it unpacks itself into two copies that then pack down and fly off in opposite directions. Herman said that they're a real-space analogue: he called them a Boyce-Tipler robot. Self-replicating, slower-than-light interstellar probes that are sent out to gather information about the universe and feed it back to a center. Only the Festival isn't just a dumb robot fleet. It carries upload processors, thousands of uploaded minds running faster than real time when there are resources to support them, downloaded into long-term storage during the long trips.'

Rachel had shuddered slightly at that, and he hugged her, misapprehending the cause of her distress. She let him, not wanting him to realize he had upset her. She'd dealt with uploads before. The first-generation ones, fresh from the meat puppet universe, weren't a problem: it was the kids that got her. Born – if you could call it that – in a virtual environment, they rapidly diverged from any norm of humanity that she could see. More seriously, their grasp of the real world was poor. Which was fine as long as they didn't have to deal with it, but when they did, they used advanced nanosystems for limbs and they sometimes accidentally *broke* things – planets, for instance.

It wasn't intentional malice; they'd simply matured in an environment where information didn't go away unless someone wanted it to, where death and destruction were reversible, where magic wands worked and hallucinations were dangerous. The real universe played by different rules, rules that their horrified ancestors had fled as soon as the process of migrating minds into distributed computing networks had been developed.

The Festival sounded like a real headache. On the one hand, an upload civilization, used to omnipotence within its own pocket universe, had decided for no obvious reason to go forth and play the galactic tourist. On the other hand, physical machinery of vast subtlety and power was bound to do their bidding at each port of call. Bush robots, for example: take a branching tree of fronds. Each bough split into two half-scale branches at either end, with flexible joints connecting them. Repeated down to the molecular level, each terminal branch was closed off with a nanomanipulator. The result was a silvery haze with a dumbbell-shaped core, glittering with coherent light, able to change shape, dismantle and reassemble physical objects at will – able to rebuild just about anything into any desired physical form, from the atomic scale up. Bush robots made the ultimate infantry; shoot at them, and they'd eat the bullets, splice them into more branches, and thank you for the gift of metals.

'I'm worried about what will happen when we arrive,' Martin admitted. He'd wrung his hands while he spoke, unconsciously emphasizing his points. 'I don't think the New Republicans can actually comprehend what's going on. They see an attack, and I can understand why – the Festival has destroyed the political and social economy on one of their colonies as thoroughly as if it had nuked the place from orbit – but what I can't see is any possible avenue to a settlement. There's not going to be any common ground there. What does the Festival want? What could make them go away and leave the Republic alone?'

'I thought you didn't like the New Republic,' Rachel challenged.

He grimaced. 'And I suppose you do? I don't like their system, and they know it. That's why I'm sitting in this cell instead of in my cabin, or on the engineering deck. But –' He shrugged. 'Their social system is one thing, but people are people everywhere you go, just trying to get along in this crazy universe. I don't like them as individuals, but that's not the same as wanting them dead. They're not monsters, and they don't deserve what's coming to them, and life isn't fair, is it?'

'You did your bit to make it that way.'

'Yes.' He dropped his gaze to the floor, focusing intently on something invisible to her. 'I wish there was an alternative. But Herman can't just let them get away with it. Either causality is a solid law, or – things break. Far better for their maneuver simply to fail, so the whole voyage looks like a cack-handed mess, than for it to succeed, and encourage future adventurers to try for a timelike approach on their enemies.'

'And if you're lashed to the mast as the ship heads for the maelstrom?'

'I never said I was omniscient. Herman said he'd try to get me out of here if I succeeded; I wish I knew what he had in mind. What are *your* options like?'

Her lips quirked. 'Maybe he nobbled my boss – he taught me never to travel at sea without a lifeboat.'

Martin snorted, obviously misunderstanding: 'Well, they say a captain always goes down with his ship – shame they never mention the black gang drowning in the engine room!'

An announcement from the helm brought Rachel back to the present: 'Jump in one-zero-zero seconds.'

'Status, please,' said Commander Murametz. Each post called out in order; everything was running smoothly. 'Time to transition?'

'Four-zero seconds. Kernel spin-down in progress; negative mass dump proceeding.' Far beneath their feet, the massive singularity at the core of the drive system was spooling down, releasing angular momentum into the energetic vacuum underlying space-time. There was no vibration, no sense of motion: nor could there be. Spin, in the context of a space drive, was a property of warped patches of space, nothing to do with matter as most people understood it.

'Commander Murametz, proceed.' The Captain stood back, hands clasped behind his back. 'Commodore, by your leave?'

Bauer nodded. 'Proceed on your initiative.'

'Transition in progress . . . we're clear. Reference frame locked.'

'No obstructions,' called Radar One. 'Um, looks like we're on the nail.'

'One-zero gees, straight in on the primary,' said Ilya. He looked almost bored; they'd rehearsed this a dozen times in the past three days alone. 'Confirm positional fix, then give me a passive scan. Standard profile.'

'Aye aye, sir. Nav confirmation; we have a star fix. Yes, we're a good bit closer to the bucket than last time. I see a waste heat dump from *Chancellor Romanoff*; they're through.' That cheered them up; even at ten gees constant acceleration, a miss of a couple of astronomical units could take hours or days to make up. 'Nothing else in view.'

'Give me a lidar shout, then. Chirped, if you please, frontal nine-zero degrees.'

'Emission starting – now. Profile steady.' The main screen of the simulation showed megawatts of laser light pouring out into the depths of space, mostly hard ultraviolet tagged with the sawtooth timing pulses of the ship's clock. 'Scan closure. Lidar shutdown.'

Radar Two: 'I've got backscatter! Range – Holy father! Sir, we're right on top of them! Range six-zero K-kilometers, looks like metal!'

Bauer smiled like a shark.

'Helm: take us to full military power in one-zero seconds. Course plus one-zero, minus four-zero.'

'Aye aye, sir, bringing course to plus one-zero minus four-zero. Two-one one gees coming up in five . . . three . . . now.' Like most regional powers, the New Republican Navy had adopted the Terran standard gee – ten meters per second squared. At full military power, *Lord Vanek* could go from a standing start to planetary escape velocity in less than sixty seconds; without a delicate balancing act, trading off the drive kernel's spin against the curvature of space around the ship, the crew would be squashed flat and broken on the floor. But carrying a drive kernel had its price – a non-FTL, fission-powered missile could, at short range, outrun or out-turn a warship hobbled by the mass of a mountain.

'Radar, get me some details on that bounce.' Mirsky leaned forward.

'Aye aye, sir.' A plot came up on the forward display. Rachel focused on the readouts, looking over the razor-scarred rolls at the base of Petty Officer Borisovitch's skull. 'Confirming . . .'

Radar Two: 'More contacts! Repeat, I have multiple contacts!'

'How far?' demanded the captain.

'They're – too close! Sir, they're very faint. Took a few seconds for the analysis grid to resolve them, in fact. They've got to be black body emitters with stealth characteristics. Range nine-zero K, one-point-three M, seven M, another at two-five-zero K . . . we're in the middle of it!'

Rachel closed her eyes. A chill ran up her spine as she thought about small robot factories, replicators, the swarm of self-replicating weapons breeding in low orbit around a distant gas giant moon. She breathed deeply and opened her eyes.

Radar Two interrupted her reverie: 'Target! Range six-point-nine M-klicks, big emission profile. Course minus five-five, plus two-zero.'

Mirsky turned to his executive officer: 'Ilya, your call.'

'Yes, sir. Designate the new contact as target alpha. Adopt convergent course for alpha, closest pass at three-zero K, full military power.'

'Aye aye, targeting alpha.'

'You expect something, sir,' Ilya said quietly. Rachel tilted her head slightly, to let her boosted hearing focus on the two senior officers at the back of the room.

'Damn right I do. Something wiped out the system defense

flotilla,' Mirsky murmured. 'Something that was sitting there, waiting for them. I don't expect anything except hostile contacts as soon as we come out of jump.'

'I didn't expect them to be this close, though.' Murametz looked troubled.

'I had to do some digging, but thanks to Inspector Mansour' – the Captain nodded in her direction – 'we know a bit about their capabilities, which are somewhat alarming. It's not in the standard intelligence digest because the fools didn't think it worth mentioning. We're up against cornucopiae, you see, and nobody back at Naval Intel bothered asking what a robot factory can do tactically.'

Commander Murametz shook his head. 'I don't know. Sir? Does it have any military bearing?'

'Yes. You see, robots can *breed*. And spawn starwisps.'

'Starwisps –' Enlightenment dawned. Ilya looked shocked. 'How big would they be?' he asked the captain.

'About half a kilogram mass. You can cram a lot of guidance circuitry into a gram of diamond-substrate nanomachinery. The launchers that fire them probably mass a quarter of a tonne each – but a large chunk of that is stored antimatter to power the neutral particle beam generators. At a guess, there could be a couple of thousand out here; that's probably what those low aspect contacts are. If you trip-wire one of them, and it launches on you, expect the starwisp riding the beam to come out at upward of ten thousand gees. But of course, you probably won't even see it unless it gets lock-on and you get some side-scattered radiation from the beam. Basically, we're in the middle of a minefield, and the mines can shoot relativistic missiles at us.'

'But –' Ilya looked horrified. 'I thought this was a standard firing setup!'

'It is, Commander,' Bauer said drily.

'Ah.' Ilya looked slightly green at the edges.

'Backscatter!' It was Radar Three. 'I have backscatter! Something is launching from target alpha, acceleration one-point-three – no, one-point-five gees. Cooking off gammas at one-point-four MeV.'

'Log as candidate one,' said Ilya. Urgently: 'Sir, humbly request permission to resume immediate control?'

'Granted,' snapped the Captain.

Rachel glanced around at the ops room stations. Officers hunched over their workstations, quietly talking into head-set microphones and adjusting brass-handled dials and switches. Mirsky walked over to the command station and stood at Ilya's shoulder. 'Get radar looking for energy spikes,' he commented. 'This is going to be difficult. If I'm right, we're in the middle of a minefield controlled by a central command platform; if we leak again, we're not getting out of here.' Rachel leaned forward too, focusing on the main screen. It was, she thought, remarkable: if this was typical of their teamwork, then with a bit of luck they might even make it into low orbit around Rochard's World.

The tension rose over the next ten minutes, as the *Lord Vanek* accelerated toward the target. Its singularity drive was virtually undetectable, even at close range (spotting the mass of a mountain at a million kilometers defied even the most sensitive gravity-wave detectors), but all the enemy strong-point had to do was switch on a pulse-doppler radar sweep and the battlecruiser would show up like a sore thumb. The first rule of space warfare – and the ancient submarine warfare that preceded it – was, 'If they can see you, they can kill you.'

On the other hand, the enemy base couldn't be sure exactly where the ship was right now; it had changed course immediately after shutting down its search lidar. Four more brief lidar pulses had swept across the ship's hull, as other members of the squadron dropped in and took their bearings: since then, nothing but silence.

'Second trace!' called Radar One. 'Another live bird moving out. Range on this one is four-seven M-klicks, vector toward lidar source three, the *Suvaroff*.'

'Confirm course and acceleration,' ordered Ilya. 'Log it as candidate two.'

'Confirm three more,' said Radar Two. 'Another source, um, range nine-zero M-klicks. Designation beta. They're thick around here, aren't they?'

'Watch out for a—'

'Third echo from local target alpha,' called Radar Two. 'Scattering relative to candidates one and two. Looks like a third missile. This one's heading our way.'

'Give me a time to contact,' Mirsky said grimly. Rachel studied him: Mirsky was a wily old bird, but even though he'd figured out what was going on, she couldn't see how he planned to pull their chestnuts out of the fire. At any moment she expected to hear the shriek of alarms as one or another observer picked up the telltale roar of a relativistic particle stream, with a beam-riding starwhisp hurtling toward them on top of it, armed with a cargo of antimatter.

Of course, it was too much to expect the New Republic's government to realize just how thoroughly they were out-classed; their cultural bias was such that they couldn't perceive the dangers of something like the Festival. Even their best naval tacticians, the ones who understood forbidden technologies like self-replicating robot factories and starwisps, didn't comprehend quite what the Festival might do with them.

The *Lord Vanek*'s chances of surviving this engagement were thin. In fact, the entire expedition was predicated on the assumption that what they were fighting was sufficiently human in outlook to understand the concept of warfare and to use the sort of weapons overeducated apes might throw at one another. Rachel had a hopeless, unpleasant gut feeling that acting without such preconceptions, the Festival would be far deadlier to the New Republican expeditionary force than they could imagine. Unfortunately, it appeared she was going to be around when they learned the hard way that interstellar wars of aggression were much easier to lose than to win.

'More backscatter. Target gamma! We have another target – range two-seven-zero M-klicks. Ah, another missile launching.'

'That's –' Ilya paused. 'One base per cubic AU? One M bases, if they're evenly distributed through the outer system.' He looked stunned.

'You don't think you're fighting *people*, do you?' asked Mirsky. 'This is a fully integrated robot defense network. And it's big. Mind-bogglingly big.' He looked almost pleased with his own perspicacity. 'The Admiralty didn't listen when I explained it to them the first time, you know,' he added. 'Eighteen years ago. One of the reasons I never made flag rank –'

'I listened,' Bauer said quietly. 'Proceed, Captain.'

'Yes sir. Solution on target alpha?'

Fire control: 'Time to range on target alpha, two-zero-zero seconds, sir.'

'Hmm.' Mirsky contemplated the display. 'Commander. Your opinion.'

Ilya swallowed. 'I'd get in close and use the laser grid.'

Mirsky shook his head, slightly. 'You forget they may have X-ray lasers.' Louder: 'Relativity, I want you ready to give me a microjump. If I give the word, I want us out of here within five seconds. Destination can be anywhere within about one-zero AUs, I'm not fussy. Can you do that?'

'Aye aye, sir. Kernel is fully recharged; we can do that. Holding at T minus five seconds, now.'

'Guns: I want six SEM-20s in the tube, armed and ready to launch in two minutes. Warheads dialed for directional spallation, two-zero degree spread. Three of them go to alpha target; hold the other three in reserve ready for launch on five seconds' notice. Next, load and arm two torpedoes. I want them hot and ready when I need them.'

'Aye aye, sir. Three rounds for alpha, three in reserve, and two torpedoes. Six birds on the rail awaiting your command. The hot crew is fueling the torpedoes now; they should be ready in about four minutes.'

'That's nice to know,' Mirsky said, a trifle too acid; the lieutenant at the gunnery console flinched visibly. 'As you were,' added the Captain.

'Proximity in one-two-zero seconds, sir. Optimum launch profile in eight-zero.'

'Plot the positions of the nearest identified mines. Show vectors on command station alpha, assuming they fire projectiles holding a constant acceleration of ten kilo-gees. Can they nail us in just four-zero seconds?'

'Checking, sir.' Navigation. 'Sir, they can't nail us before we take out that command post, unless target alpha also has a speed demon or two up his sleeve. But they'll get us one-five seconds later.'

Mirsky nodded. 'Very good. Guns: we launch at four-zero seconds to target. Helm, relativity: at contact plus five seconds, that's five seconds *after* our fire on target, initiate that microjump.'

'Launch T minus five-zero seconds, sir . . . mark.'

Rachel watched the display, a fuzzball of red pinpricks and lengthening lines. Their own projected vector, in blue, stretched toward one of the red dots, then stopped abruptly. Any second now, she guessed, something nasty was bound to happen.

Guns: 'T minus three-zero. Birds warm. Launch grid coming up to power now. T minus two-zero.'

Radar One interrupted: 'I'm picking up some fuzz from astern.'

'One-zero seconds. Launch rails energized,' added the gunnery post.

'Fire on schedule,' said the captain.

'Yes, sir. Navigation updated. Inertial platforms locked. Birds charged, warheads green.'

'Light particles!' yelled Radar One. 'Big explosion off six M-klicks, bearing six-two by five-nine! Looks like – damn, one of the cruisers bought it. I'm getting a particle stream from astern! Bearing one-seven-seven by five, sidescatter, no range yet –'

'Five seconds to launch. Launch commencing, bird one running. Lidar lock. Drive energized. Bird one main engine ignition confirmed. Bird two loaded and green . . . running. Gone. Drive energized. Bird three running –'

'Radar One, I have a lidar lock! ECM engaged from directly astern Someone's painting us. I have a range – five-two K – and –'

Mirsky stepped forward. 'Guns. I want all three spare missiles ejected straight astern now. Passive seekers, we will illuminate the targets for them.'

'Aye aye, sir. Bird four, coming up . . . green. Bird four running. Five, green, running.'

'Radar Two, we have a seeker on our tail. Range four-five K, closing at – Holy Mother of God, I don't believe it!'

'Bird six running astern. What do you want me to lock on?'

'Radar Two, feed your plot to gunnery for birds four through six to target. Guns, shoot as soon as you see a clear fix – buy us some time.'

'Aye aye, sir.' The Lieutenant, ashen-faced, hunched over his console and pushed buttons like a man possessed.

'Range to firing point on alpha?' asked Mirsky.

'Three-zero seconds, sir. You want to push the attack?' The nav officer looked apprehensive. Every watt of power they pumped at the attack salvo via the laser grid was one watt less to point at the incoming interceptor.

'Yes, Lieutenant. I'll trust you not to tell me my job.' The nav officer flushed and turned back to his console. 'Guns, what's our situation?'

'I've pumped the forward birds right up, sir, maximum acceleration the warheads will take. MECO is in one-five seconds. Soon as that happens I'll divert power to our trailers. Ah, bird one burnout in one-zero seconds.'

Rachel nodded to herself. Remembering lectures on the basics of relativistic physics, strategy in the post-Einsteinian universe, and the implications of a light cone expanding across an evenly spaced grid of points. *Any moment now the fossil light from the next shell of interceptors should reach us . . .*

'Holy Father!' shouted Radar Three. 'I have beam spillover on all sides! We're boxed!'

'Control yourself,' snapped Mirsky. 'How many sources?'

'They – they –' radar punched buttons. Red lines appeared on the forward screen. 'One-six of 'em, coming in from all points!'

'I see.' Mirsky stroked his moustache. 'Helm, are you ready with that micro jump?'

'Yes, sir.'

'Good.' Mirsky smiled, tight-lipped. 'Guns, status.'

'Bird one burnout. Boosting bird four. Bird two, bird three, burnout. I'm diverting all propulsion beam power to the second salvo. Salvo time to target, one-five seconds. Ah, we have one-seven inbound aggressors. Three outbound antimissiles.'

'Hold further fire,' ordered the Captain. 'How long until the first hostile is in range?'

'Should happen at – oh. Two seconds postcontact, sir.'

'Nav! Pull the jump forward five seconds. We'll not stay around to count coup.'

'Aye aye.'

Radar One: 'More scattering! Sir, I have . . . no, they're not going to get us in time.'

'How many, Lieutenant?'

'We're boxed. Incoming beamriders in all directions, at long range. I count –'

'Bird one detonating now! Bird two, detonating. Bird three gone. Sir, three detonations on target.'

'Jump in five. Four –'

'One-eight-point-nine K – no, one-nine K beamriders incoming!'

'Incoming number one, range one-two K and closing –'

'Confirmed kill on target alpha, oxygen, nitrogen in emission spectra.'

'Two.'

'Nine K.'

'Three-two K incoming hostiles! No, three-two and –'

'One. Jump commit.'

The red emergency lights dimmed as the main overhead lights came up. There was silence on the bridge for a moment, then Commodore Bauer cleared his throat. 'Congratulations, gentlemen,' he announced to Mirsky and his stunned ops crew. 'Of all the ships in the squadron who have run that tape so far, you are the only one to have escaped at all, much less to have taken any of the enemy down. There will be a meeting in my office at 1600 to discuss the assumptions underlying this exercise and explain our new tactical doctrine for dealing with situations like this – massively ramified robot defense networks with fire control mediated by causal channel. Then we'll run it again tomorrow and see how well you do with your eyes open . . .'

diplomatic behavior

Meanwhile, two thousand years away, a small boy lay curled in darkness, whimpering in the grip of a dream of empire.

Felix moaned and shivered and dragged the tattered blanket closer around his shoulders. The abandoned hay loft was unheated, and the gaps between the log walls admitted a furious draft, but at least it was a roof over his head. It was warmer than the stony ground. Wolves roamed the untamed wilderness, and for a lad to sleep beneath the stars at this time of year was hazardous even in normal times.

Raven roosted on the thick oak beam above Felix's head, his long black beak tucked under one wing. Occasionally, he would wake for a moment, shake his feathers out, shuffle from one foot to the other, and glance around. But as long as the door stayed barred, nothing could reach them that he couldn't deal with; and so he would rejoin his master in sleep.

Rain battered on the roof, occasionally leaking through the sods that covered the rough-cut timber, dripping to the floor in thin cold streams. The smell of half-decayed hay hung heavy in the air. Felix hadn't dared light a fire after Mr. Rabbit pointed out how dangerous that could be. There were things out there that could see heat, silent things without mouths. Things that liked to eat little boys' brains.

Felix dreamed of Imperial orders, men in shiny uniforms, and women in silky gowns; of starships and cavalry parades and ceremonies and rituals. But his dreams were invaded by a tired and pervasive cynicism. The nobles and officers were corrupt hangers-on, their women grasping harpies searching for security. The ceremonies and rituals were meaningless and empty, a charade concealing a ghastly system of institutional injustices orchestrated to support the excesses of the rulers. Dreaming of New Prague, he felt himself to be a duke or prince, mired in a dung heap, chained down by responsibility and bureaucracy, unable to move despite the juggernaut of decaying corruption bearing down on him.

When he twitched and cried out in his dream, Mr. Rabbit crawled closer and sprawled against him, damp fur rising and falling with his breath. Presently Felix eased deeper into sleep, and Mr. Rabbit rolled away, curling nose to tail to resume his nightly regurgitation and cud-chewing. If it was hard being a small boy in a time of rapid change, it was a doubly hard burden to be a meter-tall rabbit cursed with human sentience and cunicular instincts.

In the early-morning light, Felix yawned, rubbed his eyes, and stretched stiffly, shivering with cold. 'Rabbit?'

'Caaaw!' Raven flapped down from overhead and hopped closer, head cocked to one side. 'Rabbit gone to vill-lage.'

Felix blinked, slowly. 'I wish he'd waited.' He shivered, feeling a sense of loneliness very alien to a nine-year-old. He stood up and began to pack his possessions into a battered-looking haversack; a blanket, a small tin can, a half-empty box of matches, and one of the curious metal phones by which the Festival communicated with people. He paused over the phone for a moment, but eventually his sense of urgency won, and he shoved it into the pack. 'Let's play *hunt the wabbit*,' he said, and opened the door.

It was a cold, bright morning, and the ground in the abandoned farmyard was ankle deep in squelching mud. The blackened ruin of the house squatted on the other side of the quagmire like the stump of a tree struck by lightning, the Holy Father's fire. Behind it, a patch of dusty gray mud showed the depletion layer where the Festival's nanosystems had sucked the soil dry of trace elements, building something huge; it was almost certainly connected with the disappearance of the farmer and his family.

The village lay about two kilometers downhill from the farmhouse, around a bend in the narrow dirt track, past a copse of tall pine trees. Felix shrugged on his backpack and, after a brief pause to piss against the fire-blackened wall of the house, slowly headed down the road. He felt like whistling or singing, but kept his voice to himself; there was no telling what lived in the woods hereabouts, and he wasn't inclined to ignore Mr. Rabbit's warnings. He was a very serious little boy, very grown-up.

Raven hopped after him, then flapped forward heavily and landed in the ditch some way down the path. His head ducked repeatedly. 'Brrrreak-fast!' he cawed.

'Oh, good!' Felix hurried to catch up, but when he saw what Raven had found to eat he turned away abruptly and pinched the bridge of his nose until the tears came, trying not to gag. Tears came hard; a long time ago, a very long distance away, Nurse had told him, 'Big boys don't cry.' But he knew better now. He'd seen much bigger boys crying, men even, as they were stood up against the bullet-pocked wall. (Some of them didn't cry, some of them held themselves stiffly upright, but it made no difference in the end.) 'Sometimes I hate you, Raven.'

'Caaww?' Raven looked up at him. The thing in the ditch was still wearing a little girl's dress. 'Hungrrry.'

'You might be – but I we've got to find Pyotr. Before the Mimes catch us.'

Felix looked over his shoulder nervously. They'd been running scared, one jump ahead of the Mimes, for the past three days. The Mimes moved slowly, frequently fighting an invisible wind or trying to feel their way around intangible buildings, but they were remorseless. Mimes never slept, or blinked, or stopped moving.

A hundred meters closer to the village, the phone woke up. It chirped like a curious kitten until Felix rummaged through his bag and pulled it out. 'Leave me alone!' he exclaimed, exasperated.

'Felix? It's Mr. Rabbit.'

'What?' He looked at the phone, startled. Chrome highlights glinted beneath grubby oil-slick fingerprints.

'It's me. Your flop-eared friend. I'm in the village. Listen, don't come any closer.'

'Why not?' He frowned and carried on walking.

'They're here. My luck ran out; don't think I can get away. You –' The giant lagomorph's voice broke into something utterly inhuman for a moment, a rodent squeal of rage and fright. '– Behind you, too! Go crosscountry. *Run, boy.*'

The phone buzzed, disconnected. Felix raised it angrily, meaning to dash it to the ground, then stopped. Ahead of him. Raven stared at him, beady-eyed and bloody-beaked. 'Fly over the village,' Felix ordered the bird. 'Tell me what you see.'

'Caaaw!' Raven took a running leap into the air, lumbering heavily over the grass, then climbing up over the treetops. Felix looked at the phone again, mingled rage and grief in his eyes. It wasn't fair! Nothing was fair! All he wanted was to be young and carefree, and to have fun. The companions came later; at first there had been Mrs. Hedgehog as well, but she'd been killed by a random Fringe performance, electrical discharges flashing to ground from an ionosphere raped by induced solar flares. The Fringe was like that; a mindless thing, infinitely dangerous and fickle, as trustworthy as a venomous snake but sometimes capable of producing works of great beauty. (The auroral displays had lasted for weeks.)

Felix looked around, nervously. Over the hedgerow, back down the road, something seemed to move. He held the phone to his cheek. 'Somebody talk to me?'

'*Will you entertain us?*'

'I don't know how!' he burst out.

'*Tell story. Provide entertaining formal proof of correctness. Sing, dance, clap your hands.*'

'What will you do for me in return?'

'*What do you require?*' The voice on the other end of the line sounded tinny, distant, compressed through the bandwidth ligature of a causal channel.

'Bad men are after me. They throw custard pies, turn me into one of them. Can you stop them? Protect me from the Mimes?'

'*Tell story.*' It wasn't a statement or a question, it was an order.

Felix took a deep breath. He glanced up and saw Raven circling overhead. He jumped the ditch, then ducked under the first branches and began to weave his way into the woods. He talked as he walked. 'In the beginning there was a duke who lived in a palace, on the banks of the river, overlooking the only city on the world. He wasn't a very wise duke, but he did what he thought was best for his people. Then one morning, it began to rain telephones, and the world changed. This is the duke's story.'

It was a long and rambling story, and it went on for some time. How the duke's palace had been besieged by anarchist terrorists, who unleashed chaos and plastic cutlery on the town. All his soldiers deserted after looting the palace and the zoo; he escaped through a secret passage under the Curator's waiting rooms in the sub-sub-basement. The elderly duke had escaped with three trusty retainers. Grief-stricken, he had barely been able to understand what had happened to his world. Why had everything changed? A telephone chirped at him, like a curious kitten, from the rubbish in a back alley. He bent to pick it up and the motion saved his life for two renegade soldiers shot at him with their rifles. They killed Citizen Von Beck, but not before the Citizen marked them with his slow gun – for the Citizens of the Curator's Office were allowed to use forbidden weapons in the course of their duties. (Bullets from a slow gun flew on hummingbird wings, seeking their prey wherever they might flee. Bullets from a slow gun killed by stinging with their neurotoxin barbettes, like wasps with secret police insignia. They were a terror weapon, to demonstrate the horrors of unrestricted technology.)

Felix slipped down a root-woven embankment and crossed a clearing studded with green-sprouting stumps as he continued. The duke talked to the phone in his despair, and it offered him three wishes. He asked to be made young again, thinking it a bitter joke; to his surprise, his youth was magically restored. Next, he asked for companions; and he was given friends, wonderful friends, who would do anything for him and ask nothing in return. Even the third wish, the little-boy wish made in the first flush of restored youth, had been granted. None of which was exactly what he'd wanted, or would have asked for had he not been in a very disturbed state of mind at the time, but it was better than the wishes some people he'd met subsequently had made. (The kulak whose wish had been a goose that laid golden eggs, for example. It was a wonderful animal, until you held it close to a railway man's dosimeter and discovered the deluge of ionizing radiation spewing invisibly from the nuclear alchemist's stone in its gizzard. Which you only thought to do when the bloody stools became too much to bear, and your hair began to fall out in clumps.)

The duke-turned-child had walked across three hundred kilometers in the past month, living from hand to mouth. His friends had looked after him, though. Raven, who could see over and around things, told him of traps or ambushes or deadfalls before he walked into them. Mr. Rabbit hopped along at his side, and with his acute hearing, nose for trouble, and plain, old-fashioned common sense, kept him from starving or freezing to death. Mrs. Hedgehog had helped, too, bustling around, cooking and cleaning and keeping camp, occasionally fending off beggars and indigent trash with her bristles and sharp teeth. That was before the lightning storm took her.

But somewhere along the way, the little duke had begun to regain his sense of purpose – and with it, a great depth of despair. Everywhere he looked, crops rotted in the fields. Once-sober peasants upped stakes and took to the skies in mile-high puffball spheres of spun-sugar glass and diamond. Wisewomen aged backward and grew much wiser, unnaturally so – wise until their wisdom leaked out into the neighborhood, animating the objects around them with their force of will. Ultimately, the very wise lost their humanity altogether and fled their crumbling human husks, migrating into the upload afterlife of the Festival. Intelligence and infinite knowledge were not, it seemed, compatible with stable human existence.

The little duke had talked to some of the people, tried to get them to understand that this wasn't going to last forever; sooner or later, the Festival would be over, and there would be a dreadful price to pay. But they laughed at him, calling him names when they discovered who he had been in his previous existence. And then someone set the Mimes on him.

A crash of branches and a caw of alarm; Raven crunched down onto his shoulder, great claws gripping his arm hard enough to draw blood. 'Mimes!' hissed the bird. 'Nevermore!'

'Where?' Felix looked around, wide-eyed.

Something crackled in the underbrush behind him. Felix turned, dislodging Raven, who flapped heavily upward, cawing in alarm. A human shape lurched into view on the other side of the clearing. It was male, adult in size, powdery white in color from head to foot. It moved jerkily like damaged clockwork, and there was no mistaking the circular, yellowish object it held in its right hand.

'Pie-ie-ie!' croaked Raven. 'Time to die!'

Felix turned away from the Mime and put his head down. He ran blindly, branches tearing at his head and shoulders, shrubbery and roots trying to trip him up. Distantly, he heard the screaming and cawing of Raven mobbing the Mime, flapping clear of the deadly flan and pecking for eyes, ears, fingers. Just one sticky strand of orange goo from the pie dish would eat clear through bone, its disassembly nanoware mapping and reintegrating neural paths along its deadly way, to convert what was left of the body into a proxy presence in realspace.

The Mimes were broken, a part of the Fringe that had swung too close to a solar flare and succumbed to bit rot several Festival visits ago. They'd lost their speech pathways, right down to the Nucleus of Chomsky, but somehow managed to piggyback a ride on the Festival starwisps. Maybe this forcible assimilation was their way of communicating, of sharing mindspace with other beings. If so, it was misguided at best, like a toddler's attempt to communicate with a dog by hitting it; but nothing seemed to deter them from trying.

A wordless scream from behind told him that Raven had certainly distracted that particular Mime. But Mimes traveled in packs. Where were the others? And where was Mr. Rabbit, with his trusty twelve-bore and belt of dried farmer's scalps?

Noise ahead. Felix staggered to a stop. He was still holding the phone. 'Help,' he gasped into it.

'*Define help parameters.*'

A fuzzy white shape moved among the trees in front of him. It had once been a woman. Now it was powder white, except for blood-red lips and bobble nose: layers of white clothing shrouded its putrefying limbs, held together with a delicate lacework of silvery metallic vines that pulsed and contracted as it moved. It swayed from side to side as it approached, bending coquettishly at the hips, as if the base of its spine had been replaced by a universal joint. It clutched a large pie dish in both bony hands. Collapsed eye sockets lined with black photoreceptive film grinned at him as it bowed and extended the bowl, like a mother offering her spoiled son his favorite desert.

Felix gagged. The smell was indescribable. 'Kill it. Make it go away,' he whimpered. He fell back against a tree. 'Please!'

'*Acknowledged.*' The Festival voice remained dusty and distant, but somehow its tone changed. '*Fringe security at your service. How may we be of assistance?*'

The Mimes were closing in. 'Kill them!' Felix gasped. 'Get me out of here!'

'*Target acquisition in progress. X-ray laser battery coming on-line. Be advised current orbital inclination is not favorable for surgical excision. Cover your eyes.*'

He threw an arm across his face. Bones flashed in red silhouette, followed a split second later by a crash of thunder and a blast of heat, as if someone had opened the oven door of hell right in front of his face. His skin prickled as if Mrs. Hedgehog was embracing him, only all over. Trees falling in the forest, a flapping of panic-stricken wings. The flash and bang repeated itself a second later, this time behind him; then three or four more times, increasingly distant.

'Incident Control stand down. Threat terminated. Be advised you have received an ionizing radiation dose of approximately four Greys, and that this will be life-threatening without urgent remediation. A medical support package has been dispatched. Remain where you are, and it will arrive in twenty-two minutes. Thank you for your custom, and have a nice day.'

Felix lay gasping at the base of his tree. He felt dizzy, a little sick: after-images of his femur floated in ghostly purple splendor across his eyes. 'I want Mr. Rabbit,' he mumbled into the phone, but it didn't answer him. He cried, tears of frustration and loneliness. Presently, he closed his eyes and slept. He was still asleep when the spider slipped down from the stars and wove him into a cocoon of silvery not-silk to begin the task of dissolving and re-forming his radiation-damaged body yet again. This was the third time so far; it was all his own fault for making that third wish. Youth, true friends . . . and what every little boy wished for in his heart, without quite grasping that an adventure-filled life isn't much fun when you're the person who has to live it.

Martin sat on the thin mattress in his cell, and tried to work out how many days he had left before they executed him.

The fleet was six days out from the final jump to Rochard's World. Before that, they'd probably transfer supplies from the remaining support freighters and put any supernumeraries – conscripts who'd gone mad, contracted crippling diseases, or otherwise become superfluous to requirements – on board. Maybe they'd move him over and send him back with the basket cases, back to the New Republic to face trial on the capital charge of spying in the dockyard. Somehow, he doubted that his defense (of shipyard necessity) would do him much good; that snot-nosed assistant from the Curator's Office had it in for him, quite obviously, and would stop at nothing to see him hang.

That was one option. Another was that he'd be kept in the brig aboard ship until it arrived. At which point they'd realize that the cumulative clock-delay he'd bodged into the *Lord Vanek*'s fourspace guidance system had screwed the pooch, completely buggering their plan to sneak up on the Festival via a spacelike trajectory. In which case, they'd logically assume sabotage, and they'd have the saboteur already in the cells, trussed like a turkey for Thanksgiving.

Somehow, the fact that he'd succeeded, that his mission was accomplished and the threat of a wider causality violation averted, did not fill Martin with happiness. There might, he supposed, be heroes who would go to the airlock with a spring in their step, but he wasn't one of them; he'd rather be opening Rachel's bedroom door than opening that other door, learning to breathe in her muff rather than learning to inhale vacuum. It was, he supposed dismally, typical of the pattern of his life to fall in love – the kind of annoying obsession that won't go away – just before stumbling irremediably into the shit. He'd been around enough to think he had few illusions left; Rachel had edges rough enough to use as a nail file, and in some ways, they had very little in common. But being banged up alone in a tiny cell was a frighteningly lonely experience, all the lonelier for knowing that his lover was almost certainly less than thirty meters away – and completely unable to help him. Probably under suspicion herself. And however much he needed her, he didn't, in all honesty, want her in here with him. He wanted to be with her on the outside – preferably somewhere many light-years from the New Republic, acquiring a long history of having absolutely nothing to do with it.

He lay back, rolled over on his stomach, and closed his eyes. Then the toilet began talking to him in a faint, buzzing voice.

'If you can hear me, tap one finger on the deck next to the base of the toilet, Martin. Just one.'

I've lost it, he thought. *They won't bother executing me; they'll put me in one of their psychiatric zoos and let the children throw bananas.* But he reachead out a hand and tapped at the base of the stainless-steel toilet that extruded from the wall of his cell.

'That's –' he sat up, and the voice went away abruptly.

Martin blinked and looked around. No voices. Nothing else had changed in the cell; it was still too hot, stuffy, with a constant background smell of bad drains and stale cabbage. (The cabbage was inexplicable; the menu had long since shifted to salt beef and ship's biscuit, a recipe perversely retained by the New Republic's Navy despite the ready avail- ability of vacuum and extreme cold millimeters beyond the outer pressure hull of the ship.) He lay down again.

'– just one. If you can –'

He closed his eyes and, as if at a seance, rapped once, hard, on the base of the toilet.

'Received. Now tap –' The voice paused. 'Tap once for each day you've been in the tank.'

Martin blinked, then rapped out an answer.

'Do you know Morse code?'

Martin racked his brains. It had been quite a long time – 'yes,' he tapped out. A mostly obsolete skill, that low-band- width serial code set, but one that he *did* know, for a simple reason: Herman had insisted he learn it. Morse was human- accessible, and a sniff for more sophisticated protocols might easily miss something as mundane as the flnger-tapping back channel in a video call.

'If you lie with your head up against the side of the toilet bowl, you will hear me better.'

He blinked. *Bone conduction?* No, something else. The induction wires around his auditory nerves – some high-frequency source must be shorting out against the metal of the toilet, using it as an antenna! Inefficient, but if it wouldn't carry far . . .

'Identify yourself,' he signaled.

The reply came in Morse. 'AKA Ludmilla. Who watched us over dinner?'

'The boy wonder,' he tapped out. He slumped against the floor, shivering in relief. Only two people could reasonably be on the other side of the pipe, and the Curator's Office wasn't likely to authenticate his identity that way. 'What's your relay?'

'Spy drone in sewage system jammed against effluent valve. One of batch accidentally released by idiot subcurator. Told them to find you. Fuel cells in drone very low, drained by conduction telephone. Prefer Morse. Martin, I am trying to get you out. No luck so far.'

'How long till arrival?' he tapped urgently.

'Ten days to low-orbit arrival. If not released first, expect rescue day of arrival. Attempting to assert diplomatic cover for you.'

Ten days. Rescue – if they didn't stick him on a freighter under armed guard and ship him back to execution dock, and if Rachel wasn't whistling in the face of a storm. 'Query rescue.'

'Diplomatic life belt big enough for two. Power level approaching shutdown will try to send another relay later. Love you. Over.'

'I love you, too,' he tapped hopefully, but there was no reply.

A myriad of tiny gears whirred, clucked, and buzzed in a background hum of gray noise beneath a desktop. Optical transducers projected a magic-lantern dance of light on the wall opposite. The operator, gold-leafed collar unbuttoned, leaned back in his chair and dribbled smoke from his nostrils: a pipe dangled limply between his knuckles as he stared at the display.

There was a knock on the door.

'Come in,' he called. The door opened. He blinked: came to his feet. 'Ah, and what can I do for you, Procurator?'

'A m-moment of your time if I may, sir?'

'By all means. Always a pleasure to be of service to the Basilisk. Have a seat?'

Vassily settled down behind the desk, visibly uncomfortable. The shadow play of lights danced on the wall, thin blue smoke catching the red-and-yellow highlights and coiling lazily in midair. 'Would this be the, ah, our state vector?'

For a moment Security Lieutenant Sauer considered hazing the lad; he reluctantly shelved the idea. 'Yes. Not that there's much to be made of it, unless you're interested in the topology of five-dimensional manifolds. And it's only theoretical, until we arrive at the far end and relativistics come out with a pulsar map to confirm it. I'm trying to study it; promotion board ahead you know, once this affair is straightened out.'

'Hmm.' Vassily nodded. Sauer wasn't the only Navy officer expecting a promotion to come out of this campaign. 'Well, I suppose you could look on the bright side; we're most of the way there now.'

Sauer pursed his lips, raised his pipe, and sucked. 'I would never say that. Not until we know the enemy's dead and buried at a crossroads with a mouthful of garlic.'

'I suppose so. But your lads will take care of that, won't they? Meanwhile it's my people who have to come in afterward and do the tidying up, keep this sort of thing from happening again.'

Sauer looked at the young policeman, maintaining a polite expression despite his mild irritation. 'Is there something I can help with?'

'Er, yah, I think so.' The visitor leaned back. He reached into his tunic pocket and withdrew a cigar case. 'Mind if I smoke?'

Sauer shrugged. 'You're my guest.'

'Thank you!'

For a minute they were silent, lighters flaring briefly and blue-gray clouds trailing in the airflow to the ceiling vents. Vassily tried to suppress his coughing, still not quite accustomed to the adult habit. 'It's about the engineer in the brig.'

'Indeed.'

'Good.' *Puff.* 'I was beginning to wonder what is going to happen to him. I, er, gather that the last supply ships will be dropping off their cargo and heading home in a couple of days, and I was wondering if . . .?'

Sauer sat up. He put his pipe down; it had flamed out, and though the bowl was hot to the touch, it held nothing but white-stained black shreds. 'You were wondering if I could sign him over to you and put you on the slow boat home with your man in tow.'

Vassily half smiled, embarrassed. 'Exactly right, I'm sure. The man's guilty as hell, anyone can see that; he needs to be sent home for a proper trial and execution – what do you say?'

Sauer leaned back in his chair and contemplated the analytical engine. 'You have a point,' he admitted. 'But things aren't quite so clear-cut from where I'm sitting.' He relit his pipe.

'Nice tobacco, sir,' ventured Vassily. 'Tastes a bit funny, though. Very relaxing.'

'That'll be the opium,' said Sauer. 'Good stuff, long as you don't overdo it.' He puffed contentedly for a minute. 'Why do you think Springfield's in the brig in the first place?'

Vassily looked puzzled. 'It's obvious, isn't it? He violated Imperial regulations. In fact, that's just what I'd been looking for.'

'Executing him isn't going to make it easy for the

Admiralty to convince foreign engineers to come work for us, though, is it?' Sauer sucked on his cigar. 'If he was a spacer, lad, he'd have done the frog kick in the airlock already. I'll tell you what. If you insist on dragging him home on the basis of what you found on him, all that will happen is that the Admiralty will sit on it for a few months, hold an inquiry, conclude that no real harm was done, court-martial him for something minor, and sentence him to time served – on general principles, that is – and leave you looking like an idiot. You don't want to do that; trust me, putting a blot on your record card at this stage in the game is a bad move.'

'Ah, so what do you suggest, sir?'

'Well.' Sauer stubbed out his cigar and looked at it regretfully. 'I think you're going to have to decide whether or not to have a little flutter on the horses.'

'Horses, sir?'

'Gambling, Mr. Muller, gambling. Double or quits time. You *have* decided that this engineer is working for the skirt from Earth, no? It seems a justifiable suspicion to me, but there is a lack of firm evidence other than the disgraceful way she plays for him. Which, let us make no mistake, could equally well be innocent – disreputable but innocent of actual criminal intent against the Republic, I say. In any event, she has made no sign of wrongdoing, other than possessing proscribed instruments in her diplomatic bag and generally being detrimental to morale by virtue of her rather unvirtuous conduct. We have no grounds for censure, much less for declaring her *persona non grata*. And irritating though she may be, her presence on this mission was decreed by His Excellency the Archduke. So I think the time has come for you to either shit or get off the can. Either accept that Mr. Springfield is probably going to waltz free, or shoot for the bigger target and hope you find something big to pin on her so that we can overcome her immunity.'

Vassily turned pale. Perhaps it hadn't really sunk in until now; he'd overstepped his authority already, rummaging in Rachel's cabin, and either he must find a justification, or his future was in jeopardy. 'I'll gamble, sir. Do you have any recommendations, though? It seems like an awfully big step; I wouldn't want to make any mistakes.'

Sauer grinned, not unpleasantly. 'Don't worry, you won't. There're others who want her out of the way and are willing to stick their necks out a bit to help. Here's how we'll flush her cover . . .'

invitation to an execution

A ragged row of crucifixes capped the hill overlooking the road to Plotsk. They faced the narrow river that ran along the valley, overlooking Boris the Miller's waterwheel: their brown-robed human burdens stared sightlessly at the burned-out shell of the monastery on the other bank. The abbot of the Holy Spirit had gone before his monks, impaled like a bird on a spit.

'Kill them all, God will know his own,' Sister Seventh commented mockingly as she turned the doorway to face the grisly row. 'Not is what their nest father-mother's said in times gone before?'

Burya Rubenstein shivered with cold as the bird-legged hut strode along the road from Novy Petrograd. It was a chilly morning, and the fresh air was overlaid with a tantalizingly familiar odor, halfway between the brimstone crackle of gunpowder and something spicy-sweet. No smell of roast pork: they'd burned the monastery after killing the monks, not before. 'Who did this?' he asked, sounding much calmer than he felt.

'You-know-who,' said the Critic. 'Linger not thisways: understand Fringe performers hereabout more so deranged than citywise. Mimes and firewalker bushbabies. *Very* dangerous.'

'Did they –' Burya swallowed. He couldn't look away from the fringe on the hilltop. He was no friend of the clergy, but this festival of excess far outstripped anything he could have condoned. 'Was it the Fringe?'

Sister Seventh cocked her head on one side and chomped her walrus tusks at the air. 'Not,' she declared. 'This is human work. But headlaunchers have herewise been seeding corpses with further life. Expect resurrection imminently, if not consensually.'

'Headlaunchers?'

'Fringeoids with fireworks. Seed brainpan, cannibalize corpus, upload and launch map containing mindseeds to join Festival in orbit.'

Burya peered at the row of crosses. One of them had no skull, and the top of the crucifix was charred. ''M going to be sick –'

He just made it to the edge of the hut in time. Sister Seventh made it kneel while he hung head down over the edge, retching and dry-heaving on the muddy verge below.

'Ready to continue? Food needed?'

'No. Something to drink. Something stiff.' One corner of the hut was stocked with a pyramid of canned foodstuffs and bottles. Sister Seventh was only passingly familiar with human idiom; she picked up a large tin of pineapple chunks, casually bit a hole in it, and poured it into the empty can that Burya had been using as a cup for the past day. He took it silently, then topped it up with schnapps from his hip flask. The hut lurched slightly as it stood up. He leaned against the wall and threw back the drink in one swallow.

'Where are you taking me now?' he asked, pale and still shivering with something deeper than a mere chill.

'To Criticize the culprits. *This* is not art.' Sister Seventh bared her fangs at the hillside in an angry gape. 'No esthetics! Zip plausibility! Pas de preservatives!'

Rubenstein slid down the wall of the hut, collapsing in a heap against the pile of provisions. Utter despair filled him. When Sister Seventh began alliterating she could go on for hours without making any particular sense.

'Is it anyone in particular this time? Or are you just trying to bore me to death?'

The huge mole-rat whirled to face him, breath hissing between her teeth. For a moment he flinched, seeing grinning angry death in her eyes. Then the fire dimmed back to her usual glare of cynical amusement. 'Critics know who did this thing,' she rasped. 'Come judge, come Criticize.'

The walking hut marched on, carrying them away from the execution ground. Unseen from the vestibule, one of the crucified monk's habits began to smolder. His skull exploded with a gout of blue flame and a loud bang as something the size of a fist flew up from it, a glaring white shock contrail streaming behind. One more monk's mind – or what had been left of it after a day of crucifixion, by the time the headlaunch seed got to it – was on its way into orbit, to meet the Festival datavores.

The hut walked all day, passing miracles, wonders, and abominations on every side. Two thistledown geodesic spheres floated by overhead like glistening diadems a kilometer in diameter, lofted by the thermal expansion of their own trapped, sun-heated air. (Ascended peasants, their minds expanded with strange prostheses, looked down from their communal eyrie at the ground dwellers below. Some of their children were already growing feathers.) Around another hill, the hut marched across a spun-silver suspension bridge that crossed a gorge that had not been there a month before – a gorge deep enough that the air in its depths glowed with a ruddy heat, the floor obscured by a permanent Venusian fog. A rhythmic thudding of infernal machinery echoed up from the depths. Once, a swarm of dinner-plate-sized, solar-powered silicon butterflies blitzed past, zapping and sputtering and stealing any stray electrical cabling and discrete components in their path: a predatory Stuka the size of an eagle followed them, occasionally screaming down in a dive that ended with one of their number crumpled and shredded in the claws sprouting from its wheel fairings. 'Deep singularity,' Sister Seventh commented gnomically. 'Machines live and breed. Cornucopia evolution.'

'I don't understand. What caused this?'

'Emergent property of complex infocology. Life expands to fill environmental niches. Now, machines reproduce and spawn as Festival maximizes entropy, devolves into way station.'

'Devolves into –' he stared at the Critic. 'You mean this is only a *temporary* condition?'

Sister Seventh looked at him placidly. 'What made you think otherwise?'

'But –' Burya looked around. Looked at the uncared-for fields, already tending toward the state of weed banks, at the burned-out villages and strange artifacts they were passing. 'Nobody is prepared for that,' he said weakly. 'We thought it would last!'

'Some will prepare,' said the Critic. 'Cornucopiae breed. But Festival moves on, flower blossoming in light of star before next trip across cold, dark desert.'

Very early the next day, they came within sight of Plotsk. Before the Festival incursion, Plotsk had been a sleepy gingerbread market town of some fifty thousand souls, home to a regional police fortress, a jail, two cathedrals, a museum, and a zeppelin port. It had also been the northernmost railhead on the planet, and a departure point for barges heading north to the farms that dotted the steppes halfway to the Boreal Ocean.

Plotsk was barely recognizable today. Whole districts were burned-out scars on the ground, while a clump of slim white towers soared halfway to the stratosphere from the site of the former cathedral. Burya gaped as something emerald green spat from a window halfway up a tower, a glaring light that hurtled across the sky and passed overhead with a strange double boom. The smell, half gunpowder and half orchids, was back again. Sister Seventh sat up and inhaled deeply. 'One loves the smell of wild assemblers in the morning. Bushbot baby uploads and cyborg militia. Spires of bone and ivory. Craving for apocalypse.'

'What are you talking about!' Burya sat on the edge of the pile of smelly blankets from which the Critic had fashioned her nest.

'Is gone nanostructure crazy,' she said happily. 'Civilization! Freedom, Justice, and the American Way!'

'What's a merkin way?' Burya asked, peeling open a fat garlic bratwurst and, with the aid of an encrusted penknife, chopping large chunks off it and stuffing them into his mouth. His beard itched ferociously, he hadn't bathed in days, and worst of all, he felt he was beginning to understand Sister Seventh. (Nobody should have to understand a Critic; it was cruel and unusual punishment.)

A bright green glare flashed on above them, shining starkly in through the doorway and lighting up the dingy corners of the hut. '*Attention! You have entered a quarantined area! Identify yourselves immediately!*' A deep bass humming shook Burya to his bones. He cringed and blinked, dropping his breakfast sausage.

'Why not you answer them?' Sister Seventh asked, unreasonably calmly.

'Answer them?'

'*ATTENTION! Thirty seconds to comply!*'

The hut shook. Burya stumbled, treading on the wurst. Losing his temper, he lurched toward the doorway. 'Stop that racket at once!' he yelled, waving a fist in the air. 'Can't a man eat his breakfast in peace without you interfering, you odious rascals? Cultureless imbeciles, may the Duke's whore be taken short and piss in your drawers by mistake!'

The light cut out abruptly. '*Oops*, sorry,' said the huge voice. Then in more moderate tones, '*Is that you, Comrade Rubenstein?*'

Burya gaped up at the hovering emerald diamond. Then he looked down. Standing in the road before him was one of Timoshevski's guards – but not as Burya had known him back in Novy Petrograd.

Rachel sat on her bunk, tense and nervous. Ignoring the banging and clattering and occasional disturbing bumps from the rear bulkhead, she tried desperately to clear her head. She had a number of hard decisions to make – and if she took the wrong one, Martin would die, for sure, and more than that, she might die with him. Or worse, she might be prematurely bugging out, throwing away any chance of fulfilling her real mission. Which made it all the harder for her to think straight, without worrying.

Thirty minutes ago an able flyer had rapped on her door. She'd hastily buttoned her tunic and opened it. 'Lieutenant Sauer sends his compliments, ma'am, and says to remind you that the court-martial convenes this afternoon at 1400.'

She'd blinked stupidly. 'What court-martial?'

The flyer looked nonplussed. 'I don't know, ma'am. He just told me to tell you –'

'That's quite alright. Go away.'

He'd gone, and she'd hurriedly pulled her boots on, run a comb through her hair, and gone in search of someone who knew.

Commander Murametz was in the officers' wardroom, drinking a glass of tea. 'What's all this about a court-martial?' she demanded.

He'd stared at her, poker-faced. 'Oh, it's nothing,' he said. 'Just that engineer who's under arrest. Can't have him aboard when we go into battle, so the old man scheduled a hearing for this afternoon, get the business out of the way.'

'What do you mean?' she asked icily.

'Can't go executing a man without a fair trial first,' Ilya said, barely bothering conceal his contempt. He rapped his glass down next to the samovar. 'Trial's in this very room, this afternoon. Be seeing you.'

The next thing she knew she was back in her cabin. She couldn't remember getting there; she felt cold and sick. *They want to kill Martin,* she realized. *Because they can't get at me any other way.* She cursed herself for a fool. Who was behind it, how many enemies had she racked up? Was it the Admiral? (Doubtful, he didn't need the formality of a trial if he wanted to have someone shot.) Or Ilya – yes, there was someone who'd taken against her. Or the kid spook, the wet-behind-the-ears secret policeman? Or maybe the Captain? She shook her head. Someone had decided to get her, and there were no secrets aboard the ship; however discreet she and Martin had thought they'd been, someone had noticed.

The cold emptiness in her stomach congealed into a knot of tension. This whole voyage was turning into a fiasco. With what she'd learned from Martin – including his mission – there was no way the Navy could make a success of it; in fact, they'd probably all be killed. Her own role as a negotiator was pointless. You negotiate with human beings, not with creatures who are to humans as humans are to dogs and cats. (Or machines, soft predictable machines that come apart easily when you try to examine them but won't fit back together again.) Staying on was useless, it wouldn't help her deliver the package for George Cho, and as for Martin –

Rachel realized she had no intention of leaving him behind. With the realization came a sense of relief, because it left her only one course of action. She leaned forward and spoke quietly. 'Luggage: open sesame. Plan Titanic. You have three hours and ten minutes. Get started.' Now all she had to do was work out how to get him from the kangaroo court in the wardroom to her cabin; a different, but not necessarily harder task than springing him from the brig.

The trunk silently rolled forward, out from under her bunk, and its lid hinged back. She tapped away at the controls for a minute. A panel opened, and she pulled out a reel of flexible hose. That went onto the cold-water tap on her tiny sink. A longer and fatter hose with a spherical blob on the end got fed down the toilet, a colonoscopy probing the bowels of the ship's waste plumbing circuit. The chest began to hum, expelling pulses of viscous white liquid into the toilet tube. Thin filaments of something like plastic began to creep back up the bowl of the toilet, forming a tight seal around the hose; a smell of burning leaked into the room, gunpowder and molasses and a whiff of shit. Rachel checked a status indicator on the trunk; satisfied, she picked up her gloves, cap, anything else she would need – then checked the indicator again, and hastily left the room.

The toilet rumbled faintly, and pinged with the sound of expanding metal pipework. The vent pipe grew hot; steam began to hiss from the effluent tube, and was silenced rapidly by a new growth of spiderweb stuff. An overhead ionization alarm tripped, but Rachel had unplugged it as soon as she arrived in her cabin. The radiation warning on the luggage blinked, unseen, in the increasingly hot room. The diplomatic lifeboat was beginning to inflate.

*

'Don't worry. son. It'll work.' Sauer slapped Procurator Muller on the back.

Vassily forced a wan smile. 'I hope so, sir. I've never attended a court-martial before.'

'Well.' Sauer considered his words carefully. 'Just think of this as an educational experience. And our best opportunity to nail the bitch legally . . .'

Truth be told, Sauer felt less confident than he was letting on. This whole exercise was more than slightly unauthorized; it exceeded his authority as ship's security officer, and without the active support of Commander Murametz, first officer, he wouldn't have dared proceed with it. He certainly didn't have the legal authority to convene a court-martial on his own initiative in the presence of superior officers, much less to try a civilian contractor on a capital charge. What he *did* have was a remit to root out subversion by any means necessary, including authorized deception, and a first officer willing to sign on the dotted line. Not to mention an institutional enthusiasm to show the Curator's agent up for the horse's ass that he was.

They were short of time. Since coming out of their jump on the edge of the inner system, the heavy squadron had been running under total radio silence at a constant ten gees, the heavy acceleration compensated for by the space-time-warping properties of their drive singularities. (Ten gees, without compensation, would be enough to make a prone man black out; bone-splintering, lung-crushing acceleration.) There had apparently been some sort of navigation error, a really bad one which had the admiral's staff storming about in a black fury for days, but it hadn't betrayed them to the enemy, which was the main thing.

Some days ago, the squadron had flipped end over end and executed a deceleration sequence to slow them down to 100 k.p.s. relative to Rochard's World. In the early hours of this morning, they had reached engagement velocity; they would drift the last thirty light-seconds, resuming acceleration (and increasing their visibility) only within active radar range of the enemy. Right now, they were about two million kilometers out. Some time around midnight, shipboard time, they would begin their closest approach to the planet, go to full power, and engage the enemy ships – assuming they were willing to come out and fight. (If they didn't, then the cowards had conceded control of the low orbital zone to the New Republic, tantamount to abandoning their ground forces.) In any event, any action against the UN inspector had to be completed before evening, when the ship would lock down for battle stations – assuming they didn't run into anything before then.

In Sauer's view, it was a near miracle that Ilya had agreed to join in this deception. He could easily have scuppered it, or referred it to Captain Mirsky, which would have amounted to the same thing. This close to a major engagement, just detaching himself plus a couple of other officers who didn't have active duty stations to prepare was enough of a wonderment to startle him.

Sauer walked up to the table at the front of the room and sat down. It was actually the officer's dining table, decked out in a white tablecloth for the occasion, weighted down with leather-bound tomes that contained the complete letter of the Imperial Articles of. War. Two other officers followed him; Dr. Hertz, the ship's surgeon, and Lieutenant Commander Vulpis, the relativist. They looked suitably serious. Sauer cleared his throat. 'Court will come to order,' he intoned. 'Bring in the accused.'

The other door opened. Two ratings marched in, escorting Martin Springfield who, being hobbled and handcuffed, moved rather slowly. Behind them, a door banged. 'Ah, er, yes. Please state your name for the court.'

Martin looked around. His expression was pale but collected. 'What?' he said.

'Please state your name.'

'Martin Springfield.'

Lieutenant Sauer made a note on his blotter. Irritated, he realized that his pen held no ink; no matter. This wasn't an affair that called for written records. 'You are a civilian, subject of the United Nations of Earth. Is that correct?'

A look of irritation crept over Martin's face. 'No it bloody isn't!' he said. 'I keep telling you people, the UN is not a government! I'm affiliated to Pinkertons for purposes of legislation and insurance; that means I obey their rules and they protect me against infringers. But I've got a backup strategic infringement policy from the New Model Air Force which, I believe, covers situations like this one. I've also got agreements with half a dozen other quasi-governmental organizations, but none of them is entitled to claim sovereignty over me – I'm not a slave!'

Dr. Hertz turned his head and looked pointedly at Sauer; his pince-nez glinted beneath the harsh glare of the tungsten lamps. Sauer snorted. 'Let it be entered that the accused is a subject of the United Nations of Earth,' he intoned.

'No he isn't.' Heads turned. While Martin had been speaking, Rachel Mansour had slipped in through a side door. Her garb was even more scandalous than usual; a skintight white leotard worn beneath various items of padding and a bulky waistcoat resembling a flak jacket. *Almost like a space suit liner*, Sauer noted, puzzled. 'The United Nations is not a –'

'Silence!' Sauer pointed at her. 'This is a court of military justice, and I do not recognize your right to speak. Stay silent, or I'll have you thrown out.'

'And create a diplomatic incident?' Rachel grinned unpleasantly. 'Try it, and I'll make sure you regret it. In any event, I believe the accused is permitted to retain an advocate for the defense. Have you advised him of his rights?'

'Er –' Vulpis looked down.

'Irrelevant. The trial will continue –'

Martin cleared his throat. 'I'd like to nominate Colonel Mansour as my advocate,' he said.

It's working. Sauer made a pretense of scribbling on his blotter. At the back of the room, he could see Vassily's sharp intake of breath. The young whippersnapper was getting his hopes up already. 'The court recognizes UN inspector Mansour as the defendant's counsel. I am obliged to warn you that this trial is being conducted under the Imperial Articles of War, Section Fourteen, Articles of Combat, in view of our proximity to the enemy. If you are ignorant of those rules and regulations, you may indicate so and withdraw from the trial now.'

Rachel's smile broadened. 'Defense moves for an adjournment in view of the forthcoming engagement. There will be plenty of time for this after the battle.'

'Denied,' Sauer snapped. 'We need a fair trial on the record before we can execute the sentence.' *That* made her smile slip. 'Court will go into recess for five minutes to permit the defendant to brief his advocate, and not one minute longer.' He rapped on the table with his fist, stood, and marched out of the room. The rest of the tribunal followed suit, trailed by a paltry handful of spectators, leaving Rachel, Martin, and four ratings standing guard on the doors.

'You know this is just a rubber stamp? They want to execute me,' Martin said. His voice was husky, a trifle unsteady; he wrung his hands together, trying to stop them from shaking.

Rachel peered into his eyes. 'Look at me, Martin,' she said quietly. 'Do you trust me?'

'I – yes.' He glanced down.

She reached a hand out, across the table, put it across the back of his left wrist. 'I've been reading up on their procedures. This is well out of order, and whatever happens I'm going to lodge an appeal with the Captain – who should be chairing this, not some jumped-up security officer who's also running the prosecution.' She glanced away from him, looking for the air vents; simultaneously, she tapped the back of his hand rapidly. He tensed his wrist back in a well-understood pattern, message understood: *Next session. See me blink three times you start hyperventilating. When I blink twice hold breath.*

His eyes widened slightly. 'There won't be time for them to do anything before perigeon, anyway,' she continued verbally. 'We're about two astronomical units out and closing fast; engagement should commence around midnight if there's to be a shooting war.' *Got lifeboat*, she added via Morse Gode.

'That's –' he swallowed. *How escape?* he twitched. 'I'm not confident they're going to observe all the niceties. This kangaroo court –' He shrugged.

'Leave it all to me,' she said, squeezing his hand for emphasis. 'I know what I'm doing.' For the first time, there was hope in his expression. She broke contact and leaned back in her chair. 'It's stuffy in here,' she complained. 'Where's the ventilation?'

Martin looked past her head. She followed his gaze: grilles in the ceiling. She closed her eyes and squeezed shut; green raster images like a nightmare vision of a jail cell pasted themselves across the insides of her eyelids. The spy drones, remnant of the flock Vassily had unleashed, waited patiently behind the vents. They'd followed her to this room, loaded up with a little something to add interest to the proceedings. *Serve the little voyeur right*, she thought bitterly about the spy. 'I'll get you out of this,' she told Martin, trying to reassure him.

'I understand.' He nodded, a slight inclination of his head. 'You know what I, uh, I'm not so good at people things –'

She shook her head. 'They're doing this to get me to compromise myself. It's not about you. It's nothing personal. They just want me out of the way.'

'Who?'

She shrugged. 'The midranking officers. The ones who figure a short victorious war is a ticket up the promotion ladder. The ones who don't think I should be here in the first place, much less reporting back. Not after First Lamprey. I was Red Cross agent-in-place there, you know? Investigating the war crimes. Didn't leave anybody looking too good, and I think they know it. They don't want a negotiated settlement, they want guts and glory.'

'If it's just you, why's the chinless wonder from the Curator's Office in here?' asked Martin.

She shrugged. 'Two birds, one stone. Don't sweat it. If they screw this up, they can blame the Curator's cat's-paw, make the enemy within look bad. There's no love lost between Naval Intelligence and the civil secret police. If it works, they get us both out of the way. Reading the regs, they don't have authority to pull this stunt, Martin. It takes a master and commander to issue a capital sentence except in the face of the enemy, so if they do execute you, it's illegal enough to hang them all.'

'That's a great reassurance.' He forced a smile, but it came out looking decidedly frightened. 'Just do your – hell. I trust you.'

'That's good.'

Then the doors opened.

'It's working.' Sauer commented. 'She's come out to defend her minion. Now we need to maneuver her into outright defiance. Shouldn't be too hard; we have the bench.'

'Defiance?' Vulpis raised an eyebrow. 'You said this was a trial.'

'A trial of wits, ours against hers. She's consented to defend him; that means she's acting as an officer of the court. Article Forty-six states that an officer of the court is subject to the discipline of the Articles and may himself be arraigned for malfeasance or contempt of court. By agreeing to serve before our court, she's abandoning her claim of diplomatic immunity. It gets better. In about two hours, we go to stations. While we may be a charade right now, at that point *any* commissioned officer is empowered to pass a capital sentence – or even order a summary execution – because it's classified under Article Four, Obedience in the Face of the Enemy, Enforcement Thereof. Not that I'm *planning* on using it, but it does give us a certain degree of cover, no?'

Dr. Hertz removed his pince-nez and began to polish them. 'I'm not sure I like it,' he said fussily. 'This smells altogether too much of the kind of trickery the Stasis like handing down. Aren't you concerned about playing for the Curator's brat?'

'Not really.' Sauer finally grinned. 'Y'see, what I really plan on doing is to get our new advocate so thoroughly wound up she's insubordinate or something – but for the defendant himself, I'm thinking of an absolute discharge or a not guilty verdict.' He sniffed. 'It's quite obvious he didn't know he was breaking any regulations. Plus, the device he had in his possession was inactive by the time it was discovered, so we can't actually prove it was in a state fit for use at any time when he was aboard the ship. And the Admiralty will be angry if we make it hard for them to hire civilian contractors in future. I'm hoping we can keep her rattled enough not to realize there's no case to answer until we've got her out of the way; then we discharge Springfield. Which will make our young Master Muller look like a complete and total idiot, not to mention possibly supplying me with cause to investigate *him* for suspicion of burglary, pilferage of personal effects, violation of a diplomat's sealed luggage, immoral conduct, and maybe even deserting his post.' His grin became sharklike. 'Need I continue?'

Vulpis whistled quietly in awe. 'Remind me never to play poker with you,' he commented.

Dr. Hertz reinstalled his spectacles. 'Shall we resume the circus, gentlemen?'

'I think so.' Sauer drained his glass of tea and stood up. 'After you, my brother officers, then send in the clowns!'

The shipping trunk in Rachel's cabin had stopped steaming some time ago. It had shrunk, reabsorbing and extruding much of its contents. A viscous white foam had spread across the fittings of the cabin, eagerly digesting all available hydrocarbons and spinning out a diamond-phase substrate suitable for intensive nanomanufacturing activities. Solid slabs of transparent material were precipitating out of solution, forming a hollow sphere that almost filled the room. Below the deck, roots oozed down into the ship's recycling circuits, looting the cesspool that stored biological waste during the inbound leg of a journey. (By long-standing convention, ships that lacked recyclers only discharged waste when heading away from inhabited volumes of space; more than one unfortunate orbital worker had been gunned down by a flash-frozen turd carrying more kinetic energy than an armor-piercing artillery shell.)

The self-propelled trunk, which was frozen into the base of the glassy sphere, was now much lighter than it had been when Rachel boarded the ship. Back then, it had weighed the best part of a third of a tonne: Now it massed less than fifty kilos. The surplus mass had mostly been thick-walled capillary tubes of boron carbide, containers for thin crystals of ultrapure uranium-235 tetraiodide, and a large supply of cadmium; stuff that wasn't easy to come by in a hurry. The trunk was capable of manufacturing anything it needed given the constituent elements. Most of what it wanted was carbon, hydrogen, and oxygen, available in abundance in the ship's sewage-process plant. But if a diplomat needed to get away in a real hurry and didn't have a potent energy source to hand . . . well, fission, an old and unfashionable technology, was eminently storable, very lightweight, and didn't usually go bang without a good reason. All you needed was the right type of unobtanium to hand in order to make it work. Which was why Rachel had been towing around enough uranium to make two or three good-sized atom bombs, or the core of a nuclear saltwater rocket.

A nuclear saltwater rocket was just about the simplest interplanetary propulsion system that could fit in a steamer trunk. On the other side of the inner pressure hull from Rachel's cabin, the trunk had constructed a large tank threaded through with neutron-absorbing, boron-lined tubes: this was slowly filling with water containing a solution of near-critical uranium tetraiodide. Only a thin layer of carefully weakened hull plates and bypassed cable ducts held the glassy sphere and its twenty-tonne saltwater fuel tank on the other side of the bulkhead, inside the warship. The hybrid structure nestled under the skin of the ship like a maggot feeding on the flesh of its host, preparing to hatch.

Elsewhere in the ship, toilets were flushing sluggishly, the officer's shower cubicle pressure was scandalously low, and a couple of environment techs were scratching their heads over the unexpectedly low sludge level in the number four silage tank. One bright spark was already muttering about plumbing leaks. But with a full combat engagement only hours away, most attention was focused on the ship's weapons systems. Meanwhile, the luggage's fabricator diligently churned away, extruding polymers and component materials to splice into the lifeboat it was preparing for its mistress. With only a short time until the coming engagement, speed was essential.

'Court wil reconvene.' Sauer rapped on the tabletop with an upturned glass. 'Defendant Martin Springfield, the charges laid against you are that on the thirty-second day of the month of Harmony, Year 211 of the Republic, you did with premeditation carry aboard the warship *Lord Vanek* a communications device, to wit a causal channel, without permission from your superior officer or indeed any officer of that ship, contrary to Article Forty-six of the Articles of War; and that, furthermore, you did make use of the said device to communicate with foreign nationals, contrary to Article Twenty-two, and in so doing, you disclosed operational details of the running of the warship *Lord Vanek* contrary to Section Two of the Defense of the Realm Act of 127, and also contrary to Section Four of the Articles of War, Treachery in Time of War. The charges laid against you therefore constitute negligent breach of signals control regulations, trafficking with the enemy, and treason in time of war. How do you plead?'

Before he could open his mouth, Rachel spoke up. 'He pleads not guilty to all charges. And I can prove it.' There was a dangerous gleam in her eyes; she stood very straight, with her hands clasped behind her back.

'Does the accused accept that plea?' Vulpis intoned.

'The colonel speaks for me,' said Martin.

'First, evidence supporting the charges. Item: on the thirty-second day of the month of Harmony, year 211 of the Republic, you did with premeditation carry aboard the warship *Lord Vanek* a communications device, to wit a causal channel, without permission from your superior officer or indeed any officer of that ship, contrary to Article Forty-six. Clerk, present the item.'

A rating stepped forward, stony-faced, bearing a small paper bag. He shook the contents out over the tabletop; a small, black memory cartridge. 'Item one: a type twelve causal channel, embedded within a standard model CX expansion cartridge as used by personal assist machines throughout the decadent Terran sphere. The item was removed from defendant's personal assist machine by Junior Procurator Vassily Muller, of the Curator's Office on assignment to monitor the conduct of the defendant, on the thirty-second day of

Harmony as noted. A sworn deposition by the Procurator is on record. Does anyone contest the admissibility of this evidence? No? Good –'

'I do.' Rachel pointed at the small black cartridge. 'Firstly, I submit that the Junior Procurator's search of the defendant's personal property was illegal and any evidence gained from it is inadmissible, because the defendant is a civilian and not subject to the waiver of rights in the oath of allegiance sworn by a serving soldier – his civil rights, including the right to property, cannot be legally violated without a judicial warrant or an order from an official vested with summary powers subject to Article Twelve. Unless the Junior Procurator obtained such an order or warrant, his search was illegal and indeed may constitute burglary, and any information gathered in the process of an illegal search is not admissible in court. Secondly, if that thing is a causal channel, I'm a banana slug. That's a standard quantum dot storage card; if you get a competent electronic engineer in, they'll tell you the same. Thirdly, you don't have authority to hold this charade of a trial; I've been checking in the Articles, and they state quite clearly that courts-martial can only be convened by order of the senior officer present. Where's your written order from the Admiral?'

She crossed her arms and stared at the bench.

Sauer shook his head. 'The Junior Procurator has standing orders to investigate Springfield; that makes anything he does legal in the eyes of the Curator's Office. And I must register my extreme displeasure at the defense's imputation that I do not have authority to convene this court. I *have* obtained such authority from my superior officer and will use it.' Carefully, he avoided specifying precisely what kind of authority he had. 'As for the item of evidence being misidentified, we have on record a statement by the defendant to the effect that it is a causal channel, which he was asked to carry aboard by foreign parties, to wit the dockyard. As the Articles concern themselves specifically with intent, it does not matter whether the item is in fact a banana slug: the defendant is still guilty of thinking he was carrying a communications device.'

He paused for a moment. 'Let it be entered that the item of evidence was admitted.' He glared at Rachel: *Got you, you bitch. Now what are you going to do?*

Rachel glanced at Martin and blinked rapidly. Then she turned back to face the bench. 'A point of law, sir. As it happens, thinking is not generally considered the same as doing. Indeed, in this nation, which refuses to even consider the use of thought-controlled machinery, the distinction is even sharper than in my own. You appear to be attempting to try the defendant for his opinions and beliefs rather than his actions. Do you have any evidence of his actually passing on information to a third party? If not, there is no case to answer.'

'I have *exactly* that.' Sauer grinned savagely. 'You should know who he's been passing on information to.' He pointed at her. 'You are a known agent of a foreign power. Defendant has been communicating freely with you. Now, since you consented to defend him, you are acting as an officer of this court. I refer you to Article Forty-six: "Any person deputized to act as an officer of the court is subject to the discipline of the Articles." I conclude that you have courageously agreed to waive your diplomatic immunity in order to attempt to rescue your spy from the hangman's noose.'

For a moment, Rachel looked confused; she looked at Martin again, blinking rapidly. Then she turned back to the bench. 'So you rigged this whole kangaroo court as an attempt to work around my immunity? I'm impressed. I really didn't think you'd be quite this stupid – *Utah!*'

Everything happened very quickly. Rachel dropped to her knees behind her makeshift desk; Sauer made a motion toward the ratings at the back of the room, intending to have them arrest the woman. But before he could do more than open his mouth, four sharp bangs burst around the room. The overhead air-conditioning ducts split open; *things* dropped down, complex and many-armed things squirting pale blue foam under high pressure. The foam stuck to everything it touched, starting with the judge's bench and the guards at the back of the makeshift courtroom: it was lightweight but sticky, rapidly setting into a hard foam matrix.

'Get her!' Sauer shouted. He grabbed for his pistol, but somewhere along the way a huge gobbet of blue foam engulfed his arm and cemented it to his side. A strong chemical odor came from the foam, something familiar from childhood visits to the dentist. Sauer breathed deeply, struggling to dislodge the sticky mass, and the fruity, sickly stench cut into his lungs; then the world turned hazy.

Rachel knew things were going to turn pear-shaped from the moment she walked into the room. She'd seen judges in hanging mode before, back on Earth, and on a dozen assignments since then. You could almost smell it, an acrid and unreasoning eagerness to order an execution, like the stench of death itself. This board had it – and something else. A sly reserve, a smug sense of anticipation; as if the whole thing was some kind of tremendous joke, with a punch line she could only guess at.

When the security lieutenant delivered it – a half-formed, inadequate punch line, in her opinion, obviously something he'd stitched up on an *ad hoc* basis to fit the occasion – she glanced around at Martin. *Please be ready*. She blinked three times and saw him stiffen, then nod; the prearranged signal. She turned back to the bench, blinking again: green-lights rippled behind her eyelids. 'State two,' she subvocalized, the radio mike in her throat relaying the command to the drones waiting in the ventilation ducts. She turned back to the bench. The three officers sat there, glowering at her like thunderclouds on a horizon. *Buy time.*

'A point of law, sir. As it happens, thinking is not generally considered the same as doing. –' She carried on, wondering how they'd react to effectively being accused of rigging this charade; either they'd back down, or –

'I have exactly that.' The political officer in the middle, the hatchet-faced one, grimaced horribly. 'You should know who he's been passing on information to.' He pointed straight at her. *Here it comes*, she thought. Subvocalizing again: 'Luggage. Query readiness state.'

'Lifeboat closed out for launch. Fuel storage subcritical and ready. Spare reaction mass loaded. Oxygen supply nominal. Warning, delta-vee to designated waypoint New Peterstown currently 86 k.p.s., decreasing. Total available maneuvering margin 90 k.p.s.' That would do, she decided. The saltwater rocket was nearly as efficient as an old-fashioned fusion rocket; back home, it would do for an Earth-Mars return trip, surface to surface. This was pushing it a bit – they wouldn't be able to ride it back up into orbit without refueling. But it would do, as long as –

'– I conclude that you have courageously agreed to waive your diplomatic immunity in order to attempt to rescue your spy from the hangman's noose.'

She swallowed, glanced at Martin and blinked twice, the signal for 'hold your breath.' *'Luggage: prep for launch. Expect crew arrival from one hundred seconds. Launch hold at T minus twenty seconds from that time.'* Once they burned that particular bridge and jumped overboard, all she could do was pray that the bridge crew wouldn't dare light off their radar – and risk warning the Festival – in order to find her and kill her. The lifeboat was a soap bubble compared to the capital ships of the New Republican naval force.

Rachel turned her attention back to the bench and took a deep breath, tensing. 'So you rigged this whole kangaroo court as an attempt to work around my immunity? I'm impressed. I really didn't think you'd be quite this stupid – *Utah!*'

She ducked. The last word was a shout, broadcast to the drones through her throat mike. A simultaneous crackle told her the shaped-charge cutters had blown. She yanked the transparent breather hood over her face and choked it shut, then powered up her cellular IFF.

The drones swarmed in through holes in the ceiling. Spiders and crabs and scorpions, all made of carbon polymers – recycled sewage, actually – they sprayed sticky antipersonnel foam everywhere, releasing anesthetic trichloromethane vapor wherever anyone struggled. A rating made a move toward her, and her combat implants took over; he went down like a sack of potatoes before she consciously noted his existence, rabbit-punched alongside the head by an inhumanly fast fist. Everything narrowed into the gap between herself and Martin, standing wide-eyed behind a table, his arms half-raised toward her and a rating already beginning to steer him toward the door.

Rachel went to combat speed, cutting her merely human nervous system out of the control loop.

Time slowed and light dimmed; the chains of gravity weakened, but the air grew thick and viscous around her. Marionettes twirled in slow motion all around as she jumped over a table and ran at Martin. His guard began to turn toward her and throw up an arm. She grabbed it and twisted, feeling it pop out of its socket. She threw a brisk left-handed punch at the other guard; ribs snapped like brittle cardboard, and a couple of the fine bones in the back of her hand fractured with the impact. It was hard to remember – hard to think – but her own body was her worst enemy, more fragile than her reflexes would admit.

She grabbed Martin with one arm, handling him delicately as bone china; the beginning of an *oof* of air from his lungs told her she'd winded him. The door wasn't locked, so she kicked it open and dragged Martin through before it had time to rebound closed. She dropped him and spun in place, slammed it shut, then grabbed in a vest pocket for a lump of something like putty. '*Omaha*,' she shouted into her throat mike. Strobing patterns of red-and-yellow light raced over the surface of the putty – visible in her mechanized vision – and she jammed it into the doorframe and spat on it. It turned blue and began to spread rapidly, a wave of sticky liquid rushing around the gap between door and wall, setting hard as diamond.

Between the glued door, the severed intercom cables, and the chloroform and antipersonnel foam, it might be a minute or two before anyone in the room managed to raise the alarm.

Martin was trying to double over and gasp. She picked him up and ran down the corridor. It was like wading through water; she rapidly discovered it was easier to kick off with one foot, then the other, like low-gee locomotion.

A red haze at the edge of her vision told her she was close to burnout. Her peripheral nervous system might have been boosted, but for this sort of speed, it relied on anaerobic respiration, and she was exhausting her reserves frighteningly fast. At the next intersection, a lift car stood open: she lurched into it, dragging Martin behind, and tapped the button for the accommodation level in officer country. Then she dropped back to normal speed.

The doors slid shut as the lift began to rise, and Martin began to gasp. Rachel slumped against the far wall, black spots hazing her vision as she tried to draw air into straining lungs. Martin was first to speak. 'Where – did you learn –'

She blinked. A clock spiraled in the left upper quadrant of her vision. Eight seconds since she'd yelled Utah – eight seconds? Minutes, maybe. She drew a deep breath that turned into a yawn, flushing the carbon dioxide from her lungs. All her muscles ached, burning as if there were hot wires running down her bones. She felt sick, and her left hand was beginning to throb violently. 'Special. Implants.'

'Think you nearly broke a – rib, back there. Where are we going?'

'Life. Boat.' *Gasp*. 'Like I said.'

A light blinked above them. They'd crawled up one floor. One more to go.

The door opened on the right level. Rachel staggered upright. Nobody there, which was a blessing; in her present state, she didn't know if she could put a hamster in its place, much less a soldier. She stepped out of the lift, Martin following. 'My room,' she said quietly. 'Try to look at ease.'

He raised his wrists. 'Wearing these?'

Shit. Should have ripped them apart before running out of boost. She shook her head and hunted in her hip pocket, pulled out a compact gray tube. 'Stun gun.'

They ran out of luck halfway down the last corridor. A door opened and a petty officer stepped out; he moved to give them room to pass, then his jaw dropped as he realized what he was seeing. 'Hey!'

Rachel shot him. 'Hurry,' she hissed over her shoulder, and stumbled ahead. Martin followed her. Her door was ahead, just around a curve in the corridor. '*Gold*,' she called to the waiting lifeboat.

Red lights flashed overhead: the PA system piped up, a warbling alert noise. 'Security Alert! Green deck accommodation sector B, two armed insurgents on the loose. Armed and dangerous. Security to Green deck accommodation B. Alert!'

'Shit,' Martin mumbled. A pressure door began to rumble shut ten meters ahead of them.

Rachel went to combat speed again, her vision greying almost immediately. She threw herself forward: stood directly beneath the door and thrust straight up at the descending pressure barrier. Martin moved forward with glacial slowness as she felt the motors bear down on her, trying to crush her in half. He ducked and swam under the barrier. She followed him, letting go, and stayed fast, even though her hands and feet were becoming numb and a deadly warning pincushion sensation pricked at her face. The door to her cabin was two meters away. '*Juno!*' she yelled at it through her throat mike, the word coming out in a high-pitched gabble that sounded like the croaking of an aged dinosaur to her ears.

The door swung open. Martin ran through inside, but it was too late for Rachel: she couldn't see, and her knees were beginning to give way. The combat acceleration stopped, and she felt herself floating, a bruised impact along one side.

Someone was dragging her over gravel and it hurt like hell.

Her heart sounded as if it was about to explode. She couldn't get enough air.

Sound of a door slamming.

Darkness.

circus of death

The committee for the Revolution had taken over the onion-domed orthodox cathedral in Plotsk, making it the headquarters of the Commissariat for Extropian Ideology. All those who rejected the doctrine of revolutionary optimization and refused to flee the town were dragged before the tribunal and instructed boringly and at length about the nature of their misdemeanor; then they were shot, minds mapped and uploaded into the Festival, and sentenced to corrective labor – usually all at once. There weren't many of them; for the most part, the population had fled into the wilderness, transcended, or happily adopted the revolutionary cause.

Sister Seventh's hut, spun from local memories of myth and legend uploaded into the noosphere of the Festival, squatted in the courtyard outside the Revolutionary Commissariat and defecated massively. Presently, the house stood and ambled in the direction of the cherry trees that fringed the square: it was hungry, and the Bishop's liking for cherry blossom wouldn't stop it eating.

Sister Seventh wrinkled her snout with displeasure and

ambled indoors. The floor of the church was full of plaintiffs, queuing to demand this or appeal that. They stood before a kitchen table parked in the middle of the nave, behind which sat half a dozen bored-looking revolutionary functionaries. The small, frenetic human called Rubenstein waved his arms and exhorted their chairman, who was so heavily augmented with mechanical add-ons that he clanked when he walked. The subject of the exhortation seemed to be something to do with the need to reverse the previous policy of destroying the artistically illiterate. True, that priority rated low in the estimates of the Critics – after all, you can't win an argument over esthetics with a corpse – but Rubenstein's willingness to change his mind after only a day or two in her company didn't commend his artistic integrity to her. These curious, lumpen humans were so impossibly gnomic in their utterances, so lacking in consistency, that sometimes she despaired of understanding their underlying esthetic.

Sister Seventh lost herself for a while in the flux of knowledge from the Festival. It let a filtered feed of its awareness escape, titillating the Critic colony in orbit, who relayed choice tidbits her way. The Festival propagated by starwisp, that much was true. It also relied on causal channels to relay its discoveries home. Now, great Higgs boson factories were taking shape in the rings of machinery orbiting Sputnik, icy gas and dust congealing into beat-wave particle accelerators on the edge of planetary space. Thousands of huge fusion reactors were coming on-stream, each pumping out enough energy to run a continental civilization. The first batch of new starwisps was nearing readiness, and they had a voracious appetite, a tonne of stabilized antimatter each; then there were the causal channels, petabytes and exabytes of entangled particles to manufacture and laboriously, non-observationally, separate into matching batches. The first starwisps would soon take on their payloads, point their stubby noses at the void, and accelerate at nearly half a million gees, sitting atop the neutral particle beams emitted by vast launch engines in high orbit above Rochard's World. Their primary destinations were the last two stops on the Festival's route, to deliver fresh channels and a detailed report on the current visit; their other destinations – well, the Festival had been encamped for three months. Soon the traders would arrive.

Traders followed the Festival everywhere. A self-replicating, natural source of causal channels, the Festival laid down avenues of communication, opening up new civilizations to trade – civilizations which, in the wake of a visitation, were usually too culture-shocked to object to the Traders' abstraction of the huge structures the Festival had constructed and abandoned for its own purposes. More than a thousand megafortunes had been made by natives of dirt-based trader civilizations with FTL ships and just enough nous to follow the trail of the Festival; like birds in the wake of a plow turning over rich farm soil, they waited to pounce on juicy nuggets of intellectual property turned up by the passing farmer.

Now something new tickled Sister Seventh's hindbrain. She stopped beside a font and stooped to drink. A message from She Who Observes the First. *Ships coming. Festival notices. Many ships coming in silence.* Now *that* was interesting; normally, the traders would appear like a three-ring circus, flashing lights and loud music playing on all available wavelengths, trying to attract attention. Stealth meant trouble. *Forty-two vessels itemized. All with drive kernels, all with low emissions: query thermal dump to stem, reduce visibility from frontal aspect. Range seven light-seconds.*

How peculiar. Sister Seventh straightened up. Someone – no, some construct of the Festival, human-child-high, but with long, floppy ears and a glossy fur coat, eyes mounted on the sides of its rodent face – was coming in through the side door.

Sister mine. What reflex of Festival? she asked silently. Hardwired extensions patched her through the Festival's telephonic nervous system, building a bridge to her sibling.

Festival has noticed. Current activities not over; will not tolerate interference. Three Bouncers have been dispatched.

Sister of Stratagems the Seventh shivered and bared her teeth. There were few things about the Festival that scared her, but Bouncers were second on the list, right behind the Fringe. The Fringe might kill you out of random pique. The Bouncers were rather less random . . .

The leporine apparition in the aisle bounced toward her, a panicky expression on its face. Burya stopped lecturing Timoshevski and looked around. 'What is it?' he demanded.

Timoshevski rumbled forward. 'Am thinking is rabbit stew for dinner.'

'No! Please, sirs! Help!' The rabbit stopped short of them, pushing two aggrieved babushkas aside, and held out its front limbs – arms, Sister Seventh noticed, with disturbingly human hands at their extremities. It was wearing a waistcoat that appeared to consist entirely of pockets held together by zip fasteners. 'Master in trouble!'

'Are no masters here, comrade,' said Timoshevski, apparently categorizing the supplicant as inedible. 'True revolutionary doctrine teaches that the only law is rationalism and dynamic optimism. Where are you from, and where is your internal passport?'

Rabbits have little control over their facial muscles; nevertheless, this one made a passable show of being nonplussed. 'Need *help*,' it bleated, then paused, visibly gathering self-control. 'My master is in trouble. Mime hunt! They got between us, a village ago; I escaped, but I fear they're coming this way.'

'Mimes?' Timoshevski looked puzzled. 'Not clowns?' A

metallic tentacle tipped in gun-muzzle flanges uncurled from his back, poked questing into the air. 'Circus?'

'Circus of death,' said Sister Seventh. 'Fringe performance, *very* poor. If coming this way, will interfere with popular acclaim of your revolution.'

'Oh, how so?' Timoshevski focused on Sister Seventh suspiciously.

'*Listen* to her, Oleg,' growled Burya. 'She came with the Festival. Knows what's going on.' He rubbed his forehead, as if the effort of making that much of a concession to her superior knowledge was painful.

'Oh?' Wheels turned slowly behind Timoshevski's skull; evidently his plethora of augmentations took a goodly amount of his attention to run.

Sister Seventh stamped, shaking the floor. 'Mimes are boring. Say help rabbit. Learn something new, maybe stage rescue drama?'

'If you say so.' Burya turned to Oleg. 'Listen, you're doing a reasonable job holding things down. I'd like to take six of your finest – who do I talk to? – and go sort these Mimes out. We really don't need them messing things up; I've seen what they do, and I don't like it.'

A sallow-faced commissar behind Oleg shouldered his way forward. 'I don't see why we should listen to you, you pork-fed cosmopolitan,' he snarled in a thick accent. 'This isn't your revolution; this is the independent Plotsk soviet soyuz community, and we don't take any centralist reactionary shit!'

'Quiet, Babar,' said Oleg. The tentacle sticking out of his back rotated to face the easterner: a dim red light glowed from its tip. 'Burya is good comrade. If wanted force centralism on us, am thinking he would have come with force, no?'

'He did,' said Sister Seventh, but the revolutionaries ignored her.

'He go with detachment of guards. End to argument,' Oleg

continued. 'A fine revolutionary; trust him do right by this — rabbit.'

'You better be right, Timoshevski,' grunted Babar. 'Not fools, us. Am not tolerating failure.'

Sauer was out of the wardroom and into the security watch office less than a minute after regaining consciousness, cursing horribly, blinking back a painful chloroform headache, and tugging creases from his rumpled and spattered tunic. The petty officer on duty sprang to his feet hastily, saluting; Sauer cut him off. 'General security alert. I want a full search for the UN spy and the shipyard engineer immediately, all points. Pull all the surveillance records for the UN spy in the past hour on my workstation, soon as you've got the search started. I want a complete inventory on all off-duty personnel as soon as you've done that.' He flung himself down behind his desk angrily. He ran fingers through his razor-cut hair and glared at the screen set into his desktop, then hit the switchboard button. 'Get me the duty officer in ops,' he grunted. Turning around, 'Chief, what I said — I need it now. Grab anyone you need.'

'Yes, sir. Excuse me, sir, beg permission to ask — what are we expecting?'

'The Terran diplomat is a saboteur. We flushed her, but she ran, taking the engineer with her. Which might have done us all a favor, except, firstly, they're still loose, and, secondly, they're armed and aboard this ship right now. So you're to look for crazed foreign terrorists with illegal off-world technology lurking in the corridors. Is that clear?'

'Yes, sir.' The flyer looked bemused. 'Very clear, sir.'

The workstation bonged. Sauer turned to face it. Captain Mirsky stared at him inquiringly; 'I thought you were busy keeping an eye on that damned chinless wonder from the Curator's Office,' he commented.

'Sir!' Sauer sat bolt upright. 'Permission to report a problem, sir!'

'Go ahead.'

'Security violation.' Sweat stood out on Sauer's forehead. 'Suspecting a covert agenda on the part of the Terran diplomat, I arranged a disinformation operation to convince her we had her number. Unfortunately, we convinced her too well; she escaped from custody with the shipyard engineer and is loose on the ship right now. I've started a search and sweep, but in view of the fact that we appear to have armed hostiles aboard, I'm recommending a full lockdown and security alert.'

The Captain didn't even blink. '*Do it.*' He turned around, out of camera view for a few seconds. 'The operations room is now sealed.' Beyond the sound-insulating door of the security office, a siren began to wail. 'Report your status.'

Sauer looked around; the rating standing by the door nodded at him. 'Beg to report, sir, security office is sealed.'

'We're locked down in here, sir,' said Sauer. 'The incident only began about three minutes ago.' He leaned sideways. 'Found the records yet, Chief?'

'Backtracking now, sir,' said the Chief Petty Officer. 'Ah, found external – *damn*. Begging your pardon, sir, but twelve minutes ago the surveillance cameras in Green deck, accommodation block – that's where her quarters are – were disabled. An internal shutdown signal via the maintenance track, authorized by – ah. Um. The shutdown signal was authorized under your ID, sir.'

'Oh.' Sauer grunted. 'Have you traced off-duty crew dispositions?'

'Yes, sir. Nobody was obviously out of bounds during the past hour. 'Course that doesn't mean anything – worst thing a sneak would normally get for being caught without a tracking badge would be a day or two in the brig.'

'You don't say. Get a team down there now, I want that cor-ridor covered!'

Sauer didn't remember the open phone channel until the Captain cleared his throat. 'I take it you're secure for the time being,' he said.

'Yes, sir.' The Lieutenant's ears began to turn red. 'Someone disabled the sensors outside the inspector's cabin, using my security authentication. Sir, she's really put one over on us.'

'So what are you going to do about it?' Mirsky raised an eyebrow. 'Come on. I want a solution.'

'Well –' Sauer stopped. 'Sir, I believe I've located the saboteurs. Permission to go get them?'

Mirsky grinned humorlessly. 'Do it. Take them alive. I want to ask them some questions.' It was the first time Sauer had seen his captain look angry, and it made his blood run cold. 'Yes, make sure they're alive. I don't want any accidents. Oh, and Sauer, another thing.'

'Sir?'

'When this is over I want a full, written report explaining how and why this whole incident happened. By yesterday morning.'

'*Yes, sir.*' The Captain cut the connection abruptly; Sauer stood up. 'You heard the man,' he said. 'Chief, I'm taking a pager. And arms.' He walked over to the sealed locker and rammed his thumb against it; it clicked open, and he began pulling equipment out. 'You're staying here. Listen on channel nineteen. I'm going to be heading for the cabin. Keep an eye on my ID. If you see it going somewhere I'm not, I want you to tell me about it.' He pulled on a lightweight headset, then picked up a taser, held it beside his temple while the two computers shook hands, then rolled his eyes to test the target tracking. 'Is that clear?'

'Yes, sir. Should I notify the red tabs on green deck?'

'Of course.' Sauer brought the gun to bear on the door. 'Open the hatch.'

'Aye aye, sir.' There was a click as latches retracted; the rating outside nearly dropped his coffee tray when he saw the Lieutenant.

'You! Maxim! Dump that tray and take this!' Sauer held out another firearm, and the surprised flyer fumbled it into place. 'Stick to channel nineteen. Don't speak unless you're spoken to. Now follow me.' Then he was off down the corridor, airtight doors scissoring open in front and slamming closed behind him, turning the night into a jerky red-lit succession of tunnels.

The first thing she realized was her head hurt. The second . . .

She was lying in an acceleration couch. Her feet and hands were cold. 'Rachel!'

She tried to say 'I'm awake,' but wasn't sure anything came out. Opening her eyes took a tremendous effort of will. 'Time. Wassat? How long −?'

'A minute ago,' said Martin. 'What's happened in here?' He was in the couch next to her. The capsule was claustrophobically tiny, like something out of the dawn of the space age. The hatch above them was open, though, and she could just see the inner door of her cabin past it. '*Hatch, close.* I said I had a lifeboat, didn't I?'

'Yeah, and I thought you were just trying to keep my spirits up.' Martin's pupils were huge in the dim light. Above him, the roof of the capsule began to knit itself together. 'What's going on?'

'We're sitting on top of −' She paused to pant for breath. 'Ah. *Shit.* On top of − a saltwater rocket. Fission. Luggage full of − of uranium. And boron. Sort of unobtanium you need in 'mergency, stuff you can't find easily. My little insurance policy.'

'You can't just punch your way out of an occupied space-ship!' Martin protested.

'Watch me.' She grimaced, lips pulling back from her teeth. 'Sealed – bulkheads. Airtight cocoon 'round us. Only question is—'

'*Autopilot ready*,' announced the lifeboat. An array of emergency navigation displays lit up on the console in front of them.

'Whether they shoot at us when we launch.'

'Wait. Let me get this straight. We're less than a day out from Rochard's World, right? This – thing – has enough legs to get us there? So you're going to punch a neat hole in the wall and eject us, and they're just going to let us go?'

''S about the size of it,' she said. Closing her eyes to watch the pretty blue displays projected on her retinas: 'About ten thousand gee-seconds to touchdown. We're about forty thousand seconds from perigee right now. So we're going to drift like a turd, right? Pretend to be a flushed silage tank. If they light out their radar, they give themselves away; if they shoot, they're visible. So they'll let us go, figure to pick us up later 's long as we get there after they do. If we try to get there first, they'll shoot . . .'

'You're betting the Festival will finish them off.'

'Yup,' she agreed.

'*Ready to arm initiator pump*,' said the autopilot. It sounded like a fussy old man.

'M' first husband,' she said. 'He always nagged.'

'And here was me thinking it was your favorite pet ferret.' Martin busied himself hunting for crash webbing. 'No gravity on this crate?'

''S not a luxury yacht.'

Something bumped and clanked outside the door. 'Oh shit.'

'We launch in – forty-two seconds,' said Rachel.

'Hope they give us that long.' Martin leaned over and began

strapping her into the couch. 'How many gees does this thing pull?'

She laughed: it ended in a cough. 'Many as we can take. Fission rocket.'

'Fission?' He looked at her aghast. 'But we'll be a sitting duck! If they—'

'Shut up and let me work.' She closed her eyes again, busy with the final preparations.

Sneak was, of course, of the essence. A fission rocket was a sitting duck to a battlecruiser like the *Lord Vanek*; it had about four hours' thrust, during which time it might stay ahead – if the uncompensated acceleration didn't kill its passengers, and if the ship didn't simply go to full military power and race past it – but then it was out of fuel, a ballistic casualty. To make matters worse, until she managed to get more than about ten thousand kilometers away from the *Lord Vanek*, she'd be within tertiary laser defense range – close enough that the warship could simply point its lidar grid at the lifeboat and curdle them like an egg in a microwave oven.

But there was a difference between *could* and *would* which, Rachel hoped, was big enough to fly a spaceship through. Activating the big warship's drive would create a beacon that any defenders within half a light-minute or so might see. And torching off the big laser sensor/killer array would be like lighting up a neon sign saying INVADING WARSHIP – COME AND GET ME. Unless Captain Mirsky was willing to risk his Admiral's wrath by making a spectacle of himself in front of the Festival, he wouldn't dare try to nail Rachel so blatantly. Only if she lit off her own drive, or a distress beacon, would he feel free to shoot her down – because she would already have given his position away.

However, first she had to get off the ship. Undoubtedly, they'd be outside her cabin door within minutes, guns and cutters in their hands. The weakened bulkheads between the larval lifeboat and the outer pressure hull were all very well, but how to achieve a clean separation without warning them?

'Mech one. Broadcast primary destruct sequence.'

'Confirm. Primary destruct sequence for mech one.'

'*Sword*. Confirm?'

'Confirmed.'

The transponder in her luggage was broadcasting a siren song of destruction, on wavelengths only her spy mechs – those that were left – would be listening to. Mech one, wedged in a toilet's waste valve in the brig, would hear. Using what was left of its feeble power pack, it would detonate its small destruct charge. Smaller than a hand grenade – but powerful enough to rupture the toilet's waste pipe.

Warships can't use gravity-fed plumbing; the *Lord Vanek*'s sewage-handling system was under pressure, an intricate network of pipes connected by valves to prevent backflow. The *Lord Vanek* didn't recycle its waste, but stored it, lest discharges freeze to shrapnel, ripping through spacecraft and satellites like a shotgun loaded with ice. But there are exceptions to every rule; holding waste in tanks to reduce the risk of ballistic debris creation was all very well, but not at the risk of shipboard disaster, electrical short circuit, or life-support contamination.

When Rachel's makeshift bomb exploded, it ruptured a down pipe carrying waste from an entire deck to the main storage tanks. Worse, it took out a backflow valve. Waste water backed up from the tank and sprayed everywhere, hundreds of liters per second drenching the surrounding structural spaces and conduits. Damage control alarms warbled in the maintenance stations, and the rating on duty hastily opened the main dump valves, purging the waste circuit into space. The *Lord Vanek* had a crew of nearly twelve hundred, and had been in flight for weeks; a fire spray of sewage exploded from the scuppers, nearly two hundred tonnes of waste water purging into space just as Rachel's lifeboat counted down to zero.

In the process of assembling her lifeboat, the robot factory in Rachel's luggage had made extensive – not to say destructive – changes to the spaces around her cabin. Supposedly solid bulkheads fractured like glass; on the outer hull of the ship, a foam of spun diamond half a meter thick disintegrated into a talc-like powder across a circle three meters in diameter. The bottom dropped out of Rachel's stomach as the hammock she lay in lurched sideways, then the improvised cold-gas thrusters above her head kicked in, shoving the damply new-born lifeboat clear of its ruptured womb. Weird, painful tidal stresses ripped at her; Martin grunted as if he'd been punched in the gut. The lifeboat was entering the ship's curved-space field, a one-gee gradient dropping off across perhaps a hundred meters of space beyond the hull; the boat creaked and sloshed ominously, then began to tumble, falling end over end toward the rear of the warship.

On board the *Lord Vanek*, free-fall alarms were sounding. Cursing bridge officers yanked at their seat restraints, and throughout the ship, petty officers yelled at their flyers, calling them to crash stations. Down in the drive maintenance room, Commander Krupkin was cursing up a blue streak as he hit the scram switch, then grabbed his desk with one hand and the speaking tube to the bridge with the other to demand an explanation.

Without any fuss, the warship's drive singularity entered shutdown. The curved-space field that provided both a semblance of gravity and shielding against acceleration collapsed into a much weaker spherical field centered on the point mass in the engine room – just in time to prevent two hundred tons of bilgewater, and a twenty-tonne improvised lifeboat, from hammering into the rear of the *Lord Vanek*'s hull and ripping the heat exchangers to shreds.

In the Green deck accommodation block corridor, a nightmare cacophony of alarms was shrilling for attention. Lights strobed overhead, blue, red, green; blow-out alarm, gravity failure alarm, everything. Lieutenant Sauer cursed under his breath and grappled with an emergency locker door; 'Help me, you idiot!' he shouted at Able Flyer Maxim Kravchuk who, whey-faced with fear, was frozen in the middle of the corridor. 'Grab this handle and pull for your life!'

Farther up the corridor, damage control doors were sliding shut; as they closed, struts extended from their inner surfaces and extended bright orange crash nets. Maxim grabbed the handle Sauer pointed him at and yanked. Together they managed to unseal the stiff locker door. 'Get *inside*, idiot,' Sauer grunted. The blow-out alarm, terror of all cosmonauts, stopped strobing, but now he could feel the keening of the gravity failure siren deep in his bones – and the floor was beginning to tilt. Kravchuk tumbled inside the locker and began to belt himself to the wall, hands working on instinct alone. Sauer could see the whites of the man's terrified eyes. He paused in the entrance, glancing up the corridor. The UN bitch's cabin was in the next segment – he'd have to secure this one and get breathing apparatus before he could go and find out what she'd done to his ship. *It's not just the skipper who'll be asking questions*, he thought bitterly.

Sauer clambered into the locker even as the floor began to tilt sideways; but the tilt stabilized at a relatively tolerable thirty degrees. He began to feel light on his feet. *Drive must be going into shutdown*, he realized. Leaving the door open – it would close automatically if there was a pressure drop – he began systematically to pull on an emergency suit. The emergency suit was basically a set of interconnected transparent bags, with enough air to last six hours in a backpack, no good for EVA but a lifesaver inside a breached hull. 'You get dressed,' he told the frightened rating. 'We're going to find out what caused this.'

Four minutes later, Chief Molotov and four armed red-tab police arrived, laboriously cycling through the sealed-off corridor segments; the young Procurator tagged along behind them, face flushed, evidently struggling with the unfamiliar survival suit. Sauer ignored him. 'Chief, I have reason to believe there are armed saboteurs inside the next corridor segment, or the third compartment in it. When I give the signal, I want this door open and the corridor behind it cleared. I don't know what the occupants have by way of defenses, but they're definitely armed, so I suggest you just saturate with taser fire. Once we've done that, if it's empty, we move on the compartment. Got that?'

'Aye,' said Molotov. 'Any idea who's inside?'

Sauer shrugged. 'My best bet is the engineer, Springfield, and the woman from Earth. But I could be wrong. How you handle it is your call.'

'I see.' Molotov turned. 'You and you; either side of the door. When it opens, shoot anything that moves.' He paused. 'Remote override on the cabin door?'

'It's locked. Manual hinges only, too.'

'Right you are.' Molotov unslung a knapsack, began unrolling a fat cable. 'You'll want to stand back, then.' He grabbed the emergency door override handle. 'On my mark! Mark!'

The emergency door hummed up into the ceiling, and the ratings tensed, but the corridor was empty. 'Right. The cabin, lads.'

He approached the cabin door carefully. 'Says it's open to vacuum, sir,' he said, pointing to the warning lights on the door frame.

'Bet you it's a pinhole leak she's rigged to keep us out. Just get everyone into suits before we blow it.' Sauer approached and watched as Molotov attached the cable of rubbery cord to the door frame, running it alongside the hinges and then around the door handle and lock, holding it in place with tape. 'I'm going to use cutting cord. Better tell Environment to seal this corridor for a pressure drop-off until we repressurize this compartment.'

'Sir –' It was Muller, the cause of this whole mess.

'What is it?' Sauer snapped, not bothering to conceal his anger.

'I, uh –' Vassily recoiled. 'Please be careful, sir. She – the inspector – isn't a fool. This makes me nervous –'

'Keep pestering me, and I'll make you nervous. Chief, if this man makes a nuisance of himself, feel free to arrest him. He caused this whole fiasco.'

'He did, did he?' Chief Molotov glared at the Subcurator, who wilted and retreated down the passage.

'I'll get Environment to seal us off.' Sauer was on the command channel again, as Molotov retrieved some wires and a detonator, and began cabling up the explosives. Finally, he retreated a few paces down the corridor and waited. 'All clear,' said Sauer. 'Okay. Is everybody ready?' He backed up until he stood beside Molotov. 'Are you ready?' The chief nodded. 'Then *go*.'

There was a loud whip crack, and smoke jetted from the sides of the door. Then there was an unbelievably loud bang, and Sauer's ears popped. The doorway was gone. Behind it, a rolling darkness dragged at him with icy claws, howling and sucking the others out into the void. *Not a pinhole?* He tried to grab at the nearest emergency locker door, but it was already slamming shut, and he was dragged down the corridor. Something thumped him hard between the shoulders, so hard that he couldn't breathe. Everything was dark, and the pain was unbelievable. A dark cylinder spun before his eyes, and there was a ringing whistling in his ears. Plastic flapped against his face. *Must have ripped my suit*, he thought vaguely. *I wonder what happened to . . .* Thinking was hard work; he gave up and fell into a doze, which spiraled rapidly down into dreamless silence.

Vassily Muller, however, was luckier.

bouncers

The admiral sat at his desk and squinted.

Commodore Bauer cleared his throat. 'If I may have your attention, sir.'

'Huh? Speak up-up, young man!'

'We enter terminal engagement range with the enemy tonight,' Bauer said patiently. 'We have to hold the final pre-approach session, sir, to articulate our immediate tactical situation. I need you to sign off on my orders if we are to conduct the battle.'

'Very well.' Admiral Kurtz tried to sit up in his chair; Robard's helping hands behind his frail shoulders steadied him. 'You have them?'

'Sir.' Bauer slid a slim folder across the polished oak. 'If you would care to see—'

'No, no.' The Admiral waved a frail hand. 'You're a sound man. You give-ive those natives jolly what for, won't you?'

Bauer stared at his commander in mixed desperation and relief. 'Yes, sir, I will,' he promised. 'We will be in lidar range of the planetary surface in another hour, then we should be able to establish their order of battle fairly accurately. Task Group Four will illuminate and take the first blood, while the heavies stay under emission control and punch out anything we can identify after we get within close broadside range. I have the destroyer squadrons ready to go after any fixed emplacements we find in GEO, and the torpedo boats are tasked with high-delta-vee intercepts on anything fleeing –'

'Give the natives what-ho,' Kurtz said dreamily. 'Make a hill of skulls in the town square. Volley fire by platoons. Bomb the bastards!'

'Yes, sir. If you'd be so good as to sign here –'

Robard put the pen between the Admiral's fingers, but they shook so much that his crimson signature on the orders was almost completely obscured by a huge blot, like fresh blood.

Bauer saluted. 'Sir! With your permission I will implement these orders forthwith.'

Kurtz looked up at the Commodore, his sunken eyes glowing for a split second with an echo of his former will. 'Make it so! Victory is on-on our side, for our Lord will not permit his followers to come to –' A look of vast puzzlement crossed his wrinkled face, and he slumped forward.

'Sir! Are you –' The Commodore leaned forward, but Robard had already pulled the Admiral's chair back from the table.

'He's been overwrought for days,' Robard commented, reclining his charge's chair. 'I shall take him back to his bedchamber. As we approach the enemy –' He tensed. 'Would sir please accept my apologies and call the ship's surgeon?'

Half an hour later, ten minutes late for his own staff meeting, Commodore Bauer surged into the staff conference room. 'Gentlemen. Please be seated.'

Two rows sat before him, before the podium from which the Admiral commanding could address his staff and line officers. 'I have a very grave announcement to make,' he began. The folio under his right arm bent under the tension with which he gripped it. 'The Admiral –' A sea of faces upturned before him, trusting, waiting. 'The Admiral is indisposed,' he said. Indisposed indeed, if you could call it that, with the ship's surgeon in attendance and giving him a ten percent chance of recovery from the cerebral hemorrhage that had struck him down as he signed the final order. 'Ahem. He has instructed me to proceed with our prearranged deployment, acting as his proxy while he retains overall control of the situation. I should like to add that he asked me to say, he knows every man will do his duty, and our cause will triumph because God is on our side.'

Bauer shuffled his papers, trying to dismiss his parting image of the Admiral from his awareness; lying prone and shriveled on his bed, the surgeon and a loblolly boy conferring over him in low voices as they awaited the arrival of the ship's chaplain. 'First to review the situation. Commander Kurrel. What word on navigation?'

Commander Kurrel stood. A small, fussy man who watched the world with sharp-eyed intelligence from behind horn-rimmed glasses, he was the staff navigation specialist. 'The discrepancy is serious, but not fatal,' he said, shuffling the papers in front of him. 'Evidently Their Lordships' projected closed timelike path was more difficult to navigate than we anticipated. Despite improvements to the drive timebase monitors, a discrepancy of no less than sixteen million seconds crept in during our traversal – which, I might add, is not entirely inexplicable, considering that we have made a grand total of sixty-eight jumps spaced over some 139 days, covering a distance of just over 8053 light-years; a new and significant record in the history of the Navy.'

He paused to adjust his spectacles. 'Unfortunately, those sixteen megaseconds lay in precisely the worst possible direction – timewise, into the domain within which the enemy occupied our territory. Indeed, we would have done little worse had we simply made the normal five-jump crossing, a distance of some forty-four light-years. A full pulsar map correlated for spin-down indicates that our temporal displacement is some three million seconds into the future of our origin point, when it is extrapolated to the destination's world line. This is confirmed by classical planetary ephemeris measurements; according to local history, the enemy – the Festival – has been entrenched for thirty days.'

A single intake of breath rattled around the table, disbelief and muted anger mingling. Commodore Bauer watched it sharply. '*Gentlemen.*' Silence resumed. 'We may have lost the anticipated tactical benefits of this hitherto untried maneuver, but we have not entirely failed; we are still only ten days in the future of our own departure light cone, and using a conventional path we wouldn't be arriving for another ten days or so. As we have not heard anything from signals intelligence, we may assume that the enemy, although entrenched, are not expecting us.' He smiled tightly. 'An inquiry into the navigation error will be held after the victory celebrations.' That statement brought a brief round of 'ayes' from the assembly. 'Lieutenant Kossov. General status report, if you please.'

'Ah, yes, sir.' Kossov stood. 'All ships report ready for battle. The main issues are engineering failures with the *Kamchatka* – they report that pressure has been restored to nearly all decks, now – and the explosion in the waste-disposal circuits of this ship. I understand that, with the exception of some cabins on Green deck, and localized water damage near the brig, we are back to normal; however, several persons are missing, including Security Lieutenant Sauer, who was investigating some sort of incident at the time of the explosion.'

'Indeed.' Bauer nodded at Captain Mirsky. 'Captain. Anything to report?'

'Not at this time, sir. Rescue parties are currently busy

trying to recover those who were expelled from the ship during the decompression incident. I don't believe this will affect our ability to fight. However, I will have a full and detailed report for you at your earliest convenience.' Mirsky looked grim; and well he might, for the Flag Captain's ship was not expected to disgrace the fleet, much less to lose officers and crew to some sort of plumbing accident – if indeed it was an accident. 'I must report, sir, that the Terran diplomat is among those listed as missing following this incident. Normally, I would conduct a search for survivors, but in the current situation –' His shrug was eloquent.

'Let me extend my sympathies, Captain; Lieutenant Sauer was a fine officer. Now, as to our forthcoming engagement, I have decided that we will deploy in accordance with attack plan F. You've gamed it twice in exercises; now you get a chance to play it for real, this time against a live but indeterminate foe –'

A bumping on the hull brought Martin to his senses.

He blinked, hair floating in front of his eyes, and stared at the wall in front of him. It had slid past his eyes as the cold-gas thrusters tried to yank him into the ceiling, turning from solid gray into a sheet of blackness stippled with the glaring diamond dust of stars. The tides of the *Lord Vanek* had tried to yank his arms and legs off; he ached with a memory of gravity. Rachel lay next to him, her lips twitching as she communed with the lifeboat's primitive brainstem. Huge gray clouds blocked the view directly overhead, waste water from the scuppers. As he looked, yellow beacons flashed in it, rescue workers searching for something.

'You alright?' he croaked.

'Just a minute.' Rachel closed her eyes again and let her arms float upward until they almost touched the glassy overhead screen – which was much, much closer than Martin had originally thought. The capsule was a truncated cylinder, perhaps four meters in diameter at the base and three at the top, but it was less than two meters high; about the same volume as the passenger compartment of a hackney carriage. (The fuel tanks and motor beneath it were significantly larger.) It hummed and gurgled quietly with the rhythm of the life-support pipework, spinning very slowly around its long axis. 'We're making twelve meters per second. That's good. Puts us a kilometer or so from the ship . . . damn, what's going on back there?'

'Somebody on EVA? Looking for us.'

'Seems like more than one of 'em. Almost like a debris cloud.' Her eyes widened in horror as Martin watched her.

'Whatever happened, it happened after we left. If you'd triggered a blowout, we'd be surrounded by debris, wouldn't we?'

She shook her head. 'We should go back and help. We've got a—'

'*Bullshit.* They've got EVA teams suited up all the time they're at battle stations, you know that as well as I do. It's not your problem. Let me guess. Someone tried to get into your cabin after we left. Tried a bit too hard, by the look of it.'

She stared at the distant specks floating around the rear of the warship, a stubby cylinder in the middle distance. 'But if I hadn't—'

'I'd be on my way to the airlock with my hands taped behind my back, and you'd be under arrest,' he pointed out. Tired, cold, rational. His head ached; this capsule must be at a lower pressure than the ship. His hands were shaking and cold in reaction to the events of the past five minutes. Ten minutes. However long it had been. 'You saved my life, Rachel. If you'd stop kicking yourself over it for a minute, I'd like to thank you.'

'If there's anyone out there and we leave them—'

'The EVA crew will get them. Trust me on this, I figure they tried to blow their way into your cabin. Didn't check that it wasn't open to space first, and got blown a bit farther than they expected. That's what warships have away teams and jolly boats for. What we should be worrying about now is hoping nobody notices us before the final event.'

'Um.' Rachel shook her head: her expression relaxed slightly, tension draining. A certain darkness seemed to lift. 'We're still going to be entirely too close for my liking. We've got another cold-gas tank, that'll give us an extra ten meters per second; if I use it now that means we'll have drifted about 250 kilometers from the ship before perigee, but before then, they should begin maneuvering and widen the gap considerably. We've got enough water and air for a week. I was figuring on a couple of full-on burns to take us downside while they're busy paying attention to the enemy defenses, whatever they turn out to be. If there are any.'

'I'm betting on eaters, shapers.' Martin nodded briefly, then held his head still as the world seemed to spin around him. Not spacesickness, surely? The thought of being cooped up in this cubbyhole for a week with a bad case of the squirts was too revolting to contemplate. 'Maybe antibodies. Nothing the New Republic understands, anyway. Probably easy enough for us to avoid, but if you go in shooting—'

'Yeah.' Rachel yawned.

'You look exhausted.' Concern filled him. 'How the hell did you do that? I mean, back on the ship? It must take it out on you later—'

'It does.' She bent forward and fumbled with a blue fishnet, down around what would have been the floor of the cabin. Surprisingly homely containers of juice floated out, tumbling in free fall. She grabbed one and began to suck on the nozzle greedily. 'Help yourself.'

'Not that I'm ungrateful or anything,' Martin added,

batting a wandering mango and durian fruit cordial out of his face, 'but – *why*?' She stared at him for a long moment. 'Oh,' he said.

She let the empty carton float free and turned to face him. 'I'd prefer to give you some kind of bullshit about trust and duty and so on. But.' She shrugged uncomfortably in her seat harness. 'Doesn't matter.' She held out a hand. Martin took it and squeezed, wordlessly.

'You didn't blow your mission,' he pointed out. 'You never had a mission out here. Not realistically, anyway, not what your boss, what was his name?'

'George. George Cho.'

'– George thought. Insufficient data, right? What would he have done if he'd known about the Festival?'

'Possibly nothing different.' She smiled bleakly at the empty juice carton, then plucked another from the air. 'You're dead wrong; I still have a job to do, if and when we arrive. The chances of which have just gone down by, oh, about fifty percent because of this escapade.'

'Huh. Let me know if there's anything I can do to help, alright?' Martin stretched, then flinched with a remembered pain. 'You wouldn't have seen my PA would you? After—'

'It's bagged under your chair, along with a toothbrush and a change of underwear. I hit your cabin after they pulled you in.'

'You're a star,' he exclaimed happily. He bent double and began fishing around in the cramped space under the control console. 'Oh my –' Straightening up, he opened the battered gray book. Words and pictures swam across the pages in front of him. He tapped an imaginary keyboard; new images gelled. 'You need any help running this boat?'

'If you want.' She drained the second container, thrust both the empties into the bag. 'Yes, if you want. You've flown before?'

'Spent twelve years at L5. Basic navigation, no problem. If it's got a standard life-support module, I can program the galley, too. Traditional Yorkshire habit, that, learning how to cook black pudding in free fall. The trick is to spin the ship around the galley, so that the sausage stays still while the grill rotates –'

She chuckled; a carton of cranberry juice bounced off his head. 'Enough already!'

'Alright.' He leaned back, the PA floating before him. Its open pages showed a real-time instrument feed from the lifeboat's brain. (A clock in one corner spiraled down the seconds to Rachel's first programmed deceleration burn, two thousand seconds before perigee.) Frowning, he scribbled glyphs with a stylus. 'We should make it. Assuming they don't shoot at us.'

'We've got a Red Cross transponder. They'd have to manually override their IFF.'

'Which they won't do unless they're *really* pissed off. Good.' Martin tapped a final period on the page. 'I'd be happier if I knew what we were flying into, though. I mean, if the Festival hasn't left anything in orbit –' They both froze.

Something scraped across the top of the escape capsule, producing a sound like hollow metal bones rattling against a cage.

The rabbit snarled and hefted his submachine gun angrily. Ears back and teeth visible, he hissed at the cyborg.

Sister Seventh sat up and stared at the confrontation. Everyone else except Burya Rubenstein ducked; Burya stepped forward into the middle of the clearing. 'Stop this! At once!'

For a long moment the rabbit stood, frozen. Then he relaxed his stiff-backed pose and lowered his gun muzzle. 'He started it.'

'I don't care what he started: we have a job to do, and it does not require shooting each other.' He turned to the cyborg whom the rabbit had confronted. 'What did you say?'

The revolutionary looked bashful; her fully extended claws retracted slowly. 'Is not good extropian. This *creature* –' her gesture at the rabbit brought another show of teeth – 'believe cult of personality! Is counterrevolutionary dissident. Headlaunch now! Headlaunch now!'

Burya squinted. Many of the former revolutionaries had gone overboard on the personal augmentations offered by the Festival, without realizing that it was necessary to modify their central nervous systems in order to run them. This led to a certain degree of confusion. 'But, comrade, you have a personality, too. A sense of identity is a necessary precondition to consciousness, and that, as the great leaders and teachers point out, is the keystone upon which the potential for transcendence is built.'

The cyborg looked puzzled. Mirror-finished nictitating membranes flashed across her eyeballs, reflecting inner thoughts. 'But within society of mind there is no personality. Personality arises from society; therefore, individual can have no—'

'I think you misunderstand the great philosophers,' Rubenstein said slowly. 'This is not a criticism, comrade, for the philosophers are, of their essence, very brilliant and hard to follow; but by "society of mind", they were referring to the arrival of consciousness within the individual, arising from lesser pre-conscious agents, not to society outside the person. Thus, it follows that being attached to one's own consciousness is not to follow a cult of personality. Now, following another's –' He broke off and looked sharply at the rabbit. 'I don't think we will pursue this question any further,' he said primly. 'Time to move on.'

The cyborg nodded jerkily. Her fellows stood (or in one case, uncoiled) and shouldered their packs; Burya walked over to Sister Seventh's hut and climbed inside. Presently the party moved off.

'Not understand revolutionary sense,' commented the Critic, munching on a sweet potato as the hut bounced along the dirt track behind the detachment from the Plotsk soviet. 'Sense of identity deprecated? Lagomorph Criticized for affinity to self? Nonsense! How appreciate art without sense of self?'

Burya shrugged. 'They're too literal-minded,' he said quietly. 'All doing, no innovative thinking. They don't understand metaphors well; half of them think you're Baba Yaga returned, you know? We've been a, ah, stable culture too long. Patterns of belief, attitudes, get ingrained. When change comes, they are incapable of responding. Try to fit everything into their preconceived dogmas.' He leaned against the swaying wall of the hut. 'I got so tired of trying to wake them up . . .'

Sister Seventh snorted. 'What you call *that*?' she asked, pointing through the door of the hut. Ahead of them marched a column of wildly varied cyborgs, partially augmented revolutionaries frozen halfway beyond the limitations of their former lives. At its head marched the rabbit, leading them into the forest of the partially transcended wilderness.

Burya peered at the rabbit. 'I'd call it anything it wants. It's got a gun, hasn't it?'

By noon, the forest had changed beyond recognition. Some strange biological experiment had warped the vegetation. Trees and grass had exchanged leaves, so that now they walked on a field of spiny pine needles, while flat blades waved overhead; the leaves were piebald, black and green, with the glossy black spreading. Most disturbingly of all, the shrubbery seemed to be blurring at the edges, species exchanging phenotypic traits with unnatural promiscuous abandon. 'What's responsible for this?' Burya asked Sister Seventh, during one of their hourly pauses.

The Critic shrugged. 'Is nothing. Lysenkoist forestry fringe, recombinant artwork. Beware the Jabberwocky, my son. Are there only Earth native derivations in this biome?'

'You asking me?' Rubenstein snorted. 'I'm no gardener.'

'Guesstimation implausible,' Sister Seventh replied archly. 'In any event, some fringeworks are recombinant. Non human-centric manipulations of genome. Elegant structures, modified for non-purpose. This forest is Lamarckian. Nodes exchange phenotype-determinant traits, acquire useful ones.'

'Who determines their usefulness?'

'The Flower Show. Part of the Fringe.'

'What a surprise,' Burya muttered.

At the next stop, he approached the rabbit. 'How far?' he demanded.

The lagomorph sniffed at the breeze. 'Fifty kilometers? Maybe more?' It looked faintly puzzled, as if the concept of distance was a difficult abstraction.

'You said sixty kilometers this morning,' Burya pointed out, 'We've come twenty. Are you sure? The militia doesn't trust you, and if you keep changing your mind, I may not be able to stop them doing something stupid.'

'I'm just a rabbit.' Ears twitched backward, swiveling to either side to listen for threats. 'Know where master is, *was*, attacked by Mimes. Haven't heard much from him since, you bet. Always know where he is, don't know how – but can't tell you how far. Like fucking compass in my head, mate, you understand?'

'How long have you been a rabbit?' asked Rubenstein, an awful suspicion coming to mind.

The rabbit looked puzzled. 'I don't rightly know. I think I once –' He stopped talking. Iron shutters came down, blocking the light behind his eyes. 'No more words. Find master. Rescue!'

'Who is your master?' Burya demanded.

'Felix,' said the rabbit.

'Felix . . . Politovsky?'

'Don't know. *Maybe.*' Rabbit twitched his ears right back and bared his teeth 'Don't want to talk! We there tomorrow. Rescue master. Kill the Mimes.'

Vassily looked down at the stars wheeling beneath his feet. *I'm going to die*, he thought, swallowing acrid bile.

When he closed his eyes, the nausea went away a little. His head still hurt where he'd thumped it against the wall of the cabin on his way through; everything had blurred for a while, and he'd caught himself floating away on a cloud of pain. Now he had time to reflect, the pain seemed like an ironic joke; corpses didn't hurt, did they? It told him he was still alive. When it stopped hurting –

He relived the disaster again and again. Sauer checking everybody was suited up. 'It's just a pinhole,' someone said, and it had seemed so plausible – the woman had let some air out of her cabin to trip the decompression interlocks – and then the bright flash of the cutting cord proved him wrong. The howling maelstrom had reached out and yanked the lieutenant and the CPO right out of the ship, into a dark tunnel full of stars. Vassily had tried to catch a door handle, but the clumsy mitten hands of his emergency suit wouldn't grip. They'd left him tumbling over and over like a spider caught in the whirlpool when a bath plug is pulled.

Stars whirled, cold lights like daggers in the night outside his eyelids. *This is it. I'm really going to die. Not going home again. Not going to arrest the spy. Not going to meet my father and tell him what I really think of him. What will the Citizen think of me?*

Vassily opened his eyes. The whirling continued; he must be spinning five or six times a minute. The emergency suit had no thrusters, and its radio had a pathetic range, just a few hundred meters – more than enough for shipboard use, perhaps enough to make a beacon if anyone came looking for him. But nobody had. He was precessing like a gyroscope; every couple of minutes, the ship swam briefly into view, a dark splinter outlined against the diamond dust of the heavens. There'd been no sign of a search party heading his way; just that golden fog of waste water spreading out around the ship, which had been over a kilometer away before he first saw it.

It looked like a toy; an infinitely desirable toy, one he could pin all his hopes of life and love and comradeship and warmth and happiness on — one that hung forever out of reach, dangling in a cold wasteland he couldn't cross.

He glanced at the crude display mounted on his left wrist, watching the air dial tick down the hours left in his oxygen bottle. There was a dosimeter there, too, and this wasteland was hot, charged particles streaming through it at a rate that might suffice to prevent his mummified corpse decaying.

Vassily shuddered. Bitter frustration seized him: *Why couldn't I do something right?* he wondered. He'd thought he was doing the right thing, enlisting in the Curator's Office, but when he'd pridefully shown his mother the commission, her face had closed like a shop front, and she'd looked away from him in that odd manner she used when he'd done something wrong but she didn't want to chastise him for it. He'd thought he was doing the right thing, searching the engineer's luggage, then the diplomat's — but look where it had taken him. The ship beneath his shoes was a splinter against the dark, several kilometers away and getting farther out of reach all the time. Even his presence aboard the ship — if he was honest, he'd have done better to stay at home, wait for the ship (and the engineer) to return to New Prague, there to resume his pursuit. Only the news from Rochard's World, the place of exile, had filled him with a curious excitement. And if he hadn't wanted to go along, he wouldn't be here now, spinning in a condemned man's cell of memories.

He tried to think of happier times, but it was difficult. School? He'd been bullied mercilessly, mocked because of who and what his father was – and was not. Any boy who bore his mother's name was an object of mockery, but to have a criminal for a father as well, a notorious criminal, made him too easy a target. Eventually he'd pounded one bully's face into pulp, and been caned for it, and they'd learned to avoid him, but it hadn't stopped the whispering and sniggering in quiet corners. He'd learned to listen for that, to lie in wait after classes and beat the grins off their faces, but it hadn't gained him friends.

Basic training? That was a joke. A continuation of school, only with sterner taskmasters. Then police training, and the cadet's college. Apprenticeship to the Citizen, whom he strived to impress because he admired the stern inspector vastly; a man of blood and iron, unquestionably loyal to the Republic and everything it stood for, a spiritual father whom he'd now managed to disappoint twice.

Vassily yawned. His bladder ached, but he didn't dare piss – not in this suit of interconnected bubbles. The thought of drowning was somehow more terrifying than the idea of running out of air. Besides, when the air went – wasn't this how they executed mutinous spacers, instead of hanging?

A curious horror overtook him, then. His skin crawled; the back of his neck turned damp and cold. *I can't go yet*, he thought. *It's not fair!* He shuddered. The void seemed to speak to him. *Fairness has nothing to do with it. This will happen, and your wishes are meaningless.* His eyes stung; he squeezed them tightly shut against the whirling daggers of night and tried to regain control of his breathing.

And when he opened them again, as if in answer to his prayers, he saw that he was not alone in the deep.

jokers

High in orbit above Rochard's World, the Bouncers were stirring.

Two kilometers long, sleek and gray, each of them dwarfed the incoming naval task force. They'd been among the first artifacts the newly arrived Festival manufactured. Most of the Bouncers drifted in parking orbits deep in the Oort cloud, awaiting enemies closing along timelike attack paths deep in the future of the Festival's world line; but a small detachment had accompanied the Festival itself, as it plunged deep into the inner system and arrived above the destination world.

Bouncers didn't dream. Bouncers were barely sentient special units, tasked with the defense of the Festival against certain crude physical threats. For denial of service, decoherence attacks, and general spoofing, the more sophisticated antibodies could be relied on; for true causality-violation attacks, the Festival's reality-maintenance crew would be awakened. But sometimes, the best defense is a big stick and a nasty smile – and that was what the Bouncers were for.

The arrival of the New Republic task force had been

noted four days earlier. The steady acceleration profiles of the incoming warships stuck out like a sore thumb; while His Majesty's Navy thought in terms of lidar and radar and active sensors, the Festival used more subtle instruments. Localized minima in the outer system's entropy had been noted, spoor of naked singularities, echoes of the tunneling effect that let the conventional starships jump from system to system. The failure of the incoming fleet to signal told its own story; bouncers knew what to do without being told.

The orbiting Bouncer division began to accelerate. There were no fragile life-forms aboard these craft – just solid slabs of impure diamond and ceramic superconductors, tanks of metallic hydrogen held under pressures that would make the core of a gas giant planet seem like vacuum, and high-energy muon generators to catalyze the exotic fusion reactions that drove the ships. Also, of course, the fractal bushes that were the Bouncers' cargo: millions of them clinging like strange vines to the long spines of the ships.

Fusion torches providing thrust in accordance with Newtonian laws might seem quaint to the New Republican Admiralty, who had insisted on nothing but the most modern drive singularities and curved-space engines for their fleet; but unlike the Admiralty, the Festival's Bouncers had some actual combat experience. Reaction motors had important advantages for space-to-space combat, advantages that gave an unfair edge to a canny defender; a sensible thrust-to-mass ratio for one thing, and a low degree of observability for another. Ten-billion-tonne virtual masses made singularity-drive ships incredibly ponderous: although able to accelerate at a respectable clip, they couldn't change direction rapidly, and to the Festival, they were detectable almost out to interstellar ranges. In contrast, a gimbaled reaction motor could change thrust vector fast enough to invite structural breakup if the ship wasn't built to withstand the stresses. And while a fusion torch seen from astern was enough to burn out sensors at a million kilometers, the exhaust stream was very directional, with little more than a vague hot spot visible from in front of a ship.

With the much larger infrared emitter of the planet behind them, the Bouncers accelerated toward the New Republican first squadron at a bone-crushing hundred gees. Able to triangulate on the enemy by monitoring their drive emissions, the Bouncers peaked at 800 k.p.s., then shut down their torches and drifted silently, waiting for the moment of closest approach.

The operations room of the *Lord Vanek* was tense and quiet.

'Gunnery Two, ready a batch of six SEM-20s. Dial them all to one-zero-zero kilotonnes, tune the first two for maximum EMP, next three for spallation debris along main axis. Gunnery One, I want two D-4 torpedoes armed for passivee launch with a one-minute motor-on delay inlined into them.'

Captain Mirsky sat back in his chair. 'Prediction?' he muttered in the direction of Commander Vulpis.

'Holding ready, sir. A bit disturbing that we haven't seen anything yet, but I can give you full maneuvering power within forty seconds of getting a drive signal.'

'Good. Radar. Anything new?'

'Humbly report nothing's new on passive, sir.'

'Deep joy.' They were two hours out from perigee. Mirsky had to fight to control his impatience. Tapping his fingers on the arm of his chair, he sat and waited for a sign, anything to indicate that there was life elsewhere in this empty cosmos. The fatal ping of a lidar illuminator glancing off the *Lord Vanek*'s stealthed hull, or the ripple of gravitomagnetic waves; anything to show that the enemy was out there, somewhere between the battle ship squadron and its destination.

'Any thoughts, Commander Vulpis?'

Vulpis's eyes flickered around the fully manned stations in

front of him. 'I'd be a lot happier if they were making the effort to paint us. Either we've taken 'em completely by surprise, or . . .'

'Thank you for that thought,' Mirsky commented under his breath. 'Marek!'

'Sir!'

'You've got a rifle. It's loaded. Don't shoot till you see the whites of their eyes.'

'Sir?' Vulpis stared at his Captain.

'I will be in my cabin if anything happens,' Mirsky said lightly. 'You have the helm, pending Commander Murametz's or my own return. Call me at once if there's any news.'

Down in his stateroom, directly under the ops room, Mirsky collapsed into his chair. He sighed deeply, then poked at the dial of his phone. 'Switchboard. My compliments to the Commodore and if he has a spare moment? Jolly good.' A minute later, the phonescreen dinged. 'Sir!'

'Captain.' Commodore Bauer wore the expression of a very busy, very tired manager.

'I have a report for you on the, ah, annoyance. If you have time for it now.'

Bauer made a steeple of his fingers. 'If you can keep it short,' he said gloomily.

'Not difficult.' Mirsky's eyes glittered in the gaslight. 'It was all the fault of my idiot of an intelligence officer. If he hadn't managed to kill himself, I'd have him in irons.' He took a deep breath. 'But he didn't act alone. As it is, sir, in confidence, I would recommend a reprimand for my FO, Fleet Commander Murametz, if not formal proceedings – except that we are so close to the enemy that—'

'Details, Captain. What did he do?'

'Lieutenant Sauer exceeded his authority by attempting to draw out the Terran spy – the woman, I mean – by means of a faked trial. He somehow convinced Commander Murametz to cover him, damned error of judgment if you ask me: he had no job making a mess in diplomat territory. Anyway, he pushed too hard, and the woman panicked. Ordinarily this would be no problem, but she somehow –' He coughed into his fist.

Bauer nodded. 'I think I can guess the rest. Where is she now?'

Mirsky shrugged. 'Outside the ship, with the dockyard contractor. Missing, probably suited up, don't know where they are, don't know what in *hell* they thought they were doing – the Procurator's missing too, sir, and there's an embarrassing hole in our side where there used to be a cabin.'

Slowly, the Commodore began to smile. 'I don't think you need waste any time searching for them, Captain. If we found them, we'd only have to throw them overboard again, what? I suppose the Procurator had a hand in this kangaroo court, didn't he?'

'Ah, I suppose so, sir.'

'Well, this way we don't have to worry about the civilians. And if they get a little sunburned during the engagement, no matter. I'm sure you'll take care of everything that needs doing.'

'Yes, sir!' Mirsky nodded.

'So,' Bauer said crisply, 'that's tied down. Now, in your analysis, we should be entering the enemy's proximity defense sphere when?'

Mirsky paused for thought. 'About two hours, sir. That's assuming that our emcon was sufficient and the lack of active probes is a genuine indication that they don't know we're out here.'

'I'm glad you added that qualifier. What's your schedule for working up to stations?'

'We're ready right now, sir. That is, there are some inessential posts that won't lock down for another hour or so, but the ops crew and black gang are already on combat watch, and gunnery is standing by the weapons. The mess is due to send around some hot food, but in principle, we're ready for action at a moment's notice.'

'Very good.' Bauer paused and glanced down at his desk. Rubbed the side of his nose with one long, bony finger. Then he glanced up. 'I don't like this silence, Captain. It stinks of a trap.'

Martin and Rachel glanced up in reflexive terror, seeking the source of the noise.

Aboard a spacecraft, any noise from outside spells trouble – big trouble. Their lifeboat was drifting toward Rochard's World at well over solar escape velocity; a BB pellet stationary in their path would rip through them with the force of an anti-shipping missile. And while warships like the *Lord Vanek* could carry centimeters of foamed diamond armor and shock bumpers to absorb spallation fragments, the lifeboat's skin was thin enough to puncture with a penknife.

'Masks,' snapped Rachel. A mess of interconnected transparent bags with complex seals and some sort of gas tank inside coiled from the console opposite Martin and bounced into his lap; for her part, she reached behind her seat and pulled out a helmet. Yanking it on over her head, she let its rim melt into her leotard, dripping sealant down her neck. Crude icons blinked inside the visor. She breathed out, relieved, hearing the fan whine behind her right ear. Beside her, Martin was still stuffing himself into the transparent cocoon. She looked up. 'Pilot. Topside sensor view, optical, center screen.'

'Oh shit,' Martin said indistinctly.

The screen showed an indistinct blur that moved against a backdrop of pinprick stars. As they watched, the blur receded, dizzyingly fast, and sharpened into a recognizable shape. Moving.

She turned and stared at Martin. 'Whoever he is, we can't leave him out there,' he said.

'Not with a rescue beacon,' she agreed grimly. 'Pilot. Oxygen supply. Recalculate on basis of fifty percent increase in consumption. How does it affect our existing survival margin?'

An amber GANT chart flickered across the screen. 'Bags of room,' Martin commented. 'What about landfall? Hmm.' He prodded at his PA. 'I think we can make it,' he added. 'Mass ratio isn't so much worse.'

'Think or know?' she replied pointedly. 'If we get halfway down and run out of go-juice, it could put a real damper on this day-trip.'

"I'm aware of that. Let me see . . . yeah. We'll be okay, Rachel. Whoever designed this boat must have thought you'd be carrying one hell of a diplomatic bag with you. More like a wardrobe.'

'Don't *say* that.' She licked her lips. 'Question two. We take him on board. How are we going to stop him if he decides to get in the way?'

'I think you get to use your feminine wiles on him,' Martin deadpanned.

'I should have known you'd come up with something like that.' Wearily, she groped for the stun gun. 'This won't work in vacuum, you know? And it's not a good idea to use the sucker in a confined space either.'

'Talking of confined spaces.' Martin pointed to the rather basic mass detector display. 'Twelve kilometers and drifting. We don't want to be this close when they spin up for combat.'

'No, we don't,' Rachel agreed. 'Okay. I'm as ready as I'll ever be. You got confirmation on suit integrity? Once we vent, you won't be able to move much.' Martin nodded, held up a balloon-bloated glove. Rachel cranked open her oxygen regulator and yawned, deliberately, hunting the roof of the cabin for an attachment point for her survival tether. 'Okay. Pilot,

EVA cycle. Prepare to depressurize cabin.'

An alarm pinged in the operations room.

'Contact.' Lieutenant Kokesova leaned over his subordinate's shoulder and stared at the gauges on his console. Lights blinked violet and green. 'I say again, contact.'

'Accepted.' Lieutenant Marek swallowed. 'Comms, please signal captain to the ops room and condition red.'

'Aye aye, sir.' A red light began to strobe by the doorway. 'Any specifics?' asked Marek.

'Tracking. I have a definite fusion source, came up about two-zero seconds ago. I thought at first it was a sensor malfunction but it's showing blue-shifted Balmer lines, and it's bright as hell – black body temperature would be in the five-zero-zero M-degree range. Traveling at well above local stellar escape velocity.'

'Very good.' Marek tried to lean back in the command chair but failed, unable to force himself to relax that much. 'Time to get a solution on it?'

'Any minute.' Lieutenant Kokesova, tech specialist, demonstrating his proficiency once again. 'I'll see if I can pickle some neutrinos for you.'

The door opened, and the guard beside it came to attention. Lieutenant Marek spun around and saluted stiffly. 'Sir!'

'What's the situation?'

'Humbly report we have a provisional fix on one incoming, sir,' said Marek. 'We're still waiting for a solution, but we have a blue-shifted fusion torch. Looks like we're looking straight up their endplate mirror.'

Mirsky nodded. 'Very good, Lieutenant. Is there anything else?'

'Anything else?' Marek was flustered. 'Not unless something's come up –'

'Contact!' It was the same sensor op. He looked up apologetically. 'Begging your pardon, sir.'

'Describe.' It was the Captain's turn.

'Second fusion source, about two M-kilometers above and south of the first. It's tracking on a parallel course. I have a preliminary solution, looks like they're vectoring to pass us at about one-zero-zero K-klicks, decelerating from eight-zero-zero k.p.s. Time to intercept, two K-seconds.'

'Any other activity?' asked Mirsky.

'Activity, sir?'

'You know. Anomalous lateral acceleration. Jamming, comms traffic, luminous pink tentacles, whatever. Anything else?'

'No, sir.'

'Well, then.' Mirsky stroked his beard thoughtfully. 'Something doesn't add up.'

The door to the bridge opened again; Lieutenant Helsingus came in. 'Permission to take fire control, sir?'

'Do it.' Mirsky waved his hand. 'But first, riddle me this: Why by the Emperor's beard can we see two drive torches, but nothing else?'

'Ah –' Marek shut up.

'Because,' Commander Vulpis said over Mirsky's shoulder, 'it's an entrapment, Captain.'

'I don't know how you could possibly imagine such a thing; they're obviously inviting us to a dinner dance.' Mirsky grinned nastily. 'Hmm. You think they ditched a bunch of mines before they fired up the torches?'

'Quite possibly.' Vulpis nodded. 'In which case, we're going to get hit in about' – he punched at his board – 'two-five-zero seconds, sir. We won't be in range of anything you can cram on a mine for very long, but at this speed, even a cloud of sand would make a mess of us.'

Mirsky leaned forward. 'Guns. Point defense to automatic! Comms, please request an ack from the commodore's staff, and from *Kamchatka* and *Regina*. Make sure they're watching for mines.' He smiled grimly. 'Time to see what they're made of, I think. Comms, my compliments to the Commodore, and please say that I am requesting permission to terminate emission control for defensive reasons.'

'Aye aye, sir.'

Emission controls were desperately important to a warship. Active sensors like radar and lidar required an echo from a foreign body to confirm its presence; but a sufficiently distant (or stealthed) body wouldn't return an echo loud enough to pick up. Sending out the initial pulse gave away a ship's position with great accuracy to any enemy who happened to be stooging around outside the return range but within passive detection range. By approaching Rochard's World under emission control, the battle squadron had attempted to conceal themselves. The first ship to start actively radiating would make its presence glaringly obvious – painting a target on itself in the process of lighting up the enemy.

'Sir?'

'Yes, Lieutenant Marek?'

'What if there are more than two ships out there? I mean, we carry probes and a shuttle. What if we're up against some kind of larger force, and the two we can see are just a decoy?'

Captain Mirsky grinned humorlessly. 'That's not a possibility, Lieutenant, it's a near certainty.'

'Mine intercept waypoint one, four minutes.' Vulpis read off timings from the glowing nixie tubes before him. He glanced up at the command chair; Captain Mirsky, seated there, nodded.

'Weapons, arm torpedoes, stand by on missiles. Remotes, status on red, blue, orange.' Mirsky was calm and collected, and his presence was a settling influence on the otherwise tense ops room crew.

The red telephone rang, jangling. Mirsky listened, briefly,

then replaced the handset. 'Radar. You have permission to radiate.'

Radar One: 'Going active now, sir. One-zero-second pulse-doppler train, four octave agile spread, go to jamming sequence alpha afterward. Decoys, sir?'

'You may launch decoys.' Mirsky folded his hands in his lap and gazed straight ahead at the main screen. Beneath the calm exterior, he was seriously worried; he was gambling his life and his ship – and all those aboard her – on a hypothesis about the nature of their pursuers. He wasn't confident, but he was sufficiently well informed to make an educated guess about what was after them. *Maybe the UN woman had the right idea*, he thought gloomily. He glanced around the ops room. 'Commander Helsingus. Status, please?'

The bearded gunnery officer nodded. 'First four rounds loaded as per order, sir. Two self-propelled torpedoes with remote ignition patches on my board, followed by six passive-powered missiles rigged for EMP in a one-zero-degree spread. Laser grid programmed for tight point-defense. Ballistic point-defense programs loaded and locked.'

'Good. Helm?'

'Holding steady on designated fleet approach pattern, sir. No evasion authorized by staff.'

'Radar?'

Lieutenant Marek stood up. He looked tense and drawn, new lines forming around his eyes. 'Humbly report, sir, active is on cold clamp. Passive shows nothing yet, except on infrared trace, but that should give us a fix in' – he glanced down – 'about three minutes and counting. Decoy is overboard, running out to radiation rangepoint one.' The decoy – a small unpowered drone trailing behind the warship on a ten-kilometer-long tether – was preparing to radiate an EM signature identical to that of the ship: synchronized by interferometer with the active sensors aboard the *Lord Vanek*, it would help

confuse any enemy sensors as to the exact position of the battlecruiser.

'Good.' Mirsky looked at the clock beside the main forward display, then glanced down at the workstation before
him. Time for the checklist. 'At waypoint one, he prepared to
commence burn schedule one on my word. That's four-zero
gees continuous until we build up to six-zero k.p.s. then shut
down, full damping, course three-six-zero by zero by zero on
current navigation lock. Comms, notify all elements of
squadron one. Guns, at time zero plus five seconds, be prepared to drop torps one and two, on my word. Comms, signal
torpedo passive drop to Squadron One. Please confirm.'

'Aye aye, sir. One and Two' – Helsingus snapped a brass
switch over – 'are armed for passive drop at time plus five.'

'Good.'

'Time to possible mine intercept, two minutes, sir.'

'Thank you Nav Two, I can see the clock from here.' Mirsky
gritted his teeth. 'Helm, status.'

'Program locked. Main engine is available for burn in five-
zero seconds, sir.'

'Radar, update.'

'We should pick 'em up in about two minutes, sir. No emissions –' Lieutenant Marek stopped. 'What's that?'

Radar Two: 'Contact, sir! Lidar registers ping one. Waiting
for –'

An alarm shrilled. 'Something just pinged us, sir,' said
Marek.

Everybody except the radar techs were staring at Mirsky. He
caught Helsingus's eye and nodded. 'Track beta.'

'Aye aye, sir. Guns Two, track beta.' An almost impercepti-
ble thump shuddered through the structure of the
battlecruiser as the main axial launch coil spat twenty tonnes
of intricately machined heavy metal and fuel out through the
nose of the ship. A second bump signaled the release of the

second torpedo. Drifting unpowered, cold but for their avionics packages, they would wait behind when the *Lord Vanek* began to accelerate.

'Minus three-zero seconds,' called Nav Two.

'Beg to report on the contact, sir,' said Marek.

'Speak, Nav.'

'We managed to get a look at the pulse train on the contact, and it looks, um, strange. Noisy, if you follow my meaning; they've done a good job of concealing their recognition signature.'

'One-zero seconds.'

'All posts switch to plan two,' said Captain Mirsky. 'Nav, pass that contact info on to *Kamchatka* and *Ekaterina*. Get anything you can off them.' He picked up the phone to notify his squadron captains of the impending change of plan.

'Aye aye, sir. Plan two burn commencing in five . . . two, one, now.' There was no change evident in the ops room, no shaking or shuddering or sudden leaden-limbed feeling of acceleration, but inside the guts of the starship, the extremal black hole twisted in sudden torment; the *Lord Vanek* fell forward at full military acceleration, four hundred meters per second squared, more than forty gees.

Another alarm trilled. Nav: 'Full scan running.' Twenty gigawatts of laser light beamed out in all directions, a merciless glare bright enough to melt steel at a range of kilometers. Down in the bowels of the ship, heat exchanges glowed redhot, flashing water into saturated high-pressure steam and venting it astern; this close to combat, running out the huge, vulnerable heat exchangers would be suicidal.

Guns: 'Track beta launch commencing.' This time a real bump-and-grind made the ship shudder; the two missiles Helsingus had preloaded back when they'd been on the track alpha heading. As they hurtled ahead of the ship, a tenth of its total laser output focused up their tails, energizing their reaction mass.

This was the time of maximum danger, and Mirsky did his best to maintain a confident demeanor for the benefit of his crew. As the Commodore had put it in the privacy of his staff briefing room: 'If they're smart, they'll send out just enough assets to make us reveal ourselves, then use whatever they've got in orbit to dump a snowstorm of mines in our path. They know where we're going; that's half the problem of pinpointing us. When we start radiating they'll get their solution – and it'll be a question of how much pounding they can hand out, and how much we can take.'

Attacking a fixed point – in this case, the low-orbit installations around a planet – was traditionally reputed to be the hardest task in deep-space warfare. The defenders could concentrate forces around it and rapidly bring defensive missile and laser screens to bear on anyone approaching; and if the attackers wanted to know just what they were attacking, they'd have to hang out high-energy signposts for the defenders to take aim on.

Seconds later, Mirsky breathed a quiet sigh of relief. 'Point defense reports all quiet, sir. We're inside their envelope, but they don't seem to have dropped a minefield.' Drifting mines wouldn't follow the deceleration curve of the enemy ships; they'd come slamming in way ahead of the warships that had dropped them overboard at peak velocity.

'That's good,' Mirsky murmured. His eyes focused on the two red points on the main plotting screen. They were still decelerating, painfully fast; almost as if they were aiming for a zero-relative-velocity slugging match. The *Lord Vanek*'s two missiles crawled toward them – in reality, boosting at a savage thousand gees, already over 1000 k.p.s. Presently, they shut down and coasted, retaining only enough reaction mass for terminal maneuvering when they got within ten seconds of the enemy. Ahead of the *Lord Vahek*, the glinting purple crosses of the unpowered torpedoes fell forward toward the enemy.

A minute later, Gunnery Two spoke up. 'I've lost missile one, sir. I can ping it, but it doesn't respond.'

'Odd –' Mirsky's brow furrowed; he glanced at the dooms-day clock. The battlecruiser was closing on the destination at a crawl, just 40 k.p.s. The enemy was heading toward them at better than 200 k.p.s., decelerating, but their thrust was drop-ping off – if this continued, closing unpowered at 250 k.p.s., their paths would intersect in about 500 seconds, and they'd be within missile-powered flight range 200 seconds before that. These long, ballistic shots weren't expected to cause real damage, but if they came close, they would force the enemy to respond. But missile one had been more than 50,000 kilome-ters from the target –

'Humbly reporting, I've lost missile two as well, sir.'

'That doesn't make sense,' muttered Helsingus. He glanced at the plot: a flurry of six more missiles, all fired from the *Kamchatka*, was closing in on their target: ranging shots all, with little chance of doing any damage, but –

Point Defense: 'Sir, problem on deck one. Looks like – humbly report a debris impact, sir, lost a scattering of eyeballs on the lidar grid but nothing broke the inner pressure hull.'

'Looks like they've got bad dandruff,' Mirsky commented. 'But their point defense is working. Torpedoes?'

'Not yet, sir,' said Helsingus. 'They've only got about five-zero-zero k.p.s. of delta-vee. Won't be in position to light off for, ah, eight-zero more seconds.' Drifting toward the enemy almost 100 k.p.s. faster than the warship that had launched them, the torpedoes nevertheless had relatively short legs. Unlike the missiles, they had their own power plant, radar, and battle control computers, which made them valuable assets in event of an engagement – but they accelerated more slowly and had a lower total acceleration budget.

Radar Two: 'Humbly report I think I spotted something,

sir. About one-zero-zero milliseconds after missile two dropped off, detector three trapped a neutrino pulse; impossible to say for sure whether it came from the target or the missile, but it looked fairly energetic. Ah, no sign of any other radiation.'

'Most peculiar,' Mirsky murmured under his breath: an extreme understatement. 'What's our range profile?'

'Torpedo range in six-zero seconds. Active gunnery range in one-five-zero seconds; contact range in four-zero-zero seconds. Closest pass two-zero K-kilometers, speed on the order of two-six-zero k.p.s. assuming no maneuvering. Range to target is one-zero-five K-kilometers on my mark, now.'

'Hah.' Mirsky nodded. 'Gentlemen, this may look preposterous, but I have a problem with the way things are going. Helsingus, your two torpedoes – torch 'em off straight at bogey one.'

'But they'll go ballistic short of –'

Mirsky raised a warning hand. 'Just do it. Helm, option three-two. Signal all ships.' Once again, he picked up the phone to the Commodore's battle room to confer with his flag officer.

'Aye aye, sir.' The display centered on Rochard's World shifted, rolling; the orange line representing *Lord Vanek*'s course, hitherto straight in toward the planet, began to bend, curving away from the planet. The red lines showing the course of the two incoming enemy ships were also bending, moving to intercept the *Lord Vanek* and her five sister ships; meanwhile the twelve dots of blue, representing the torpedoes the squadron had dropped overboard almost two minutes earlier, began to grow outward.

Live torpedoes were not something any starship captain wanted to get too close to. Unlike a missile – essentially a tube full of reaction mass with a laser mirror in its tail and a warhead at the other end – a torpedo was a spacecraft with its own power plant, an incredibly dirty fission rocket, little more than a slow-burning atom bomb, barely under control as it spewed a horribly radioactive exhaust stream behind it. It was also the most efficient storable-fuel rocket motor available, without the complexity of fusion reactors or curved-space generators. Before the newer technologies came along, early-twenty-first-century pioneers had used it for the first crewed interplanetary missions.

'Fish are both running, sir. Ours are making nine-six and one-one-two gees respectively; general squadron broadside averages ninety-eight. They should burn out and switch to sustainer in one-zero-zero seconds and intersect bogeys one and two if they stay on current course in about one-fivezero seconds. Guidance pack degradation should still be under control by then, we should be able to do terminal targeting control.'

'Good,' Mirsky said shortly. Heading in on the *Lord Vanek* on a reciprocal course, the enemy ships might well be able to start shooting soon: but the torpedoes would get in the way nicely, messing up the clear line of sight on the *Lord Vanek* while threatening them. Which was exactly what Mirsky was hoping for.

There was something extremely odd about the two ships, he noted. They weren't following any kind of obvious tactical doctrine, just accelerating in a straight line, pulsing with lidar as they came – homing in blindly. There was no sign of sneaky moves. They'd lurched out and begun pinging away like drunken fools playing a barroom computer game, throwing away the advantage of concealment that they'd held. *Whoever was driving those birds is either a fool or –*

'Radar,' he said softly. 'Saturation cover forward and down. Anything there?'

'I'll look.' Marek gulped, getting the Captain's drift immediately. If these two were hounds, flushing their game out of hiding, something would be drifting in quietly from ahead. Not mines dropped at peak velocity, but something else. Maybe something worse, like a brace of powered torpedoes. 'Um, humbly suggest optical scan as well, sir?'

'It can't fix us for them any better,' Mirsky grunted. 'They know where we are.'

Radar Two: 'Sir, nothing on mass. Nothing within two light-seconds ahead or down. Small amount of organic debris – we passed through a thin cloud of it back at waypoint one, picked up a couple of scratches on the nose – but no sign of escorts or weapons.'

'Sir, we are all clear ahead,' said Lieutenant Marek.

'Well, keep looking then.' Mirsky looked down at his hands. They were tightly entwined in his lap, veins standing out on their backs, old hands, the fine hair at his wrists turning gray. 'How did I get this far?' he asked himself quietly.

His workstation pinged. 'Incoming call for you, sir,' it said.

'Damn.' He punched up the image. It was Commodore Bauer.

'I'm busy,' he said tersely. 'Torpedo run. Can it wait?'

'I don't think so. There is something very flaky going on. Why do you think they aren't shooting?'

'Because they've already shot at us, but the bullets haven't arrived yet,' Mirsky said through gritted teeth.

Bauer stared at his Flag Captain for a moment, wordless agreement written on his face. Then he nodded. 'Get us the hell out of here, Captain. I'll tell the rest of the squadron to follow your lead. Just give me as much delta-vee as you can between us and those – whatever.'

Radar Two: 'Time to torpedo closest approach, eight-zero seconds. Sir, there are no signs that wolf one or two has seen the fish. But they're well within sensor range if they're using something equivalent to our G-90s.'

'Understood.' Mirsky paused. Something was nagging at

the back of his mind; a nasty sense of having forgotten something. That neutrino pulse, that was it. Neutrinos meant strong nuclear force. So why no flash? 'Guns, load up twelve SEM-20s for tail drop at shortest intercept course. Assuming they come in from behind.' He glanced back at his screen, but the commodore had hung up on him without waiting.

'Aye aye. Birds loaded.' Helsingus seemed almost happy, twitching levers and adjusting dials. It was the nearest thing to pleasure Mirsky remembered the dour gunnery officer showing since his dog had disappeared. 'Ready at minus one-zero seconds.'

'Helm.' Mirsky paused. 'Prepare to execute plan bugout on my command.'

An alarm warbled at the radar desk. 'Beg to report sir,' began the petty officer on duty, face whey-pale: 'I've lost *Prince Vaclav*.'

Faces looked up in shock all around the room. 'What do you mean, lost it?' snapped Vulpis, bypassing the operational pecking order. 'You didn't just lose a battlecruiser –'

'Sir, she's stopped responding. Stopped accelerating, too. I can see her on plot, but there's something wrong with her –' The radar operator paused. 'Sir, I can't get an IFF heartbeat out of her. And she's reflecting way too much energy – something must have ripped the front off her emission control coating.'

'Helm. Execute plan bugout,' Mirsky snapped in the sudden silence that followed the report.

'Aye aye, sir, bugout it is.' Lieutenant Vulpis began flipping switches in a frenzy.

A fundamental problem with combat in space was that if things began to go wrong, they could do so with dizzying speed – and to make matters worse, catastrophe would only become visible to a ship that was so deep into the enemy's powered-missile envelope that escape was nearly impossible. Mirsky had gamed this situation repeatedly with Bauer and the other fleet captains; plan bugout was the result. It was a lousy plan, the only thing to commend it being the fact that all the alternatives were worse. Something had just reached out across ninety thousand kilometers and bushwhacked a battle-cruiser. This wasn't entirely unexpected; they were here to fight, after all. But they hadn't seen any missiles, only their own birds and the debris from the blow-out drifting in ahead of them, and the fine drizzle of organic 'dandruff' from the enemy ships – and in active mode, the *Lord Vanek*'s lidar could pin down a missile at almost a light-second, three hundred thousand kilometers. If the enemy had a beam weapon of some kind that was capable of trashing a capital ship at that range, nearly two orders of magnitude greater than their own point-defense energy weapons, they were already too damned close. All they could do was turn side-on and go to emergency thrust, generating a vector away from the enemy before they could respond.

Radar Two: 'Torpedo intersect in four-zero seconds. Wolves one and two still tracking on course, acceleration down to one gee.'

'Well, that's nice to know. Mr. Helsingus, I would appreciate it if you'd be so good as to prepare a warm welcome for anything our friends try to send after us. I don't know just what they threw at *Prince Vaclav*, but I don't propose to give them time to show us. And if you gentlemen will excuse me for a minute, I have a private call to make.' Mirsky pulled on his headset and pushed down on the antisound lever. 'Comms, get me the Commodore.' His earpieces clicked. 'Sir?'

'Have you started bugout?'

'Yes, sir. The *Prince Vaclav*—'

The screech of the decompression alarm cut through his ears like a knife. 'By the numbers, damn you!' yelled Mirsky. 'Suit up!' He yanked off his headset. Officers and men dashed to the emergency locker at the rear of the compartment and pulled their gear on, stumbled back to man posts while their backups followed suit. The ops room had already cycled onto its emergency supply, along with all the main nerve centers of the ship, but Mirsky wasn't one to take chances. Not that being suited up would count for much protection in ship-to-ship combat, but decompression was another threat entirely, one dreaded aboard any starship almost as much as fire or Hawking radiation. 'Damage control, talk to me,' he grunted. A passing CPO held out a suit for him; he stood up and pulled it on slowly, making sure to double-check its status display.

'Humbly report a big pressure drop on A deck, sir. Critical decompression, we're still venting air. Ah, humbly report there appears to be some damage to lidar emitter quadrant three.'

'You make sure everybody's buttoned down. Guns, Radar, where do we stand?'

Radar One: 'Torpedo intercept in one-five seconds. Bogey holding course, due to pass inside our terminal engagement envelope for two-zero seconds in one-two-zero then drop behind.'

Helsingus nodded. 'All tubes loaded,' he reported.

'Damage Control: Patch into life support and find out what the hell is loose.'

'Got it already, sir. I've got some kind of contamination, source inside life support one: weird organic molecules, low concentration. Also, er, localized outbreaks of fire. It's mostly around A deck. The lidar grid damage is localized, around where the debris strike happened. Ah, I have one-six crew marked down on the status board. A deck segment two is open to space, and they were all inside at the time.'

Gunnery: 'Five seconds to torpedo terminal boost phase.'

'Let's dazzle 'em now,' said Helsingus. 'Grid to full power.'

'Aye aye, sir, full multispectral shriek in progress.'

Helsingus leaned sideways and muttered into his headset; Radar One muttered back. There was some mutual adjustment of switches as radar relinquished priority control on the huge phased-array laser grid that coated the warship, then Helsingus and his two assistants began entering instructions.

The *Lord Vanek* boosted at right angles to the two enemy craft, accelerating away from the two silent pursuers on a ripple of warped space-time. The two saltwater-fission torpedoes, bright sparks behind, accelerated toward the enemy warships like a pair of nuclear fireworks. Now the tight-packed mosaic of panels that covered much of the *Lord Vanek*'s cylindrical bulk began to glow with the intense speckled purity of laser light. A thousand different colors appeared, blending and clashing and forming a single brilliant diadem of light; megawatts, then gigawatts of power surged out, the skin of the ship burning like a directional magnesium flare. The glow built up, and most of it flowed out in two tightly controlled beams, intense enough to cut through steel plate like a blowtorch at a range of a thousand kilometers.

Simultaneously, the flight of torpedoes throttled up to maximum thrust, weaving erratically as they closed the final three thousand kilometers to the onrushing enemy ships. Hurtling in ten times faster than an ICBM of the pre-space age, the rockets jinked and wove to avoid the anticipated pointlasers, relying on passive sensors and sophisticated antispoofing algorithms to cut through the expected jamming and countermeasures of the enemy ships. They took barely thirty seconds to close the distance, and found the enemy point defense to be almost non-existent.

From the ops room of the *Lord Vanek*, the engagement was undramatic. One of the pursuer points simply disappeared, replaced by an expanding shell of spallation debris and hot gases energized by an incandescent point far brighter than any conventional fission explosion; with the ship's hull blown wide and drive mountings shattered, the antimatter bottle spilled its contents into a soup of metallic hydrogen, triggering a mess of exotic subnuclear reactions. But only one of the torpedoes struck home; the other eleven winked out.

'Humbly report got more neutrino pulses, sir,' called the radar op. 'Not from the one we nailed –'

Mirsky stared at the main screen. 'Damage control. What about A deck?' he demanded. 'Helm. Everyone else running on bugout?'

'A deck is still empty to space, sir. I sent a control team, but they aren't reporting back. Pressure's dropping in the number four recycler run, no sign of external venting. Um, I'm showing a major power drain on the grid, sir, we're losing megawatts somewhere.'

'Bugout message was sent a minute ago, sir. So far they're all –' Vulpis cursed. 'Sir! *Kamchatka*'s gone!'

'Where, dammit?' Mirsky leaned forward.

'Another IFF drop-off,' called radar. 'From –' The man paused, eyes widening with shock. '*Kamchatka*,' he concluded. On the main plot at the front of the bridge, the Imperial ships' vectors were lengthening, up to 300 k.p.s. now and creeping up steadily. The target planet hung central, infinitely far out of reach.

Mirsky glanced at his first officer. Ilya stared back apprehensively.

'With respect, sir, they're not fighting any way we know –'

Red lights. Honking sirens. Damage Control shouting orders into his speaking horn. 'Status!' roared Mirsky. 'What's going on, dammit?'

'Losing pressure on B deck segment one, sir! No readings anywhere on segment three from A down to D deck. Big power fluctuations, distribution board fourteen compartment D-nine-five is on fire. Ah, I have a compartment open to space and another compartment on fire in B-four-five. I can't get through to damage control on B deck at all and all hell has broken loose on C deck –'

'Seal off everything above F,' ordered Mirsky, his face white. 'Do it *now*! Guns, prep decoys two and three for launch –'

But he was already too late to save his ship; because the swarm of bacteriasized replicators that had slammed into A deck at 600 k.p.s. – cushioned in a husk of reinforced diamond – and eaten their way down through five decks into the ship, were finally arriving in the engineering spaces. And eating, and breeding . . .

Vassily's voice quavered with a nervous, frightened edge that would have been funny under other circumstances. 'I am arresting you for sabotage, treason, unlicensed use of proscribed technologies, and giving aid and comfort to the enemies of the New Republic! Surrender now, or it will be the worse for you!'

'Shut up and grab the back of that couch unless you want to walk home. Martin, if you wouldn't mind giving him a leg down – that's right. I need to get this hatch shut –'

Rachel glanced around disgustedly. There was a beautiful view; stars everywhere, a terrestrial planet hanging huge and gibbous ahead, like a marbled blue-and-white hallucination – and this idiot child squawking in her ear. Meanwhile, she was clinging with both hands to the underside of the capsule lid, and with both feet to the pilot's chair, trying to hold everything together. When she'd poked her head up through the hatch and seen who was clinging to the low-gain antenna, she'd had half a mind to duck back inside again and fire up the thrusters to jolt him loose; a stab of blind rage made her grind her teeth together so loudly a panicky Martin had demanded to know if her suit had sprung a leak. But the red haze of anger faded quickly, and she'd reached out and grabbed Vassily's arm, and somehow shoved his inflated emergency suit in through the hatch.

'I'm coming down,' she said. Clenching her thighs around

the back of the chair, she clicked the release catch on the hatch and pulled it down as far as she could, then locked it in position. The cabin below her was overfull: Vassily obviously didn't have a clue about keeping himself out of the way, and Martin was busy trying to squirm into the leg well of his seat to make room. She yanked on her lifeline, dropped down until she was standing on the seat of her chair, then grabbed the hatch and pulled it the rest of the way shut. She felt the solid ripple-click of a dozen small catches locking home on all four sides. 'Okay. Autopilot, seal hatch, then repressurize cabin. Martin, not over there – that's the toilet, you really don't want to open that – yes, that's the locker you want.' Air began hissing into the cabin from vents around the ceiling; white mist formed whirlpool fog banks that drifted across the main window. 'That's great. You, listen up: you aren't aboard a Navy ship here. Shut up, and we'll give you a lift downside; keep telling me I'm under arrest, and I might get pissed off enough to push you overboard.'

'Urp.'

The Junior Procurator's eyes went wide as his suit began to deflate around him. Behind the seats, Martin grunted as he rifled through the contents of one of the storage lockers. 'This what you want?' He punted a rolled-up hammock at Rachel. She rolled around in her seat and stuck one end of it to the wall behind her, then let it unroll back toward Martin. He drifted out of the niche, narrowly avoided kicking their castaway in the head and managed to get the other end fastened. 'You! Out of that suit, into this hammock. As you may have noticed, we don't have a lot of room.' She pressed the release stud, and her helmet let go of her suit and drifted free; catching it, she shoved it down behind her seat, under the hammock. 'You can unsuit now.'

Martin peeled halfway out of his own suit, keeping his legs and lower body in the collapsed plastic bag. Vassily floated out of his niche, struggling with the flaccid bladder of his helmet: Martin steered him into the hammock and managed to get his head out of the bag before he managed to inhale it. 'You're –' Vassily stopped. 'Er, thank you.'

'Don't even *think* about hijacking us,' Rachel warned darkly. 'The autopilot's slaved to my voice, and neither of us particularly wants to take our chances with your friends.'

'Er.' Vassily breathed deeply. 'Um. That is to say –' He looked around wildly. 'Are we going to die?'

'Not if I have anything to do with it,' Rachel said firmly.

'But the enemy ships! They must be—'

'It's the Festival. Have you got any idea what they are?' asked Martin.

'If you know anything about it, you should have told the Admiral's staff. Why didn't you tell them? Why—'

'We *did* tell them. They didn't listen,' Rachel observed.

Vassily visibly struggled to understand. Ultimately, it was easier to change the subject than think the unthinkable. 'What are you going to do now?'

'Well.' Rachel whistled tunelessly through her front teeth. 'Personally I'd like to land this lifeboat somewhere near, say, Novy Petrograd, book the honeymoon suite in the Crown Hotel, fill the bathtub with champagne and lie in it while Martin feeds me caviar on black bread. However, what we actually do next really depends on the Festival, hmm? If Martin is right about it—'

'Believe it,' Martin emphasized.

'– the Navy force is going to quietly disappear, never to be seen again. That's what comes of assuming that everyone plays by the same set of rules. We're just going to drift on through, then fire up our motor for a direct landing, meanwhile squawking that we're neutral at the top of our voices. The Festival isn't what your leaders think it is, kid. It's a threat to the New Republic – they got that much right – but they don't understand what *kind* of threat it is, or how to deal with it Going in shooting will only make it respond in kind, and it's better at it than your boys.'

'But our Navy is good!' Vassily insisted. 'They're the best navy within twenty light-years! What would you anarchists do? You don't even have a strong government, much less a fleet!'

Rachel chuckled. After a moment, Martin joined in. Gradually their laughter mounted, deafening in the confined space.

'Why are you laughing at me?' Vassily demanded indignantly.

'Look.' Martin hunched around in his chair until he could lock eyes with the Procurator. 'You've grown up with this theory of strong government, the divine right of the ruling class, the thwack of the riding crop of firm administration on the bare buttocks of the urban proletariat and all that. But has it occurred to you that the UN system also works, and has maybe been around for twice as long as the New Republic? There's more than one way to run a circus, as I think the Festival demonstrates, and rigid hierarchies like the one you grew up in are lousy at dealing with change. The UN system, at least after the Singularity and the adoption of the planetary unconstitution –' He snorted.

'Once, the fringe anarchists used to think the UN was some kind of quasi-fascist world government. Back in the twentieth and twenty-first centuries, when strong government was in fashion because the whole planetary civilization was suffering from future shock, because it was approaching a Singularity. After that passed, though – well, there weren't a lot of viable authoritarian governments left, and the more rigid they were, the less well they could deal with the aftereffects of losing nine-tenths of their populations overnight. Oh, and the cornucopiae: it can't be pleasant to run a central bank and wake up one morning to discover ninety percent of your taxpayers are gone and the rest think money is obsolete.'

'But the UN is a government—'

'No it isn't,' Martin insisted. 'It's a talking shop. Started out as a treaty organization, turned into a bureaucracy, then an escrow agent for various transnational trade and standards agreements. After the Singularity, it was taken over by the Internet engineering task force. It's not the government of Earth; it's just the only remaining relic of Earth's governments that your people can recognize. The bit that does the common-good jobs that everyone needs to subscribe to. World-wide vaccination programs, trade agreements with extrasolar governments, insurer of last resort for major disasters, that sort of thing. The point is, for the most part, the UN doesn't actually *do* anything; it doesn't have a foreign policy, it's just a head on a stick for your politicians to rant about. Sometimes somebody or another uses the UN as a front when they need to do something credible-looking, but trying to get a consensus vote out of the Security Council is like herding cats.'

'But you're –' Vassily paused. He looked at Rachel.

'I *told* your Admiral that the Festival wasn't human,' she said tiredly. 'He thanked me and carried right on planning an attack. That's why they're all going to die soon. Not enough flexibility, your people. Even trying to run a minor – and horrendously illegal – causality-violation attack wasn't that original a response.' She sniffed. 'Thought they'd turn up a week before the Festival, by way of that half-assed closed time-like path "to avoid mines and sleepers". As if the Eschaton wouldn't notice, and as if the Festival was just another bunch of primitives with atom bombs.'

A red light winked on the console in front of her. 'Oh, look,' said Martin.

'It's beginning. Better strap yourself in – we're way too close for comfort.'

'I don't understand. What's going on?' asked Vassily.

Martin reached up to adjust a small lens set in the roof of the cabin, then glanced over his shoulder. 'Can you juggle, kid?'

'No. Why?'

Martin pointed at the screen. 'Spine ships. Or antibodies. Subsentient remotes armed with, um, you don't want to know. Eaters and shapers and *things*. Nasty hungry little nanomachines. Gray goo, in other words.'

'Oh.' Vassily looked ill. 'You mean, they're going to—'

'Come out to meet the fleet and take a sniff, by the look of it. Unfortunately, I don't think Commodore Bauer realizes that if he doesn't make friendly noises, they're all going to die; he still thinks it's a *battle*, the kind you fight with missiles and guns. If they *do* decide to talk — well, the Festival is an infovore. We're perfectly safe as long as we can keep it entertained and don't shoot at it. Luckily, it doesn't understand humor; finds it fascinating, but doesn't quite get it. As long as we keep it entertained it won't eat us; we may even be able to escalate matters to a controlling intelligence that can let us off the Bouncers' hook and let us land safely.' He reached into the bag of equipment he'd dredged out of the locker behind the seats. 'Ready to start broadcasting, Rachel? Here, kid, put this on. It's showtime.'

The red nose floating in the air in front of Vassily's face seemed to be mocking him.

the telephone
repairman

Sitting in a highly eccentric polar orbit that drifted almost sixty thousand kilometers above the provincial township of Plotsk, the Festival'ss prime node basked fat and happy at the heart of an informational deluge. The pickings in this system were sparse compared to some of the previous ports of call on its itinerary, but Rochard's World was still unusual and interesting. The Festival had chanced upon few primitive worlds in its travel, and the contrast with its memories of them was great.

Now, as the first starwisps departed — aimed forward at new, unvisited worlds, and back along its track to the hot-cores of civilization where it had stopped before — the Festival took stock. Events on the ground had not gone entirely satisfactorily; while it had accrued a good body of folklore, and not a little insight into the social mores of a rigidly static society, the information channels on offer were ridiculously sparse, and the lack of demand for its wares dismaying. Indeed, its main source of data had been the unfortunate minds forcibly uploaded by some of the more dissolute, not to say amoral, fringe elements. The Critics, with their perennial instinct to explain and dissect, were moaning continuously — something about the colony succumbing to a disastrous economic singularity — but that sort of thing wasn't the Festival's problem. It would soon be time to move on; the first tentative transmissions from Trader clades had been detected, burbling and chirping in the Oort cloud, and the job of opening up communications with this civilization was nearly done.

Each of the hundreds of starwisps the high-orbit launchers were dispatching carried one end of a causal channel: a black box containing a collection of particles in a quantum-entangled state with antiparticles held by the Festival. (By teleporting the known quantum state of a third particle into one of the entangled particles, data could be transmitted between terminals infinitely fast, using up one entangled quantum dot for each bit.) Once the starwisps arrived at their destinations, the channels would be hooked into the communications grid the Festival's creators had set out to construct. No longer limited by the choke point of the Festival's back channel to its last destination, the population of Rochard's World would be exposed to the full information flow of the polity it belonged to.

Out toward Sputnik, the Festival took note of some activity by Bouncers. They seemed to be clearing up a small mess: a handful of slow, inefficient ships that had approached without warning and opened fire on the Bouncers with primitive energy weapons. The Bouncers responded with patient lethality; anything that menaced them died. Some small craft slipped by, evidently not involved in the assault; a number of the second wave broke and ran, and they, too, were spared. But for the most part, the Festival ignored them. Anyone so singlemindedly hostile as to attack the Festival was hardly likely to be a good source of information: as for the others, it would have a chance to talk to them when they arrived.

*

The air in the lifeboat was foul with a stench of sweat and stale farts. Rachel sat hunched over her backup console, staring unblinkingly at the criticality monitors while the rocket howled and rumbled beneath them: while a single output jitter might kill them before she could even blink, it made her feel better to go through the motions. Besides, she was totally exhausted: as soon as they touched down she had every intention of sleeping for three days. It had been fourteen hours since they escaped from the *Lord Vanek*; fourteen hours on top of a day and a sleepless night before. If she stopped making the effort to stay awake –

'Riddle this interrogative.' The creature on the screen snapped its tusks, red light gleaming off fangs like blood. 'Why not you Bouncers accept?'

'I couldn't possibly place myself further in their debt,' she said as smoothly as she could manage. *Neutron flux stable at ten kilobecquerels per minute*, warned her implants. A hundred chest X rays, in other words, sustained for four hours during the deceleration cycle. The lifeboat's motor shuddered beneath her like something alive. Vassily's hammock swung behind her. He'd fallen asleep surprisingly fast once she convinced him they weren't going to throw him overboard, exhausted by the terror of four hours adrift spent waiting to die. Martin snored softly in the dim red light of the comms terminal, similarly tired. *Nothing like learning you aren't about to die to make you relax*, she thought. Which was why she couldn't sleep yet –

'No debt for payment in kind,' said the strange creature. 'You bear much reduction of entropy.'

'Your translation program is buggy,' she muttered.

'Is so interrogative? Suppose, we. Reiterate and paraphrase: question why you do not attack Bouncers like other ships?'

Rachel tensed. 'Because we are not part of their expedition,' she said slowly. 'We have different intentions. We come in peace. Exchange information. We will entertain you. Is that understood?'

'Ahum. *Skreee* –' the thing in the screen turned its head right around to look over its shoulder. 'We you understand. Will Bouncers of notify peaceful intent. You part are not of not-old administrative institution territoriality of planet?'

'No, we're from Earth.' Martin stopped snoring: she glanced sideways. One eye was open, watching her tiredly. 'Original world of humans,' she clarified.

'Know about Dirt. Know about you-mans, too. Information valuable, tell all!'

'In due course,' Rachel hedged, acutely aware of the thickening air in the capsule. 'Are we safe from the Bouncers?'

'Am not understanding,' the thing said blandly. 'We are will notify Bouncers of your intent. Is that not safety?'

'Not exactly.' Rachel glanced at Martin, who frowned at her and shook his head slightly. 'If you notify the Bouncers that we are not attacking them, will that stop them from eating us?'

'Ahum!' The creature blinked at her. 'Maybe not.'

'Well, then. What *will* stop the Bouncers from attacking us?'

'*Skree* – why worry? Just talk.'

'I'm not worrying. It's just that I am not going to tell you everything you want to know about me until I am no longer at risk from the Bouncers. Do you understand that?'

'Ha-*frumph!* Not entertaining us. Humph. A-okay, Bouncers will *not* eat you. We have dietary veto over theys. Now tell all?'

'Sure. But first –' She glanced at the autopilot monitor. 'We're running low on breathable air. Need to land this ship. Is that possible? Can you tell me about conditions on the ground?'

'Sure.' The creature bounced its head up-down in a jerky

parody of a nod. 'You not problem, land. May find things changed. Best dock here first. We Critics.'

'I'm looking for a man,' Rachel added, deciding to push her luck. 'Have you installed a communications net? Can you locate him for us?'

'May exist. Name?'

'Rubenstein. Burya Rubenstein.' A noise behind her; Vassily rolling over, his hammock swinging in the shifting inertial reference frame of the lifeboat.

'Excuse.' The creature leaned forward. 'Name Rubenstein? Revolutionary?'

'Yes.' Martin frowned at her inquiringly: Rachel glanced sideways. *I'll explain later*, she thought at him.

'Knows Sister Burya. Sister Seventh of Stratagems. You business with have the Extropian Underground?'

'That's right.' Rachel nodded. 'Can you tell me where he is?'

'Do better.' The thing in the screen grinned. 'You accept orbital elements for rendezvous now. We take you there.'

Behind her, Vassily was sitting up, his eyes wide.

The admiral didn't want to board the lifeboat.

'D-d-d-d-' he drooled, left eye glaring, right eye slack and lifeless.

'Sir, please don't make a fuss. We need to go aboard now.' Robard looked over his shoulder anxiously, as if half-expecting red-clawed disaster to come stooping and drooling through the airlock behind him.

'N-ever surrr –' Kurtz found the effort too much; his head flopped forward onto his chest.

Robard hefted his chair, and pushed forward, into the cramped confines of the boat. 'Is he going to be alright?' Lieutenant Kossov asked fussily.

'Who knows? Just show me somewhere to lash his chair and we'll be off. More chance of getting help for him down –'

Sirens honked mournfully in the passage outside, and Robard winced as his ears popped. Kossov reached past another officer wearing the braid of a lieutenant commander and yanked the emergency override handle: the outer door of the lifeboat hissed shut. 'What's going on?' someone called from up by the cockpit.

'Pressure breach in this section! Doors tight!'

'Aye, doors tight. Is the Admiral aboard?'

'Yes to that. You going?'

In answer, the deck heaved. Robard grabbed a stanchion and held on one-handed, bracing the Admiral's wheelchair with another hand as the lifeboat lurched. A rippling bang of explosive bolts severed its umbilical connection to the stricken warship, then it was falling – falling through a deliberately opened gap in the ship's curved-space field, which was otherwise strong enough to rip the small craft apart. Officers and a handful of selected enlisted men struggled to seize anchor points as whoever was in the hot seat played a fugue on the attitude thrusters, rolling the lifeboat out from behind the warship. Then the drive cut in with a gentle buzzing hiss from underfoot, and a modicum of weight returned them to the correct plane.

Robard bent to work on the wheelchair with a length of cable. 'Someone help me with the Admiral,' he asked.

'What do you need?' Lieutenant Kossov peered at him, owlish behind his pince-nez.

'Need to tie this chair down. Then – where are we landing? Is there a doctor aboard this boat? My master really needs to be taken to a hospital, as soon as possible. He's very ill.'

'Indeed.' The Lieutenant glanced at him sympathetically, then his gaze wandered to the somnolent Admiral. 'Give me that.'

Robard passed him the other end of the cable, and together they secured the wheelchair to four of the eye bolts that dotted the floor. Around them, the other surviving officers were taking stock of the situation, neatly unfolding emergency deceleration hammocks from overhead lockers and chatting quietly. The atmosphere aboard the lifeboat was subdued, chastened; they were lucky to be alive, ashamed not to be aboard the stricken battlecruiser. The fact that most of the survivors were officers from the admiral's staff didn't go amiss; the real warriors remained at their posts, trying valiantly to halt the plague that was eating the ship around them. In one corner, a junior lieutenant was sobbing inconsolably at the center of an embarrassed circle of silence.

The Admiral, oblivious to everything around him, mumbled and coughed querulously. Kossov leaned forward attentively. 'Is there anything I can do for you, my Admiral?' he asked.

'I fear he's beyond our help,' Robard said sadly. He rested a gentle hand on Kurtz's shoulder, steadying the Admiral in his chair. 'Unless the surgeons can do something —'

'He's trying to talk,' Kossov snapped. 'Let me listen.' He leaned close to the old warrior's face. 'Can you hear me, sir?'

'A-a —' The Admiral gargled in the back of his throat.

'Don't excite him, I implore you! He needs rest!'

Kossov fixed the servant with a baleful eye. 'Be silent for a minute.'

'— Aah, arr — we — 'oing?'

Robard started. 'Humbly report we are on our way down to the planetary surface, sir,' said the Lieutenant. 'We should be arriving in the capital shortly.' Nothing about the rest of the fleet, the disposition of which was anything but likely to arrive in the colonial capital.

'Ood.' The Admiral's face relaxed, eyelids drooping. ''Amprey. 'Ive'm wha' for.' He subsided, evidently exhausted by the effort of speaking.

Robard straightened up: his eyes met those of the

Lieutenant. 'He never gives up,' he said calmly. 'Even when he ought to. It'll be the death of him one of these days . . .'

Riding a chicken-legged hut through a wasteland that had recently gone from bucolic feudalism to transcendent posthumanism without an intervening stage, Burya Rubenstein drifted through a dream of crumbling empires.

The revolutionaries were ideologically committed to a transcendence that they hadn't fully understood – until it arrived whole and pure and incomprehensible, like an iceberg of strange information breaking the surface of a frozen sea of entropy. They hadn't been ready for it; nobody had warned them. They had hazy folk memories of Internets and cornucopiae to guide them, cargo-cult assertions of the value of technology – but they hadn't felt the elephant, had no sense of the shape the new phenomena took, and their desires caused new mutant strains to congeal out of the phase space of the Festival machinery.

Imagine not growing up with telephones – or faxes, video conferencing, on-line translation, gesture recognition, light switches. Tradition said that you could send messages around the world in an eyeblink, and the means to do so was called e-mail. Tradition didn't say that e-mail was a mouth morphing out of the nearest object and speaking with a friend's lips, but that was a more natural interpretation than strange textual commands and a network of post-office routers. The Festival, not being experienced in dealing with Earth-proximate human cultures, had to guess at the nature of the miracles being requested. Often, it got them wrong.

Burya knew all about communications; his grandfather had dandled him on his knee and passed on legends his own grandfather had told him, legends about management information systems that could tell the management everything they could possibly know about the world and more, legends about the strange genii of human resources that could bring forth any necessary ability at will. Some of the more wired dissidents of Novy Petrograd had cobbled together something which they, in turn, called a management information system: cameras squatted with hooded cyclopean eyes atop the garrets and rooflines of the city, feeding images into the digital nervous system of the revolution.

Before he'd left Plotsk, Burya had spent some time with Timoshevski. Oleg had applied the leeches to Burya's engorged sense of importance, reminding him that he was only a high official within the Novy Petrograd soviet, that the soviet, in turn, was only a benign parasite upon the free market, a load-balancing algorithm that would be abandoned when the true beauty of the level playing field could be established. Oleg had also applied the worms, which itched furiously (and occasionally burned) as they established contact with Burya's nervous system. He'd had to inquire pointedly as to the origins of Burya's strange sense of bourgeois incrementalism in order to goad his erstwhile colleague into accepting the upgrade, but in the end, Rubenstein had seen no alternative. Given his currently peripatetic occupation, he'd be sidelined by the Central Committee if he stayed out of touch much longer. And so it was that his head itched abominably, and he was plagued by strange visions as the worms of the Committee for State Communications forged a working relationship with his brain.

When Burya slept, he dreamed in rasterized false-color images, scanned from the rooftops of the capital. The revolution, eternally vigilant, multi-tasked on his lateral geniculate body, rousting slumbering synapses to recognize suspicious patterns of behavior. Burya found it both disturbing and oddly reassuring to see that the city, for all the changes wrought by the revolution, continued. Here a youth darted from shadow to shadow, evidently on a midnight assignation with his sweetheart; there a grimmer kind of conspiracy fomented, dogs fighting over the bones of temporal responsibility as a block warden stalked a resented houseowner with murder in his eye. Houses grew and fissioned in slow motion, great sessile beasts prodded hither and yon by their internal symbionts. It was all unspeakably alien to him: an eerie half-life crawling over the once-familiar city, echoes of the way he'd lived for years, lying like a corpse in an open casket. Even the searing light of a nighttime shuttle landing at the field outside the city couldn't bring it back to a semblance of the life he'd known.

Burya dreamed, too, of his own family; a wife he hadn't seen in fourteen years, a five-year-old son whose chubby face blurred with distance. (Internal exile was not a sentence of exclusion from family, but she came from solid middle-class stock, had disowned him upon hearing of his sentence and been granted a legal separation.) A helpless, weak loneliness – which he cursed whenever he noticed it in waking life – dogged his heels. The revolutionary junta had barely affected the course of events; it provided a nucleus for the wilder elements to coagulate around, a lens to focus the burning rays of resentment on the remains of the ancien régime, but in and of itself, it had achieved little. People suddenly gifted with infinite wealth and knowledge rapidly learned that they didn't need a government – and this was true as much for members of the underground as for the workers and peasants they strove to mobilize. Perhaps this was the message that the Critic had been trying to drum into him ever since his abduction from the offices of the revolutionary soviet – the revolution he had been striving for didn't need him.

On the second morning of the search for Felix, Burya awakened exhausted, limbs aching and sore, feet half frozen, in one corner of the walking-hut. Sister Seventh was elsewhere, snuffling and crashing in the undergrowth beside the path. Bright polymer-walled yurts clung to the fringes of the clearing they'd camped in. A growth of trees around them struggled defiantly beneath huge shelf fungi that threatened to turn them into many-colored outcroppings. All around them grew gigantic ferns and purple-veined cycads, interstellar colonists planted by the unseen gardeners of the Festival fleet. Small mouselike creatures tended the ferns, bringing them scraps of decaying matter and attaching them to the sundewlike feeding palps that sprouted from their stems.

According to the presingularity maps, they should have passed a village two kilometers ago, but they'd seen no sign of it. Instead, they'd passed beneath a huge drifting geodesic sphere that had turned the sunset to flame overhead, making one of the cyborg militia shout and fire wildly into the air until Sergeant Lukcas yelled at him and took his gun away. 'It's a farm, pighead,' he'd explained with heavy-handed irony, 'like what you grew up on, only rolled into a ball and flying around the sky. And if you don't stop shooting at it, we'll use your head the same way.' Some of the guards had muttered and made signs to avert the evil eye – in one case using a newly functional set of mandibles – and the rabbit walked with his ears laid flat along his head for half a kilometer before they made camp, but there were no further untoward incidents before the end of the road. But now the road had definitely come to an end.

The posse had made good progress along the Emperor's metaled highways to reach this point; but ahead of them, the Lysenkoist forest was attempting to assimilate the road. Small, eyeless rodents with fine pelts gnawed mindlessly at the asphalt surface, extruding black pellets that were swarmed over by not-ants the size of grasshoppers. Tall clay structures not unlike termite mounds dotted the open spaces between the ferns: they hummed quietly with a noise like a million microscopic gas turbines.

The campfire crackled ominously and belched steam as Mr. Rabbit threw scraps of dead, fungus-riddled wood on it. Burya yawned and stretched in the cold air, then stumbled off to find a tree to piss behind. Bedrolls stirred on the ground, militiamen grumbling and demanding coffee, food, and sexual favors from a nonexistent cook. There was a gout of flame and the rabbit jumped backward, narrowly missing a soldier who howled curses; the road castings were highly inflammable.

After pissing, Burya squatted. It was in this undignified position that Sister Seventh, in an unusually avuncular mood, found him.

'Greetings of morning and good micturations to you! News of outstandingness and grace bring I.'

'Harrumph.' Burya glared at the giant rodent, his ears meanwhile flushing red with the effort of evacuation. 'Has anybody told you it isn't polite to stare?'

'At what?' Sister Seventh looked puzzled.

'Nothing,' he muttered. 'What's this news?'

'Why, of importance nothing.' The Critic turned away innocently. 'Of pleasing symmetry –'

Burya gritted his teeth, then began fumbling about for leaves. (This was something that had never been mentioned in the biographies of the famous revolutionaries, he noted vaguely; being attacked by bears and pursued by bandits or Royal mounted police was all very exciting and noteworthy, but the books never said anything about the shortage of toilet paper in the outback, or the way there were never any soft leaves around when you needed them.) 'Just the facts.'

'Visitors! My sibling's nest overflows with a bounty of information.'

'Visitors? But –' Burya stopped. 'Your siblings. In *orbit*?'

'Yes!' Sister Seventh rolled forward and over, waving her stubby legs in the air briefly before tumbling over with a loud thud. 'Visitors from space!'

'Where from?' Burya leaned forward eagerly.

'The New Republic.' Sister Seventh grinned amusedly,

baring huge, yellowed tusks. 'Sent fleet. Met Bouncers. There were survivors.'

'Who, dammit!' He gritted his teeth angrily as he yanked his trousers up.

'Ambassador from Earth-prime. One other-else-who component-wise is part of her hive. And ambiguosity. They inquire for you, yourself. Want to meet?'

Burya gaped. 'They're coming *here*?'

'They land at our destination. Soon.'

The lifeboat was dark, hot, and stank of methane; the waste gas scrubber had developed an asthmatic wheeze. By any estimate, the life-support loop was only good for another day or so of breathable air before they had to retreat into their suits – but long before then, the passengers would have to face the perils of reentry.

'Are you sure this is safe?' asked Vassily.

Rachel rolled her eyes. 'Safe, he asks,' muttered Martin. 'Kid, if you wanted safe, you should have stayed home when the fleet left port.'

'But I don't understand – you've been talking to those aliens. They're the enemy! They just killed half our fleet! But you're taking orbital elements and course correction advisories from them. Why are you so trusting? How do you know they won't kill us, too?'

'They're not the enemy,' Rachel said, patiently prodding away at the autopilot console. 'They never were the enemy – at least, not the kind of enemy the Admiral and his merry band expected.'

'But if they're not your enemy, you must be on their side!' Vassily glanced from one of them to the other, thoroughly spooked now.

'Nope.' Rachel carried on prodding at the autopilot. 'I wasn't sure before, but I am, now: the Festival isn't anything like you think it is. You guys came out here expecting an attack by a foreign government, with ships and soldiers, didn't you? But there are more things out in this universe than humans and their nations and multinational organizations. You've been fighting a shadow.'

'But it destroyed all those ships! It's hostile! It —'

'Calm down.' Martin watched him cautiously. *Ungrateful little shit: or is he just terminally confused?* Rachel's easy conversation with the Critics had unsettled Martin more than he liked to admit, almost as much as her unexpectedly successful rescue attempt. There were wheels within wheels here, more than he'd expected. 'There are no sides. The Critics aren't enemies; they aren't even part of the Festival. We tried to tell your people to expect something totally alien, but they wouldn't listen.'

'What do you mean?'

'The Festival isn't human, it isn't *remotely* human. You people are thinking in terms of people with people-type motivations; that's wrong, and it's been clear that it's wrong from the start. You can no more declare war on the Festival than you can declare a war against sleep. It's a self-replicating information network. Probe enters a system: probe builds a self-extending communications network and yanks the inhabited worlds of that system into it. Drains all the information it can get out of the target civilization, then spawns more probes. The probes carry some parasites, uploaded lifeforms that build bodies and download into them whenever they reach a destination — but that's not what it exists for.'

Vassily gaped. 'But it attacked us!'

'No it didn't,' Martin replied patiently. 'It isn't intelligent; analyzing its behavior by adopting an intentional stance is a mistake. All it did was detect an inhabited planet with no telephone service at a range of some light-years and obey its instructions.'

'But the instructions — it's war!'

'No, it's a bug fix. It turns out that the Festival is just a — a telephone repairman. Like a robot repairman. Only it doesn't repair mere telephones — it repairs holes in the galactic information flow.' Martin glanced sideways at Rachel. She was wrestling with the autopilot, getting the landing burn sequence keyed in. It was a bad idea to distract her at a time like this; better keep the young nuisance occupied.

'Civilizations rise and fall from time to time; the Festival is probably a mechanism set in place a few millennia ago to keep them in touch, built by an interstellar culture back in the mists of time. When it detected a hole in the net it maintains, it decided to fix it, which is why it set up to do business in orbit around Rochard's World, which is about as isolated and cut off as it's possible to be.'

'But we didn't ask for it,' Vassily said uncertainly.

'Well, of course not. Actually, I think it's strayed outside its original maintenance zone, so every system it discovers in this sector warrants a repair job: but that's not necessarily all there is to it. Part of the repair process is a rapid exchange of information with the rest of the network it connects to, a flow that runs in two directions. Over time, the Festival has become more than a mere repair service; it's become a civilization in its own right, one that blooms like a desert flower — briefly flourishing in the right environment, then curling up into a seed and sleeping as it migrates across the deserted gulf light-years between oases. Telephone switches and routers are some of the most complicated information-processing systems ever invented — where do you think the Eschaton originally came from?

'When the Festival arrived at Rochard's World, it had a 250-year communications deficit to make good. That repair — the end of isolation, arrival of goods and ideas restricted by the New Republic — caused a limited local singularity, what in our business we call a consensus reality excursion; people went a little crazy, that's all. A sudden overdose of change; immortality, bioengineering, weakly superhuman AI arbeiters, nanotechnology, that sort of thing. It isn't an attack.'

'But then – you're telling me they brought unrestricted communications with them?' he asked.

'Yup.' Rachel looked up from her console. 'We've been trying for years to tell your leaders, in the nicest possible way: information wants to be free. But they wouldn't listen. For forty years we tried. Then along comes the Festival, which treats censorship as a malfunction and routes communications around it. The Festival won't take no for an answer because it doesn't have an opinion on anything; it just is.'

'But information isn't free. It can't be. I mean, some things – if anyone could read anything they wanted, they might read things that would tend to deprave and corrupt them, wouldn't they? People might give exactly the same consideration to blasphemous pornography that they pay to the Bible! They could plot against the state, or each other, without the police being able to listen in and stop them!'

Martin sighed. 'You're still hooked on the state thing, aren't you?' he said. 'Can you take it from me, there are other ways of organizing your civilization?'

'Well –' Vassily blinked at him in mild confusion. 'Are you telling me you let information circulate freely where you come from?'

'It's not a matter of permitting it,' Rachel pointed out. 'We had to admit that we couldn't prevent it. *Trying* to prevent it was worse than the disease itself.'

'But, but lunatics could brew up biological weapons in their kitchens, destroy cities! Anarchists would acquire the power to overthrow the state, and nobody would be able to tell who they were or where they belonged anymore. The most foul nonsense would be spread, and nobody could stop it –' Vassily paused. 'You don't believe me,' he said plaintively.

'Oh, we believe you alright,' Martin said grimly. 'It's just – look, change isn't always bad. Sometimes freedom of speech provides a release valve for social tensions that would lead to revolution. And at other times, well – what you're protesting about boils down to a dislike for anything that disturbs the *status quo*. You see your government as a security blanket, a warm fluffy cover that'll protect everybody from anything bad all the time. There's a lot of that kind of thinking in the New Republic; the idea that people who aren't kept firmly in their place will automatically behave badly. But where I come from, most people have enough common sense to *avoid* things that'd harm them; and those that don't, need to be taught. Censorship just drives problems underground.'

'But, terrorists!'

'Yes,' Rachel interrupted, 'terrorists. There are always people who think they're doing the right thing by inflicting misery on their enemies, kid. And you're perfectly right about brewing up biological weapons and spreading rumors. But –' She shrugged. 'We can live with a low background rate of that sort of thing more easily than we can live with total surveillance and total censorship of everyone, all the time.' She looked grim. 'If you think a lunatic planting a nuclear weapon in a city is bad, you've never seen what happens when a planet pushes the idea of ubiquitous surveillance and censorship to the limit. There are places where –' She shuddered.

Martin glanced at her. 'You've got somewhere specific in mind to –'

'I don't want to talk about it,' she said tersely. 'And you should be ashamed of yourself, winding the boy up like that. Either of you two noticed the air stinks?'

'Yeah.' Martin yawned widely. 'Are we about—'

'– I am not a –' A thundering chorus of popping noises sounded outside the cabin. '– boy!' Vassily finished with a squeak.

. 'Belt up, kid. Main engine coming on in five seconds.'

Martin tensed, unconsciously tightening his belt. 'What's our descent curve?'

'Waypoint one coming up: ten-second course adjustment, one-point-two gees. We sit tight for four minutes or so, then we hit waypoint two, and burn for two hours at two and a quarter gees – this ends 'bout four thousand klicks elevation relative to planetary surface, and we'll hit atmosphere sixteen minutes later at about four k.p.s. We'll have some reaction mass left, but I really don't want to power up the main engine once we're in air we'll have to breathe afterward; so we're going to drop the propulsion module once we're suborbital and it'll kick itself back into a graveyard orbit with the last of its fuel.'

'Er.' Vassily looked puzzled. 'Four k.p.s. Isn't that a bit fast?'

'No it's –' A high-pitched roar cut into Rachel's explanation, jolting everything in the capsule back toward the rear bulkhead. Ten seconds passed. 'It's only about Mach 12, straight down. And we'll have dropped the engines overboard, first. But don't worry, we'll slow up pretty fast when we hit the atmosphere. They used to do this sort of thing all the time during the Apollo program.'

'The Apollo program? Wasn't that back in the days when space travel was *experimental*?' Martin noticed that where Vassily was gripping the back of his chair, the lad's knuckles had turned white. *How interesting.*

'Yeah, that was it,' Rachel said casually. ''Course, they didn't have nuclear power back then – was it before or after the Cold War?'

'Before, I think. The Cold War was all about who could build the biggest refrigerator, wasn't it?'

'Cold War?' piped Vassily.

'Back on Earth, about four, five hundred years ago,' Rachel explained.

'But they were doing this, and they couldn't even build a steam engine?'

'Oh, they could build steam engines,' Martin said airily. 'But they powered them by burning rock oil under the boilers. Fission reactors were expensive and rare.'

'That doesn't sound very safe,' Vassily said dubiously. 'Wouldn't all that oil explode?'

'Yes, but Earth is an early population three planet, and quite old; the isotope balance is lousy, not enough uranium-235.'

'Too damn much if you ask me,' Rachel muttered darkly.

'I think you're trying to confuse me, and I really don't like that. You think you're so sophisticated, you Terrans, but you don't know everything! You still can't keep terrorists from blowing up your cities, and for all your so-called sophistication you can't control your own filthy impulses – meddling fools by politics, meddling fools by nature!'

Another burp from an attitude control thruster. Rachel reached over and grabbed Martin's shoulder. 'He's got us nailed.'

'Aye up, 'e's got us bang to rights. It's a fair cop, guv.'

Vassily glanced from one of them to the other in bewilderment; his ears began to glow bright red. Rachel laughed. 'If that's meant to be a Yorkshire accent, I'm a Welsh ferret, Martin!'

'Well, I'd be pleased to stuff you down my trousers any day of the week, my dear.' The engineer shook his head. Out of the corner of his eye, he noted Vassily's glow spreading from ears to neck. 'You've got a lot to learn about the real world, kid. I'm surprised your boss let you out on your own without a minder.'

'Will you stop calling me a child!'

Rachel hunched around in her chair and stared at him. 'But you are, you know. Even if you were sixty years old, you'd still be a child to me. As long as you expect someone or something else to take responsibility for you, you're a child. You could fuck your way through every brothel in New Prague, and you'd *still* be an overgrown schoolboy.' She looked at him sadly. 'What would you call a parent who never let their children grow up? That's what we think of your government.'

'But that's not why I'm here! I'm here to protect the Republic! I'm here because –'

The main motor went critical and spooled up to full power with a deep bass roar, rattling the capsule like a tin can in a hurricane. Vassily was shoved back into his hammock, gasping for breath; Rachel and Martin subsided into their seats, slugged by a solid twenty meters per second of acceleration – not the five-hundred-kilo chest-squishing gorilla of re-entry, but enough force to make them lie back and concentrate on breathing.

The engine burned for a long time, carrying them away from the drifting wreckage of battle, toward an uncertain rendezvous.

delivery service

The houses of two spent Bouncer ships drifted toward the edge of the system, tumbling end over end at well over stellar escape velocity. They didn't matter anymore; they'd done their job.

Behind them, the wreckage of the New Republican home fleet scattered like ashes on a searing hot wind. Two-thirds of the ships bubbled and foamed, engineering segments glowing red-hot as the disassembler goop stripped them down; bizarre metallic fuzz sprawled across their hulls, like fungal hyphae drilling through the heart of dead and rotting trees. Almost all of the other warships were boosting at full power, pursuing escape trajectories that would take them back into deep space. The space around Rochard's World was full of screaming countermeasure signals, jammers and feedback howlers and interferometry decoys and penaids that − unknown to their owners − were proving as effective as shields slung over the backs of tribesmen fleeing in the face of machine-gun fire. A scattering of much smaller, slower ships continued to decelerate toward the planet ahead, or coasted slowly in. For the most part the remaining Bouncers ignored these: lifeboats weren't generally troublemakers. Finally, coasting in from a range of astronomical units, came the first trade ships of the merchant fleet that followed the Festival around. Their signals were gaily entertaining, flashy and friendly: unlike the New Republic, these were not ignorant of the Festival, its uses and hazards.

But the Festival barely noticed the approaching trade fleet. Its attention was directed elsewhere: soon it would give birth to its next generation, wither, and die.

Antimatter factories the size of continents drilled holes in the fiery solar corona, deep in the curved-space zone just outside the photosphere of Rochard's star. Huge accelerator rings floated behind their wake shields, insulated by kilometers of vacuum; solar collectors blacker than night soaked up solar energy, megawatts per square meter, while masers dumped waste heat into the interstellar night overhead. Every second, milligram quantities of antimatter accumulated in the magnetic traps at the core of the accelerators. Every ten thousand seconds or so, another hazardous multigram payload shipped out on a beam-riding cargo pod to the starwisp assembly zone around Sputnik. There were a hundred factories in all; the Festival had dismantled a large Kuiper body to make them and placed the complex barely a million kilometers above the stellar surface. Now the investment was paying off in raw energy, a million times more than the planetary civilization had been able to muster.

The starwisps weren't the Festival's only cargo, nor were the Fringe and the Critics the only passengers to visit the planetary surface. Deep in the planetary biosphere, vectors armed with reverse transcriptase and strange artificial chromosomes were at work. They'd re-entered over the temperate belt of the northern continent, spreading and assimilating the contents of the endogenous ecology. Complex digestive organs, aided by the tools of DNA splicing and some fiendishly complicated expression control operons, assimilated and dissected chromosomes from everything the package's children swallowed. A feedback system – less than conscious but more than vegetable – spliced together a workable local expression of a design crafted thousands of years ago; one that could subsist on locally available building blocks, a custom saprophyte optimized for the ecology of Rochard's World.

Huge Lamarckian syncitia spread their roots across the pine forest, strangling the trees and replacing them with plants shaped like pallid pines. They were fruiting bodies, mushrooms sprouting atop the digested remains of an entire ecosystem. They grew rapidly; special cells deep in their cores secreted catalytic enzymes, nitrating the long polysaccharide molecules, while in the outer bark long, electrically conductive vessels took shape like vegetable neurons.

The forest parasite grew at a ferocious rate, fruiting bodies sprouting a meter a day. It was a much longer-term project than the rewiring of the incommunicado civilization that the Festival had stumbled across; and one more grand than any of the sentient passengers could have imagined. All they were aware of was the spread of intrusive vegetation, an annoying and sometimes dangerous plague that followed the Festival as closely as did the Mimes and other beings of the Fringe. Come the dry season, and the Festival forest would become a monstrous fire hazard; but for now, it was just a sideshow, still sprouting slowly toward its destiny, which it would reach around the time the Festival began to die.

Fifty kilometers above the ocean, still traveling at twelve times the speed of sound, the naval lifeboat spread its thistledown rotors behind the shock front of re-entry and prepared to autorotate.

'Makes you wish the Admiralty'd paid for the deluxe

model,' Lieutenant Kossov muttered between gritted teeth as the capsule juddered and shook, skipping across the ionosphere like a burning sodium pellet on a basin of water. Commander Leonov glared at him: he grunted as if he'd been punched, and shut up.

Thirty kilometers lower and fifteen hundred kilometers closer to the coast of the northern continent, the plasma shock began to dissipate. The rotors, glowing white at their tips, freewheeled in the high stratosphere, spinning in a bright blurring disk. Lying in an acceleration couch in the cockpit, the flight crew grappled with the problem of landing a hypersonic autogyro on an airfield with no ground control and no instrument guidance, an airfield that was quite possibly under siege by hostiles. Robard's blood ran cold as he thought about it. Reflexively, he glanced sideways at his master: a life dedicated to looking after the Admiral had brought him to this fix, but still he looked to him for his lead, even though the old warhorse was barely conscious.

'How does he look?' Robard asked.

Dr. Hertz glanced up briefly. 'As well as can be expected,' he said shortly. 'Did you bring his medications with you?'

Robard winced. 'Only his next doses. There are too many pill bottles –'

'Well then.' Hertz fumbled with his leather bag, withdrew a pre-loaded syringe. 'Was he taking laudanum? I recall no such prescription, but . . .'

'Not to my knowledge.' Robard swallowed. 'Diabetes, a dyskinesia, and his um, memory condition. Plus his legs, of course. But he was not in *pain*.'

'Well, then, let's see if we can wake him up.' Hertz held up the syringe and removed the protective cap. 'I would not normally so brutalize an old man before landing, especially one who has suffered a stroke, but under the circumstances –'

Twelve kilometers up, the autogyro dropped below Mach 2. Rotors shedding a disk of thunderous lightning, its ground track angled across the coast; where it passed, animals fled in panic. The lifeboat continued to lose altitude while Hertz administered his wake-up injection. Less than a minute later, the craft dropped to subsonic speed, and a new keening note entered the cabin. Robard glanced up instinctively.

'Just restarting the aerospikes,' Kossov mumbled. 'That way we can make a powered touchdown.'

The Admiral groaned something inarticulate, and Robard leaned forward. 'Sir. Can you hear me?'

The lifeboat flew sideways at just under half the speed of sound, a bright cylinder of fire spurting from the tips of the rotor disk that blurred around its waist. The copilot repeatedly tried to raise Imperial Traffic Control, to no avail; he exchanged worried glances with his commander. Trying to land under the missile batteries of the Skull Hill garrison, with no word on who was holding the city below, would be nerve-racking enough. To do so in a lifeboat short on fuel, with a desperately sick admiral aboard –

But there was no breath of search radar bouncing off the lifeboat's hull. Even as it rose over the castle's horizon, drifting in at a sedate four hundred kilometers per hour, there was no flicker of attention from the ground defense batteries. The pilot keyed his intercom switch. 'The field's still there even though nobody's talking to us. Visual approach, stand by for a bumpy ride.'

The Admiral muttered something incoherent and opened his eyes. Robard leaned back in his seat as the rotor tip aerospikes quietened their screeching roar, and the pilot fed the remaining power into the collective pitch, trading airspeed against altitude. 'Urk.' Lieutenant Kossov looked green.

'*Hate* 'copters,' mumbled the Admiral.

The motors shut down, and the lifeboat dropped,

autorotating like a fifty-ton sycamore seed. There was a brief surge of upward acceleration as the pilot flared out before touchdown, then a bone-jarring crunch from beneath the passenger compartment. A screech of torn metal told its own story; the lifeboat tilted alarmingly, then settled back drunkenly, coming to rest with the deck tilted fifteen degrees.

'Does that mean what I think it means?' asked Robard.

'Shut up and mind your business,' grated Commander Leonov. He hauled himself out of his couch and cast about. 'You! Look sharp, man the airlock! You and you, break open the small-arms locker and stand by to clear the way.' He began to clamber down the short ladder to the flight deck, hanging on tight despite the fifteen-degree overhang, still barking out orders. 'You, Robot or whatever your name is, get your man ready to move, don't know how long we've got. Ah, Pilot-captain Wolff. I take it we're on the field. Did you see any sign of a welcoming committee?'

The pilot waited while Leonov backed down the ladder, then followed him down to the deck. 'Sir, humbly report we have arrived at Novy Petrograd emergency field, pad two. I was unable to contact traffic control or port air defense control before landing, but nobody shot at us. I didn't see anyone standing around down there, but there are big changes to the city – it's not like the briefing cinematograph. Regret to report that on final approach we ran a little short of fuel, hence the bad landing.'

'Acceptable under the circumstances.' Leonov turned to the airlock. 'You there! Open the hatch, double quick, ground party will secure the perimeter immediately!'

The Admiral seemed to be trying to sit up. Robard cranked up the back of his wheelchair, then leaned down to release the cables securing it in place. As he did so, the Admiral made a curious chuckling noise.

'What is it, sir?'

'Heh – 'omit commit. Heh!'

'Absolutely, sir.' Robard straightened up. Fresh air gusted into the confines of the lifeboat; someone had tripped the override on the airlock, opening both hatches simultaneously. He could smell rain and cherry blossoms, grass and mud.

Lieutenant Kossov followed the ground party through the airlock, then ducked back inside. 'Sir. Humbly report, ground party has secured the site. No sign of any locals.'

'Hah, good. Lieutenant, you and Robot can get the old man down. Follow me!' Leonov followed the last of the officers – the flight crew and a couple of lieutenant commanders Robard didn't recognize, members of the Admiral's staff or the bridge crew – into the airlock.

Together, Robard and Lieutenant Kossov grunted and sweated the Admiral's wheelchair down a flimsy aluminum stepladder to the ground. Once his feet touched concrete, Robard breathed in deeply and looked around. One of the lifeboat's three landing legs looked wrong, a shock absorber not fully extended. It gave the craft an oddly lopsided appearance, and he knew at once that it would take more than a tankful of fuel to get it airborne again, much less into orbit. Then his eyes took in what had happened beyond the rust-streaked concrete landing pad, and he gasped.

The landing field was less than two kilometers from the brooding walls of the garrison, on the outskirts of the scantily settled north bank of the river. South of the river, there should have been a close-packed warren of steep-roofed houses, church spires visible in the distance before a knot of municipal buildings. But now the houses were mostly gone. A cluster of eldritch silvery ferns coiled skyward from the former location of the town hall, firefly glimmerings flickering between their fractally coiled leaves. The Ducal palace showed signs of being the worse for wear; one wall looked as if it had been smashed by a giant fist, the arrogant bombast of heavy artillery.

The Admiral slapped feebly at the arm of his chair. 'Ot right!'

'Absolutely, my lord.' Robard looked around again, this time hunting the advance landing party. They were halfway to the control tower when something that glowed painfully green slashed overhead, making the ground shake with the roar of its passage.

'Enemy planes!' shouted Kossov. 'See, they've followed us here! We must get the Admiral to cover, fast!' He pushed Robard aside and grabbed the handles of the wheelchair, nearly tipping it over in his haste.

'I say!' Robard snapped, angry and disturbed at his position being usurped. He cast a worried glance at the sky and decided not to confuse the issue further; the Lieutenant's behavior was unseemly, but the need to get the admiral to safety was pressing. 'I say, there's a path there. I'll lead. If we can reach the tower –'

'You! Follow us!' Kossov called to the perimeter guards, confused and worried ratings who, thankful at being given some direction, shouldered their carbines and tagged along. It was a warm morning, and the Lieutenant wheezed as he pushed the wheelchair along the cracked asphalt path. Robard paced along beside him, a tall, sepulchrally black figure, hatchet-faced with worry. Weeds grew waist high to either side of the path, and other signs of neglect were omnipresent; the field looked as if it had been abandoned for years, not just the month since the invasion. Bees and other insects buzzed and hummed around, while birds squawked and trilled in the distance, shamefully exposing the locals' neglect of their DDT spraying program.

A distant rumble prompted Robard to glance over his shoulder. Birds leapt into the sky as a distant green brightness twisted and seemed to freeze, hovering beneath the blind turquoise dome of the sky. 'Run!' He dashed forward and threw himself into the shade of a stand of young trees.

'What?' Kossov stopped and stared, jaw comically dropping. The green glare grew with frightening, soundless rapidity, then burst overhead in an emerald explosion. A noise like a giant door slamming shut pushed Robard into the grass: then the aircraft thundered past, dragging a freight train roar behind it as it made a low pass over the parked lifeboat and disappeared toward the far side of the city. Bees buzzed angrily in his ears as he picked himself up and looked wildly around for the Admiral.

The Lieutenant had been knocked off his feet by the shock wave; now he was sitting up, cradling his head gingerly. The wheelchair had remained upright, and a loud but slurred stream of invective was flowing from it. "Orson swiving 'role'erian cocksu'ing *ba-a-stards*!' Kurtz raised his good arm and shook a palsied fist at the sky. 'You 'evolushunary shit'll get yours! Ouch!' The arm flopped.

'Are you alright sir?' Robard gasped nervously.

"Astard *stung* me,' Kurtz complained, drooling on the back of his wrist. 'Damn bees.' An angry buzzing veered haywire around Robard, and he whacked at it with his dirt-stained gloves.

'I'm sure you'll be alright, sir, once we get you to the control tower and then the castle.' He inspected the mashed insect briefly, and froze. Red, impact-distorted letters ridged its abdomen with unnatural clarity. He shuddered and smeared the back of his glove on the ground. 'We'd better move fast, before that plane decides we're the enemy.'

'You take over,' said Kossov, clutching a reddened handkerchief to his forehead. 'Let's go.' Together they turned and pushed on toward the control tower, and beyond it the uncertainties of the Ducal palace and whatever had become of the capital city under the new order.

*

Eighty kilometers away, another lifeboat was landing.

Rachel shook herself groggily and opened her eyes. It took her a moment to realize where she was. Re-entry had been alarmingly bumpy; the capsule was swinging back and forth with a regular motion that would have made her nauseous if her vestibular dampers hadn't kicked in. There was a moan from behind her seat and she glanced sideways. Martin was waking up visibly, shaking his head, his face going through a horrible series of contortions and twitches. Behind her, Vassily moaned again. 'Oh, that was terrible.'

'Still alive, huh?' She blinked at the viewscreen. Black smears obscured much of it, remnants of the ablative heat shield that had melted and streaked across the cameras on the outside of the hull. The horizon was a flat blue line, the ground half-hidden beneath a veil of clouds as they descended beneath the main parasail. An altimeter ticked down the last two thousand meters. 'Say yes if you can wriggle your toes.'

'Yes,' said Martin. Vassily just moaned. Rachel didn't bother to inquire further after their health; she had too many things to do before they landed. It could all get very messy very fast, now they didn't have an engine.

Pilot: Plot range and heading to rendezvous waypoint omega. A map overlay blinked on the viewscreen. They were coming down surprisingly close, only a few kilometers out from the target. *Pilot: Hard surface retromotor status, please.* More displays; diagnostics and self-test maps of the landing motor, a small package hanging in the rigging halfway between the rectangular parachute and the capsule roof. Triggered by radar, the landing turbine would fire a minute before touchdown, decelerating the capsule from a bone-crushing fifty-kilometer-per-hour fall and steering them to a soft touchdown.

'I could do with a drink,' said Martin.

'You'll have to wait a minute or two.' Rachel watched the screen intently. One thousand meters.

'I can't feel my toes,' Vassily complained.

Oh shit. 'Can you wriggle them?' asked Rachel, heart suddenly in her mouth. She'd never expected a third passenger, and if the hammock had landed him with a spinal injury –

'Yes.'

'Then why the fuck did you say you couldn't feel them?'

'They're cold!'

Rachel yawned; her ears popped. 'I think we just depressurized. You must have your toes on top of the vent or something.' The outside grew hazy, whited out. Ten more seconds, and the wispy cloud thinned, peeling back to reveal trees and rivers below. A dizzying view, the ground growing closer. She gritted her teeth. Next to her, Martin shuffled for a better view.

'*Attention. Landing raft inflation.*' A yellow python wrapped itself around the bottom of the capsule and bloated outward, cutting off her viev of the ground directly below. Rachel cursed silently, looked for a clearing in the trees. The forest cover was unusually dense, and she tensed.

'Over there.' Martin pointed.

'Thanks.' Using the side stick, she pointed out the opening to the autopilot. *Pilot: make for designated landing ground. Engage autoland on arrival.*

'*Attention. Stand by for retromotor ignition in five seconds. Touchdown imminent. Three seconds. Main canopy separation.*' The capsule dropped sickeningly. '*Motor ignition.*' A loud rumbling from above, and the fall stopped. The clearing below lurched closer, and the rumbling grew to a shuddering roar. '*Attention. Touchdown in ten seconds. Brace for landing.*'

Trees slid past the screen, implacable green stems exfoliating purple-veined leaves the size of books. Martin gasped. They dropped steadily, like a glass-walled elevator on the side of an invisible skyscraper. Finally, with a tooth-rattling bump, the capsule came to rest.

Silence.

'Hey, guys.' Rachel shakily pushed the release buckle on her seat belt. 'Thank you for flying Air UN, and may I take this opportunity to invite you to fly with us again?'

Martin grunted and stretched his arms up. 'Nope, can't reach it from here. Got to unbelt first.' He let his arms flop down again. 'Feel like lead. Funny.'

'All it takes is eight hours in zero gee.' Rachel rummaged in the storage bins next to her leg well.

'I think I understand you Terrans now,' Vassily began, then paused to let the tremor out of his voice before continuing. 'You're all mad!'

Martin looked sidelong at Rachel. 'He's only just noticed.'

She sat up, clutching a compact backpack. 'Took him long enough.'

'Well. What do we do now? Make with the big tin opener, or wait for someone to pass by and yank the ring pull?'

'First' – Rachel tapped icons busily on the pilot's console – 'we tell the Critics that we're down safely. She said she'd try to help us link up. Second, I do *this*.' She reached up and grabbed the top edge of the display screen. It crumpled like thin plastic, revealing the inner wall of the capsule. A large steamer trunk was half-embedded in the bulkhead, incongruous pipes and cables snaking out of its half-open lid.

'I knew it!' Vassily exclaimed. 'You've got an illegal—'

'Shut up.' Rachel leaned forward and adjusted something just inside the lid. 'Right, now we leave. Quickly.' Standing up, she unlocked the overhead hatch and let it slide down into the capsule, taking the place of the screen. 'Give me a leg up, Martin.'

'Okay.' A minute later, all three of them were sitting on top of the lander. The truncated cone sat in a puddle of yellow inflatable skirts, in the middle of a grassy meadow. To their left, a stream burbled lazily through a thick clump of reeds; to their right, a row of odd, dark conifers formed a wall against the light. The air was cold and fresh and smelled unbearably clean. 'What now?' asked Martin.

'I advise you to surrender to the authorities.' Vassily loomed over him. 'It will go badly with you if you don't cooperate, but if you surrender to me I'll, I'll –' He looked around wildly.

Rachel snorted. 'What authorities?'

'The capital –'

Rachel finally blew her top. 'Listen, kid, we're stuck in the back of beyond with a dead lifeboat and not a lot of supplies, on a planet that's just been hit by a type three singularity, and I have just spent the past thirty-six hours slaving my guts out to save our necks – all of them, yours included – and I would appreciate it if you would just *shut up* for a while! Our first priority is survival; my second priority is linking up with the people I've come here to visit, and getting back to civilization comes third on the list. With me so far? Because there are *no* civil authorities right now, not the kind you expect. They've just been dumped on by about a thousand years of progress in less than a month, and if your local curator's still sitting at his desk, he's probably catatonic from future shock. This planetary civilization has *transcended*. It is an ex-colony; it has ceased to be. About the only people who can cope with this level of change are your dissidents, and I'm not that optimistic about them, either. Right now, *we* are your best hope of survival, and you'd better not forget it.' She glared at Vassily, and he glared right back at her, obviously angry but unable to articulate his feelings.

Behind her, Martin had clambered down to the meadow. Something caught his attention, and he bent down. 'Hey!'

'What is it?' Rachel called. The spell was broken: Vassily subsided with a grumble and began hunting for a way down off the capsule. Martin said something indistinct. 'What?' she called.

'There's something wrong with this grass!'

'Oh shit.' Rachel followed Vassily down the side of the pod – two and a half meters of gently sloping ceramic, then a soft landing on a woven spider-silk floatation bed. 'What do you mean?'

Martin straightened up and wordlessly offered her a blade of grass.

'It's –' She stopped.

'Rochard's World is supposed to have an Earth-normal biosphere, isn't it?' Martin watched her curiously. 'That's what it said in my gazetteer.'

'What *is* that?' asked Vassily.

'Grass, or what passes for it.' Martin shrugged uncomfortably. 'Doesn't look very Earth-normal to me. It's the right color and right overall shape, but—'

'Ouch. Cut myself on the damned thing.' Rachel dropped it. The leaf blade fluttered down, unnoticed: when it hit the ground it began to disintegrate with eerie speed, falling apart along radial seams. 'What about the trees?'

'There's something odd about them, too.' A crackling noise from behind made Martin jump. 'What's that?'

'Don't worry. I figured we'd need some ground transport, so I told it to make some. It's reabsorbing the capsule –'

'Neat luggage,' Martin said admiringly. The lifeboat began to crumple inward, giving off a hot, organic smell like baking bread.

'Yeah, well.' Rachel looked worried. 'My contact's supposed to know we're here. I wonder how long . . .' She trailed off. Vassily was busily tramping toward the far side of the clearing, whistling some sort of martial-sounding tune.

'Just who is this contact?' Martin asked quietly.

'Guy called Rubenstein. One of the more sensible resistance

cadres, which is why he's in internal exile here – the less sensible ones end up dead.'

'And what do you want with him?'

'I'm to give him a package. Not that he needs it anymore, if what's happened here is anything to go by.'

'A package? What kind of package?'

She turned and pointed at the steamer trunk, which now rested on the grass in the middle of a collapsing heap of structural trusses, belching steam quietly. '*That* kind of package.'

'That kind of –' His eyes gave him away. Rachel reached out and took his elbow.

'Come on, Martin. Let's check out the tree line.'

'But –' He glanced over his shoulder. 'Okay.'

'It's like this,' Rachel began, as they walked. 'Remember what I said about helping the people of the New Republic? A while ago – some years, actually – some people in a department you don't really need to know much about decided that they were ripe for a revolution. Normally we don't get involved in that kind of thing; toppling regimes is bad ju-ju even if you disapprove of them or do it for all the right moral reasons. But some of our analysts figured there was a chance, say twenty percent, that the New Republic might metastasize and turn imperial. So we've been gearing up to ship power tools to their own home-grown libertarian underground for a decade now.

'The Festival . . . when it arrived, we didn't know what it was. If I'd known what you told me once we were under way, back at Klamovka, I wouldn't be here now. Neither would the luggage. Which is the whole point of the exercise, actually. When the aristocracy put down the last workers' and technologists' soviet about 240 years ago, they destroyed the last of the cornucopiae the New Republic was given at its foundation by the Eschaton. Thereafter, they could control the arbeiter classes by restricting access to education and tools and putting tight bottlenecks on information technology. This luggage, Martin, it's a full-scale cornucopia machine. Design schemata for just about anything a mid-twenty-first-century postindustrial civilization could conceive of, freeze-dried copies of the Library of Congress, all sorts of things. Able to replicate itself, too.' The tree line was a few meters ahead. Rachel stopped and took a deep breath. 'I was sent here to turn it over to the underground, Martin. I was sent here to give them the tools to start a revolution.'

'To start a –' Martin stared at her. 'But you're too late.'

'Exactly.' She gave him a moment for it to sink in. 'I can still complete my mission, just in case, but I don't really think . . .'

He shook his head. 'How are we going to get out of this mess?'

'Um. Good question.' She turned and faced the melting re-entry capsule, then reached into a pocket and began bringing out some spare optica spybots. Vassily was aimlessly circling the perimeter of the clearing. 'Normally, I'd go to ground in the old town and wait. In six months, there'll be a merchant ship along. But with the Festival—'

'There'll be ships,' Martin said with complete assurance. 'And you've got a cornucopia, you've got a whole portable military-industrial complex. If it can make us a lifeboat, I'm sure I can program it to manufacture anything we need to survive until we've got a chance to get off this godforsaken hole. Right?'

'Probably.' She shrugged. 'But first I really ought to make contact, if only to verify that there's no point in handing the luggage over.' She began to walk back toward the lander. 'This Rubenstein is supposed to be fairly levelheaded for a revolutionary. He'll probably know what –' There was a distant cracking sound, like sticks breaking. At the other side of the clearing, Vassily was running back toward the luggage. 'Shit!'

Rachel dragged Martin to the ground, fumbled for the stunner in her pocket.

'What is it?' he whispered.

'I don't know.'

'Damn. Well, looks like they've found us, whoever they are. Nice knowing you.' A large, hunched thing, hugely, monstrously bipedal, lurched into the clearing: a vast mouth like a doorway gaped at them.

'Wait.' Rachel held him down with one hand. '*Don't* move. That thing's wired like a fucking tank, sensors everywhere.'

The thing swung toward the lander, then abruptly squatted on its haunches. A long, flat tongue lolled groundward; something big appeared at the top of it and stepped down to the meadow. It swept its head from side to side, taking in the decrepitating lifeboat, Vassily hiding behind it, the rest of the clearing. Then it called out, in a surprisingly deep voice. 'Hello? We arrive not-warfully. Is there a Rachel Mansour here?'

Well, here goes. She stood up and cleared her throat. 'Who wants to know?'

The Critic grinned at her, baring frighteningly long tusks: 'I am Sister Seventh. You come in time! We a crisis have!'

People began gathering outside the Ducal palace around evening. They came in ones and twos, clumped shell-shocked beneath the soot-smeared outer walls. They looked much like any other citizens of the New Republic; perhaps a bit poorer, a bit duller than most.

Robard stood in the courtyard and watched them through the gates. Two of the surviving ratings stood there, guns ready, a relic of temporal authority. Someone had found a flag, charred along one edge but otherwise usable. The crowd had begun to form about an hour after they raised it to fly proudly in the light breeze. The windows might be broken and the furniture smashed, but they were still soldiers of His Imperial Majesty, and by God and Emperor there were standards, and they would be observed – so the Admiral had indicated, and so they were behaving.

Robard breathed in deeply. Insect bite? A most suspicious insect, indeed. But since it had stung the Admiral, his condition had improved remarkably. His left cheek remained slack, and his fingers remained numb, but his arm –

Robard and Lieutenant Kossov had borne their ancient charge to the control tower, cursing and sweating in the noonday heat. As they arrived, Kurtz had thrown a fit; choking, gasping, choleric, thrashing in his wheelchair. Robard had feared for the worst, but then Dr. Hertz had come and administered a horse syringe full of adrenaline. The Admiral subsided, panting like a dog: and his left eye had opened and rolled sideways, to fix Robard with a skewed stare. 'What is it, sir? Is there anything I can get you?'

'Wait.' The Admiral hissed. He tensed, visibly. ''M all hot. But it's so clear.' Both hands moved, gripping the sides of his wheelchair, and to Robard's shock the old man rose to his feet. 'My Emperor! I can walk!'

Robard's feelings as he caught his employer were impossible to pin down. Disbelief, mostly, and pride. The old man shouldn't be able to do that; in the aftermath of his stroke, he'd been paralyzed on one side. Such lesions didn't heal, the doctor had said. But Kurtz had risen from his chair and taken a wobbly step forward –

From the control tower to the castle, events had moved in a dusty blur. Requisitioned transport, a bouncing ride through a half-deserted town, half the houses in it burned to the ground and the other half sprouting weird excrescences. The castle, deserted. Get the Admiral into the Duke's bedroom. Find the kitchen, see if there's anything edible in the huge underground larders. Someone hoisted a flag. Guards on the gate. Two timid serving women like little mice, scurrying from hiding and curtsying to the service they'd long since been broken to. A cleaning detail, broken furniture ruthlessly consigned to the firewood heap that would warm the grand ballroom. Emergency curtains – steel-mesh and spider-silk – furled behind the tall and shattered windows. Guards on the gate, with guns. Check the water pipes. More uniforms moving in the dusty afternoon heat. Busy, so busy.

He'd stolen a minute to break into Citizen Von Beck's office. None of the revolutionary cadres had got that far into the castle, or survived the active countermeasures. All the Curator's tools lay handy; Robard had paused to check the emergency causal channel, but its entropy had been thoroughly maximized even though the bandwidth monitor showed more than fifty percent remaining. His worst suspicions confirmed, he made liberal use of the exotic insecticides Von Beck had stocked, spraying his person until the air was blue and chokingly unbreathable. Then he pocketed a small artifact – one that it was illegal on pain of death for anyone not of the Curator's Office to be in possession of – left the room, locked it behind him, and returned to the duties of the Admiral's manservant.

The aimless cluster outside the Ducal palace had somehow metamorphosed into a crowd while he'd been busy. Anxious, pinched faces stared at him: the faces of people uncertain who they were, bereft of their place in the scheme of things. Lost people, desperately seeking reassurance. Doubtless many would have joined the dissident underground; many more would have made full use of the singular conditions brought about by the arrival of the Festival to maximize their personal abilities. For years to come, even if the Festival vanished tomorrow, the outback would be peopled by ghouls and wizards, talking animals and sagacious witches. Some people didn't want to transcend their humanity; a life of routine reassurance was all they craved, and the Festival had deprived them of it. Was that an army greatcoat lurking at the back of the square? A sallow-faced man, half-starved, who in other circumstances Robard would have pegged for a highwayman; here he was just as likely to be the last loyal dregs of a regiment that had deserted *en masse*. Snap judgments could be treacherous.

He looked farther. Dust, rising in the distance, perhaps half a mile away. *Hmm*.

The grand hallway opened from the front doors and led to the main staircase, the ballroom, and numerous smaller, more discreet destinations. Normally, a manservant would have used a small side entrance. Today, Robard strode in through the huge doors that normally would have welcomed ambassadors and knights of the realm. Nobody watched his dusty progress across the floor, treading dirt into shattered tiles and bypassing the shattered chandelier. He didn't stop until he reached the entrance to the Star Chamber.

'— other leg of lamb. Damn your eyes, can't you knock, man?'

Robard paused in the doorway. The Admiral was sitting at the Governor's desk, eating a platter of cold cuts — very cold, preserved meats and pickles from the cellar — with Commander Leonov and two of the other surviving staff officers standing attentively by. 'Sir. The revolutionary guards are approaching. We have about five minutes to decide whether to fight or talk. Can I suggest you leave the rest of your meal until after we have dealt with them?'

Leonov rounded on him. 'You bounder, how dare you disturb the Admiral! Get out!'

Robard raised his left hand and turned it over, revealing the card he held. 'Have you ever seen one of these before?'

Leonov turned white. 'I – I—'

'I don't have time for this,' Robard said brusquely. To the Admiral; 'My lord?'

Kurtz stared at him with narrowed eyes. 'How long?'

Robard shrugged. 'All the time I've been with you, my lord. For your own protection. As I was saying, a crowd is moving in our direction from the south bank, over the old bridge. We have about five minutes to decide what to do, but I doubt we will make any friends by shooting at them.'

Kurtz nodded. 'I will go and talk to them, then.'

Now it was Robard's turn to stare. 'Sir, I believe you should be in a wheelchair, not arguing with revolutionaries. Are you quite sure—'

'Haven't felt this good in, oh, about eight years, young feller. The bees around here pack a damned odd sting.'

'Yes, you could say that. Sir, I believe you may have been compromised. The Festival apparently has access to a wide range of molecular technologies, beyond the one that's done such a sterling job on your cerebrovascular system. If they wanted—'

Kurtz raised a hand. 'I know. But we're at their mercy in any event. I will go down to the people and talk. Were any of the crowd old?'

'No' Robard puzzled for a moment. 'None that I saw. Do you suppose—'

'A cure for old age is a very common wish,' Kurtz observed. 'Dashed slug-a-beds want to be shot by a jealous husband, not a nurse bored with emptying the bedpan. If this Festival has been granting wishes, as our intelligence put it . . .' He stood up. 'Get me my dress uniform, Rob – oh. You, yes you, Kossov. You're my batman now Robard here outranks you all. And my medals!'

Leonov, white as a sheet, still hadn't stopped shaking. 'It's alright,' Robard said sepulchrally. 'I don't usually have people executed for being rude to me.'

"Sir! Ah – yes, sir! Um, if I may ask –'

'Ask away.'

'Since when is an Invigilator of the Curator's Office required to disguise himself as a manservant?'

'Since –' Robard pulled out his pocket watch and glanced at it – 'about seven years and six months ago, at the request of the Archduke. Really. Nobody *notices* a servant, you know. And His Excellency –' Kossov returned bearing the trappings of high office. Leonov ushered Robard out onto the landing while the Admiral dressed. 'His Excellency is not in *direct* line to the throne. If you take my meaning.' Leonov did, and his sharp intake of breath – combined with the stress analyzers wired into his auditory nerves – told Robard everything he needed to know. 'No, His Majesty had no expectation of a coup; the Admiral is unquestionably loyal. But his personal charisma, fame as a hero of the Republic, and wide popularity, made his personal safety a matter of some importance. We can use him here.'

'Oh.' Leonov thought for a while. 'The revolutionaries?'

'If he pushes them, they'll crumble,' Robard said decisively. 'All their strongest supporters have long since fled; that's the nature of a singularity. If they don't' – he tapped his pocket – 'I am licensed to take extraordinary measures in the defense of the Republic, including the use of proscribed technologies.'

Leonov dabbed at his forehead with a handkerchief. 'Then it's all over. You'll break the revolutionaries by force or by politics, install His Excellency as governor pro tem, and in six months time it will all be over, bar the shouting.'

'I wouldn't say that. Even if the woman from Earth was right – and I am inclined to think she was telling the truth about the Festival not being interested in planetary conquest as we understand it, in which case this whole expedition has been a monstrously expensive mistake – we've lost two-thirds of the population. We can never get rid of the pernicious virus of bandwidth that they've infected this planet with; we may have to abandon the colony, or at the very least institute quarantine procedures. The bloody revolutionaries have *won*, here, the djinn is well and truly out of the bottle. Everything our ancestors fought for, torn up and scattered to the winds! A virus of eternal youth is loose in the bees, and the streets are paved with infinite riches. It devalues everything!' He stopped and took a deep breath, disturbed by the degree of his own agitation. 'Of course, if we can suppress the revolutionary cadres here in New Petrograd, we can mop up the countryside at our leisure . . .'

The door to the Star Chamber opened to reveal Admiral Kurtz standing there, resplendent in the gold braid, crimson sash, and chestful of medals that his rank dictated. He looked a decade younger than his age, not two decades older: patrician, white-haired, the very image of a gentleman dictator, reassuringly authoritarian. 'Well, gentlemen! Shall we review the crowds?' He did not stride – wasted leg muscles saw to that – but he walked without a hand at either elbow.

'I think that would be a very good idea, sir,' said Robard.

'Indeed.' Leonov and the senior Curator fell into step behind the admiral as he walked toward the staircase. 'The sun is setting on anarchy and disarray, gentlemen. Only let my tongue be silver and tomorrow will once again be ours.'

Together, they stepped into the courtyard to address the sheep who, did they but know it, had already returned to the fold.

An amber teardrop the size of a charabanc perched on the edge of a hillside covered in the mummified bones of trees. Ashy telegraph poles coated in a fine layer of soot pointed at the sky; tiny skeletons crunched under Burya Rubenstein's boots as he walked among them, following a man-sized rabbit.

'Master in *here*,' said Mr. Rabbit, pointing at the weirdly curved lump.

Rubenstein approached it cautiously, hands clasped behind his back. Yes, it was definitely amber – or something closely resembling it. Flies and bubbles were scattered throughout its higher layers; darkness shrouded its heart. 'It's a lump of fossilized vegetable sap. Your master's dead, rabbit. Why did you bring me here?'

The rabbit was upset. His long ears tilted backward, flat along the top of his skull. 'Master *in* here!' He shifted from one foot to the other. 'When Mimes attack, master call for help.'

Burya decided to humor the creature. 'I see –' He stopped. There *was* something inside the boulder, something darkly indistinct. And come to think of it, all the trees hereabouts were corpses, fried from the inside out by some terrible energy. The revolutionary guards, already spooked by the Lysenkoist forest, had refused to enter the dead zone. They milled about downslope, debating the ideological necessity of uplifting non-human species to sapience – one of them had taken heated exception to a proposal to giving opposable thumbs and the power of speech to cats – and comparing their increasingly baroque implants. Burya stared closer, feeling himself slip into a blurred double vision as the committee for state communications worms fed their own perspective to him. There was something inside the boulder, and it was thinking, artlessly unformed thoughts that tugged at the Festival's cellular communications network like a toddler at its mother's skirt.

Taking a deep breath, he leaned against the lump of notamber. 'Who are you?' he demanded noiselessly, feeling the smooth warm surface under his hands. Antennae beneath his skin radiated information into the packetized soup that flooded in cold waves through the forest, awaited a reply.

'*Me-Identity: Felix. You-Identity: ???*'

'*Come out of there with your hands above your head and prepare to submit your fate to the vanguard of revolutionary justice!'* Burya gulped. He'd meant to send something along the lines of 'Can you come out of there so we can talk?', but his revolutionary implants evidently included a semiotic de-referencing stage that translated anything he said – through this new cyberspatial medium – into Central Committee sound bites. Angry at the internal censorship, he resolved to override it next time.

'*Badly hurt. No connection previous incarnation. Want/need help metamorphosis.'*

Burya turned and leaned his back against the boulder. 'You. Rabbit. Can you hear any of this?'

The rabbit sat up and swallowed a mouthful of grass. 'Any of what?'

'I've been talking to, ah, your master. Can you hear us?'

One ear flicked. 'No.'

'Good.' Burya closed his eyes, settled back into double vision, and attempted to communicate. But his implant was still acting up. '*How did you get here? What are you trying to achieve? I thought you were in trouble*' came out as 'Confess your counter-revolutionary crimes before the tribunal! What task are you striving to accomplish in the unceasing struggle against reactionary mediocrity and bourgeois incrementalism? I thought you were guilty of malicious hooliganism!'

'Fuck,' he muttered aloud. 'There's got to be a bypass filter –' Ah. '*Sorry about that, my interface is ideologically biased. How did you get here? What are you trying to achieve? I thought you were in trouble.'*

An answer slowly burbled up and out of the stone; visual perceptions cut in, and for a few minutes Burya shook in the grip of a young lad's terrified flight from the Fringe.

'Ah. So. The Festival mummified you pending repairs. And now you're ready to go somewhere else – where? What's that?'

Another picture. Stars, endless distance, tiny dense and very *hot* bodies sleeping the dreamless light-years away. Bursting in a desert storm of foliage on a new world, flowering and dying and sleeping again until next time.

'Let me get this straight. You used to be the governor. Then you were an eight-year-old boy with some friendly talking animals under some kind of geas to 'lead an interesting life' and have lots of adventures. Now you want to be a starship? And you want me, as the nearest delegate of the Central Committee for the revolution, to help you?'

Not exactly. Another vision, this time long and complex, burdened by any number of political proposals that his implant irritatingly attempted to convert into plant-yield diagrams indicating the progress toward fruition of an agricultural five-year plan. 'You want me to do *that*?' Burya winced. 'What do you think I am, a free agent? Firstly, the Curator's Office would shoot me as soon as look at me, much less listen to what they'd view as treason. Secondly, you're not the governor anymore, and even if you were and proposed something like this, they'd sack you faster than you can snap your fingers. In case you didn't notice those fireworks yesterday, that was the Imperial fleet – what's left of it – shooting it out with the Festival. Thirdly, the revolutionary committee would be queuing up to shoot me, too, if I proposed something like this. Never underestimate the intrinsic, as opposed to ideological, conservatism of an idea like revolution once it's got some momentum behind it. No, it's not practical. I really don't see why you waste my time with such a stupid proposal. Not at –'

He stopped. Something downslope was making a lot of noise, thrashing through the kill zone left by the X-ray laser battery. 'Who's there?' he asked, but Mr. Rabbit had vanished in a tuft of panicky white tail fur.

A telephone-pole tree toppled slowly over before the thrashing, and strange, chicken-legged mound lurched into view. Sister Seventh sat in the hut's doorway, glaring intently at him. 'Burya Rubenstein!' she yelled. 'Come here! Resolution achieved! Cargo retrieved! You have visitors!'

Expecting a momentous meeting, Rachel cast her eyes around the hillside: they took to the air and flew on insectile wings, quartering the area for threats.

The trees hereabouts were dead, charred by some terrible force. Martin watched anxiously as she rummaged in the corpulent steamer trunk. 'What's that?' he asked.

'Cornucopia seed,' she said, tossing the fist-sized object at him. He caught it and inspected it curiously.

'All engineering is here,' he marveled. 'In miniature.' Several million billion molecular assemblers, a kilowatt of thin-film solar cells to power them, thermodynamic filtration membranes to extract raw feedstocks from the environment, rather more computing power than the whole of the pre-Singularity planetary Internet. He pocketed the seed, then looked at her. 'You had a reason . . .?'

'Yup. We're not going to have the original for much longer. Don't let the kid see it, he might guess what it is and flip his lid.' She continued forward. There was some kind of boulder near the crest of the hill, and a man was leaning against it. The Critic's house lurched forward, crashing and banging toward it. 'If that's who I hope it is –'

They started up the rise. The trees hereabouts were all dead. Martin stumbled over a rounded stone and kicked at it, cursing: he stopped when it revealed itself to be a human skull, encrusted with metallic fibrils. 'Something bad happened here.'

'Big surprise. Help me steer this thing.' The steamer trunk, now running on fuel cells, was proving balky and hard to control on the grassy slope: half the time they had to drag it over obstacles. 'You got any holdouts?'

Martin shrugged. 'Do I look like a soldier?'

She squinted at him for a moment. 'You've got enough hidden depths, dearie. Okay, if it turns nasty, I'll handle things.'

'Who's this guy you're supposed to be seeing, anyway?'

'Burya Rubenstein. Radical underground journalist, big mover and shaker in the underground. Ran a soviet during a major worker's strike some years ago; got himself exiled for his pains, lucky they didn't shoot him.'

'And you're planning to hand –' Martin stopped. 'Ah, so that's what you were planning. That's how you were going to start a revolution here, before the Festival made it all last year's news.' He glanced over his shoulder, but Vassily was nowhere to be seen.

'Not exactly. I was just going to give them the tools to do so if they wanted to.' She wiped her forehead on the back of a hand. 'Actually, it's been a contingency plan for years, only we never quite had a good enough reason to do it – initiation of force, that kind of thing. Now, well, the whole game's changed. Far as I can tell, Rubenstein's lot survived the transition to a postscarcity economy; they may be the nearest thing to civil authorities on this two-bit backwater colony right now. When the Festival gets bored and moves on, they may not be able to survive without a cornucopia. Assuming, of course, that they didn't ask the Festival for one straight off.' The luggage surged forward, getting a grip on the ground, and she stopped talking for a while to concentrate on steering it up the hill.

'So what was your exit strategy?' Martin asked, walking along behind her.

'Exit strategy? We don't need no stinking exit strategy! Just – deliver this. Then melt into the chaos. Find somewhere to live. Settle down till trade resumes. Ship out. You?'

'About the same. Herman has a way of catching up after a while. Uh, did you have anywhere in mind to—'

'Small town called Plotsk.' She jerked her head sharply. 'First things first. I need to deliver the package. Then we need to ditch laughing boy somewhere safe where he can't follow us, hmm? Aside from that, I was wondering if – well. About us.'

Martin reached out and took her free hand. 'Wondering if you were going to get rid of me?'

She stared at him. 'Mm. Why – am I going to have to?'

Martin took a deep breath. 'Do you *want* to get rid of me?'

She shook her head.

Martin gently pulled her toward him, until she leaned against him. 'Me neither,' he murmured in her ear.

'Two of us stand a better chance than one, anyway,' she rationalized. 'We can watch each other's backs, it's going to be hairy for a while. Plus, we may be stuck here for some time. Years, even.'

'Rachel. Stop making excuses.'

She sighed. 'Am I that transparent?'

'You've got a worse sense of duty than –' She pulled back a little, and he stopped, seeing the warning glint in her eyes. Then she began to laugh quietly, and after a moment he joined her.

'I can think of much worse people to be stranded with in the middle of a backwater recovering from a revolution, Martin, believe me—'

'Okay, I believe you, I believe you!' She leaned forward and kissed him hard, then let go with a smile.

The luggage was rolling smoothly now, and the slope of the ground was flattening out. The boulder above them glowed yellow in the afternoon light; and the man who'd been leaning against it was deep in animated arm-waving conversation with the huge Critic. As they approached, he turned to face them: a wiry, short man with bushy hair, a goatee, and the antique affectation of pince-nez. Judging by the state of his clothing he'd been on the road for some time. 'Who are you?' he demanded aggressively.

'Burya Rubenstein?' Rachel asked tiredly.

'Yes?' He glared at her suspiciously. 'You have countermeasures!'

'Parcel for Burya Rubenstein, care of the Democratic Revolutionary Party, Rochard's World. You wouldn't believe how far it's come or how many hoops I've had to jump through to get it to you.'

'Ah –' He stared at the trunk, then back at Rachel. 'Who did you say you were?'

'Friends from Old Earth,' Martin grunted. 'Also hungry, dirty, shipwrecked survivors.'

'Well, you won't find any decent hospitality here.' Rubenstein swept a hand around the clearing. 'Old Earth, did you say? Now that *is* a long way to come with a parcel! Just what exactly is it?'

'It's a cornucopia machine. Self-replicating factory, fully programmable, and it's yours. A gift from Earth. The means of production in one handy self-propelled package. We hoped you might feel like starting an industrial revolution. At least we did before we found out about the Festival.' Rachel blinked as Rubenstein threw back his head and laughed wildly.

'Just what exactly is that meant to mean?' she demanded irritably. 'I've come forty light-years, at not inconsiderable risk, to deliver a message you'd have murdered for six months ago. Don't you think you could explain yourself?'

'Oh, madam, please accept my apologies. I do you a disservice. If you'd delivered this even four weeks ago, you'd have changed the course of history – of that I have no doubt! But you see' – he straightened up and his expression grew sober – 'we have had such devices since the first day of the Festival. And for all the good they've done us, I'd just as soon never have set eyes on one.'

She looked back at Rubenstein. 'Well, that confirms it. I suppose you've got time to fill me in on what's been going on here while I've been engaged in this fool's errand?' she demanded.

'We held the revolution about, ah, three weeks ago.' Burya circled the steamer trunk, inspecting it. 'Things did not go according to plan, as I'm sure our friend the Critic here will explain.' He sat down on the chest. 'Eschaton only knows what the Critics are doing here in the first place, or indeed the Festival. We – nobody – was ready for what happened. My dreams are co-opted by committee meetings, did you know that? The revolution ran its course in two weeks: that's how long it took for us to realize nobody *needed* us. Emergent criticality. The Sister here has been showing me the consequences – bad consequences.' He hung his head. 'Survivors of the fleet have landed at the capital, they tell me. People are flocking to them. They want security, and who can blame them?'

'So let me get this straight.' Rachel leaned against the huge amber boulder. 'You changed your mind about wanting to change the system?'

'Oh no!' Burya stood up agitatedly. 'But the system no longer exists. It wasn't destroyed by committees or soviets or worker's cadres; it was destroyed by people's wishes coming true. But come, now. You look as if you've been through a battle! There are refugees everywhere, you know. Once I sort out my business here, I will return to Plotsk and see what I can do to ensure stability. Perhaps you'd like to come along?'

'Stability,' Martin echoed. 'Um, what business? I mean, why are you here? We seem to be quite a way from civilization.' That was a huge understatement, as far as Rachel could see. She leaned back and looked down at the forest dispiritedly. To come all this distance, only to find that she was three weeks too late to change history for the better: that the Festival had dropped an entire planetary society, such as it was, into an informational blender and dialed the blades to FAST; it was all a bit too much to appreciate. That, and she was *tired*, mortally tired. She'd done her best, like Martin. Three weeks. *If Martin had failed . . .*

'There's someone inside that boulder,' said Rubenstein.

'What?' A complex three-dimensional model of the hillside spread out before Rachel's distributed spy-eyes. There was Vassily, working his way up the far side of the slope. Here was Martin. And the boulder –

'The occupant.' Burya nodded. 'He's still alive. Actually, he wants to join the Festival as a passenger. I can see why; from his point of view, it makes sense. But I think the emergency committee might disagree – they'd rather see him dead. The reactionary forces in the capital would disagree for other reasons: they'd want him back. He used to be the planetary governor, you see, until too many of his private, personal wishes came true. Dereliction of duty.' Rubenstein blinked. 'I wouldn't have believed it, but.'

'Ah. So what's the real problem with him joining the Festival?'

'Getting their attention. The Festival trades information for services. He's told it everything he knows. So have I. What are we to do?'

'That's preposterous,' said Martin. 'You mean, the Festival will only accept fare-paying passengers?'

'Strange as this may seem, it's how the Fringe and the Critics first came aboard. The Critics still pay their way by providing higher-level commentary on whatever they find.' Burya sat down again.

Martin yelled. 'Hey! Critic!'

On the lower slopes of the hill, Sister Seventh sat up. 'Question?' she boomed.

'How are you going home?' Martin shouted at her.

'Finish Critique! Exchange liftwise.'

'Can you take a passenger?'

'Ho!' Sister Seventh ambled up the slope of the hill. 'Identity interrogative?'

'Whoever's in this vitrification cell. Used to be the planetary governor, I'm told.'

The Critic shambled closer. Rachel tried not to recoil from her clammy vegetable-breathy presence. 'Can take cargo,' Sister Seventh rumbled. 'Give reason.'

'Um.' Martin glanced at Rachel. 'The Festival assimilates information, no? We came from the fleet. I have an interesting story to tell.'

Sister Seventh nodded. 'Information. Useful, yes, low entropy. Is passenger—'

'Vitrified,' Burya interrupted. 'By the Festival, apparently. Please be discreet. Some of my colleagues would disapprove, and as for the reactionaries –'

Some sixth sense made Rachel turn around. It was Vassily: he'd circled around the far side of the hill for some reason, and now she saw that he was clutching a seemingly bladeless handle. His expression was wild. 'Burya Rubenstein?' he gasped.

'That's me. Who are you?' Rubenstein turned to face the new arrival.

Vassily took two steps forward, half-staggering, like a marionette manipulated by a drunk. 'I'm your son, you bastard! Remember my mother yet?' He raised his power knife.

'Oh *shit*.' Rachel suddenly noticed the fuzz of static that was even now plucking at her implants, trying to tell them this wasn't happening, that there was nobody there. Things became clearer, much clearer. She wasn't the only person with high-level implants hereabouts.

'My son?' Rubenstein looked puzzled for a moment, then his expression cleared. ''Milla was allowed to keep you after I was exiled?' He stood up. 'My son –'

Vassily swung at Rubenstein, artlessly but with all the force he could muster. But Burya wasn't there when the knife came down; Martin had tackled him from behind, ramming him headfirst into the ground.

With a shrill screech, the power knife cut into the lid of the cornucopia, slicing through millions of delicate circuits. A numinous flickering light and a smell of fresh yeast rose up as Vassily struggled to pull the blade out. A superconducting monofilament, held rigid by a viciously powerful magnetic field, the knife could cut through just about anything. Martin rolled over on his back and looked up just as Vassily, his face a slack mask, stepped toward him and raised the knife. There was a brief buzzing sound, and his eyes rolled up: then Vassily collapsed across the chest.

Arms and chest burning, Rachel lowered the stun gun and dropped back into real-world speed. Panting, heart racing. *Do this too often and die.* 'Bloody hell, wasn't there *anybody* aboard the fleet without a covert agenda?' she complained.

'Doesn't look like it.' Martin struggled to sit up.

'What happened?' Burya looked around, dazed.

'I think –' Rachel looked at the trunk. It was outgassing ominously: the power knife had cut through a lot of synthesis cells, and evidently some of the fuel tanks were leaking faster than the repair programs could fix them. 'It could be a bad idea to stay here. Talk about it on the road to Plotsk?'

'Yes.' Burya rolled Vassily off the trunk and dragged him a few paces. 'Is he really my son?'

'Probably.' Rachel paused to yawn for air. 'I wondered a bit. Why he was along. Couldn't have been a mistake. And then, the way he went for you – programmed, I think. Curator's Office must have figured, if revolution, you'd be central. Bastard child, disgraced mother, easily recruited. Credible?'

Sister Seventh had ambled up and was sniffing at the

vitrification cell occupied by the nearly late Duke Felix Politovsky. 'I told Festival passenger upload now-soon,' she rumbled. 'You tell story? Honor credit?'

'Later,' said Martin.

'Okay.' Sister Seventh gnashed at the air. 'You got overdraft at the mythology bank. I fix. Go Plotsk, now-soonish?'

'Before the luggage goes bang,' Martin agreed. He stood up a trifle drunkenly, winced as he transferred his weight onto one knee. 'Rachel?'

'Coming.' The dark spots had almost vacated her visual field. 'Okay. Um, if we can tie him up and put him in that walking hut of yours, we can work on his brainwashing later. See if there's anything more to him than a programmed assassin.'

'I agree.' Burya paused. 'I didn't expect this.'

'Neither did we,' she said shortly. 'Come on. Let's get away before this thing blows.'

Together they stumbled away from the fizzing revolutionary bomb and the last unchanging relic of the ancien regime, back down the hillside that led toward the road to Plotsk.

epilogue

Once news of Admiral Kurtz's miraculous appearance in the Ducal palace spread into the city, a tenuous curtain of normality began to assert itself. The revolutionary committees centered on the Corn Exchange watched the situation with alarm, but the common people were less unenthusiastic. Most of them were bewildered, disoriented, and deeply upset by the strangeness of the times. Those who weren't had for the most part already left the city; the survivors huddled together for comfort amidst the ruins of their certainties, eating manna from the Festival's machines and praying.

Kurtz's mysterious burst of good health continued; as Robard had noticed earlier, diseases of senescence were extremely rare among the survivors of the Festival, and for good reason. Acting on the Curator's advice, the Admiral magnanimously announced an amnesty for all progressive elements and a period of reconstruction and collective introspection. Many of the remaining revolutionaries took the opportunity to melt into the crowded camps or leave the city, in some cases taking cornucopia seeds with them. Rochard's World was thinly colonized, an almost unknown wilderness starting just three hundred kilometers beyond the city. Those who could not stand to watch a return to the old *status quo* took to the roads.

Also at the behest of the Curator's Office, the Admiral made no attempt to send militia forces after them. There would be time for dealing with miscreants later, Robard pointed out. Time enough after they'd starved through the coming winter.

A few more lifeboats made it down intact, cluttering the landing field behind the palace. Regular light shows lit up the sky with blue streaks of light; departing spawn of the Festival. Babushkas in the street looked up, made the sign of the evil eye, and spat in the gutter as the evil time passed. Some of the passing wisps bore the encoded essence of the old Duke; but few people knew and fewer cared. Gradually, the Festival's orbiting factories reached the end of their design life and shut down: slowly, the telephones stopped ringing. Now, people used them to call each other up. It was good to talk, and scattered families and friends rediscovered one another through the directionless medium of the phone network. The Curator fretted, and finally concluded that there was nothing to be done about it. Not until contact with the father planet resumed, in any event.

Things happened differently in Plotsk. The outlying township lay cut off from the capital by landslides and bizarre, dangerous structures that had rendered the roads impassable. Here, the revolutionary committee wound down until it was now a local provisional council, now a town governance. Peasants began to squat in the many abandoned farms around the town, second and third sons gifted by a sudden superfluity of soil. Strangers drifted in, fleeing chaos in smaller settlements, and there was space for everybody. Comrade Rubenstein of the Central Committee announced his intention to settle; after a heated row with the governance, he agreed to stick to publishing a newsletter and leave matters of ideology to less mercurial souls. He moved into Havlicek the Pawnbroker's apartment above the gutted shop on Main Street, along with a young man who said little and was not seen in public for the first week, providing much fertile material for wagging tongues. Strange structures burbled and steamed in the small courtyard behind the shop, and rumor had it that Rubenstein dabbled in the strange arts of technological miracle-working that had so upset the state sometime ago – but nobody disturbed him, for the local constabulary were in the pay of the governance, who had more sense than to mess with a dangerous wizard and revolutionary ideologue.

Another strange couple took over a tenement above Markus Wolff's old hardware store. They didn't talk much, but the bearded man demonstrated a rearkable aptitude with tools. Together they rebuilt the store, then opened for business. They kept a small stock of locks and clocks and rebuilt telephones and more exotic gadgets, racked in the age-blackened oak cabinets within the shop. These they traded for food and clothing and coal, and tongues wagged about the source of the miraculous toys that they sold so cheap – items that would have cost a fortune in the capital of the father world; never mind a backwoods colonial town. The supply seemed never-ending, and the sign they hung from the shop front was daringly close to subversive: ACCESS TO TOOLS AND IDEAS. But this didn't provoke as much comment as the conduct of his partner; a tall, thin woman with dark hair cut short, who sometimes went about bareheaded and unaccompanied, and frequently ran the shop when her husband was absent, even serving strangers on her own.

Back before the Festival, their conduct would have been sure to arouse comment, perhaps even a visit by the police and a summons to the Curator's Office. But in these strange times nobody seemed to care: and the radical Rubenstein was a not-infrequent visitor to their shop, procuring interesting components for his printing mechanism. They evidently had dangerous friends, and this was enough to deter the neighbors from snooping too much – except for the widow Lorenz, who seemed to feel it was her duty to pick a quarrel with the woman (who she suspected of being a Jewess, or unwed, or something equally sinister).

Over the nine months following the Festival, summer slid into the cold, rainy depths of autumn: the sun hid its face, and winter settled its icy grip into the ground. Martin spent many evenings rooting through the supply of metal bar stock he'd collected during the summer, feeding pieces to the small fabricator in the cellar, trying his hand at toolmaking with the primitive mechanical equipment to hand. Diamond molds, electric arc furnace, numerically controlled milling machine – these, his tools, he spun from the fabricator, using them in turn to make artifacts that the farmers and shopkeepers around him could understand.

While Martin worked at these tasks, Rachel kept house and shop together, rooted out clothing and food, bought advertising space in Rubenstein's broadsheet, and kept her ears to the ground for signs of trouble. They lived together as man and wife, meeting nosy neighborly inquiries with a blank stare and a shrug meaning *mind your own business*. Life was primitive, their resources and comfort limited both by what was available and by the exigencies of leading an inconspicuous existence; although after winter began to bite, Martin's installation of insulating foam and heat pumps kept them so warm that one or two of the more daring neighbors developed an unwelcome tendency to hang around the shop.

One chilly morning, Martin awoke with a headache and a dry mouth. For a moment he couldn't recall where he was: he opened his eyes and looked up at a dingy white curtain.

Someone murmured sleepily and rolled against him. *How did I get here? This isn't my shop. This isn't my life* – the sense of alienation was profound. Then memory came sluicing back like a flash flood, damping down the dusty plains. He rolled over and reached out an arm, hugged her sleeping shoulders against his chest. Distant emitters twittered to the back of his head: all the wards were in place. Rachel muttered and twitched, yawning. 'Awake?' he asked softly.

'Yeah. Ah. What time is it?' She blinked against the morning light, hair tousled and eyes puffy with sleep, and a stab of affection thrilled through him.

'After dawn. Bloody cold out here. 'Scuse me.' He hugged her once, then slid feet first through the bed-curtains, out into the frigid bedroom. The frost had scrawled its runes inside the windowpanes. Trying to keep his feet off the wooden floor, he twitched on his felt slippers then pulled out the chamber pot and squatted. He pulled on chilly outerwear from the clothesline inside the canopy bed, then went down into the cellar to inspect the charcoal burner that still glowed, peltier cells generating power for the small manufacturing plant's overnight milling run. Draw water, boil it, and soon they'd have coffee – a miraculous luxury, notwithstanding that it was ersatz, produce of a cornucopia machine. Maybe in a week or two the geothermal tap would be providing a bit more heat; for now, any temperature above freezing was a win in the face of the fierce steppe winter.

Rachel was up, floor creaking underfoot, yawning as she pulled on her chemise and underskirts. He stomped downstairs to rake out the oven and light a new fire; his hands were too cold, and he rubbed them hard to get the circulation going. *Morning market, isn't it?* He thought. *Lots of farmers. Maybe make some sales.* Then he almost pinched himself. *What am I turning into?* Cold ashes tumbling into a tin bucket as he scraped behind the fire grate. Something rustled behind him.

He glanced around. Rachel was clad for outdoors: her volumi-
nous brown dress covered her to the soles of her boots, and
she'd tied her hair up in a head scarf, knotted tightly under her
chin after the local fashion. Only her face was exposed. 'You
going out?' he asked.

'Market this morning. I want to buy some bread, maybe a
chicken or two. They're not going to be so easy to come by if
we leave it any longer.' She glanced away. 'Brr. Cold today, isn't
it?'

'We should be warming up in here by the time you get
back.' He finished laying coals in the grate and used a small,
familiar piece of magic: light blossomed fast, spread hungrily
across the anthracite surfaces. He turned his back to the oven.
'Should be a lot of sales today. Money –'

'I'll draw some from the till.' She leaned close, and he
wrapped his arms around her. Reassuring and solid, embedded
within the guise of a local artisan's wife. She leaned her chin on
his shoulder with long familiarity.

'You're looking good this morning. Wonderful.'

She smiled a little, and shivered. 'Flatterer. I wonder how
much longer we're going to be able to stay here?'

'Be able to? Or have to?'

'Um.' She considered for a moment. 'Is it getting to you?'

'Yes. A bit.' He chuckled quietly. 'I caught myself thinking
like a shopkeeper this morning, while I was cleaning out the
grate. It'd be so easy to slip into a routine. It's what, eight
months now? Living the quiet life. I could almost see us settling down here, raising a family, sinking into obscurity.'

'It wouldn't work.' She tensed under his hands, and he
rubbed at her shoulders. 'We wouldn't age right. They'll open
up travel again in the new year, and then, well. I've done child
rearing, too. It wouldn't work, trust me. Be glad of that
reversible vasectomy. Or had you thought what it'd be like to
be on the run with a baby in tow?'

'Oh, I know about that.' He carried on moving his hands in small circles until she relaxed slightly. Thick fabric moved under his fingertips, many layers of it against the cold. 'I know. We need to move on, sooner rather than later. It's just so . . . quiet. Peaceful.'

'Graveyards are quiet, too.' She pulled back to arm's length and stared at him, and once again he held his breath: because when she did this, he found her unbearably beautiful. 'That's what the New Republic is all about, isn't it? This isn't a good place to live, Martin. It isn't safe. The town's in shock; collectively they're all in a fit of denial. All their wishes granted, for three months, and it wasn't enough! When they wake up, they'll reach for the security blanket. The place will be crawling with Curator's Office informers, and this time you don't have an Admiralty contract and I don't have a diplomatic passport. We'll have to move on.'

'And your employers –' He couldn't continue.

'Easy come, easy go.' She shrugged. 'I've taken leave of absence before. This isn't leave; it's lying low, waiting to exit a hot zone. But if we could only make it back to Earth, there are lots of things I'd like to do with you. Together. There'll be room to make plans, then. Here, if we stay, someone else will plan everything for us. Along with everybody else.'

'Alright.' He turned back to the cooker: a healthy red glow rippled beneath the coals that the adiabatic heater had goosed into combustion. 'Today, the market. Maybe this evening we can think about when to –'

There was a pounding at the front door.

'What is it?' Martin shouted. Leaving the stove, he shambled through into the cold, dark shop: paused at the door. Opened the letterbox. 'Who's there?'

'Telegram!' piped a breathless voice. 'Telegram for Master Springburg!'

With a rattle of bolts, Martin slid the door a jar. Blinding white snow, and a red-uniformed post office runner boy who stood staring up at him. 'Telegram? For the toolsmith?'

'That'd be me,' he said. The boy waited: Martin fumbled for a tip, a few kopecks, then closed the door and leaned against it, heart pounding. A *telegram!*

'Open it!' Rachel loomed over him, eyes anxious with hope and surprise. 'Who is it from?'

'It's from Herman –' he opened the envelope and, mouth dry, began to read aloud:

TO: MARTIN SPRINGFIELD AND RACHEL MANSOUR,
   CONGRATULATIONS ON YOUR BABY.

   I UNDERSTAND THE CHILD WAS BORN IN ORBIT AROUND ROCHARD'S WORLD, AND SHORTLY DEPARTED IN VARIOUS DIRECTIONS. WHILE I APPRECIATE THAT YOU ARE BOTH TIRED, YOU MIGHT BE INTERESTED TO KNOW THAT I HAVE AN IMPORTANT BUSINESS VENTURE OPENING BACK HOME. IF YOU'D LIKE TO BE INVOLVED, TWO TICKETS ARE WAITING FOR YOU AT THE CENTRAL POST OFFICE IN NOVY PETROGRAD.

   PS: I GATHER SPRING IS AN UNHEALTHY SEASON IN PLOTSK. PLEASE DON'T TARRY.

Later that day, the old Wolff hardware store caught fire and burned down to the ground – the victim, local rumor had it, of neglect by its feckless owner. He had last been seen leaving town in a hired sleigh, accompanied by his fancy woman and a small carpetbag. They were never seen again in Plotsk, but vanished into the capital city like a drop of ink in the blue ocean: lost in the turbulence and excitement surrounding the arrival of the first civilian starship since the Festival departed, a tramp freighter from Old Calais.

They weren't really lost: but that, as they say, is another story. And before I recount it, I have some wishes I would like you to grant me . . .

IRON SUNRISE

Charles Stross

The stunning follow-up novel to *Singularity Sky*

When the planet of New Moscow was brutally destroyed, its few survivors launched a counter-attack against the most likely culprit: the neighbouring system of trade rival, New Dresden. But New Dresden wasn't responsible and, as the deadly missiles approach their target, Rachel Mansour, agent for the interests of Old Earth, is assigned to find out who was.

The one person who does know is a disaffected teenager who calls herself Wednesday Shadowmist. But Wednesday has no idea where she might be hiding this significant information. Time is limited and if Rachel can't resolve this mystery it will mean annihilation of an entire world . . .

THE ALGEBRAIST

Iain M. Banks

It is 4034 AD. Humanity has made it to the stars. Fassin Taak, a Slow Seer at the Court of the Nasqueron Dwellers, will be fortunate if he makes it to the end of the year.

The Nasqueron Dwellers inhabit a gas giant on the outskirts of the galaxy, in a system awaiting its wormhole connection to the rest of civilisation. In the meantime, they are dismissed as decadents living in a state of highly developed barbarism, hoarding data without order, hunting their own young and fighting pointless formal wars.

Seconded to a military-religious order he's barely heard of – part of the baroque hierarchy of the Mercatoria, the latest galactic hegemony – Fassin Thak has to travel again amongst the Dwellers. He is in search of a secret hidden for half a billion years. But with each day that passes a war draws closer – a war that threatens to overwhelm everything and everyone he's ever known.

NEWTON'S WAKE

Ken MacLeod

The explosive stand-alone epic of galactic conflict and human folly from a true master of far-future space opera. *Newton's Wake* charts the struggle for human survival in a universe dominated by post-human intelligence.

Centuries ago, space settlers and soldiers fled to the stars from the sentient AI war machines that engulfed Earth. They colonized Eurydice, a planet whose rocks contain traces of its own war constructs. Long-dormant war machines which are beginning to stir . . .

RINGWORLD'S CHILDREN

Larry Niven

Larry Niven's sequence of Ringworld novels is one of the classic works of science fiction. Winner of both the Hugo and Nebula awards, it is a towering imaginative achievement – as extraordinary as the world on which it is set.

The Ringworld is dying. And this time even Louis Wu, captive of the hyper-intelligent alien Tunesmith, may be unable to save it. Even if Louis can escape he will then have to survive in a galaxy ravaged by interstellar war and deadly political intrigue. For the Ringworld is no longer a secret and entire civilisations now battle to control its power.

The victorious race that conquers the Ringworld will conquer the galaxy . . . and no one will be able to stop them.

But Louis Wu is going to try.